STORY
OF
BEFORE

Born in London, Susan Stairs has lived in Ireland since early childhood. Involved in the art business for many years, she has written extensively about Irish art and artists. She received an MA in Creative Writing from University College Dublin in 2009 and was shortlisted for the Davy Byrnes Irish Writing Award in the same year. She lives in Dublin with her family. *The Story of Before* is her first novel.

Praise for *The Story of Before*:

'*The Story of Before* is a bewitching read, a book that transports you back to the world of childhood, where everything outside of yourself is a mystery to be unraveled. Beautifully observed, the novel conjures up the landscape of nineteen-seventies Dublin as effectively as a time machine. I can't recommend it highly enough' Kathleen MacMahon, author of *This is How it Ends*

'A single event can occur in a lifetime of a family that will change utterly the heart that keeps it beating… Stairs has made it all the more absorbing by writing in the assured voice and sensibility of a young girl' *Sunday Independent*

'Stairs revels in sharp physical description, tinged with implication… Familiar and unsettling… An assured debut' *The Sunday Times*

'With this moving and evocative novel, Stairs has won her spurs as an emerging new voice in Irish quality women's fiction' *Irish Independent*

'As literary Ireland continues to await the definitive novel of Celtic-tiger Ireland, first-time novelist Susan Stairs has swept in under the radar to pique our interest with a pre-tiger-era story which makes for perhaps more beguiling reading' *Sunday Business Post*

'An astoundingly assured piece of work which is beautifully written, poignant and compelling' *Yorkshire Evening Post*

'A tale of childhood secrets and lies with a wonderful sense of time and place' *Bookseller*

'*The Story of Before* is a mesmerising psychological coming-of-age novel' *Irish Examiner*

'Susan Stairs' debut novel is causing a stir for its accurate depiction of Ireland in the 70s, its sustained suspense, and powerful, moving story' *Irish Daily Star*

'The deftly drawn characters and perfect pace and tone make this a beautiful book with a real heart that stays with you long after you have turned the last page' *Gazette*, Basingstoke

'Stunning' *Image* magazine, Ireland

'*The Story of Before* is a wonderful and touching read which tugs at the heartstrings and reminds us how precious life can be' *InDaily*, Adelaide

'A wonderfully evocative book with a beautiful dusting of magic brushed through each page' www.rozz.ie

THE
STORY
OF
BEFORE

SUSAN STAIRS

x

CORVUS

Published in trade paperback in Great Britain in 2013 by Corvus,
an imprint of Atlantic Books Ltd.

This paperback edition published in Great Britain in 2014 by Corvus,
an imprint of Atlantic Books Ltd.

10 9 8 7 6 5 4 3 2 1

A CIP catalogue record for this book is available from the British Library.

Ppaperback ISBN: 978 0 85789 908 8
E-book ISBN: 978 0 85789 909 5

Printed and bound by CPI Group (UK) Ltd, Croydon, CR0 4YY.

Corvus
An imprint of Atlantic Books Ltd
Ormond House
26–27 Boswell Street
London
WC1N 3JZ

www.corvus-books.co.uk

For my family

Have patience with everything unresolved in your heart
and try to love the questions themselves...
Do not search for the answers,
which could not be given to you now,
because you would not be able to live them.
And the point is, to live everything.
Live the questions now.
Perhaps then, someday far in the future,
you will gradually, without even noticing it,
live your way into the answer.

~ Rainer Maria Rilke ~

ONE

The others used to say I was psychic. They said I could sense stuff before it happened. But I'm not sure there was anything special about me at all. I was just a bit more observant than they were. They never paid proper attention to what was going on around them, whereas I was always on the lookout for clues.

I remember the first time they noticed. We were watching *The Waltons* and John Boy had gone up the mountain with his daddy to shoot a turkey for dinner. I just knew he wouldn't be able to do it. When I said as much to the others, they started shouting at the telly, egging him on, wanting to prove me wrong. But I don't think they understood that the turkey posed no threat, and that John Boy Walton would never hurt a creature unless he, or one of his family, was in danger.

'You'll get your blood soon,' I told them. I knew the way these things worked; the programme makers wouldn't want us to think that John Boy was a complete chicken. So, later in the episode, when his daddy was in danger of being mauled to death by a wounded bear, it was obvious to me that John Boy would pull the trigger.

'Told you so,' I said, trying to sound all knowledgeable and wise after the deed was done and the others were left wondering how I 'knew'.

Of course, I didn't always get it right. But if you asked the others today, they'd tell you about the times I did. Times when I predicted what we each would get for Christmas, or which one of his collection of ties Dad would wear on a Sunday, or what we'd be having for dessert after dinner.

So I wonder today how no one else could see the bad thing coming. Not that I knew back then what the bad thing was. And if I had – if I'd known one of us was going to die – would there have been anything I could've done to prevent it? I play it all back in my mind, over and over. The clues were all there. But maybe they're a lot easier to spot when you know the answer.

The snow was really deep that January. Almost as soon as we heard Big Ben ringing out from the telly downstairs, and a recorded studio audience rumbling through a tuneless version of 'Auld Lang Syne', a blizzard began. Not soft – like in romantic films when it 'snows' to make everything seem so pretty and pure – but wild and relentless and hard. Snow with no remorse. It was instantly obvious to all of us that this was snow like we'd never seen it before.

We watched from the front bedroom, our faces buffed with the freezing air that seeped through the panes of the huge picture window. Our knees were shoved up against the tepid ridges of the radiator and our teeth left bite-marks on the white metal slats of the Venetian blinds that none of us ever owned up to. The snow fell so fast that it covered our garden in minutes. We watched it blanket our neighbours' slated roofs and tarmacked driveways. It shrouded the concrete road of our keyhole-shaped cul-de-sac, secreting the cement pathways, circular manhole covers and grass verges. Billions of feather-light flakes fused to form a glistening coverlet that turned the whole of Hillcourt Rise into a vast, crystalline wonderland. Our estate had been virginized. It was hard to believe how quickly it transformed; how its grey, pebbledash, territorial markings disappeared and it looked like we lived on one enormous, open-plan plot. We could hardly distinguish one house from the other.

Earlier that evening, Mam had said we could stay up for the countdown. Kev was asleep upstairs in his cot. At one and a half, he hadn't a clue what night of the year it was. We lay on the sunburst rug in front of the fire – my brother Mel, just thirteen, sister Sandra, twelve, and me, Ruth, eleven – with a crate of mandarin oranges and a newly opened box of Black Magic to keep us going. By half past nine, we'd already grown bored, but none of us would allow ourselves to admit it.

There was nothing on the telly. At least nothing we found even mildly entertaining. On one channel, a troupe of thick-thighed dancers wearing way too much make-up pranced across a glittery stage, and on another, a huddle of tartan-and-tweed-clad diddley-eyes plucked and wheezed their way through one whingey ballad after another. There might've been a Western on too; back then there seemed to be cowboys and Indians galloping across cactus-dotted deserts every time we turned on the telly. I only ever watched them if I found one of the chiefs attractive.

The Black Magic kept us going for a while, but after all the soft ones were gone and only the hard toffees were left, things began to disintegrate. I was accused of taking more than my share, but it was only that I'd saved mine up in a little pile, instead of wolfing each one down as soon as I picked. And the others were miffed right from the start because they didn't even like dark chocolate in the first place. They still ate it – it was chocolate after all – but without any real pleasure. I preferred dark chocolate to milk, and liked to savour it; I could make a bar of Bourneville last a whole week. And I didn't see why I should gorge just to make the others feel less greedy.

To ease the tension, Dad suggested a game of Scrabble at about half past ten, forgetting that we rarely got beyond the first triple word score. That night was no different. We hadn't been playing long when the board mysteriously toppled over. Because no one owned up, we were collectively punished.

'I don't care what night it is,' Mam said, stage-managing the hunt for the plastic letters that were sprinkled all over the shag-pile, and waving the glass of sherry she'd been sipping since teatime. 'That's the end of it.'

Our pleas were ignored. Gathering my stash of chocolates and a couple of mandarins into the folds of my nightdress, I followed the others out of the room. Stopping at the door, I looked Dad square in the eye.

'Happy New Year,' I said, trying my best to sound sincere. He looked sort of uneasy. Things had been tense between Dad and me since Christmas night. 'It's OK if we stay up for the bells, isn't it?' I asked in a low voice. It wasn't really a question; I knew he wouldn't say no.

'Well . . . I . . .' he mumbled, glancing at Mam as she nodded along with the music on the telly. 'I . . . suppose so . . . As long as you don't wake your brother.'

The others were waiting on the stairs, dangling limbs through the serpentine curves of the wrought iron banisters.

'Well?' they both asked.

I gave them a frown; I didn't want them to think it'd been easy.

'It's OK,' I told them, as sternly as I could manage. 'We can stay up till next year.'

We spent the next hour in Mel's room, playing I-spy and hangman and X's and O's without incident. Then Sandra finally accused Mel of cheating when he overtook her lead on the scoresheet I was keeping and we waited in a sort of sulky silence till we could hear the midnight bells. We gathered on the landing to listen and I crept into Mam and Dad's room to sneak a look at Kev as he slept. That's when I noticed the snow. I whispered to the others to follow me in and we sat on the bed together to watch the blizzard thicken. We wrapped the candlewick bedspread tight around our shivering bodies and tried to count the soft flakes that stuck silently to the glass, soundproofing us in to our cotton-wool cocoon. The houses of the estate turned into glittering ice palaces and the huge oval-shaped emerald of the green disappeared under a cover of crystal-white. Though the novelty of ringing in the new year wore off five minutes into January, our attention was held fast by the snow. If I could hold back time, that's where I'd stop it. I wouldn't allow that year to begin at all.

I sometimes think about the inhabitants of Hillcourt Rise, going about their normal business that night with no clue everything was about to change. And the ones whose actions that coming year would matter are the ones who stand out in my mind.

Shayne Lawless. I can see him now. Balancing on a battered tea-chest, pissing a stream of snow-melting urine through the slanted open window of his tiny attic room. Pissing in controlled spurts to the rhythm of 'Bohemian Rhapsody' as it blasted from the teak-veneered hulk of his radiogram. Shayne, whose shoulder-length hair looked and smelled like dried tobacco leaves, and whose close-set eyes never seemed to focus on anything in particular. Shayne pissed out his window almost every night; there was a five- or six-foot long stripe on the slates where the moss never grew.

Of course, I didn't really see Shayne that night; his roof wasn't visible from our front bedroom. But I like to think the snow would've made no difference to his nightly ritual. And I'm sure the fact that it was New Year's Eve hardly even registered. The only thing that would've been important to him at that moment was lifting the needle when the gong sounded at the end so he could listen to the song once more from the top. I think his radiogram was probably the best friend Shayne ever had. It was almost an antique, but it served its purpose loyally. He'd thumped it up the narrow staircase to his lair the afternoon a brand-new, cherry-red Sanyo portable record player was delivered to his house by a starry-eyed, balding man, sporting a stomach that spilled out over the waistband of his slacks. Yet another man Liz Lawless insisted her son call 'Uncle'.

And Bridie Goggin. What would it please me to believe she was up to that New Year's Eve? Stripping clean, white sheets from the un-slept-in spare beds she'd made up in anticipation weeks before Christmas; re-wrapping pink tissue paper round the bone china teacups she'd taken out for the festivities and never used; or maybe clutching the jade-green telephone receiver to her huge chest, podgy tears dredging paths through her pan-sticked cheeks, so thankful for the two-minute Happy New Year phone call from one of her grown-up children.

Tracey Farrell and Valerie Vaughan: in Valerie's bedroom, swapping fantasies about pin-up pop stars. Trading exaggerated secrets about boys they pretended they couldn't stand and grouping girls into pink-paged, biro-ed lists of 'Friends' and 'Enemies'. In their brushed nylon nightdresses, rolling on the super-soft wool carpet, or lolling on the lavender satin eiderdown of Valerie's luxurious double bed, blithely exposing inches of their flesh, imagining that this was how it felt to be grown up. These were the things that made them happy, that enabled them to exist within the confines of the world their circumstances had created.

And I mustn't forget David O'Dea, with his slender, smooth-skinned fingers sliding across the keys of his piano. Yes, even at midnight on New Year's Eve. Eyes half-closed, head tilted to the left, shoulders faltering over his instrument like waves, unsure of when to crash. His parents probably stood behind him that night, perhaps having popped the champagne Mr O'Dea won in the local golf club four-ball. It's likely their gaze fixed on the back of his head, and they reminded themselves of their leniency in allowing his fair hair to curl a whole inch over his collar. While upstairs their high-achieving twin daughters wrote spiteful entries about each other in their lockable diaries, Mr and Mrs O'Dea wore satisfied smiles on their faces and sipped their champagne, secure in the knowledge that this would be another good year because they'd always done right by their children.

I can still hear the snow; the absolute, all-concealing silence of it. It rings in my ears and spreads like a virus through my body. Like it did that night. I felt it first in my feet, creeping up through my veins and capillaries and arteries, making me shiver in a way I never had before.

'Something bad's going to happen this year,' I announced to the others, closing my eyes, afraid I might go snow-blind. They bunched themselves in around me, waiting for me to elaborate, but that was all I had. It was no more than a feeling, but one I felt I had to share.

The snow continued for days, piling high in six-foot drifts. While our parents moaned and shovelled, we made proper snowmen that survived for almost three weeks. Some dads walked to work, but most didn't make it in at all. All over the estate, abandoned Cortinas and Hillmans hibernated, their metal mounds sugared over and decorated with the filigree, fork-like footprints of starving birds. On the news we watched aerial shots of city traffic chaos, stranded commuters, and helicopter milk-and-bread drops all over our albino country. And it was announced – to our delirious delight – that the school holidays would be extended by one whole week.

We were snowed-in.

And while those old enough to understand the hardship the snow brought wore worried frowns on their faces when they looked out their windows, we wore hats and gloves and wellies without complaining, and repeatedly slid our backsides down the sloping entrance to Hillcourt Rise.

And when eventually the blanket melted, and everything went back to the way it had been, we were astonished at how patchy and grubby it looked underneath.

We never saw snow like that again.

TWO

The Big Freeze saw us into our final few months in Hillcourt
Rise. Mam thought we'd be living there forever. I suppose
when we first moved in we all did; the house was her dream
come true. Before that, we'd been living on South Circular
Road, a busy stretch of seven hundred houses and shops that
ran from Portobello – a stone's throw from Dublin city –
through Dolphin's Barn, Rialto and Kilmainham, all the way
to the Phoenix Park.

Our house stood on the curving stretch between Griffith
Barracks – a former prison building hidden behind thick,
grey-stone walls – and the Player Wills cigarette factory. It
had been Gran's house, the place where our dad had grown
up. Gran never got to see me; she went downhill very quickly
in the end and died a month before I was born. I often studied

photos of her: plump and rosy and twinkly-eyed with Dad as a baby in her arms; and one with Mel and Sandra on her lap, her withered hands circling their chubby baby bodies, her false-teeth smile stretching the papery skin of her hollow-cheeked face. And although they hardly remembered her, I still felt a certain pang of jealousy that she'd known them, and I wished she'd hung on long enough to meet me. She was the last of our grandparents; both sets were dead before I came into the world.

To Mel and Sandra and me, the house was our home. To Mam it was cold, draughty and old-fashioned. In the seventies, to be old-fashioned was a sin. Some of the houses on our road had been modernized over the years: chequerboard quarry tiles buried under patterned lino; ornate skirtings prised off and replaced with smaller, plainer versions; period fireplaces ripped out to make way for cement monsters covered in beige and brown tiles. Our house had undergone no such transformation, much to Mam's disappointment. She dreamed lustfully of semi-detached streamlined living: double-glazing, a fitted kitchen, crazy-paving patio, built-in wardrobes with louvre doors. Instead, she received the penance of living in the century-old birthplace of the man she married. She found much to complain about: the sash windows she couldn't open without Dad's help; the lack of a 'proper' kitchen (it seemed fine to us – she went in and meals came out); the ten-foot-high ceilings that made the place impossible to heat.

Although Dad was a painter and decorator, he rarely did any painting or decorating in our house. 'The cobbler's children always go barefoot,' Mam would sigh, eyeing the half-used paint tins stacked in a corner of the backyard. The same faded flock wallpaper that covered the sitting room walls in Dad's boyhood photos was still hiding damp patches in the plaster, thirty years later. Mam regularly washed down the woodwork with vinegar, tut-tutting as she went along, but it made little difference to the yellowed gloss. Dad would come whistling through the door in the evenings in a draught of tobacco and turpentine, his thick black hair, moustache and sideburns salted with paint flecks. He'd take the stairs two at a time, wriggling out of his petrol blue, button-through overalls on the landing. Twenty minutes later, he'd emerge from the bathroom smelling of Old Spice and he'd flop down in his favourite flowery armchair, ready to scan the small ads in the *Evening Press*. Once Dad crossed the threshold, he was no longer: *Michael P Lamb, Painter & Decorator – 'No Job Too Small'*; he was: *Mick Lamb, Husband & Father – 'No Jobs At All'*.

Mam was a country girl, born in Wicklow in a cottage somewhere out past the Sugarloaf Mountain. She'd spent her childhood roaming fields and meadows, and what she hated most about where we lived was the fact that we had nowhere to play. Out the back was a tiny concrete yard, completely out of proportion to the size of the house. Gran had sold off more than half the original garden to a mechanic who'd built an eyesore of a shed on it years before we were born. At the front of the house we did have some outdoor space, but it was only a tiny railed-in patch of grass, bordered with purple and yellow crocuses in spring, and plump, dark pink roses in summer.

Traffic hummed up and down South Circular Road at all times of the day: dusty, navy double-decker buses; enormous, clanking lorries; and cars in dull shades of grey or brown. Mam often wiped black carbon dust from the silver-painted railings in the morning, only to find they were filthy again by late afternoon. Not that she was worried about us inhaling it; nobody knew the dangers of leaded petrol back then. What annoyed her was the dirt, the way it grubbied our fingers so that we left black streaks all along the dado rail in the hall, contributing to her never-ending housework.

So it came about that Mam's constant but good-natured nagging won out – the day arrived when we learned we were moving to the suburbs. To a house in an estate called Hillcourt Rise. Mam's trump card came in the form of our baby brother, Kevin. At thirty-nine, I guess she'd presumed her child-bearing days were over. But when she discovered she was pregnant with something we heard her describe as 'an afterthought', she decided it was quite definitely time to go. It was going to be hard enough getting used to night feeds and nappies after ten years, without worrying about keeping an eye on us three.

'They need somewhere safe to play, Mick,' I'd strained to hear her saying to Dad one evening after dinner. We were used to hearing whispers between the two of them while they were washing and drying at the kitchen sink and we were supposed to be doing our homework at the table. I used to imagine they'd won the sweeps, and were desperately trying to keep it from us for fear we'd demand new bicycles, roller skates, and holidays to Disneyland. Or that one of us was terminally ill (it was always me) and they couldn't bring themselves to break the news.

'And some kids to play with,' she said, her yellow rubber-gloved hands smoothing over her rounding belly. 'What do you think?' It was a question she'd asked him many times before, and one he usually ignored.

Dad looked out the window, stroking his moustache and breathing hard up his nose. I could tell he was thinking about it this time. And so could Mam. She held her head to one side with her eyebrows raised and her mouth ready to curve into a smile. Then finally Dad let out a sort of false sigh as he turned and put his arm around her.

'I think you've finally won, Rose,' he said, pulling her close. Mam let out a little shriek and kissed him noisily on the cheek. Then he whispered something into her ear, and she hugged him tight around his waist.

I didn't let on to the others for a while, but the next Friday evening when I saw Dad sorting through tins of paint and brushes out the back, I knew the preparations had begun and we were in for a weekend of chores. I said as much to the others and, as usual, they were suitably impressed when, the following morning, Dad handed us three brushes and a bucket of magnolia and told us to get to work brightening up the back wall of the shed.

'I think we're moving house,' I said, as we sloshed paint over the grey concrete.

'Don't be stupid,' said Mel. He stood back to look at our progress, scrunching up his face. 'Wish Dad had given us bigger brushes. We'll be ages. And get a move on, you two,' he ordered, mimicking Mam. 'I've done most of it.'

'Why would we be moving house?' asked Sandra, absently wiping her brush over and back across the same square foot of wall. 'Where would we go?'

'I don't know,' I said, reaching up as far as I could. 'Maybe to a house that isn't so old. With a big back garden.'

'Hope you're wrong,' said Mel from behind us. 'All that grass to cut. And I'd be the one made to do it.' He shouldered his way between us, anxious to prove he could stretch up further towards the top of the wall than Sandra. Mel was finding it hard to accept that his younger sister was the same height as him and he raised himself up on his toes whenever she stood near. In some seaside photos, his face had a manic, glacial expression as he tried to puff himself up for the duration of the pose while Sandra smiled sweetly, completely unaware of his desperation. With their similar fair skin and hair, blue eyes and gangly limbs, they were often mistaken for twins. By contrast, my small, slightly chubby build and dark colouring brought about expressions of surprise that I could even be distantly related to them, let alone be part of the same family.

THREE

We nearly killed Shayne Lawless the day we moved into Hillcourt Rise. He ran in front of our car and Dad had to jam on the brakes. He looked in at us – the newcomers – with his giddy eyes and grinning mouth just inches from the bonnet. Dad cursed under his breath, holding his hairy hands up as if to say sorry, even though it wasn't his fault. A tiny stream of sweat ran down his neck, under the loosened collar of his white shirt, and his washed-out eyes in the rear-view mirror implored us not to tell Mam. She wasn't with us for the actual move; we'd had to leave her in the hospital with our new baby brother.

It was a sweltering July day in the hottest summer for years. I was ten years old. Mam and Dad had signed the contract for the house that morning in a solicitor's office on Merrion Square, leaving me, Mel and Sandra to wait in the car. We were on our summer holidays from school, and for some reason there was no one able – or perhaps willing – to look after us. As soon as they'd been handed the keys to forty-two Hillcourt Rise, Mam told Dad it was time, and they'd walked quickly along the east side of the square to Holles Street Maternity Hospital, where, fifteen minutes later, Kevin shot out like a bullet. Well, he was number four. They thought they'd timed it all to perfection and that we'd be nicely settled into our new house before he arrived. But Kev was impatient to get out into the world and didn't want to wait any longer. So Dad could be forgiven for being a bit distracted that evening as he drove behind the removal lorry into the estate.

The events of that day are obviously memorable: new brother, new house, new neighbours. But another thing took place that morning in Merrion Square Park that was to mark the day out in my mind. Something a lot more strange and frightening. I kept quiet about it at the time; it wasn't something I wanted to share. The day would come when I'd think maybe what happened had been some kind of warning. But by then, it was already too late.

Dad had pulled in under the shadowy, dark green tangle of trees that dipped over the park railings, rushing around to help Mam as she tried to heave herself and her ballooning stomach out of the car. She was making a huge effort to breathe regularly, taking long streams of warm air up through her nose, waiting a few seconds, then pushing them out steadily through the 'O' of her pursed lips. In the last few weeks, her movements had slowed. She tired easily. Often, she went to bed in the afternoons and we had to wait longer for our dinner. Occasionally, Dad even had to make it and bring it up to her on a tray. When Mel grumbled once that the mashed potato had black bits in it, he was made to do the washing up *and* the drying.

Dad pushed his head through the open window, his chin showing the marks of a rushed shave. 'Won't be long. Just have to sign for the new house and get the keys.' Then, leaning in further, he whispered, 'And for God's sake, behave yourselves. Your mother doesn't need any of your carry on today.' He looked at me. 'You'll let me know if there's been any trouble, Ruth?'

I nodded my head with a mixture of pride and apprehension; while I was used to the role of informer, I was mindful that both Mel and Sandra were bigger and stronger than me, and were expert at giving Chinese burns.

'I'm *so* thirsty,' Mel complained. 'I'll *die* if I don't get a drink.'

'Pity about you,' Dad said. 'But don't worry. We'll all go to the funeral.'

I watched the way they crossed the road, Mam using Dad like a crutch and keeping one hand on the underside of her huge belly. The beige smock she wore was one she'd made herself, using a pattern that came free with *Woman's Way*. The heat of her body against the even hotter PVC of the car seat had caused a dark stain to emerge on her back. Against the sandy fabric, it reminded me of an oasis in the middle of a desert. Without thinking, I said as much to Sandra. She frowned at me, her eyebrows straight golden lines above her sea-blue eyes.

'It's just sweat, Ruth,' she said. 'It's hot, or haven't you noticed?'

Her nose was sunburned, a new, pink layer peeping through the curls of peeling skin. She bit at her bottom lip with her front tooth, the one she'd chipped at my last birthday party, when, in the rush to get the Rice Krispie cakes, someone (we never discovered who, but I always suspected Brainbox – our cousin, Trevor) pulled her chair from under her as she was about to sit down, and she walloped her chin off the edge of the kitchen table. She blamed me because it was my party. Mam said she was lucky she didn't break her jaw. Her lip biting had since become a habit, the sharp edge of the tooth often drawing blood. She'd scraped her red-gold hair into an untidy ponytail that morning, tying it with a purple bobble to match the bib-front shorts with the heart-shaped buttons she'd begged Mam to make for her. It hadn't taken much persuasion; Mam loved to sew. Most evenings she sat in front of the telly in the wickerwork armchair, eyes darting from needle to *Kojak* or *Columbo* or whoever, and back again, as she hemmed or cross-stitched as perfectly as any machine. She always got it spot on with Sandra; everything she made for her seemed to fit exactly right. I was more hit and miss, perhaps because I was small, and not as graceful or perfectly proportioned. So I was thankful that the last few months had limited her output to cute romper suits for the new baby and huge tent-like dresses for herself.

The second Mam and Dad had left to get the keys, Mel started. He began by flicking toast crusts into Sandra's hair. Because we'd been late leaving, we were allowed to eat our breakfast in the car, and Mel had saved up his crusts for ammunition. Being the eldest, he had that air of supreme authority that he thought the eleven months he spent as an only child entitled him to for life. I don't think he ever forgave our parents for diluting his one hundred per cent share of their attention and he used up huge amounts of energy trying to get it back. He always got the best reaction from Sandra. He'd given up on me, but my big sister was easily provoked. I saw the relationship she enjoyed with Mel as like a sort of earthquake graph: long periods of inactivity combined with spells of minor movement that progressed towards massive eruptions. I saw myself as something of a dormant volcano: one whose silence was effectively guaranteed, but should never really be taken for granted.

Mel and Sandra's squabble soon reached Wimbledon proportions. Back and forth between the two of them the ball of accusations flew. Mel jumped into the driver's seat, twisting the knob that made it recline.

'Ouch! You're leaning on my knees,' Sandra whined.

'Move over then,' Mel told her.

'No, I don't want to. Lift the seat.'

'Make me.'

I felt the warmth of the glass against my cheek and wished I'd brought a book. I'd wanted to, but Dad had said we were late already and there was no time to be rummaging around in tea-chests for stuff that was already packed. Thirty seconds would hardly have made a difference, but I'd said nothing. Dad wasn't much of a reader – except for newspapers – and didn't understand my compulsive need to escape into an imaginary world. I felt he should have though; he knew what Mel and Sandra were like. I thought it unfair that he expected me to put up with them when I didn't have the necessary distractions.

Soon, the stuffy atmosphere of the car became too much. Sandra opened a door and jumped out. Mel was next. In seconds, my face was cutting through the morning air as I ran behind them, through the gates, and into the park. I had on my new Clark's sandals and a pair of white knee socks, the toes of which quickly became sodden and green from the dewy grass. The sky was clear of clouds and sort of hazy, with that early-morning promise of all-day blue. It seemed higher than usual, as if it needed to raise itself up to avoid the treetops and the roofs of the four-storey Georgian terraces lining the square. I knew we wouldn't get in trouble for leaving the car. I think it was a sense that things were shifting, changing; and punishments were always difficult to give out when normal routines weren't being followed.

Mel found a red plastic ball and tried to involve me in a game, but I wasn't interested. Besides, my open-toed sandals were hardly suitable for playing football. Sandra was willing, despite their earlier bickering. So I left them to it and wandered off in among the trees and bushes to explore, hoping I might be lucky this time. I regularly dreamed of discovering a hoard of gold coins hidden in undergrowth, or some priceless ancient treasure stuffed inside a hole in a tree. I climbed in under a holly bush, its waxy, spiked leaves pricking my back through the thin cotton of my dress. The sound of Mel and Sandra grew faint, drowned out by the thick, green growth on one side and the low rumble of traffic from around Merrion Square on the other.

It was much darker in there. Sunlight barely found its way through. High above, the trees had twined and twisted their branches together and only tiny flashes of blue showed through. It smelled old and damp and sort of rotten. A crumpled newspaper, a few crushed cans and a broken bottle lay at the base of a tree, and in the middle of a small clearing, hundreds of matches lay scattered around a circle of blackened stones. I listened. The place was silent. I trudged through last years' autumn leaves, still crisp in deep, rusty piles under my feet, and was glad when I reached the railings. I could see out to the square from there. I found a gap in the hedge, squatted down and nestled myself into its cover where I could watch the people passing by.

I felt safe there. I was in a place of my own. Unseen and unheard. The best place. At home, I was used to finding some seemingly inaccessible spot to hide myself away for a while: in the cupboard under the stairs; on the bottom shelf of my wardrobe; in the space between the back of the couch and the radiator. I think I sometimes needed to find a place away from the constant tug-of-war of family couplings. Mam and Dad formed one pair, Mel and Sandra the other. In truth, I understood there was no way to break through the intertwining links that had been created well before I'd been born.

I began counting shoes and legs. Brown shoes, black shoes, bare legs, trouser legs. It was easy enough for a while. But it grew complicated when a group of chattering office girls breezed past in a criss-cross of rubber platforms, straw wedges, flapping blue jeans and orange nylons. After a while, my legs grew stiff from squatting, so I stretched out each one in turn for a few seconds, before realizing that I really needed to wee. I was well used to going behind bushes; on Sunday drives, Dad regularly had to pull over someplace for one or other of us. And although I was quite good at holding it, I didn't want to take the chance this time. I'd no way of knowing how much longer Mam and Dad might be. And anyway, this was the perfect place to go. I stood up and moved backwards, away from the gap and further behind the hedge. Then I reached up under my dress, pulled down my pants and bent my knees again.

Just then, a blackbird flew down beside me. Even in the murky light, his feathers had a kind of sheen and I could clearly see the bright orange-yellow of his beak and eyes. He cocked his head left and right then he fluttered up, settled on a low branch about ten feet away, and started to sing. My wee rushed onto the mess of old leaves and undisturbed black earth in a steady, hot flow. Although there was no one else to hear, the splashing made me feel embarrassed and I was glad the birdsong drowned most of it out. A slight wind swished through the leaves and the screech of an ambulance siren came and went from somewhere out beyond the square. When I was nearly done, I fixed my eyes on the blackbird, willing him to keep singing for the last few seconds. As my wee slowed to a trickle, the cold air found its way under my dress, creeping up my legs and around my middle. I shivered. At the very last drop, like somehow he knew, the blackbird stopped and the place fell silent.

I didn't move. I was suddenly scared. I was still staring at the blackbird but I couldn't see him any more; he was just a dark, blurry blob. My gaze had shifted. My eyes were focused on something behind him now and what I realized I was looking at made my skin start to prickle and crawl. There was movement in the tree. A faint swaying in the branches behind the blackbird.

I wasn't alone at all.

What I saw was a foot. A large foot. In a muddy black boot that had a strap and a silver buckle. And close beside it, another one, kicking lamely against the tree trunk. Above them was a pair of mucky, brown corduroy trousers, then, further up, a dark red shirt and around it, a grubby black coat.

The prickle on my skin turned to a burning flood that seeped through my body and thump-thumped in my head. Hard as I tried to convince myself that someone might've put together a sort of scarecrow for a joke, I knew this collection of limbs and clothes had to belong to a person.

A man.

A stranger.

I couldn't bring myself to look into his face but I knew if I did he'd be looking straight at me. I thought I'd been all alone. Hidden away. But he must have been there the whole time. Watching. He'd seen me pulling down my pants. And now he had a full view of me pissing in the undergrowth. I shouldn't have gone off on my own. I shouldn't have followed the others out of the car in the first place. I had to get back to them. My wee had stopped but my pants were around my ankles; I'd have to pull them up before I could run. But if I stood to do that, I'd expose my thighs and maybe my bum and I didn't want him to see any more than he already had. I'd have to be careful. And quick.

Keeping my eyes down, I reached in under the folds of my dress. I hooked my fingers around one leg of my pants and deftly stepped out of them, leaving them behind, cherry pink against the dark earth. I was running before I even stood up. Galloping over tangled roots and kicking sprays of crispy leaves in the air, I didn't look back. I leaped over the circle of black stones but one of my knees buckled when I landed and I stumbled and part crawled the last few feet. I dragged myself under the holly bush and back out onto the grass. My breath wheezed in and out of my throat and goosepimples raced up my legs and arms. I felt dizzy and my chest hurt. The sunlight was blinding and I squinted against it as I looked around.

The park was deserted. There was no sign of Sandra or Mel.

The red ball lay in the middle of the grass and I ran towards it, expecting them both to materialize. I tapped it with my foot, but it was burst and bumped only a couple of inches over the ground.

I spun around. Selfish as Mel was, I didn't think he'd have left without me. They had to be hiding. I didn't know what frightened me more: the fact that I was all alone, or the fact that they might be watching me from some secret viewing point, like that man in the tree. I began looking around trunks, even thin ones they couldn't possibly be behind, my feet clumping awkwardly across the grass as if they weren't properly connected to my body.

Then I remembered the reason we were there, and wondered if Mam and Dad were finished getting the keys. What if they'd all gone off to the new house without me? If, in their panic to get everything done on time, they hadn't noticed I'd been left behind. I ran along the path, trying to remember the way we'd come in. Then I started to pray. I'd been lost before when I was five, on a Sunday trip to Brittas Bay. I still hate the feel of sand between my toes.

When I eventually found the car, it was empty. I stood beside it for as long as it took me to say the Our Father, then ran back into the park. I thought how much I hated Mel and Sandra for leaving me on my own. Back again where I'd left them, I sank to the ground and started to cry. It was all their fault; if they hadn't left the car, I'd never have followed.

I lay down on the grass. The damp soaked up through my dress, and my bum felt really cold without my pants. Above me, a lone cloud hung in the blue sky, ragged and forlorn. The shape of it reminded me of the stain on the back of Mam's smock and the horrible way Sandra had sneered at how I'd described it. Then I remembered something.

I jumped to my feet.

This was a park we'd come to before. When Mam was having her check-up at the baby hospital.

I knew what had happened. I was sure of it. I began walking across the park, pretty certain where the entrance nearest the hospital was. And as I got closer to it, I saw them. Dad, Mel and Sandra. Holding hands. Swinging into the park with smiles across their faces. When there was no sign of Mam, I knew I'd been right.

'Guess what?' Sandra asked when I reached them. She was sort of breathless and her face was all flushed. And her feet danced about, as if she badly needed to go to the toilet. She was trying not to smile.

'Mam's had the baby,' I said quietly.

Her face crumpled into a frown and she stopped moving. 'How did you know?'

'I just guessed,' I said. 'I knew the hospital was near here.' My breath caught in my throat. 'Why . . . why did you leave me in there on my own?'

'It was only for a few minutes. We couldn't find you anywhere.' She squinted her eyes at me. 'You weren't *crying*, were you?'

I shook my head. 'No, why would I be?'

'We haven't seen it yet or anything,' she said. 'So don't think you've been left out.' She started walking. Then she looked back with a smirk. 'We just found out first, that's all.' I stuck my tongue out and made a face but she just laughed and skipped off down the path.

'It's a boy,' Mel announced blankly. I could tell he was put out; his authority was threatened.

'It was all a bit sudden, love,' Dad said, taking my hand. 'But Mam's fine, baby's fine. The nurses'll look after them. We've a lot more to get through today.' He let out a big sigh, as if he'd had more than enough already.

As I'd suspected, we didn't get in trouble for leaving the car. On another day, our disobedience would've been the priority, and we'd have been punished. That day, it wasn't even noticed. Dad's eyes were fixed on the distance, in a sort of vacant, unseeing way, like he wasn't sure who he was. He'd just witnessed his fourth child coming into the world, and was shortly to leave the place of his own birth for ever. That night, he'd be sleeping in a strange room.

As we walked through the park back to the car, I was angry. Dad could've waited until he'd found me. He didn't have to go and tell the others about the baby first. Was it any wonder I tried to predict things when everything seemed to happen without me? And the fact that I had a new brother didn't make me feel any less alone; I knew there was far too much of an age gap for us to become an inseparable pair.

'Where were you, anyway?' Sandra asked as we got back into the car.

'Nowhere. Just looking around.' I couldn't tell. I was too afraid. If I kept it to myself, I could pretend it hadn't happened. The others would be sure to make a meal of it if I told them. They'd rub it in my face in front of Dad, seeing as I'd been the one supposed to be keeping an eye on them.

The removal men were waiting for us when we got back and Dad made us stay in the car while he supervised the stacking of our belongings into the big green truck. It didn't take long for trouble to start. Mel invented a game which involved each of them pinching the other's arm and seeing who could last the longest without screaming. When Sandra got tired of it, she began waving out at the removal men and collapsing into giggles whenever they waved back. I wished Mam was with us. And part of me wished our baby brother hadn't been born. Not yet. Not today. Not at the exact time I was being watched by that man in the park. What would Mam say if she knew? I leaned my head against the window and closed my eyes. And though I hadn't seen the stranger's face, I couldn't help imagining what it might look like.

The others grew even more giddy on the drive to our new house. They wondered out loud what lay in store for us in Hillcourt Rise and asked Dad questions he couldn't possibly answer. How many families lived there? How many children? What were they like? What sort of games did they play? They jumped about in their seats, rolled the windows up and down and found the most ridiculous things amusing. Sandra thumped me on the shoulder each time she made what she thought was a funny joke, hoping to make me laugh. After a while, she succeeded. We forgot to dislike each other and I found myself caught up in the excitement. But when Dad said we were nearly there, I told her to leave me alone. I didn't want to be distracted by her silly games. She might have thought moving was something to laugh about but I didn't. I wasn't as sure as she and Mel were about making friends and becoming part of a whole new neighbourhood. And I still felt more than a bit uneasy after the episode in the park. I thought about Mam. She'd been the one who'd wanted to move more than any of us and now she was missing our first day.

We drove up a hill lined with low stone walls, topped with spiky black railings. On either side, thin, leafy trees supported by tall stakes had been planted every few feet. At the top, a white metal sign attached to a wall said *Hillcourt Rise* in big, black curly letters. Dad turned left and slowed down. Mel and Sandra could barely contain themselves. A huge green opened out in front of us, dotted with bushes and cherry trees . . . and kids. A big gang of them. As we drove along, I could see some of them turning their heads to follow us while others lay on the grass or continued with their games of chasing and football.

It was just then that Dad nearly knocked Shayne Lawless down. I don't know if he ran out in front of us deliberately or not, but either way, he made sure he got our attention.

Some of the houses in the estate faced directly onto the green, but others, like number forty-two, were set further away, in small cul-de-sacs. As soon as we'd pulled into the driveway, Mel and Sandra asked if they could go and play. They took the relief on Dad's face as a 'yes' and didn't wait for him to answer. I watched them trying to outrun each other, Sandra's hair flying and Mel's hands slapping against his thighs. When they got to the green, they ran across the grass like a pair of racehorses.

'Off you go, Ruth,' Dad said. 'Grand big green space for you all to play on.'

I stood and looked over at the gathering. Some boy stripped off his T-shirt and threw it in the air. I could tell he was showing off because of us. And I knew Sandra would get involved. I watched her pick up the T-shirt and run, disappearing into a small group of bushes. I turned away and left them to it, walking into our new house for the first time to try and find some underwear. I'd had enough of green spaces for one day.

FOUR

Hillcourt Rise sat on an incline just outside the village of Kilgessin, only five miles south west of Dublin city, but a world and a half away from South Circular Road. The estate was about ten years old when we moved in, so most of the families living there were already well established. Solidly built, red brick and pebbledash with three bedrooms and long back gardens, the houses were regarded as a home for life; most people who moved in never expected to leave. Number forty-two, we learned, was the first to come up for sale since the estate was built. The father of the family who lived there had been offered a too-good-to-turn-down job someplace in America called Conneddy Cut. I heard Dad complaining about them to our Auntie Cissy on the phone: 'Took the carpets and curtains! Would you believe it! What would they be doing with the carpets and curtains from this place in shaggin' Conneddy Cut?'

We were all sorry they hadn't taken the kitchen wallpaper to shaggin' Conneddy Cut too. Apparently Mam had told Dad it was a dirt-catcher and had to go. It had a sort of dimply texture with a pattern of loops and triangles in dark purple, yellow and green. The kitchen cupboards were the colour of Fanta, and I don't think even Dad could have lived with that level of mismatching. He said walking into the room gave him a shaggin' headache. It was one job that couldn't be avoided. So, after breakfast on the first morning, he handed us a bucket of warm water, two sponges and a scraper. He told Sandra and me to soak the walls, and Mel to scrape off the paper.

'Shouldn't he be doing this?' Mel asked, exhausted after five minutes. 'It's not fair. I want to go out on the green.'

'Me too,' Sandra agreed. 'I told Tracey and Valerie I'd be out after breakfast.' She said their names as if they'd been best friends forever. Although she was my sister, I saw Sandra as more like a friend I might invite over from school, someone I connected with occasionally for a couple of hours, then happily forgot about for weeks. I think Mam and Dad were disappointed that she and I hadn't formed a strong sisterly bond, especially as there was only a year between us, and it had been assumed we'd be close. But we were different in many ways. Sandra was more physical than I was. She preferred football and rounders to reading and drawing, and saw things like cycling and skipping as competitive sports, whereas I regarded them as enjoyable pastimes.

For all her boyishness, though, Sandra was a bit of a girly-girl underneath. She often experimented with the bits and bobs the Avon lady persuaded Mam to buy. Once I'd caught her at the mirror in our bedroom, trying to glue a pair of false eyelashes to her lids with a tube of Bostik. She begged me not to tell – and I didn't – but she still blamed me when Mam found out. I tried telling her It was fairly obvious she'd been up to something, as her eyes were all red and sticky, but she never believed me.

And if Mel ever brought a friend home from school, Sandra would badger them for ages, sitting with them to watch telly and insisting on joining in whatever game they were playing. Then she'd get changed into a different outfit and parade around, flicking her hair over her shoulders.

Mel picked a fight with Sandra about who should soak and who should scrape and ended up chasing her out to the back garden. While they screamed and shouted at each other, I carried on with the job of removing the wallpaper. Soon I found that if I picked carefully at a loose corner, a whole strip would come away in one piece, exposing a clean, light pink surface. I liked doodling, but my efforts were usually confined to copybook pages. The huge expanse I'd just revealed was calling out to be drawn on. So, while the others continued their fight in the garden, I ran upstairs to get the set of markers I'd hidden under my pillow as soon as we'd arrived. I'd had to keep them away from Sandra; she was always taking the red one to colour in her nails.

When I came back down I could hear muffled screams from outside and guessed Mel was sitting on top of Sandra. I stared at the bare wall. I didn't think about what to draw. I just found myself taking the brown marker and running it up then down, in two long, straight lines about six inches apart and filling the space between with whirls and spirals. I topped it off with shorter, criss-crossing brown lines and little green oval shapes dotted here and there. I'd drawn a tree. The trunk, the branches, the leaves.

Then I climbed up on a chair and drew another branch, longer than the others, and on it I began to draw the man. I did the outline of his body, then his dark red shirt, his mucky brown trousers, his buckled shoes. After that, I drew the blackbird and I put little notes around him so you could tell he was singing. Then, before I even knew it, I was drawing the man's face. I gave him dark, staring eyes, thick black eyebrows and a half-open, twisted mouth.

I jumped down and looked up at what I'd done. I hadn't wanted anyone to know about the man and yet here he was now, almost life-size on our kitchen wall. I hadn't planned to draw him. It was like something had taken over me and made me do it. And now I wished I hadn't.

'What the hell is that?' Mel asked as he and Sandra burst back into the kitchen.

'Nothing. Just a picture,' I told him.

'I don't like the look of him,' Sandra said. 'He's sort of . . . weird.'

'Good job he's going to be papered over,' Mel said with a laugh. He waved the scraper in the air out of Sandra's reach and tried to smooth down the cow's lick in his hair with the other. He was obsessed with flattening it. He spent ages every morning trying to beat it down, trying everything he could lay his hands on in the bathroom, even toothpaste. But nothing ever worked.

'Maybe you should ask Dad for some of that paste when he mixes it,' Sandra jeered at him. 'It might work on your stupid cow's lick.'

'Take the bloody scraper if you want,' he said, throwing it across the floor.

'It's OK,' she sniffed, plunging her sponge into the bucket. 'I think I prefer the soaking anyway.'

Mel picked up the scraper again and raised it over her head, his face scrunched up like a walnut. I'd seen that look before. And it hadn't ended well.

'*Stop!*' I shouted. 'Or I'll tell Dad you said "bloody".'

He gave me a glare and got back to the job without a word. But I ended up doing most of the work. I could feel the eyes of the man on me the whole time, so I worked extra fast to get away from his stare.

Mam came home with Kevin three days later. Dad hadn't allowed us to go in and see her in the hospital. He said she didn't need us lot on top of her so Auntie Cissy had come to mind us when he went in to visit. The first thing Mam said when she walked in the door was, 'Would you look at the state of Ruth's hair! It's a disgrace!'

It was true. The plaits she'd insisted on doing the morning we moved were still there – just about. Ribbonless, the straggly ends matted and stuck with stuff they'd dangled in throughout the last few days: butter, tomato sauce, wallpaper paste. 'Did no one think to give it a brush?' she asked. 'Not even you, Cissy? What must the neighbours think?'

Auntie Cissy looked at me with her shark eyes. 'Sorry, Rose,' she answered, in her robot voice. Cissy was Dad's older sister. She wasn't a very good minder. Of course, the others loved her; she let them do whatever they wanted, while she sat at the kitchen table repeatedly tucking her lank hair behind her ears, reading Sherlock Holmes books she borrowed from the library. Cissy was married to Uncle Frank, but they had no children. I used to think it was just as well, as she would've made a terrible mother. She hardly even looked at Kev.

We, on the other hand, couldn't contain our excitement, and pushed each other out of the way as we tried to get the best view of the latest addition to the family. He was tiny, with wrinkled fingers and puffy eyes, and thick black hair like Dad's. We stroked his cheeks and held his hands and laughed when he yawned, showing off his tiny pink tongue. There was a fight about which one of us should be allowed to hold him first and Mam raised her eyes, saying she wondered when the novelty would wear off.

'Probably when his nappy needs changing,' Dad said.

In the days and weeks that followed, I often awakened to the sound of screeching at six o'clock in the morning. Even though she was breastfeeding, Mam got up out of bed and brought Kev downstairs. She liked to sit in her bright, clean kitchen, surrounded by all her brand-new appliances. She'd pestered Dad for a pop-up toaster and a shiny electric kettle, the kind that turned itself off when the water was boiled. They took pride of place on the white worktop and she polished them every day. I often examined my reflection in the silver surface of the toaster. She said she loved the new wallpaper with its smooth, washable pattern of golden onions and copper pots. I'd been relieved when Dad had papered over the man in the tree. But I never forgot he was there. I felt his eyes on me whenever I sat at the table. It was like he'd followed me all the way from the park to Hillcourt Rise.

Mam would let me hold Kev while she made tea and toast. I'd try and shush him, rocking him in my arms and sliding my stockinged feet across the lino. Then she'd sit down at the formica table, using her free hand to eat and drink while her other arm held Kev as he hungrily sucked away. I'd sit on the chair opposite, with my chin in my hands, watching the new addition to our family and trying to remember what it had been like without him. I couldn't. It was if he'd always been there.

The hot weather continued, and for our first few weeks in Hillcourt Rise, the days ran together, sticky and sweet, like a stream of warm custard poured from a jug. The others each fell in love with someone different almost every day. I'd sit on the edge of the green, able to watch them both from a distance for the very first time. Mel showing off in front of the girls and Sandra flirting with Shayne Lawless. When we'd lived on the South Circular, we'd always been on top of one another. If they were playing on the path outside our house, I was only ever a few feet away, sitting on the front step or spying on them with my nose squashed up against the window of the front room. On the green of Hillcourt Rise, however, I found I could see things in new and altogether more interesting ways.

FIVE

The first person I got to know in Hillcourt Rise was Bridie Goggin. She lived next door in number forty-three. Her husband, Dick, had died suddenly from a 'clot in the brain' about a year before we arrived. They had three teenagers when they made the move to Dublin from Naas, in County Kildare, so they weren't the typical Hillcourt Rise family. And by the time we came, their children had left home.

Bridie made it her business to welcome us to the neighbourhood, bringing a homemade Victoria sponge, oozing jam and cream, to our door the day we moved in. And when Mam came home with Kev, she left a wicker basket of fruit, with a real pineapple and big, furry peaches. It only took a day or two before I'd wormed my way into Bridie's house. I knew she'd like me; I was quiet and wouldn't interrupt the flow of her chatter. When things got too noisy in our house (as they often did) I'd slip in to Bridie's, knowing there'd be a cushion under my bum and a coconut macaroon in my mouth almost as soon as I walked in the door.

Dick Goggin had been a bank manager in the nearby village of Westgorman. From the crystal-framed photographs on Bridie's glass-topped telephone table, I saw that he'd been a big rhino of a man with a purple face and a halo of snow-white hair. Bridie was always re-arranging the photographs, glancing at herself in the hall mirror as she did so, patting her lacquered nest of spun-gold hair and applying yet another coat of tangerine lipstick.

Her house was full of knick-knacks and boxes of stuff that she never used like china tea sets, fancy tablecloths and embroidered pillowcases. But for all their contents, the rooms seemed kind of cold and empty. We often saw her at night through her windows, wandering about in her dressing gown, drawing the heavy curtains like some sort of sad old ghost. Arriving into mass on Sundays, I'd scan the crowded church for her big fur hat and lead Mam to the pew behind her. While Father Feely's bumblebee voice thrummed up through the dusty, dead air, I'd spend a happy hour fiddling with the clawed paws and tail of Bridie's fox fur stole.

One sluggish afternoon, not much more than a week after we'd moved in, Bridie asked me to help deadhead the roses in her front garden. The air that day was thick with a kind of gluey heat that made me feel like I was wrapped in cling film. From the beginning, Bridie had made good use of me, securing my help with jobs around the house, in return for tasty delights from her well-stocked kitchen cupboards. As she set about showing me how to snip off the withered roses and gather them into a pile, someone began rattling the gate to get our attention. I looked up and saw Shayne Lawless, swinging something around that made a *whupp-whupp* noise as it slashed through the warm, hazy air. The neck of his pea green T-shirt was torn at the seam, as if he'd wrenched himself away from someone's tight grasp, and through the rip I could see the tanned skin of his chest and the flash of a silver St Christopher medal. His skin, hair and eyes were a light, toffee brown colour and this, along with his jerking, puppet-like movements, made him look like a life-sized wooden Pinocchio.

Bridie walked over to the gate, pulling off her gardening gloves, finger by finger. 'Stop that at once!' she said. 'You'll have someone's eye out!'

Shayne continued, right in front of her face, creating a sort of current that lifted the curls off his grimy forehead every few seconds. 'Yer brother around?' he asked me, his gaze unconnected with mine. His right hand hung lazily over the top of Bridie's gate and I noticed lines of black dirt under his fingernails. He was about average size for a twelve-year-old, but could've passed for any age between ten and fourteen. It was as if various parts of him were growing at different speeds: his nose was still snub and babyish, while his eyes were sunken and grey-rimmed, like they belonged to an old man.

'No,' I said. 'He's gone to get the messages for my mam. But my sister'll be out when she's finished the ironing.' I immediately regretted the amount of detail I gave him.

'Wooo-oooh,' he sang. 'Where'd ye live before? Walnut Grove?'

Little House on the Prairie was one of my favourite programmes and I fancied myself as something of a Laura Ingalls: kind of thoughtful and smart, with my hair in plaits and a closer relationship with my father than my brother and sister. So I didn't take kindly to his scorn. I moved closer, planning to say something sarcastic, but all I could do was stare. He tilted back his head and smiled knowingly at me, showing surprisingly even white teeth, and an inch-long raised scar, like a glistening worm, on the underside of his chin. My nose picked up his scent: a mix of wet earth, cigarette smoke and strawberry bubble gum.

'Off you go,' Bridie said, shooing him away. 'Go on. Away with you! And give that here, whatever it is.'

Shayne smiled and let his plaything slip out of his fingers. Then he laughed as it sailed over the gate and through the air, landing with a thump on Bridie's huge, batch-loaf bosoms. Terror spread across her face when she looked down. Lying between her bosoms was a snake. She was hysterical.

'Ruth! Help me!' she screamed, fluffing at the snake with her raw-sausage fingers. But her actions only made it slither underneath the front of her peacock-patterned dress. Shayne made a run for it. 'Come back you!' she called, her eyes filling with tears.

But he was already belting up towards the green. Bridie pulled out the front of her dress like a tent and did a little dance on the driveway, causing the snake to slip down past her stomach and thighs before bouncing out from between her mottled legs onto the warm, sticky tarmac. Holding a hand to her chest, she bent to have a look. 'Oh dear God!' she whispered breathily. 'Is it dead? *Ruth! Tell me!* Is it dead?'

I bent down to inspect it. The snake was over a foot long, yellowish-green, with a white criss-cross pattern all down its back. Its head and tail curled in opposite directions and out of its mouth lolled a blood red, forked tongue. It was clearly a rubber reptile, and not a very realistic one when I looked at it closely. But Bridie didn't have her glasses on and she found it difficult to see details without them. I tipped it with my toe, making it spring forward half an inch. Bridie jumped.

'Get rid of it! We have to get rid of it!'

'It's OK,' I said flatly. 'It's just rubber.'

If Bridie had been a shade more clever, she might've detected my disappointment. Not because the snake was rubber, but because I'd told her. If I'd let on it was real, I could have been the hero and had the run of the biscuit tin for weeks. All those coconut macaroons . . .

'*Rubber*? You mean it's not real?' She shook a shiver out of her body. 'Well of all the . . .'

I picked up the snake and tossed it onto the soft heap of dead roses, where it sank into the ragged petals like a corpse in a satin-lined coffin.

'I need to go in for a sit-down, dear. I feel a bit faint,' said Bridie with a whimper. 'Let run wild, he is. Mother takes no notice. No notice whatsoever. And her clicking around in her high-heeled boots.'

Shayne Lawless was such a pig. How could Sandra like him? And I didn't care for the sound of his mother either. Mothers weren't supposed to wear high-heeled boots. They were for teenagers, or Elton John, or the girls who danced on *Top of the Pops* every Thursday night – people who wanted to be noticed. Sandra would probably wear high-heeled boots when she was older. For the moment, she had to content herself with doing cartwheels in front of Shayne Lawless every day on the green. Even when she was wearing a dress.

Bridie went inside. I got down on my hunkers and lifted the snake up by its tail. Laying it out on the grass, I pinched its silly-looking tongue between my thumb and forefinger and carefully snipped it off with the sharpened blades of the clippers Bridie called her 'secateurs'.

Later on, I slipped both tongue and body into the space beneath the loose bottom of my red satin-lined musical jewellery box.

In the days that followed, I lingered longer on the edge of the green and soon learned the names and faces of all the kids. There was Valerie Vaughan. She was twelve and lived in number twenty-one with her parents and two younger brothers. Their house had leaded windows, a brass number on a grey marble plaque beside the door, and a white carriage lantern hanging from a big fancy pole in the front garden. Mrs Vaughan made you take your shoes off at the front door if you were ever asked inside and there was a 'don't touch!' sort of feeling in all the rooms. Mr Vaughan – Paddy – worked for a big builders' suppliers, and was always away, 'sourcing timber products in eastern Europe' according to Valerie.

She was tall for her age and annoyingly mature. Her full face was spattered with fat freckles like grains of brown sugar, and she wore braces on her teeth. She wasn't allowed to eat sticky things like Kalypso bars or Lucky Lumps, insisting, 'I prefer fruit anyway', and chomping noisily on apples like a horse, even eating the core. Her thick, auburn hair was always scraped back off her face into a ponytail that swished from side to side as she walked. Tiny emerald studs sparkled in her ears and she wore her name in swirly gold letters on a chain around her neck, as if to remind us all who she was. As a rule, Valerie ignored her two brothers out on the green, but she sprang to their defence if anyone upset them. Mrs Vaughan – Nora – paid for her daughter to take tennis lessons at a local club. Valerie had the most expensive Slazenger racquet you could buy, one with a zipped, navy leather cover, and she practised on the road outside her house, in full tennis whites, with Tracey Farrell.

There were six children in the Farrell family, Tracey being the eldest, and Mrs Farrell – Geraldine – was pregnant with number seven when we arrived. Tracey was rarely seen without a younger brother or sister clinging on to some part of her body, leaving her clothes permanently blotched with hardened patches of saliva and snot. Often she was left in charge of the whole litter on the green for hours, screaming at them crazily for the slightest offence.

She was the bossiest person in Hillcourt Rise. Even more so than Sandra or Mel. Small for her age, and what would be described as 'painfully thin', she had limp black hair that was never allowed to grow past her chin. Her skin bruised easily and pale blue veins ran close to its surface. I couldn't look at her limbs without thinking about the bones that lay under their scant covering of flesh. There was something about her that made me imagine Mr and Mrs Farrell in bed, touching each other, and Tracey falling out into the world from between her mother's short legs. I could never regard her as being totally clean.

The twins, Tina and Linda O'Dea, lived in number ten. They hated each other, and their older brother David, and it was clear both of them wished they'd been born an only child. They were identical and very pretty in a Disney sort of way, with large grey-blue eyes that dominated their heart-shaped faces, flushed pink cheeks and rippling, strawberry-blonde hair. They both fought to be the supreme O'Dea daughter, a battle neither of them was ever going to win. Mel routinely tried to make an impression on them and blamed his cow's lick for their lack of interest. He accused Sandra of doing the same thing with Shayne Lawless.

'You're such an embarrassment,' he said to her. 'Can you not see you're making a show of yourself? Ask Ruth what you look like.'

It was another blue-sky day. Sandra sat on our garden wall, kicking her heels against the pebbledash, shielding her eyes from the sun. We were waiting for Mam to bring Kev out, so we could wheel him around the estate while she got some work done. Mel was bent to the ground, carefully lacing up his new sand-coloured desert boots, convinced his choice of footwear would melt one or other of the twin's frozen hearts.

'How would Ruth know? She's never even properly on the green,' Sandra said, flicking her hair over her shoulder. I was hoping not to be drawn in, but Mel persisted.

'You've seen her, haven't you?' he asked me.

I chewed at the inside of my cheek, peering down at the teeny red spiders we called 'bloodsuckers' racing about on the top of the wall. 'I don't know,' I said.

''Course you have! You notice stuff. And you're always spying on us!'

Sandra slid off the wall, rubbing invisible dust from the bum of her denim skirt. 'Yeah, you are always spying on us.' Her eyes narrowed, ready for interrogation. But Mam interrupted, bumping the pram down the front step. 'I'm wheeling,' Sandra announced.

'Didn't you wheel the last time?' Mam said. 'I think it's Ruth's turn.'

Sandra shrugged, giving me her best 'I-don't-care look'. 'Yeah, well,' she sniffed, 'but you have to bring him onto the green.'

Mam stood in the garden, arms folded and looking tired with blue-ish half-moons under her pale eyes. The frilly apron she'd made and embroidered the words 'Home Sweet Home' on was tied loosely around her waist, and she wore Dad's tan suede slippers. On top of her head, as always, three carefully wound circles of hair were held in place with silver, spring-loaded hair clips. Every evening, before Dad came home, she'd release the clips and run her fingers through the curls they'd created. Then she'd pat some powder on her nose and colour in her lips with Desert Dawn.

'He should sleep for a while,' she said. 'Bring him back when he wakes.'

If it wasn't for Kev, I don't think I'd have ventured onto the battlefield of the green so soon. Perhaps not at all. But that afternoon, I trundled his pram over the daisies and buttercups like a chariot, screened from the eyes of the assembled gang by its shield of navy and chrome. Some of the kids sat cross-legged on the grass, others sprawled out on their backs, and it was obvious they'd all just been to the shop – everyone was sucking on a Kool Pop. Tracey Farrell was the first to approach.

'He's not supposed to be lying on his back,' she announced, poking her head in under the hood of the pram. 'My mam says they can choke and die if they do.'

I turned my back on her and busied myself making a daisy chain, tying it around my wrist. Kev let out a whimper, so I got up to check on him. He looked like a troll version of Dad, with his jet-black hair and sticky-out ears.

'What's his name?' I heard someone ask from behind.

It was David O'Dea, arriving out of nowhere as if he'd been beamed up, *Star Trek*-style. He tried to smile and ran his fingers through his fringe. At fourteen, David was the oldest of the green gang. He was always perfectly dressed. He looked like he'd been born to wear a uniform, with his shoes unscuffed and his clothes crisp and spotless, as if they'd been specially made to fit. He wore his casual check shirts with the top button closed and his Levi's with creases ironed into the legs. His clear skin was slightly tanned all year round, with an even covering of fine, bleach-blond hair and chocolate moles of varying sizes dotted across his face and arms. On his right wrist he wore a plaited, red leather strap, fastened with a brass stud that he kept snapping open and shut when he spoke. David had the best poker face of anyone I've ever known. I never really knew what he was thinking. Most of the time, I just had to guess.

'Hmm . . . Stairway to Kevin,' he said, when I answered him. I knew he was expecting me to ask him what he meant but I said nothing. I soon learned David often said strange things.

'How old is he?' he asked.

'He was born the day we moved in,' I blurted.

'So he's lived here his whole life?'

'I . . . I suppose so . . . but it's only been about three weeks.'

'Still his whole life, though.'

I wasn't sure if I should disagree, but before I could say anything, he turned and walked towards the gang. I followed, fixing my eyes on the buttoned back pocket of his jeans. Shayne Lawless spat out the bit of plastic Kool Pop wrapper he'd been chewing when he saw me approach.

'Hope it's not goin' to start screamin',' he said, tipping his head in the direction of the pram. 'Ye can bring it home if it does.'

Sandra laughed and shoved Shayne's shoulder. Any excuse to touch him. Tracey ran over, two or three little ones dragging out of her skirt. She shook them off and put her hands on her hips, tossing her hair as if it was long enough to flick over her shoulders.

'We're playing chasing,' she announced, pointing at me. 'She's on!'

The gang scattered across the grass and in behind the small trees, shrieking and whooping, then falling quiet. Shayne hung back. Facing me, he held his arms out from his sides, shaking his hands, palm sides up. 'Well? What's the matter?' he taunted. 'Afraid ye won't be able to catch me?'

The others waited at a distance: Sandra, Tracey and the twins, dancing around in a circle; Valerie jogging on the spot; Mel squatting, brushing grass from his precious desert boots. Kev began to squirm and I held fast to the pram handle. I looked up at the sky. It had never seemed so far away, like one in a Western: overpowering and vast and almost too blue. The sun beat down on Shayne's ragged head, his face tilted to the ground, his skittering eyes looking up from under his arched brows.

'Don't worry, he won't bite,' David whispered, looking into the pram. 'Shayne's not as partial to the taste of blood as I am.' He turned and gave me a creepy sort of smile and I wheeled Kev away from him. David O'Dea was making me uncomfortable. And he seemed to be enjoying it.

I was just about to start the chase when an ear-splitting cry ripped through the air. Kev was letting me know he was hungry. He wriggled wildly, kicking off his blanket, his face like a shrivelled tomato. Shayne slapped his hands over his ears.

'Jeeeesus! Get it out of here!' he screamed.

I tried rocking the pram gently, but it was hopeless. The game was over before it had begun; I didn't know if I was disappointed or relieved. I could run as fast as Mel if I wanted to, but I wasn't sure if that was speedy enough to catch Shayne.

'Right! Sandra's on!' Tracey shouted. The others readied themselves for the chase, except David, who was lying flat out on the grass now, tracing letters in the air with his forefinger.

'By the way,' Shayne said with a laugh, making sure everyone could hear, 'how's me snake? Hope ye looked after it.'

David sat bolt upright, his face as alert as a curious pup's.

I took a hard, deep breath, puffing myself up to my full height. 'Oh yes,' I said. 'I took care of it all right. I flushed it down Bridie Goggin's toilet.'

SIX

We'd all just sat down to dinner the next evening when the doorbell rang. Dad rolled his eyes and forked another chunk of liver into his mouth, pushing himself up out of his chair.

'God's sake!' he moaned, chewing. 'What time is this to call? Remind me to disconnect that bell, Rose. It's too shaggin' loud.' He tucked his loose shirttails into his slacks, then wiped his mouth and moustache with the back of his hand.

Since we'd moved in, the doorbell had caused Dad no end of irritation. Back on the South Circular, we'd had a brass knocker in the shape of a horseshoe, which had never proven to be very effective. It couldn't be heard from the kitchen and I think Dad liked it that way. But in Hillcourt Rise, there was no escaping the *drrriiing drrriiing*. We could even hear it in the back garden. And we soon became familiar with the usual suspects who called every week. On Tuesdays, it was the swarthy, sullen pools man, with his chipped front teeth and sellotaped glasses, and his red pencil stub tucked behind his ear. Wednesdays, it was Pat, the chirpy vegetable man who always added a free cabbage or cauliflower to Mam's order (never something edible, like a couple of mandarins, or a Granny Smith). And on Friday evenings, the constantly worried-looking Mrs Shine, collecting the church dues in a nylon bag. Father Feely made it his business to visit his parishioners on a regular basis too. I usually hid in my wardrobe when I heard his droning voice rising up through the house, terrified he might ask me questions I couldn't answer or insist I dance a reel for him which had happened to Sandra the first time he called. She, of course, revelled in Father Feely's delight, high-stepping her way across the shag-pile, through the hall, and out into the front garden, while he clapped his hands and tra-la-la-ed some awful diddly-eye tune.

'We're not buying anything, Mick,' Mam said over her shoulder, as Dad went to see who it was. He was easily persuaded by door-to-door sellers. Since we'd moved in, he'd already bought a set of cork tablemats that went all warped and wobbly the first time we used them, and a car air-freshener in the shape of a strawberry that Mam threw in the bin because the smell of it made her sneeze.

'I know, I know,' Dad muttered.

I sliced my liver into thin strips, arranging them in a pattern of squares around my plate. Sandra and Mel swallowed lumps without chewing and, by the looks on their faces, I could tell they were kicking each other under the table.

Dad was at the door for ages. We could hear a husky voice, going high then low, like a singer practising their scales, and Dad mumbling 'Mmms' and 'Uh-huhs' in harmony. I tried to place the voice. It wasn't any of the usual suspects, and it definitely wasn't Bridie – she was much more shrill, and she never called at dinnertime, anyway. She would've considered it rude.

'God only knows what useless article he'll come away with this time,' Mam said. 'Should've answered it myself.' She sighed and told us to eat up.

I began piling up my liver strips to see how tall a structure I could make before they toppled over. Anything was better than actually eating it. But I soon got distracted. I could feel the man watching. Though he was trapped beneath the layer of vinyl wallpaper, I still had a feeling he could see me. I glanced up at the wall and was sure I spotted a sort of eye shape in the middle of an onion like he'd poked a hole through and was watching me picking at my dinner. I imagined he might tear his way out of his paper prison one night while we were in our beds. He'd creep upstairs and kick at Mam and Dad's door, the buckles on his boots glinting in the moonlight. I could see myself peeping out at him, my mouth open wide in a silent scream and . . .

'Ruth!' I dropped my fork and it clattered loudly on my plate. Mam was frowning at me. 'Stop playing with your liver,' she said. 'For God's sake, just eat it up!'

Sandra was about to whisper something to Mel when we heard Dad calling from the front door.

'Ruth! Come here for a minute.'

The others widened their eyes. Dad's voice sounded different, softer, almost persuasive. Not like Dad at all. I jumped down from the table, certain it was the encyclopedia man at the door. He'd called the previous week and I'd nearly succeeded in pestering Dad into signing up for *The How and Why Library of Childcraft Encyclopedias* – all fifteen volumes. He'd said he'd be back, and now, I thought, here he was, and Dad was finally coming round to the idea. He just needed my final seal of approval.

When I got to the door, Dad was leaning back against the doorframe, his feet crossed over one another and his hands in his trouser pockets. I immediately suspected I'd been wrong; his pose was too relaxed, not at all suggestive of someone about to sign up to a couple of years of weekly instalments.

'There you are, Roo,' he said. He'd never called me Roo in front of anyone before, apart from Mam or the others, and even then, only on really special occasions, like my birthday, or the day I won first prize in school for my project on the life cycle of the butterfly.

'This is Mrs Lawless,' he said, smiling, 'Shayne's mammy. She wants to ask you something.'

I chewed at the inside of my mouth. It hurt a bit, but at least it tasted better than the liver. I looked at the woman standing at the door. She had her arms folded across her chest, one foot on the drive, and the other planted firmly on our porch step. She was dressed in sky-blue denim, her jeans tucked into knee-high, tan zipped boots, and the sleeves of her Wrangler jacket rolled up to her elbows. Her hair was black with reddish roots and permed into loose, frizzy spirals that curled against her cheeks and down around her neck. A large orange and purple feather hung from one ear, twirling and bobbing with her slightest movement so that it looked like she had a small exotic bird resting on her shoulder.

'Hiya,' she said, with a smile that was all mouth and no eyes. 'Nothin' to worry about, love, but d'ye know where my Shayne's snake might be?' She had a cigarette voice – throaty and smoky and sort of rough – and from her accent I knew she was from somewhere down the country. All her sentences ended on a high note, making everything she said sound like a question. 'See, 'twas a present from his uncle Joe. Brought it back from Orlando, so he did. It's kinda special to Shayne, y'know.' Her eyes were icy-blue, outlined with thick black lines. She blinked a lot when she looked at me, waiting for an answer.

'Well, do you have his snake or not?' Dad asked me. 'Don't keep Liz waiting all day.' He turned to her. 'Kids!' he said with a laugh, as if I wasn't there.

'Sure, who'd have them?' she said, stepping fully up onto the porch and leaning down. I could see her white, blobby bosoms peeping out from the V of her stretchy black top, and the silver-tipped horn on a leather string that nestled between them. 'I'm not going to eat ye,' she said with a laugh, showing me her teeth. I could tell she was trying very hard to be nice. Not much about her was pretty, but I could see how some people might think she was attractive. And the way she hid nothing made you think she was happy with who she was and couldn't care less if you liked her or not.

In my head, I weighed up my options. I'd seen the way Mel tried hard to keep lies going to avoid getting into trouble, and how his elaborate weavings always unravelled. But I considered myself smarter than my big brother.

Liz began tapping her toe on our brown porch tiles. From next door came a scraping sound as Bridie came out and began sweeping her already spotless driveway. I could see her bum wiggling from side to side out of the corner of my eye and knew she was earwigging. As far as she was concerned, I'd tossed the snake out with the heap of dead roses.

'I threw it away,' I said.

Liz Lawless took a long sniff of air in through her nose and shot Dad a piercing look.

'Go and finish your dinner,' he blurted, shuffling his feet. I happily skipped back to the table.

Mam wanted to know what was going on. When I told her, she shook her head. I readied myself for a good giving out to, but instead she said what a stupid woman Liz Lawless was to be coming round here looking for trouble when she should be spending her time putting manners on her son.

'I've heard more than enough about those two already,' she said. 'All kinds of gallivanting going on there, by all accounts.

That child seems to have more uncles than any of us have had hot dinners.' She pointed a finger at me. 'And speaking of hot dinners, eat up. That's the best of liver.'

I complained it was cold now, and that it wasn't my fault I'd had to leave the table to talk to Liz Lawless. Mam tut-tutted and shook her head. She knew she could make me sit in front of it all night and I still wouldn't eat it. 'Oh, all right then,' she said. 'Just leave it.' At least I had Liz Lawless to thank for something. 'But no rice pudding,' she added.

Dad spent another few minutes at the door before he came back into the kitchen. He plonked himself back down in his chair with a puff and ate what was left of his dinner. 'Glad I sorted that out,' he said, after a few minutes of chewing. He looked over at me. 'And what have you got to say for yourself?'

'Bridie was scared,' I said. 'She thought it was real. I had to get rid of it.'

'You should've handed it back. You'd have to feel sorry for him. No daddy in the house to keep him in order. That snake must've meant a lot to him.' Mam raised her eyes to heaven. 'Anyhow,' Dad continued, 'I said I'd touch up the mammy's kitchen, you know, give it a lick of paint. Just to make up for it. Least we can do for her.'

I expected Mam would say something, but she just sat looking at Dad as he hacked at his liver. Mel and Sandra wolfed down their dessert and ran outside. As soon as they were out of the room, Mam set a bowl of the rice pudding in front of me, as I knew she would, and I ate it in silence.

When I looked over at Dad, I noticed that his neck was very red. All the way from his chin to the curly black hair that poked out of his shirt.

The next Sunday, we went for a picnic to the Phoenix Park. After we'd eaten all the corned beef sandwiches and jam sponge, Mel and Sandra ran off to try and catch one of the deer. Mel said it'd be easy – all you had to do was grab hold of their antlers. I stretched myself out on the tartan rug beside Kev, closing my eyes and pretending to fall asleep.

'How long do you think that job's going to take?' I heard Mam say after a few minutes had gone by.

'What job's that?' Dad asked after a pause. I imagined his eyebrows turning into big hairy question marks, his whole face distorted from pretend puzzlement. Even *I* knew what Mam was talking about.

'For that woman,' she said. 'The Lawless woman.'

'Oh! That one. God, love . . . I don't know.' He drew breath in between his teeth, then blew it out again with a *swoosh*. 'Couple of Saturdays should do it, I'd say.'

'Remember we've plenty of half tins in the shed,' she said.

I opened one eye ever so slightly. From behind the screen of my eyelashes, I saw Dad press a finger into the cake crumbs. He rolled them about then flicked them onto the grass.

'We do indeed, Rose my love,' he said. 'Her kitchen might turn out like a patchwork quilt, but at least we won't be forking out for fresh paint.'

'For God's sake, I'm just trying to save us a few bob, Mick. I mean, you're not getting paid for it, so it makes sense, doesn't it?'

'Whatever you say. Look, I know you're not happy about it, but we don't want to fall out with the neighbours and we only after moving in.'

'Well, I suppose so,' she said. 'But don't be making a habit of it.'

'Would you look at the two of them,' Dad said. 'Dead to the world.'

Mam tucked Kev's blanket around his little legs.

'Do you think they're happy?' she asked. 'I mean, do you think we did the right thing, moving?'

I breathed in and out more deeply and squirmed a bit to make my 'sleep' more authentic.

'No doubt about it,' Dad said, stroking my hair. 'Best decision we ever made.'

Mam said nothing. I wondered why she'd asked if moving had been the right thing. Maybe she wasn't sure any more. It was obvious she didn't like the idea of Dad painting the Lawlesses' kitchen for free. I felt a bit guilty; it wouldn't have happened if I hadn't lied about the snake. But then again, I'd seen the way Dad had acted with Liz at the door, and how he was all red when he came back to the table. Maybe he'd have offered to paint her kitchen even if there'd been no mention of the snake at all.

SEVEN

August came around, and with it the horrible realization that summer wasn't going to last forever. We'd almost forgotten that we'd have to go back to school. And not the one we'd been used to; a new one – Kilgessin National. Mam had enrolled us as soon as the offer on our house had been accepted but, at the time, September seemed so far away we were quite sure it would never arrive.

I was in fifth class, and found myself sharing it with the twins, Tina and Linda, and Aidan Farrell. Like most of his brothers and sisters, Aidan had started school much too early; he was nearly a whole year younger than me. Geraldine Farrell's insistence on rushing her offspring out from under her feet meant that in almost every room of Kilgessin National, a Farrell was responsible for slowing progress. Along with Tracey and

Shayne, Mel and Sandra were in sixth class. They'd started school together when they were little – Mam thought it'd be easier that way.

One Saturday, a few weeks after school started, Dad asked Mel to help him carry the paint around to the Lawlesses' house after breakfast so he could get started on the job. Sandra had already left to go to her first Irish dancing lesson in the church hall. She'd spent ages deciding what to wear until Mam went to the bedroom and made her mind up for her. She sat sulking on the stairs, picking at the raised seam of the stretchy, maroon slacks she hated while she waited for Tracey and the twins to call for her as arranged. Just before half past nine the doorbell rang and I watched the four of them link arms and skip down the driveway. Mam had half-heartedly tried to get me to join them. She knew right well she'd never persuade me to go, but I suppose she thought it was her duty to at least attempt to encourage me.

As soon as Sandra left, I went upstairs to the bedroom and took my jewellery box down from the top of the wardrobe. Before I opened it, I examined the almost invisible Sellotape seal I'd stuck across the opening; as far as I could make out, it was still intact. I was sick of Sandra going through my stuff and then denying it. At least this way, there was proof if she'd been at it. I lifted the loose bottom and, very carefully, took Shayne's snake and placed it in the patch pocket of my skirt. I left the tongue sitting on its little bed of cotton wool, thinking it looked like a teeny tiny version of the snake itself. I closed the box, applied a fresh piece of Sellotape, and put it back in the wardrobe.

I touched the snake in my pocket. I liked the way it felt: sort of wet-but-dry. I'd decided to go outside, hoping maybe I'd see Shayne on the green. I imagined myself talking to him, looking him right in the eye, all the while squishing the rubbery length of the snake in my fingers.

Mam was kneeling on the stairs, hoovering. It was one of her Saturday jobs, and one she did even if the steps didn't look dusty at all. She'd taken the long metal pipe off the hoover and was, with great concentration, moving the short plastic bit of the tube from side to side over the carpet's pattern of orange and yellow autumn leaves. 'Where are you off to?' she shouted over the roar of the hoover.

'Just outside for a while,' I said, directly into her ear as I clambered past and tried not to get tangled up in the flex.

'Don't go far. Kevin's due to wake soon and I want you to keep an eye on him while I wash my hair.'

Mam usually washed her hair at night-time when she had a bath. She only washed it in the morning if she wanted to put it in curlers for the day, and that only meant one thing.

'Who's minding us?' I shouted. 'Please don't say it's Auntie Cissy.'

Mam frowned and switched off the hoover. 'What do you mean, "who's minding us"?'

'Babysitting,' I said. 'You are going out tonight, aren't you?'

She raised an eyebrow. 'No secrets with you, are there?

And it's not Cissy, by the way. We've decided to let you mind yourselves for a change.'

'Mind ourselves?' I said, grinning. 'You mean . . . you're leaving us on our own?' I could hardly believe it.

'You needn't get too excited,' she said, waving the hoover tube at me. 'We're only going down to The Ramblers for a quiet drink. I think I deserve to escape for a couple of hours now that Kevin is on the bottle.'

I could've thought of better places to escape to than the smelly old Ramblers. Dad had taken us in one Sunday after mass. We'd perched on the rickety barstools, swigging warm Cidona straight from the bottle. Old men with flat caps and gaps in their teeth drank pints of Guinness in grubby alcoves of the bar, throwing remarks at each other across the stinking, yellow fug that passed for air. I didn't like the place at all.

Halfway down the stairs I stopped. 'What if he wakes up?'

'I'll leave a bottle just in case,' she said. 'I'm sure you'll be able to cope. You can sort out who does what among yourselves.' She made it sound easy. I groaned as I pictured us trying to 'cope'. She pretended to lash out at me with the tube of the hoover. 'Go on away with you,' she said, trying to sound cross. Then she turned and switched the machine on again, her bum wiggling from side to side as she attacked the carpet once more.

Outside, everything appeared grey. There was little difference between the colour of the roads and the walls and the sky. Since summer had ended, the place had taken on a sort of settled stillness that hung over the houses like a damp blanket. It was cold. I fastened the tusk-shaped toggles of my brown duffle coat and pushed my hands deep into its pockets. I thought about pulling my hood up but I'd taken out my weekday plaits and I liked the way my hair was all rippled, flowing over my shoulders and down my back. The wet grass on the green made my shoes slick and shiny, as if I'd spent ages polishing them. I stopped for a moment, lifting each foot and twisting it left and right to admire the effect.

'Mmm, what nice shoes you have my dear . . .' It was David, appearing out of nowhere again, clicking his wristband open and shut. 'All the better to kick you to death with.'

My insides jumped but I took a deep breath and managed not to show him that he'd scared me.

'Ha ha. Very funny,' I said.

'Thank you, kind lady. So appealing that my humour is appreciated.' He came up close to me. 'And what's this, pray tell?' he said, flicking at my hair with his long, slender fingers. 'Why, I think even Rapunzel herself would be jealous.'

While I was glad he'd noticed my hair, I didn't care for the way he touched it, as if it was tainted with an infectious disease. I stepped away, eyeing him up and down. He was smiling but I couldn't tell if he was trying to be funny or not. I got the feeling he was acting, pretending to be something he wasn't. In one of Mel's *Strange But True* books, I'd read about people who burst into flames without matches or fire being anywhere near them. For some reason, I could imagine that happening to David. There was something strange going on inside him and it made me uneasy.

'And where is Rapunzel off to this fine morning?' he asked.

I hated the way he was speaking. Like he was in some kind of stupid play.

'Nowhere,' I said, beginning to walk away.

He followed after me. 'Nowhere? A most intriguing answer, don't you think?'

'Not really.' I squeezed the snake in my pocket. I had to think of some way of getting rid of him. 'Actually, I . . . I . . . I'm going down to the Lawlesses'.' I began to run.

'Well then!' he said, breaking into a kind of trot. 'I shall accompany you. I wish to speak to Master Lawless myself.' He kept up with me as I sprinted along towards Shayne's house. 'And what has you calling on them at this early hour, pray?'

I pushed open the gate and gritted my teeth. 'I . . . I just want to see how my dad's getting on. See if he needs any help. He's painting their kitchen.'

'Ah yes,' he said, tapping on the door. 'I heard. The mysterious case of the disappearing snake.' He gave me a narrow, sideways glance and I swallowed hard.

'Ye're here bright and early for a Saturday, aren't ye?' Liz said to David when she opened up. She held a brown and orange striped mug in one hand and a thick slice of well-buttered toast in the other. She yawned. 'Don't think he's even awake yet. Go on up anyway.' David took the stairs two at a time and she watched after him before turning to me with a cold look in her eyes. 'Yer Dad's busy,' she said, chewing her toast noisily. 'Do ye want me to give him a message or what?'

'I . . . uh . . . I just wanted to ask him if he needed any . . . help.' I tried to look past her into the kitchen, hoping Dad might see me at the door. She took another bite and frowned.

'Help, is it? Sure, isn't yer brother here to help him?' She wore a white bobbly jumper with a row of red hearts across the chest and a low rounded neck. The kind of jumper you were supposed to wear a blouse under. A dribble of tea had left a wormy brown stain down its front, and a line of toast crumbs had collected in the crease between her bosoms. 'Go on,' she said, slurping from her mug and nodding in the direction of the kitchen. 'Ye can go in and say hello, I suppose.'

She led the way into the kitchen. Her jeans were rolled up at the ankles and her feet were bare, showing purple-painted nails that curled over the tops of her toes. The place smelled of cigarettes, rotten vegetables and disinfectant. The door to the front room was open and I glanced inside as I passed. The seat cushions from the brown couch were all out of place, as if someone had been searching under them and not bothered to put them back properly. On a low coffee table in front of the fireplace, glasses with various levels of dregs stood around a big brass ashtray overflowing with twisted butts.

'What're *you* doing here?' Mel asked when I stepped into the kitchen.

Dad was leaning against the countertop, smoking, and drinking tea. He straightened himself up when he saw me and stubbed his cigarette out in the sink. He didn't even have his overalls on. 'Something wrong?' he asked.

'I came to see if you needed any help, that's all. I thought you'd have started by now.'

'Just about to,' he said, tipping his head back to drain his mug.

'And we don't need your help,' Mel said, prising open a paint tin with a knife. 'You'd only be in the way.'

Liz gave me one of her no-teeth smiles. 'Well! That was a wasted journey, then. I'll see you out so.'

'Wait,' I said. 'I . . . I really need to go to the toilet.'

'Sure, can't you run on home and go?' Dad said. 'You'll be there in two minutes.'

'But . . . I'm bursting. I really need to go now.'

Dad looked at Liz. 'I'm sorry, is it all right if she . . . ?'

'Go on!' she said, with a false little laugh. 'Top of the stairs.' She followed me out to the hall, then lowered her voice: 'Ye'll be able to have a good nose around while ye're up there. That's what you're here for, isn't it?'

I felt like pulling the snake out of my pocket, flinging it at her and telling Dad he didn't have to paint her kitchen after all. Why had I felt the need to say I'd thrown the snake away anyway? When Liz had called to the door, I could've admitted I had it. But there was something about her that sort of forced me to lie, as if it was what she expected. Producing the snake might've made her like me, and I realised now that I didn't want her to.

All the bedroom doors were open, and none showed any signs of life. The first had a big double bed with lacy pillowcases and a plum-coloured velvet headboard. Clothes and towels were tangled up in balls and tossed all over the floor, and the scuffed toe of a cowboy boot peeked out from under the fringes of the bedspread. In the next room there was a small unmade bed, a huge white wardrobe with oval shaped mirrors on the doors, and a black plastic chair piled high with a tower of yellowing magazines. I presumed this was Shayne's room, as the third bedroom was stuffed almost to the ceiling with cardboard boxes and junk. The bed was visible, but only just. But if the room with the white wardrobe was Shayne's, why wasn't he in there? And where was David? Confused, I began to look around the landing.

Then I saw it: a narrow, twisting, uncarpeted staircase that led towards the ceiling. Shayne's room was in the attic.

Before I'd thought about it, I found myself on the top step, staring at the words 'Go Away' that were carefully written in green marker on the door. I could hear the low buzz of mumbling coming from behind it and was trying to make out what was being said when David opened it up. His face didn't register even mild surprise.

'Well, if it isn't Rapunzel herself, come to dangle her hair out the window and wait for her prince to ride by.'

'What the hell's *she* doin' here?' Shayne asked.

'I fear the fair maiden hath followed me,' David said. 'We met out in the meadow, did we not?'

'Did ye not read what it says on the door?' Shayne asked me.

'I . . . I was looking for the bathroom. Your Mam said it was at the top of the stairs.'

'Hardly all the way up here, is it?' he said. His hair stuck out from his head in thick tufts and he wore only a pair of striped pyjama bottoms.

'How come your room's up here?' I asked.

'Just is.' He scratched his chest and stared at me.

'But why don't you have one of the other rooms? Why is yours up here?'

'I dunno, do I?' he said, annoyed. 'Cos me ma got me uncle Keith to make it, all right?'

I'd seen Uncle Keith once or twice. He wore blue overalls like Dad that hung loose from his bony body, and heavy brown boots with metal heels that clicked as they hit the ground. He had a droopy, untidy moustache and gingery-blond hair that looked as if he'd hacked at it with a blunt scissors in the dark – short and spiky on top and long and straggly, like a dirty dog's tail, down his back. He was always hauling boxes of stuff into the house from his van, whistling tunes I didn't recognize.

'You must be able to see loads from your window,' I said, trying to peer past him. 'The mountains, maybe? Can I have a look?'

'No.'

'Please? I have to go home soon. I'll only be a second.'

He looked at David, who raised his eyebrows and shrugged.

'Hurry up,' Shayne said with a loud sigh.

The first thing that struck me was how secret it felt. How I imagined a nest might feel to a baby bird. This was a place apart, a place that didn't feel connected to anything; not to the house, not to the estate, not even to the rest of the world.

Things could happen here. Hidden things. It was in the air; I could smell it.

The ceiling was painted midnight blue and it sloped on either side like a tent. The window set into it was open, and I stepped up on the tea-chest underneath to have a look outside. Staring out over the place where we lived, I wondered if this was how God felt when he looked down at the world from Heaven. I could see the whole of Hillcourt Rise. To the right was the green, where I spied a few of the Farrells in the care of Aidan, running around with their arms outstretched, bumping into each other on purpose. Their mother was standing at the end of their drive, arms folded, chatting to Nora Vaughan. I saw Bridie on her way back from Mealy's Mini Market, squeezed into a sheepskin coat and hauling a string bag full of groceries. I saw people in their back gardens, children on swings, dads raking leaves, mams hanging washing on lines. And to the left, way beyond the open fields behind the estate, the Dublin Mountains rose and fell in waves of brown and purple.

David and Shayne stood out on the tiny landing, laughing loudly in between low whispers. I jumped down from the tea-chest and looked at the narrow bed with its thin brown blanket, grubby, daisy-patterned sheets and white pillowcase mottled with ancient, yellow-brown dribble stains. The headboard was made of chipboard covered with a layer of varnished wood, lumps of which had been hacked away with something sharp. Against it, a single photograph dangled from a curling strip of Sellotape. It showed a much younger, chubbier Shayne beside a smiling, beefy man in a black leather jacket. 'Uncle Joe' it said, in scribbly biro on the white border.

Looking at it made me feel bad that I had the snake. I reached into my skirt pocket and closed my hand around the clammy rubber. I didn't like the feel of it against my fingers any more. I straightened myself up and turned to leave, but before I did, I swung around and thrust the snake underneath his filthy pillow.

That night, Mam and Dad came downstairs in a waft of perfume and aftershave while we were watching *The Generation Game*. Mam spent ages going on about Kev: how often we should check on him, what to do if he woke up, when to give him his bottle. I tried to listen but was distracted by Mel; he was all jumpy and fidgety and kept darting his eyes over to the sideboard where Mam and Dad had said there was a box of Maltesers for us to share. As soon as they left for The Ramblers, he grabbed the sweets out of the drawer and ripped off the cellophane. Naturally, Sandra had a fight with him over them, but she settled down once *Starsky and Hutch* came on. It was one of her favourites. She'd stuck posters of both cops on our wall, though I couldn't understand how she found either of them even remotely attractive.

We had about half an hour of peace and then Kev woke up. Sandra brought him downstairs and tried to give him his bottle but he didn't seem to want it. Then I took him in my arms and walked around the room, gently rocking him from side to side. Mel sighed loudly every time I passed in front of the telly so I went out into the hall. As I paced up and down, I laid my cheek against his soft, warm head and hummed a tune. He seemed to like that and after about ten minutes he was fast asleep.

I had my foot on the bottom step of the stairs when the doorbell rang, loud and long. Kev's arms flew out from his sides and his eyes opened wide. He stared at me for a second then began to scream. Mel came rushing out to open the door, and I wasn't a bit surprised when I saw Shayne standing on the step.

'Thanks for waking him up,' I said.

'Who? Me? What did I do?' he asked, coming into the house.

'You know Mam said not to allow anyone in,' I said to Mel.

'So what? It's only Shayne. She won't mind.'

'Oh yes she will. She said no one.'

'Shut up you,' he said and Shayne smiled, stuck his tongue out at me and punched Mel on the arm. Mel gave him a playful push and then Sandra appeared, her eyes lighting up. She bit at her bottom lip and went all stupid, as if she'd lost any bit of sense that she had. Kev continued to cry, his face growing redder by the second and I groaned as I made my way upstairs. Mel and Shayne continued hitting each other in a sort of mock fight while Sandra looked on, mesmerized. I was just on the top step when I heard a familiar voice.

'It's only me! I have something nice for you to share.' It was Bridie. She stepped into the hall wearing an ivy-patterned apron over her turquoise trouser suit and carrying a doily-covered plate that held a pyramid of deep-pink meringues, each one sandwiched together with a squelch of thick cream. 'Thought you children might like a few of these,' she said, waving the plate under Sandra's nose. 'Made two-dozen this afternoon, I did. And would you believe they didn't have caster sugar in Mealy's? Had to knock into the presbytery and borrow some from Father Feely's housekeeper. Remind me to drop a plate of them into him before mass tomorrow, Ruth.' She looked around the hall. 'Ruth? Where's Ruth?'

'Up here, Bridie,' I whispered from the top of the stairs.

'There you are! I should've known you'd be the one trying to settle your baby brother. The poor mite. I heard him screaming the place down and I knew your mammy and daddy were out so I—' She stopped mid-sentence when she realized Shayne was there. She looked him up and down. 'And what are *you* doing here?'

Shayne made a face at her and she stiffened, her bosoms expanding as she breathed heavily up through her nose. I crept quickly to the bedroom and settled Kev back into his cot. I gave him a kiss and stroked his cheek and I knew it wouldn't be long till he fell asleep again. I closed the door and heard some sort of a scuffle coming from the hall. I got to the top step just in time to see Bridie making a lunge at Shayne. He laughed in her face, ducking out of her way, but his elbow caught the edge of the plate in her hand. She tried to steady it but it was no use – I watched, almost in slow motion, as each and every one of her pink meringues slid off and landed on the floor with a plop. The doily followed, floating gently through the air like a crocheted flying saucer before coming to rest on the bristles of the welcome mat inside our front door.

Shayne sniggered. Sandra dug her tooth even harder into her lip and cast her eyes up to the ceiling. Mel looked down at the pile of broken meringues and splattered cream, his shoulders slumped in grief at the sheer waste of it all. I understood his despair; we'd been so close to such a plate of treats. Even though they were ruined now, they looked so good: the cream whipped to exactly the right thickness, the broken, crispy shells revealing a sticky, marshmallow-type goo that would've been absolutely melt-in-the-mouth divine.

I wondered who'd be the first to speak. It was one of those moments where no one quite knew what to say. The doily fluttered in the breeze that blew in through the open door, before its movement was killed by the stomp of a big brown shoe.

It was Dad. With Mam behind him. Home early for some reason, their faces hard and stony even before they fully took in the scene. Dad frowned, his eyebrows becoming one long, black caterpillar. He walked straight into the meringue mess before anyone could warn him.

'What the . . . ?' he said, lifting each of his feet in turn.

I shrank back from the top of the stairs, not wanting to be part of whatever was about to happen. But Mam didn't even ask for explanations. She took one look at Shayne and almost shouted, 'Get out of here, you! You've no business being in our house.'

Shayne grinned up in my direction and I slunk even further back into the shadows. Then he bounced out the front door, and in the silence of the hall we heard his pounding feet echo around the cul-de-sac.

'I . . . I'll go and get something to clean up this mess,' Bridie said, all flustered, clumsily attempting to slop dollops of broken meringue and cream onto the plate.

'It's fine, Bridie,' Mam snapped. 'You go on home. There's obviously been enough action here for one day.' She glared at Dad like the whole thing was his fault. He rolled his eyes and mumbled something under his breath. We were in for it.

As silently as I could, I tip-toed back across the landing into Mam and Dad's room and hopped into their bed, snuggling down under the cold sheets and pulling the layers of blankets in around my body. I lay in the centre, my head in the dip between their pillows, listening to the sound of Kev's breathing. I strained to hear what was happening downstairs but there weren't even any muffled murmurings. It seemed as if nothing was being said at all. After a few minutes, Mel and Sandra were marched upstairs. I heard the light being flicked on in our bedroom.

'Where's Ruth?' Mam asked. Her voice had a *don't-mess-with-me* sound.

Sandra mumbled something about me putting Kev to bed. I started to breathe as deeply as I could and curled myself into a tight ball. When Mam came into the room, she didn't even call me; she was fully convinced I was fast asleep. I heard her walking over to Kev's cot to check on him, then she switched on the lamp and began to get undressed. It was only about half past nine, much earlier than she usually went to bed on a Saturday. I reckoned she must've been really mad.

Dad came upstairs and into the room. I heard him undo the buckle of his belt, whip it angrily from the loops of his trousers and toss it on the chair in the corner. He pulled off his shoes and kicked them under the bed where they clunked against the cardboard box of photographs that had been shoved there when we first arrived in Hillcourt Rise. He was saying nothing, but making so much noise that you'd have to have been deaf not to figure out he was angry.

'Don't be so childish,' Mam said in a loud whisper. 'You've no one to blame but yourself.'

I didn't understand. For what? For the crushed meringues and the fact that Shayne was in our hall when they arrived home?

'What did I do?' Dad wanted to know.

I shifted a little in the bed, aware that people are never completely still when they're asleep.

'Sshh,' Mam said. 'You'll wake them both.' There was a pause, then she said, 'And you know right well what you did.'

'Jesus, woman! This is shaggin' ridiculous.'

'Eyes out on stalks. I'm surprised you didn't spill your pint down your front. It's no wonder that paint job took the length it did.'

The hangers in the wardrobe rattled as Dad hung up his jacket. Mam sat down on the bed and felt for her nightdress under the pillow.

'Lift Ruth into her own bed,' she ordered. 'And be careful not to wake her.'

Dad did as he was told. I felt the cold air on my body when he pulled down the blankets. He slid one hand under my knees and the other under my back, heaving me up and into his arms. I made sure to flop my limbs like a rag doll. I did deadweight really well; no one would've suspected I was wide-awake. I could smell the awful stench of The Ramblers from his hair.

'I didn't know where to look, Rose,' he whispered. 'Sure no one could help it, the way she was dressed.'

'*Undressed*, you mean.' She rustled about in the dressing table drawer. 'If it was someone attractive, I might even understand. But *Liz Lawless?*' If Dad felt my body stiffen, he didn't seem to notice. 'And then we come home to find that brat of hers in the house!'

Dad carried me into my room. He laid me in my bed where I kept up the pretence that I was asleep, ignoring Sandra as she whispered my name through the darkness at regular intervals for at least five minutes. Not long after,

Kev woke up again and screamed for what must have been two full hours.

The next morning, we got ready for mass in silence. Mam said she was too tired to go because she'd been up half the night with Kev. But there'd been plenty of other occasions when it had been hard to get Kev to sleep and still she went to mass. I said nothing to the others, but I knew it was partly because she was mad at Dad for looking at Liz Lawless in The Ramblers.

Later that afternoon, after we'd given up hope of going for a Sunday drive, Mam began her sewing and Dad fell asleep behind *The Sunday Independent*. I watched part of a Western on telly with the others. There didn't seem to be any Indians in it at all, and I was rarely interested in the cowboys, except maybe Blue Boy from *The High Chaparral*. So I left them to it and went to get Kev from his cot when he woke from his afternoon sleep. He was round about three months old now and beginning to be a bit more fun. He loved being played with so I brought him downstairs to the kitchen and slid up and down on the lino with him in my arms. He seemed to like that for a while but soon grew bored and began to whimper. I tried to make him smile, wriggling my fingers to tickle him as I held his firm and chubby body. He just stared at me with his glassy eyes and dribbled down the front of his baby-gro.

It was a dull and dreary day outside, and inside it wasn't much brighter. I wished something would happen that might cheer everyone up and make Mam and Dad start talking again. I thought about doing something bad so that they'd have to discuss my punishment with each other, and then maybe they'd forget about the night before. But then I realized that not only might it bring Mam and Dad together, it could have a similar effect on Mel and Sandra. They adored watching me get into trouble and I wasn't in the mood for their gloating.

I started to make funny faces at Kev. He gurgled and cooed and his cheeks grew round and fat and then he showed off his toothless gums.

He was smiling! For the very first time!

I held his head close to my neck, twirling around and around the room. Everything spun past in a blur of colour and light and though Kev was enjoying it, I soon got dizzy and had to stop. I flopped down at the table and the onions and pots on the wallpaper danced in front of my eyes. Then I wondered if the man was watching me and I had to turn away. But Kev kept looking at the wall. His eyes got that intense look, the one where it seemed he was staring at something that nobody else could see. Then he started to cry.

I took him into the sitting room, announcing that he'd smiled his first smile. Mam took him in her arms and gave him a cuddle. Dad reached over and rubbed her shoulder. She didn't look at him, but I could tell she wasn't that angry with him any more. Mel found the news far from interesting, just uttering a quiet 'Oh' before turning back to the telly. Sandra said with a sulk that she didn't believe me; she thought Kev was far too young to be smiling. But Mam said she wasn't surprised, and that she had a feeling Kev was one of those babies that was in a hurry to do everything in life as quickly as possible.

EIGHT

Shayne took charge of preparations for the Hallowe'en bonfire in Hillcourt Rise. From early October, he seemed to be in full control of the operation, organizing the collection of wood and stashing it away in piles in the side passage of his house. He did allow David to help, but no one else got a look in. Mel tried his best to get involved but, to be fair, he wasn't really up to the job. His previous experience seemed a little pathetic compared to the celebration that Shayne appeared to have in mind. Back in our old house, getting ready for Hallowe'en usually meant making toffee apples, carving a lantern from the biggest turnip Mam could find in the vegetable shop, and whacking the daylights out of a hairy coconut with a hammer so we could taste the dribble of milk we found inside. In Hillcourt Rise, Hallowe'en was all about the bonfire on the green.

In the weeks leading up to the big night, we began to see Shayne and David loitering outside the Vaughans' house each evening after school, waiting for Valerie's dad to arrive home in his van. Paddy Vaughan had easy access to heaps of discarded timber in the builders' suppliers and was more than happy to add off-cuts to the stash pile that the boys had started to assemble. We soon learned that there'd been a bonfire on the green every Hallowe'en since the estate was built. The first year was, we were told, as much about getting rid of rubbish left behind by the builders as it was about celebrating the night of the living dead. By the time we came along, it had become a huge community event. With each fresh delivery from Paddy Vaughan's van, the excitement increased. Shayne took possession of the wood with a seriousness that was almost comical, cradling the lengths as though they were precious gold bars. He'd run his fingers along them and when he was satisfied that each piece met his standard, he'd hand it on to David who carried it over his shoulder to the pile.

Paddy, for his part, seemed just as excited about the plans, saluting the boys as he swung into his driveway each evening, and tugging thoughtfully at his curly red beard while they studied the contents of his van. When they'd carried away their haul, he'd chuckle to himself and lay his huge hands across his fat stomach. I was surprised at first that Mr and Mrs O'Dea let David be part of the preparations at all. But I think they were happy enough to allow him tiny slivers of 'freedom' as long as it didn't interfere with his piano practice.

Bridie referred to David as 'that lovely O'Dea boy'. She couldn't understand why he hung around with Shayne.

'It's his poor parents I feel sorry for,' she said to me one afternoon.

We were in her kitchen, making a Hallowe'en brack. Shop-bought ones, she said, were full of nasty ingredients and tasted like damp cardboard. I wondered how she knew what damp cardboard tasted like, but I didn't ask. She'd answered the door to Pat, the vegetable man, and while she was paying him what she owed, she'd spied David trailing behind Shayne, carrying piles of timber across the green. She chattered away while I busied myself choosing from the selection of gaudy rings she kept in a black velvet purse. Picking out the ring for the brack was an important job. After I'd tried them all on, I settled on one with a large emerald stone and an adjustable gold band, wrapped it tightly in a square of greaseproof paper, and popped it into the bowl of doughy mixture.

Bridie scampered over, her feet bulging out of the orange sling-backs she'd insisted on squeezing on as soon as she'd heard the doorbell ring. 'My Dick said they had a child prodigy on their hands the very first time he heard him practising his Chopsticks,' she said. 'A child prodigy. And look at him now. Under the thumb of that Lawless gurrier. And him trying to corrupt your brother too,' she said, taking the butter wrapper and rubbing it vigorously over the inside of the cake tin. 'All that upset, landing in that Saturday night.' She set the tin down. 'There now, that's ready for you.'

She eyed me closely, breathing heavily as I slopped the mixture into the tin in two big mounds. The flesh-coloured lumps looked just like Liz Lawless's bosoms. I took the wooden spoon and bashed them flat.

'And tell me, has your daddy finished painting their kitchen?'

'I . . . I think so.'

'Well, at least that's something. The less contact there the better.'

The night before Hallowe'en, Mam had the dinner almost ready when she discovered we'd no brown sauce.

'I'll walk to the shop with Kev and get some HP,' I said, knowing Dad couldn't eat shepherd's pie without it.

'Would you, love?' She took her purse from behind the kettle and handed me a folded pound note.

'And can I get my mask?' I asked. The others had already got theirs and had been teasing me that there'd be none left in Mealy's if I didn't hurry up.

''Course you can. Here, take this in case you haven't enough,' she said, handing me a fifty pence piece.

It was cold outside and I made sure Kev was tucked up snug and warm under the pram cover. In the middle of the green the bonfire was already taking shape. Small sticks and old chair legs leaned against each other in a sort of tepee shape. Larger pieces lay waiting to be broken up and added to the pile: a three-legged coffee table; a small yellow-painted chest of drawers; a black leather armchair with curly springs and clouds of orange sponge bursting through its split seat cushion. And then there were the various lengths and chunks of splintered planks and odd-shaped bits of board that Paddy had donated. There hadn't been any rain for days and all the timber was dry as bone. It was going to be a huge blaze.

As I came up out of the cul-de-sac I could see, on the far side of the green, Shayne and David sitting on Vaughans' wall, waiting for Paddy to come home. I knew they saw me but they didn't let on, and when I was almost at the lane, I looked back to see them nudging each other, clearly finding something very funny.

Mealy's Mini Market was about five minutes' walk from our house. Just before the hill down to the village, a lane led into both Churchview Park – a semi-circle of bay-windowed, detached bungalows with huge front gardens, built a few years before Hillcourt Rise – and Cherrywood – a brand-new, sprawling estate of yellow-bricked houses. At the end of the lane, to the right, stood the shops. As well as Mealy's, there was Boylan's Butchers and Sheila's Fashions. Boylan's window display was always the same: kidneys and sausages in silver dishes decorated with bits of plastic parsley and fake tomatoes. Bridie said Sheila Dowd was stretching it when she used the word 'fashions' to describe her shop, but she still bought the odd hideous dress there. Most of the clothes Sheila stocked were years old and none of us would've been seen dead wearing them. The window was permanently covered with yellow cellophane to stop the clothes on display from fading, and the two models behind the glass looked like crazy mental patients, with their badly fitting bowl-cut wigs and limbs twisted in towards their bodies.

Mrs Mealy was alone in the shop when I walked in, weighing quarters of bulls-eyes into brown paper bags. She was tiny; only her head and shoulders showed above the tiled counter. Her hair was screwed into such a tight bun that her eyebrows were pulled halfway up her forehead, making her look permanently surprised. A line of sharpened pencils sat in the top pocket of her pale blue shop coat, and along her lapels she kept a selection of brown and gold hairpins, each of which eventually ended up on her head at some stage throughout the day. Bridie said it was because a customer once found a hair in between their slices of cheddar cheese and Mrs Mealy never wanted to go through that sort of humiliation again, especially since it'd been someone from Churchview Park.

Kev had fallen asleep on the walk, so I'd left him in his pram outside the shop. It was far too much trouble to try and bump the wheels up the concrete step and force the door open with my bum. It wasn't as if Mrs Mealy would be goo-ing and gaa-ing over him anyway. When I asked for the HP, she made a big deal of screwing the lid back on the jar of bulls-eyes. She huffed and puffed taking the bottle down and then walloped it onto the counter. And when I said I wanted to buy a mask, she tried to frown and muttered something about Mr Mealy hanging things up too high. She took a sweeping brush and, holding it like a sword, stabbed it up towards the row of masks hanging above her head. When she eventually managed to unhook the one I wanted, I was finally able to admire it close up. It was a devil's face: deep, fiery red, with black-rimmed eyeholes and dark green lips.

After I paid, I shoved the HP in my coat pocket, hung the mask on my wrist and went back outside. Plumes of coal smoke puffed from the chimneys of Cherrywood and Churchview Park, the smell crawling up my nose and stinging the back of my throat. I passed the mountain of briquette bales, orange gas bottles and bundles of fire sticks that were piled up against the wall. The days were getting colder; it would soon be winter. It was almost dark already though it was barely half past five.

I blinked so I could adjust to the soft grey light outside after the blinding fluorescent tubes in the shop. I blinked again.

The pram was gone.

I stood looking at the spot where I'd left it, convinced my eyes were foggy and blurred from the smoky air and it would reappear if I just kept staring.

But all I saw in front of me was an empty space.

I spun around. And around again. I opened my mouth then closed it. I wanted to scream but I couldn't.

I pressed my face to Boylan's window and peered inside. Only the butcher boy was there, wiping a bloody cloth over the chopping board. The lights were out in Sheila's Fashions, the *closed* sign on the door.

I started to shake. I knew I had to run but I didn't know where to. Which direction? What road?

I was still trying to decide when I realized I'd already taken off and my wobbly legs were carrying me back towards Hillcourt Rise.

My feet slapped hard against the concrete, pounding out his name in my head as I ran. *Kev Kev Kev Kev.* The lane seemed wider, darker; the walls loomed higher. I bolted straight down the middle, away from the deep banks of shadow that seeped out from either side.

Why would someone take him?

I could already see Mam's face. I could hear her shouting. *Don't be ridiculous, Ruth. What do you mean he's gone?*

My chest heaved as I gulped cold air into my lungs and sprinted even faster. *Kev Kev Kev Kev . . .*

I burst out of the lane into Hillcourt Rise. I'd no idea what I was doing. Whoever had him could've gone through Churchview or Cherrywood. They could be anywhere. I could hear a voice in my head. *A baby boy was taken from outside Mealy's Mini Market, Kilgessin at about half past five this evening.* I willed it to go away but it continued. *Gardai would like to speak to anyone who was in the area at the time. Any information, however insignificant, could be vital to their investigations and will be . . .*

I tried to think of Kev's face, his laugh, his cry, anything to get the voice to go away. It couldn't go as far as that, could it? Not the news. It wasn't going to be on the news. It wasn't real, was it?

I would find him. I had to. I shouldn't have left him outside. It was all my fault. Was he really gone? Maybe someone took him by mistake? Maybe it was a joke? But who would play a joke like that? Who would be that heartless, that utterly horrible? That . . .

Then I saw him.

David.

Rattling the pram at speed towards Shayne, his lolloping legs kicking high in the air behind him.

I raced across the corner of the green, reaching the path just in time to grab hold of his arm and pull him to a stop outside the Vaughans'. I shoved him away as roughly as I could and he stumbled against the wall.

'What the *hell* do you think you're doing?' I screamed at him. *'Are you mental or what?'*

'Take it easy. It was just a joke,' he said, rubbing at his shoulder. He glanced at Shayne. 'We . . . I . . . I didn't mean any harm.'

I ripped off the pram cover and there was Kev, wrapped in his blanket, fast asleep.

'A *joke*?' I asked, my voice rising. 'You think that's *funny*?'

Before he could answer, Shayne butted in. 'Told ye she wouldn't like it, didn't I? But ye just wouldn't listen.' His eyes were hard and dull like old pennies, even under the warm glow of the fancy carriage lamp. He slid from the wall and leaned against it, shoving his hands in the pockets of his jeans. He shook his head. 'Think ye know everythin', O'Dea, don't ye? Big eejit.'

David shuffled, clicking the stud on his wristband and staring at Shayne. He had that look again, the one that made me think about people who burst into flames. He bit at his lip then he turned to me. 'I'm sorry, OK?' he said. I held tight to the pram handle as I listened. 'It was . . . I mean . . . look, I'm sorry. That's all.'

It was strange hearing him speak normally, with no weird accent or odd words.

'How could you think something like that was funny?' I asked. 'How would you like it if you thought your sisters were in danger? Would you think that was a joke?'

He stared at me, then glanced again at Shayne and was about to say something, but at that second Paddy Vaughan arrived home in his van. He swerved into the driveway, beeping the horn and nearly hitting the garage door. He jumped out, beaming at the boys, his stomach wobbling under his shirt.

Shayne came away from the wall and moved towards the Vaughans' gate, patting the hood of Kev's pram as he passed. 'Sure there's no harm done anyways, is there?' he said and went to see what Paddy had brought home for the bonfire. I caught David's eye and though there was sorrow in his gaze, I couldn't be certain that was all he was feeling. I was sure he was hiding something, that his face wasn't showing all that he felt inside. He followed Shayne, keeping his head down. My heart beat so fast I could feel it in my throat.

I leaned in to the pram and stroked Kev's face. I felt sick at the thought that he could've been hurt. David had been running so fast, the pram might easily have toppled over. I wanted to believe it was all a joke, but if David really was sorry, he had a weird way of showing it.

He hadn't once looked in at Kev or asked if he was all right.

I was still shaky as I started to walk home. I decided not to tell Mam what had happened. Or anyone. There was no point in worrying them. Kev was OK despite his ordeal. And I was sure Mam would give out, even though she often left the pram outside the shops herself. *But I'd always be keeping an eye*, she'd say, and I knew I'd end up thinking it was my fault. I felt bad enough without anyone else making me feel worse.

I carried on towards the cul-de-sac. Kev was awake now, making little gurgling noises. He squirmed and struggled and loosened his blanket, so I leaned in to tuck it back around his legs. He smiled up at me and I tickled him under his chin.

'Who's the sweetest wittle angel?' I said. 'Who's the best wittle boy in the wo—'

I heard footsteps behind me. I didn't want anyone to hear my baby talk so I stopped and busied myself with Kev's blanket, waiting for them to pass. But no one did.

I threw a quick glance over my shoulder. Nothing. Not a sign of anyone. Only the weak, hazy glimmer of the nearest streetlamp and the faint *bong-bong* of church bells.

I pushed the pram a few feet. Then I was sure I heard steps again. I flicked my head around but the path was dark and empty behind me. My mind was playing tricks; my head was all muddled after the scare I'd had. I squeezed the pram handle and was about to carry on when, without warning, a figure leapt out at me from behind a gatepost, arms and legs flailing like crazy.

'*Boooooooooo!*' Then high-pitched shrieking laughter.

I screamed, terrified.

'Who's a little angel then? Hahaha! Who's the best little wittle baby boy?' A fierce, ugly face leered in to my own, all red and green and black. The devil's face. My devil. My mask.

It was Shayne. He pulled the mask off his head and held it out to me. 'Ye dropped it. I just wanted to give it back.' He was trying hard not to laugh. I took the mask, shoved it under the pram cover and went to push past him. I didn't want to even look at him. But he'd wedged his foot under one of the pram wheels and it wouldn't budge.

'Ah, come on! I was only havin' a laugh! And ye got your mask back, didn't ye?' Though I said nothing, my face showed him how I was feeling. 'Jesus! Sorry! I didn't think ye'd be like that. I thought ye'd like a laugh after what O'Dea did.'

'Get your foot out from under the wheel,' I said. 'I'd like to bring my brother home.'

'Look, don't mind O'Dea. He doesn't know what he's doin' half the time.'

'It was a horrible thing to do.'

'I know. It was stupid! I told him not to do it. I should've stopped him but he . . . well . . . ye know what he's like.'

I clenched my teeth and gripped the handle tighter. He was right up close to me and I could feel his hot breath on my face. I tried to walk but his foot was still under the wheel. He grabbed my wrist, his fingers warm and dry on my skin. 'Listen, thanks for givin' me snake back that time. I never said, but I found it under me pillow. I kind of knew all along ye hadn't thrown it down Goggin's jacks.' He'd softened his voice and his words sort of whistled in my ear. 'But I was wonderin' if . . . ye know . . . ye had the tongue? I mean, it's missin', and me uncle Joe's comin' tomorrow to do the fireworks and I don't want him to go mental when he sees the snake. Cost him a fortune, so it did. That's what me ma says, anyways.'

I swallowed. If he thought I was going to let him have the tongue after what he'd just done, he thought wrong. I shook my head. 'Never saw it. Not sure if it even had a tongue.'

His grasp tightened slightly on my wrist. 'It did. It definitely did. Ye're tellin' lies again. I know it.'

I heard a car coming around the corner and looked over my shoulder. 'There's my dad,' I said. 'Let me go.' I tried to pull away.

'If ye find it, ye better hand it over.' He squeezed hard before releasing me then walked backwards a couple of steps so he could look into my face. His eyes had a kind of desperate look in them but I stared past him and carried on quickly towards home.

Dad was climbing out of the car when I got to the gate.

'At the shop, were you?' he asked, leaning in to get his rolled up *Evening Press* from the dash.

'Yeah,' I said, and I coughed to get the shake out of my voice. 'Getting you some HP. It's shepherd's pie tonight.'

He rubbed his hands together. 'Best news I've had all day.' He peeped in under the pram hood and tickled Kev under his chin. 'And how's the little fella? Did he enjoy his jaunt to the shops?'

'He's . . . he's fine,' I said, blinking back tears. 'Not a bother on him.'

My insides were hot and fiery when I thought about what David had done. The fright of it all was only hitting me now as Dad helped me into the hall with the pram. I had to keep telling myself to calm down, that it was OK, that Kev hadn't been hurt.

Mam put a mountain of shepherd's pie in front of me but I couldn't eat much, so Dad cheerfully scraped my leftovers onto his plate and dribbled them with a river of HP. Then Kev started crying and I jumped up, offering to see to him. I picked him up and cuddled him close. He smelled of baby lotion and fresh air, and his warmth seeped into my chest. While I rocked him in my arms and hummed softly in his hot little ear, I stared at the wall and wondered if the man underneath could tell I was upset. No one else had noticed so I must've hidden it well. But I couldn't help thinking he knew.

David O'Dea was nasty. And Shayne wasn't much better after the way he scared me too. I didn't know which of them I disliked more. But it angered me a lot that despite what Shayne had done, I hadn't hated the flow of his breath on my face. Or the grip of his fingers, tight around my wrist.

On Hallowe'en night, as soon as it was dark, the three of us went outside. Mel met up with the rest of the boys and Sandra skipped off with the twins. She'd made it clear she didn't want to be seen with me, mainly because I'd decided not to go overboard with the dressing up. I wore just the devil mask, my dark grey slacks and a black polo neck jumper of Dad's. She'd wanted me to wear a length of red ribbon for a tail but I said no. She said I looked stupid but I didn't care. I preferred to go around by myself anyway.

Bridie's was the first house I went to. Despite my plaits dangling out from behind my mask, she had no idea who I was.

'And who's the little devil?' she asked, genuinely puzzled. It was only when I asked her had she sliced the brack I'd help her make that she realized who I was. 'Ruth! I'd never have guessed it was you!' she said, getting all excited. She reached in to her hall table then thrust a plate of brack under my nose, making sure the biggest, thickest slice was the nearest to me and giving me a big wink when I took it. I slid my mask up to the top of my head and bit into the brack, pretending to be completely surprised at finding the ring buried in the middle. 'Well, now! You'll be married within the year!' she laughed, flinging a whole net of monkey nuts into my bag along with a bunch of red grapes, a handful of Iced Caramels and two large Jaffa oranges. I slipped the ring on my finger, squeezed it tight, and went on my way.

Out on the green, a throng was beginning to gather. Shayne was dancing around the unlit bonfire, wearing Liz's fringed suede waistcoat, a pair of cowboy boots like the ones I'd seen peeping out from under Liz's bed, and a purple feather stuck behind his ear. David sat on the black leather armchair, dressed in his normal smart clothes, unconcerned at the scene around him. He had one of Paddy's offcuts on his knees and was using it as an imaginary keyboard, tapping his fingers across its surface, his hair falling over his eyes as he 'played'. He made a face over at me, acting as if my disguise had given him a fright, then he laughed really loud and stared at me for ages.

My plastic bag rustled as I walked, its contents banging against my knees. The inside of my mask became damp and warm as I breathed, and I kept having to push it to the top of my head so I didn't feel like I was going to suffocate. As I went along the path, I held out my hand to admire the emerald stone in the ring. I loved the way it flashed and glittered like a cat's eye in the moonlight. I was glad Bridie had made sure I got it. Sandra might demand the one from our own brack, but she could hardly make me hand over this one too. Bridie had been wrong about her brack though; shop-bought tasted much better than homemade. I spat out the bite I'd taken and tossed the remainder of the slice over a wall.

When I called to David's house, Mr O'Dea answered the door. He glanced up from the folded newspaper he was reading then stared at me when I asked him to 'help the Hallowe'en party', as if he'd no idea what night it was. So I said it again, in case my voice had been a bit muffled coming from behind my mask. He scratched his head and called for Mrs O'Dea, who came to the door carrying a brown speckled banana and four brazil nuts, which she dumped in the bottom of my bag without saying a word.

As I went from house to house, the crowd on the green continued to grow. More parents came and stood around chatting, stamping their feet against the cold. Some kids gathered in small groups, heads bowed as they looked into each other's bags, while others ran in and out of the trees and bushes, whooping and shrieking with excitement. I made my way over, satisfied now that I'd done my bit to help the Hallowe'en party. The bonfire was sure to be lit soon and I didn't want to miss the first burst of flame.

David was relaxing in the armchair now, his long legs fully stretched out and his hands behind his head. Shayne sat on the ground, picking through his bag. Every couple of seconds he looked up from his task, throwing glances towards the entrance to the estate. He wasn't the only one waiting for Uncle Joe. I was looking forward to his arrival too, almost more interested in seeing him than his firework display.

As I walked closer to the crowd, Shayne caught sight of me then turned his head away. Sandra galloped up, plonked herself down beside him and helped herself to his stash of goodies. He said something to her and they both laughed and she glanced over to make sure I was looking. Then there was a huge surge towards the bonfire as Paddy – self-appointed chief firelighter – beamed and made a big show of taking a box of matches from the top pocket of his overcoat and sliding them open.

'Stand back, now! Stand back!' he shouted, getting down on his hunkers. He leaned in and stretched his arm through the gaps in the timber pile to the tepee-shaped bit in the middle. After only a couple of seconds, the flame took hold and the bonfire was ablaze. A cheer went up and some of the adults started to clap. The dry wood hissed and popped as it burned, sending grey smoke curling up through the night like straggly wisps of witch's hair.

Shayne stood as close to the flames as the heat would allow. The light on his face showed up the flaking lines of white paint that he'd daubed across each cheek. I wondered had he deliberately chosen not to wear a mask, or had his homemade disguise been forced upon him because Liz wouldn't give him the money to buy one. The glass beads on the fringes of his waistcoat shone in the firelight, causing tiny sparks to dart out from his body with every breath that he took. A golden line edged each feature of his face: his snub nose, his pointed chin, his flickering eyelashes, and his lips moving in and out as he sucked on a mouthful of sticky sweets.

As I watched him through my eyeholes, I thought about the snake tongue sitting on its cotton wool bed in my jewellery box and wondered was it bad to feel so good about having something that he wanted. Then, with a sudden twist of his head, he caught me staring straight at him. My breath dampened the inside of my mask and made a whooshing noise that swam all around my head and I felt like I was underwater, about to drown. I was glad he couldn't see my face.

Half an hour went by and still there was no sign of Uncle Joe.

'I don't know, OK?' Shayne shouted when Sandra asked again what time the fireworks were starting. He began to pace around the bonfire, picking monkey nuts from his bag and flinging them into the flames. David still hadn't left the leather armchair despite Mel and a few others trying to pitch him out of it so they could toss it onto the flames. Shayne went over to him a couple of times and kicked at the base of the chair, mumbling under his breath and keeping an eye on the entrance to the estate.

Mam and Dad came onto the green, with Kev fast asleep in his pram, and before long, Geraldine and Nora arrived, closely followed by Mr Farrell – Clem – and the rest of the Farrells. Even Mr and Mrs O'Dea ventured out, but they left their front door open and stood on the edge of the green. Mr O'Dea surveyed the crowd, one hand holding his pipe and the other tucked into the front of his camel hair coat. After about five minutes, he turned towards home and Mrs O'Dea followed, her head down and her arms folded tight across her chest.

I began glancing up at Shayne's face every time a car came into the estate, but his expression didn't change. Not even when

Uncle Keith drove by in his battered grey van with Liz in the passenger seat. I thought they might stop, but they just sped down to the house and disappeared inside. Dad came over and stood close to me, rubbing his hands together. 'Doesn't look like we're going to get any fireworks,' he said quietly.

'No,' I said, pulling my mask off. 'Bonfire's good though.' I shook my bag of goodies in front of his face. 'And I got loads of stuff for later.'

'Great.' He crouched down beside me. 'Now . . . what would you say,' he whispered, his eyes darting over to Mam, 'if I was to . . . you know . . . stand in for Uncle Joe?'

My skin prickled. 'What do you mean?'

He rested his hands on his knees and looked into my face. 'Come on! You must have some idea.'

I'd always thought Dad's eyes were pure blue, but as I looked into them, I saw they were heavily flecked with green. It might've been the firelight, or the fact that it was night-time, but whatever it was, it scared me that I'd never noticed before.

I looked over to the group of adults and watched how Clem stood behind Geraldine like a shadow, only moving when she moved, only smiling after she let out a snort of laughter.

'You can't guess then?' Dad asked me.

I shook my head.

'Well, then, let's go and ask Kev, will we?'

'What's Kev got to do with it?'

He straightened up and led me over to the pram.

'You'll see.'

When we reached the group, Geraldine was going on about hospitals and how she was looking forward to having Farrell number seven in the next few weeks. Nora hung onto her every word, nodding and smiling and trying to butt in each time Geraldine took a breath. But she lost vital seconds trying to remember what she was about to say, and Geraldine always got in before her, leaving Nora waiting in hope, yet again, for the next available break in the conversation.

Dad bent down and took a brown paper package from the wire tray at the bottom of the pram. He gave it to me to hold. 'Go on! Open it up.'

I carefully undid the green string that had been wound around it many times and tightly knotted into a bow.

'Now! What do you think of that?' he asked, when the paper fell away.

In my hands was a small collection of fireworks. I'd never seen fireworks in real life before but I knew that's what they were. They looked like the sticks of dynamite the Coyote sometimes used when he tried to blow up the Roadrunner.

'Uncle Con got them for us,' Dad whispered. 'Make sure you don't tell anyone where they came from, though, or he might get into trouble.'

Uncle Con was our cousin Trevor's dad. He went to Belfast a lot because of his job and was able to get stuff that we couldn't get in Dublin.

'Are we going to set them off now?' I asked.

'Might as well,' he smiled. 'We've waited long enough for this Uncle Joe.' He took them from me and walked over to a clear spot on the far side of the bonfire, gesturing to Paddy and Clem. 'Make a good space now. And keep the kids well back.'

My eyes searched for Shayne. For a moment I thought he'd gone home, fed up with waiting. But then I spotted him, curled up in the armchair while David stood behind him looking at his watch and shaking his head.

Dad wasted no time. In seconds, the first firework zipped high into the sky above our heads, exploding with a crack into a perfect globe of a million sizzling sapphires. Each one blazed brighter than the stars for a few brilliant seconds before fizzling out into tiny plumes of smoke that disappeared into the night. Then, after another whoosh, a gigantic umbrella of sparkling rubies and emeralds opened up and rained down through the velvet black of the sky. One after another the fireworks shot up and burst into bloom, suspended in the air above the rooftops of Hillcourt Rise. When Dad shouted 'Last one!' everyone clapped and cheered. Kev woke and Mam took him in her arms, and with the final bang he buried his face in her neck and began to cry.

Dad was beaming when all the kids ran up to him to say thanks. Then Paddy shook his hand, patted him on the back and said, 'Good job, Mick, good job.' And Mam laughed when Nora tried to cheer Kev up by tickling him under his chin and making faces that only made him scream even louder. Sandra was sitting on the ground with Valerie, Tracey and the twins, shouting everyone down and thinking she was great because it was her dad who'd put on the fireworks display.

I looked over and saw that the leather chair was empty. Mel and some other boys began lumping it over until they reached the bonfire, where they managed to lift it a few inches off the ground and topple it into the middle of the blaze. At first it seemed to kill the fire, deadening the orange light and silencing the sound of the snapping sparks. But then the flames began to feed on their fresh supply of fuel and they roared into life. They licked at the black skin, curling and peeling it back to reveal a skeleton of sponge and springs and timber, which they gorged on until the entire chair was swallowed up.

Everyone moved back from the inferno, but I stayed as close as I could bear. There was something scarily exciting about the way the chair disappeared, how the flames reduced it to nothing. Fire was the surest way to get rid of things. You could throw something in the bin, but it could be rescued; break it into bits, but still be able to put it back together. Fire was for stuff you were certain you didn't want any more.

I stood with my back to a tree, my heart racing with the thrill of being so close to something so destructive. Then, quietly, from behind me, Shayne came walking towards the bonfire he'd spent so much time putting together. His eyes caught mine as he passed, glistening sharp and wet in the firelight. He stopped only a few feet from the blaze, arms dangling like twigs, legs thin as broom handles in his oversized boots. He threw me a look over his shoulder, then slowly, deliberately, I saw him draw his beloved snake from the pocket of his waistcoat. He cradled it in his hands, stroking his fingers along the full length of its body. Then he took it by its tail, twirled it around in the air and let it go, sending it deep into the heart of the flames.

NINE

After Hallowe'en night, no one saw Shayne for ages. Mel said he heard he had a contagious disease – chicken pox or measles or something – but Mam wouldn't allow him to call down and find out, in case it was true and we all ended up catching whatever it was that he had.

'I don't want any of us getting the measles,' she said. 'Especially Kevin. What if it spreads to the Farrells? And Geraldine only after having the new baby?'

It was a girl. Fiona, they called her. Every afternoon, on our way home from school, Tracey moaned about how much she cried or how often she had to be fed or what the stuff in her nappies smelled like. Sandra always tried to come up with similar complaints about Kev, but Tracey wouldn't be outdone. Fiona, she argued, was the Most Annoying Baby Ever.

I couldn't stop wondering about Shayne and why we hadn't seen him around. I started imagining that Uncle Keith had taken him off on a job down the country, or that Liz had decided to bring him on a holiday somewhere warm where she could sip cocktails all day long and happily show off her bosoms in a skimpy swimsuit. But I knew it was far more likely he was lying in his little attic room, covered in crusty spots and vomiting into a plastic bucket on the floor beside his bed. I nearly felt sorry for him. I kind of felt bad that Uncle Joe hadn't turned up like he was supposed to. Shayne must've been really upset about it, getting rid of the snake like that. I was glad it was gone though; now there was no proof that I'd lied about throwing it away. Having the tongue wasn't of much use any more but I decided to hang on to it all the same. I didn't need to be inspecting it as often as I had done so I took it out of my jewellery box and placed it at the back of my underwear drawer.

One morning on our way to school we were early enough to catch David at the bus stop and I asked him, casually, if he'd seen Shayne or knew why he hadn't been around. He stared at the sky. 'Can't say that ah do, chile,' he said, clicking the stud on his wristband. 'Ain't seen hide nor hair o' that there cotton-pickin' nincompoop for, oh, nigh on ten days, ah reckon.'

'Haven't you called down to him or anything?' I wanted to know, choosing not to comment on his latest accent.

'See, now, that's the thing. That's the darnedest thing. Mother O'Dea, she been plain nasty this past few weeks.' He held up his hands. 'Fingers played down to the bone. Down to the bone, ah say. Why ah—'

'So you haven't seen him, then?'

'No, ma'am. Now looky here! If it ain't the omnibus, come to take me for some schoolin'.' He hopped onto the bus when it pulled up, swinging the briefcase he used as a schoolbag and nodding to the conductor, who managed a weak smile. 'So long, now, chile! Remember me to your momma,' he sang as the bus pulled away.

We stood and watched as he waved like a queen from the upstairs back seat.

'He's so funny, isn't he?' Sandra said.

'Yeah,' I said. 'He's funny all right. Funny peculiar.'

Later that evening, while Mam was feeding Kev, I told her I was nipping into Bridie's for a while. I couldn't last any longer wondering why Shayne hadn't been around.

'Dinner in fifteen minutes,' she said. 'Don't be late.'

'What is it?' I asked.

'Steak and kidney pie.'

No need to hurry back then, I said to myself as I slipped out the door.

I noticed Bridie's curtains were still open but there was no sign of her in the front room. She was probably in the kitchen, making herself supper. She never seemed to eat dinner, it was always 'supper', or 'something light', like a mushroom omelette, or a salad of ham and sliced boiled eggs and tomatoes that she cut into little crown shapes using the gadget she got with her Green Shield stamps.

I ran silently on my toes all the way to the Lawlesses' with a freezing wind in my face. The house was in darkness when I arrived, blinds closed and curtains drawn, but somehow I knew it wasn't empty. I noticed the top pane of glass in Liz's bedroom window was broken. A scrap of a plastic bag had been stretched across it and stuck down with ragged strips of brown tape. I was thinking about knocking on the door, studying the curly pattern of scratches around the keyhole, when a loud noise made me jump. It was the unlocked door to the side passage banging against its frame in the wind. I felt strangely secure as I slipped through it and began to feel my way along the pebbledashed side of the house. It was much darker away from the orange light of the streetlamps and I had to be careful not to trip over the bits of leftover timber on the ground, the pieces that hadn't made it into the bonfire. When I reached the back door I moved my fingers over its peeling varnish until I found the handle. It turned easily and the bitter smoky-fruity-bleachy smell flooded up my nose as I stepped into the kitchen.

A spooky glow lit the room, heightening the edges of everything with a silvery fuzz. It was cold. Freezing. The whole place felt damp. I crept through the open door to the hall and stood beside the stairs where the light was stronger and coming from above. Shivering now, and almost wishing I hadn't come, I heard the sound of shaky breathing and when I looked up, a dazzling beam shone straight into my eyes.

'What d'ye want?' It was Shayne, his voice calm and low, with no sign of fear, or even surprise, that I'd snuck into his house.

'Stop blinding me with that torch and maybe I'll tell you.'

He aimed the light onto the floor, where it showed up a circle of the crimson, rose-patterned carpet. I blinked a couple of times before I could see him properly. He was sitting hunched and pale at the top of the stairs, looking thinner than before. His feet were bare and his St Christopher medal swung against the dirty front of his vest. He rubbed at his face with the back of his hand.

'Have you got the chicken pox?' I asked.

'Do I look like I have?'

'Or measles?'

'What're ye on about? I don't have the chicken pox. Or measles. Or anythin'.'

'Why haven't you been in school, then?'

He stood up and came down to the hall. 'Shuddup,' he whispered. 'Ye'll wake me ma.'

'Is she the one who's sick?'

'No. She's not sick, she's . . . well . . . she's . . . Yeah, maybe she is sick, I dunno.'

'What's wrong with her? Why's she asleep? And why don't you just switch on some lights?'

He swivelled the torch in his hand, the beam bouncing wildly off the walls. 'Jesus! Twenty questions. And what the hell are ye doin' here anyways?'

I followed him into the kitchen.

'Mel said you were sick but Mam wouldn't let him come down in case he caught the disease.'

'I don't have a bloody disease.'

'I know that now, don't I? But I didn't two minutes ago and now I—'

'Wanted to make sure I was OK? Very nice of ye, I must say.'

'I don't see why you have to be so mean about it.'

'Ye couldn't have just knocked on the door, could ye?'

'Would you have answered?'

He bit at the edge of the torch. Lit from below, his nose was a dark triangle and black rings sat under his eyes. A tiny piece of the black rubber rim came away in his teeth and he spat it across the room. Outside, the side door walloped against its frame, breaking the silence that hung between us. He set the torch on the table, opened a cupboard and took out a box of Rice Krispies. I asked again why he didn't just turn on the light.

''Cos me uncle Keith's gone,' he said, lifting a bottle of milk from the fridge.

'Oh,' I said after a pause, not sure how that answered my question. 'Where?'

He poured his cereal into a brown bowl then sloshed in the milk, spilling pools of it onto the counter. 'How would I know?'

'You mean . . . gone? For good?'

He nodded.

I watched him crunching, barely finishing one mouthful

before spooning in another. 'What's that got to do with the lights?' I asked.

'He paid the bill, didn't he? Me ma said we have to go easy now he's gone. She doesn't want them to cut us off again.'

That must've been why the house was so cold. I'd heard Dad moaning when we'd had to get a fill of oil to heat the radiators. And he was never done complaining about the cost of electricity. But I guessed he always found the money to pay the bills because our house was always warm and bright. I wondered why Liz didn't go out and get some sort of a job instead of lying in bed, but I didn't say anything. I picked up the torch and shone it around the kitchen. Plates and bowls crusted with dried food were piled in towers on the draining board and the sink was filled with dirty glasses and mugs. An empty whiskey bottle lay on its side on the counter, wedged between an open tin of beans and a frying pan holding half a shrivelled sausage on a bed of thick, grey grease.

'Why did he go?'

'Dunno. They had a big scrap up in her room. Took all his stuff and hasn't been back. She's been in bed mostly since, so I get to stay at home.'

'Doesn't she mind you missing school?'

He crunched for ages then shook his head. 'She can't make me go.'

'When did he leave?' I asked.

'Hallowe'en.'

'But I saw him in his van on Hallowe'en night with your

mam. When we were waiting for your. . .' I trailed off. He slurped the last of the milk from the bowl.

'After that. Thanks to yer da's little fireworks display.'

'What's that got to do with anything?'

'Ye don't get it, do ye?' he sneered. 'Me ma thought me uncle Joe had come back when she saw the fireworks. She went crazy when she found out it was yer da, and me uncle Keith went mental. Said he was sick of it. Said it was "Joe this" and "Joe that" the whole time. Then he smashed his fist through the window and threw all his stuff in a bag.'

'You can hardly blame my dad for that.'

He screwed up his face. 'His fireworks were crap, so they were. Everyone said so.'

'You're just jealous.'

'Think what ye like.'

'It's true. Just because your uncle Joe didn't turn up. You should be grateful, not blaming my dad that your uncle Keith's gone. It's not his fault.'

'Ye think he's great, don't ye? Ye'd swear he was bloody Superman the way yer goin' on. And me ma said he was a rubbish painter too. Look at the state of it.'

I waved the torch around. Dad's paintwork did look shabby in places. Behind the sink was flecked with splatters of dirty water, and I made out a pattern of black scuffmarks beside the back door, as if someone had kicked at the wall.

'That's nothing to do with him and you know it,' I said. 'Paintwork doesn't keep itself clean.'

'Yeah . . . well . . . believe what ye like.'

'She got it done for nothing, didn't she? And all because of a stupid snake.'

'All because you lied about havin' it, ye mean.'

'I gave it back, didn't I?'

'Too late, though. If ye'd given it back earlier yer da wouldn't've been down here paintin', would he? Did ye ever think of that? And me ma said he was aaawful slow. Said he could've been finished in a day if he'd wanted –' he narrowed his eyes – 'but for some reeeason . . . he took aaages . . . like he was draaaggin' it out.'

I didn't like what he was saying. Liz's blobby bosoms came into my head. And the way Mam had accused Dad of staring at them in The Ramblers.

'I . . . I have to go,' I said. 'My dinner'll be ready.' I felt guilty for mentioning food, even though he'd been mean to me. Bad and all as steak and kidney pie was, it was a lot better than a bowl of Rice Krispies in a cold, dark, dirty kitchen.

'Right,' he said, slapping his bowl on top of the tower in the sink and clattering his spoon in after it. 'Anyways, it was just as well me uncle Joe didn't turn up. I didn't want him to see the tongue was missin'.'

I felt even worse when he said that. I almost blurted out that I still had it, that it was safe at the back of my underwear drawer. But there was no point. It was no good to anyone now.

I stepped outside, stuffing my hands into the sleeves of my cardigan. He shone the torch down the passageway as I left, dipping my face down to escape the biting wind. Then he whispered loudly after me, 'What're ye havin'?'

'What do you mean?' I called back.

'For dinner. What are ye havin' for dinner?'

'Oh,' I said. 'Steak and kidney pie.'

He said nothing, just shone the torch directly into my face for a couple of seconds then switched it off and everything went black.

December came and by Christmas Eve the excitement in the house was high, but, as usual, it was flattened out a bit by the arrival of Auntie Cissy and Uncle Frank. We always knew what our presents would be. Each year, without fail, they gave me some kind of storybook, and Sandra got a doll that fell apart by Stephen's Day. Mel, being their favourite, always received an expensive set of Dinky cars that none of us was allowed to touch.

Frank was, like Cissy, tall, thin and pale, and he never wore any colour but brown. His trousers flapped about his ankles and slid up his legs whenever he sat down, revealing large portions of white skin, curiously free of hair. He did everything very slowly. Even when he blinked, it took ages for his paper-thin lids to wash over his chocolate-button eyes. And when he ate, his teeth – also brown – chewed in a circular way, like a cow's, forever and ever, until he finally swallowed his food with a huge gulp that made his Adam's apple bob up and down. Mam referred to Frank as 'The Drip', and said it had to be more than simply a coincidence that fixing them was his profession. 'And always touting for business,' she'd complain. 'Does he ever go anywhere without that blessed ladder strapped to the roof of his car? Sure if we wanted him to take a look at our gutters, wouldn't we just ask?' Dad said Frank had to be like that because roofs and gutters weren't things you thought about every day and if people weren't reminded, they'd never get them seen to at all. There was never any harm in him taking a quick look, he said.

When they arrived, Mam took the presents from Cissy and did her usual trick of pretending we couldn't have them until the morning. After listening to our protests, she 'gave in' and handed me the bag. Frank and Cissy's presents were the only ones we were allowed to open before Christmas Day. Cissy seemed to put a similar amount of effort into wrapping our presents as she did into choosing them. She didn't use any tape, just bundled a sheet of paper around each one, the way they wrapped the meat in Boylan's.

'*Stories for Girls*. Thanks, Auntie Cissy,' I said, flicking through the newspapery pages of tiny words and spidery black and white drawings.

'Thanks for the doll,' Sandra said. Then she whispered in my ear, 'It's exactly the same as the one they gave me last year.'

She was right. It was a cheap version of a Sindy with ridiculously long legs, both of which were bound to fall off before teatime. Mel was delighted with his haul, as usual, and sat cradling his box of shiny new cars.

Uncle Frank insisted on having a look at the roof, so while he went outside with Dad, Mam poured a glass of sherry for herself and Cissy. After a few minutes, Dad returned. Frank trailed behind with a long face.

'Well, the gutters are sound as a pound,' Dad said. 'Nothing for Frank to do there.' He laughed, trying to lighten the mood, but rolled his eyes at Mam behind Cissy's back.

'That's great news altogether,' Mam said, in spite of The Drip's disappointment. 'Will you have a glass of whiskey, Frank? And a mince pie?'

'We left the ladder up, Rose,' Dad said. 'Frank wants to take a good look at the roof before he goes. Thought a couple of slates might be a bit loose, didn't you, Frank?'

After he took a sip of whiskey and swallowed a bite of well-chewed pie, Frank nodded, then no one said anything for ages. I was so bored, I started reading *Stories for Girls*. Sandra began undressing her doll. Mel opened his box of cars, then thought better of it and carefully closed it again. I wished Kev wasn't asleep; at least he'd liven things up a bit. I was trying hard to make myself concentrate on a dull story about an injured sheepdog when, from somewhere outside, we heard thumping, followed by a muffled clatter, then something smashing to the ground.

Frank looked up from his whiskey glass. 'Sounded like a tile falling,' he announced cheerfully.

Dad went over to the window and peered through the blind. ''That'd be a bit of a coincidence, wouldn't it?' he said. 'Can't see anything, but I'll go and take a look.'

'Maybe it's Santa and the reindeer!' Mam said, smiling at us. 'Checking up on you three before tonight!'

Before we got to the front door, we heard shouting.

'What the bloody hell do you think you're doing?' Dad was yelling when we got outside. 'Get down off my roof now! Do you hear me? Now!'

'What on earth's going on, Mick?' Mam asked.

'It's that bloody Lawless kid, I know it. Up Frank's ladder if you don't mind! Would you shaggin' credit it? He's after knocking down a loose slate! What sort of a . . . He could've killed someone.'

'For God's sake!' Mam said. 'Are you sure it was him?'

'He was forever messing on my ladder when I was doing that job for his mother. You don't know the half of it. This'd be his idea of a joke.'

'Is he still up there?'

'Not for long he's not. I'm going up after him.'

'Sure what good is it going up to him? Let him come down himself. He can't stay up there for ever.'

'I'll shaggin' well throw him over my shoulders and carry him down if I have to.'

'Be careful, Mick. Do you hear me? Take it easy.'

'Jesus, woman, what do you take me for? I'm up and down ladders every day of the week. I think I know what I'm doing.'

'But you've had a few drinks.'

'All the better to steady my nerves then.'

Mam had her arms folded across her chest and a stormy look on her face. 'That little . . .' she said, shaking her head. 'Nothing but trouble.'

Cissy joined us. 'What's going on? Is everything all right, Rose?' she asked in her sleepy, flat voice. I'd often thought if tortoises could talk, they'd sound exactly like Auntie Cissy.

'Fine, Cissy. Everything's fine,' Mam said. 'Go on back in to Frank. Finish your sherry and then we'll . . . Jesus Christ! Oh my God! Mick!'

Like all of us, Mam was watching as Dad's foot slipped from the third step of the ladder. He managed to hang on for a second or two but then he lost his grip. He let out a low moan when he hit the ground. Mam ran over to him. 'Don't, Mick, don't,' she said, when he tried to get up. 'Lie still.' She told Cissy to go inside and phone Dr Crawley from Churchview Park. Cissy's mouth dropped open and her eyes grew all cloudy, so Mam told her to leave it and asked Sandra to phone instead. She ordered Mel upstairs to get a pillow and a cover for Dad, and instructed me to stand at the bottom of the ladder and wait to see if Shayne came down.

Dad lay on the driveway covered with Sandra's frilly-edged yellow eiderdown. Cissy stood beside him saying 'Oh God' over and over and clutching at her throat with her bony hands. Then Frank finally came to the door, glass in hand, and slowly surveyed the scene. 'You'll be needing a few slates replaced, then?' he said, and took another sip of his drink.

'Go back inside and sit down, Frank,' Mam snapped. 'You too, Cissy. There's nothing we can do till the doctor gets here.' She stroked Dad's hand and told Mel to go inside and keep them entertained. 'Is there any sign of him coming down yet, Ruth?' she asked.

I ran my eyes up the length of the ladder, along the roof's edge and across to Bridie's. All I could see, perched on top of our chimney, was the dark shape of a bird. Shayne was nowhere to be seen. He'd managed to escape without us noticing. He'd probably jumped down to the garage roof. From there it would've been an easy enough drop to freedom. Before I could tell Mam he was gone, Dr Crawley arrived. He made a big deal of getting down on his hunkers and he prodded and poked at Dad for ages. Mam kept asking him questions but he answered none of them until he'd finished his examination. Then he stood up and declared there was no major damage done and that Dad would be as right as rain with a few Disprin and a bit of rest.

'Oh, thank God,' Mam said, tucking the eiderdown tighter around Dad, as if he was going to be sleeping the night out on the driveway.

We couldn't get rid of Cissy and Frank for ages. They seemed to think they had to stay longer than usual because of Dad's accident, even though Mam kept saying things like: 'Looks as if it could get icy out there tonight' and 'God, I can't wait to get into my bed. I'm exhausted.'

'You're not going to let him get away with it, are you?' Cissy kept asking. 'Surely you'll go and have a word with the lad's mother?'

'Look,' Mam said. 'It's more trouble than it's worth. That woman wouldn't listen. We've no proof who it was anyway. And I won't have our Christmas destroyed. Let's be grateful Mick is all right and leave it at that.'

'I wouldn't stand for it,' said Cissy.

'Shouldn't be allowed to happen,' said Frank.

'We'd have been down to complain straight away, wouldn't we, Frank?'

'That we would. Straightaway. Sure you could've been killed going up after that . . . that . . . hooligan.'

'Well, if you hadn't been so anxious to find something wrong with our roof in the first place . . .' Mam said, her voice sounding cross and impatient.

Frank stiffened, picked up his glass, drained it in one gulp and thumped it down hard on the table. Then he stood up and buttoned his jacket. 'Well. We'll be off now. Are you right, Cis?'

Cissy looked wounded as she fussed about with her hat and gloves. 'Happy Christmas,' she sniffed. 'Hope you'll feel better soon, Mick.'

Mam and I saw them to the door. When we went back inside, Mel was sitting with his legs crossed like Uncle

Frank, the empty whiskey glass to his lips, and Sandra was nodding her head like Auntie Cissy. Dad told them to stop because his back hurt when he laughed. Mam tried to look angry but we all knew there was a smile hovering on her lips. 'Go and check on Kev, Ruth,' she said. 'Bring him down if he's awake.'

I went upstairs and tiptoed in to the room. It was almost dark, sort of dusty-grey, and I was sure I could sense he was awake. But when I looked in the cot, he was fast asleep. As my eyes adjusted, I made out the rise and fall of his little chest and heard the short, shallow sound of his breathing. The faint sound of a choir singing 'Silent Night' filtered up from the telly downstairs and I softly hummed along, running my finger over the curve of Kev's cheek. He looked so peaceful. I was glad he'd slept through all the commotion earlier on.

I heard Dad laughing and the others talking. I strained to hear what they were saying but their voices were just a low hum mixed in with the sound of the telly. I wished Kev wasn't asleep. I wanted to take him downstairs and have fun with him. I tickled his neck and under his arms and he started to squirm and stretch. He always got cranky if he woke up too quickly, so I looked out the window to give him time.

Through the slats of the blinds, Christmas trees twinkled from the halls and sitting rooms of Hillcourt Rise. I thought about what might be happening in the houses. I imagined all the Farrells running around like mice, and Geraldine flicking them away with a tea towel while she tried to stuff the turkey. And in the Vaughans', Valerie, cool and unexcited, reading some boring book by the fire. I wondered where Shayne was now. And what about David? An icy quiver ran down my spine as though I could sense someone's eyes on my back. But not like when I imagined the man watching me from behind the wallpaper. It was different to that. It was closer. More alive.

I turned to look at Kev. He yawned, then kicked his legs like crazy and let out a muffled little squeal. I reached in to pick him up.

Then I froze.

In the dark, shadowy corner by the wardrobe, something moved. I was sure of it.

My eyes were inches away from Kev's. I tried to look up without lifting my head, without whatever – whoever – it was knowing I'd seen. But Kev grabbed my hair and yanked it hard. I pulled against his grip, wincing at the pain, trying to see into the corner. But it was no use. He wriggled about, twining my hair even tighter through his sweaty fingers.

I reached in to prise his fists open. My face was flaming now. Only seconds had passed though it felt like forever.

I was almost free from his grasp. I jerked my head back.

At that instant there was a scuffling and a scrambling and the last glimpse of something bolting out the door.

It was a body. A person. Someone.

Someone had been there all the time. Someone had been watching Kev. Watching me.

Fear held me back for a moment. Then anger took over and I whipped Kev from the cot. I held him close and went out to the landing.

The window at the top of the stairs was wide open.

I scanned the flat roof of the garage, my ears straining for some sort of sound: the thump of feet hitting the ground or the noise of footsteps on the driveway. But only silence hung in the air.

I knew what had happened. Whoever had been crouched in the corner watching Kev was the person who'd climbed up Uncle Frank's ladder. It would've been easy to get in through the landing window from the garage roof. The latch was broken and Mam was forever asking Dad to fix it.

Who was it? What did they want? What did they want with Kev? They were there to scare him.

To scare us.

Dad had said it was Shayne. But he was only guessing. He hadn't seen enough to be certain. It might've been him. But it might not. What would've happened if I hadn't gone up to check on Kev? If I'd left it even a few seconds later?

I squeezed Kev tighter. He struggled against me. My eyes stung and a wave of dread washed through me. The same dread I'd felt when Kev had gone missing from outside the shop. When David had . . . David. It could've been him.

I sped downstairs and pushed open the sitting room door, bursting to tell what had happened. But something about the scene that met my eyes made me stop. Mam was poking at the coal, sending sparks up the chimney, her face all gold and soft in the firelight. She smiled when she saw me, winking at the open tin of Quality Street that sat on the floor beside her like a box of precious jewels. Dad was stretched out in his favourite chair, another glass of whiskey in his hand and his feet resting on a cushion he'd placed on the coffee table. Mel and Sandra were kneeling beside the couch, heads bent over something on the floor. As I stepped closer, I saw that the box of Dinky cars had been opened and not only was Mel playing with them, he was allowing Sandra to handle them as well. And there was a cartoon on the telly.

I handed Kev to Mam and she snuggled her face in his neck. I couldn't bring myself to tell them. Not now. Probably not ever. It was bad enough that Dad had fallen and could've been seriously hurt. I didn't want there to be any more upset. Kev was safe. There was no harm done. I wasn't going to mention it to anyone. I didn't want to think about it again. I curled up on the rug in front of the fire and I didn't say a word.

TEN

I wondered often about that night and who it might've been in the room. In the weeks and months that followed, I studied Shayne and David's faces closely whenever I saw them, hoping for some telltale sign. Sometimes I was sure I could detect a glimmer of guilt in Shayne's eyes if I happened to mention Kev's name, but it was hard to tell. Other times I could swear David's actions were a cover for some sort of shame. But I was just guessing. Every move he made or word he uttered seemed to be an act, so it was impossible to know.

David went to Grangemount, the secondary school a couple of miles away. Each afternoon he had to do at least an hour of piano practice when he came home and Shayne would usually wait for him on the green. As spring turned into summer, and the evenings grew brighter, there was rarely a day when I didn't see them together. Most boys David's age wouldn't have been keen to hang around with someone in primary school. But David was strange anyway, so no one questioned it.

I wasn't sure how deep their friendship ran, though. One afternoon, I saw them wrestling, rolling around on the grass. They might have been play-acting but it was difficult to tell. Some of the punches they were throwing seemed fairly hard. And another day, not long after we got our summer holidays from school, they had a stick-fight in among the trees, grunting and lunging at each other until Shayne flung his weapon down and stormed off on his bike, pedalling down the hill with his hands stuffed in his pockets.

Later that evening, I saw them swinging out of a cherry tree on the green, laughing and joking, so I guessed that whatever had happened between them earlier had been forgotten. Then Bridie came out of her house and trotted up the path towards them, waving an oven glove and shaking her head. 'Get down out of that, the pair of you!' she shrieked. 'You'll snap those branches! Go and find some other tree to swing out of!' She stood waiting for them to obey. 'Did you hear me? Off you go now. Off!' They slid to the ground and ran off towards the shops, David in front and Shayne trying hard to keep up.

The next day, the news of what had happened was all over the estate. They'd found another tree to swing from all right: the huge copper beech that stood in the middle of the churchyard. Though it was enormous, it wasn't a difficult tree to climb. Its branches began barely two feet from the base of the trunk. Once you stepped up, there were plenty of places to get a footing and you could find yourself high above the ground in minutes.

It was Bridie who told me. She was beside herself, seeing as she was the one who'd told them to find some other tree to swing from.

David had fallen and broken his wrist.

That, she said, was the end of the 'prestigious piano competition' he'd been practising for since the start of the year.

'Will his wrist not be healed up before the competition?' I asked. I was sitting in her kitchen, enjoying tea and coconut macaroons.

She gave me a look. 'It's tonight, dear. The competition is tonight.'

'Oh,' I said. I thought about it for a moment. 'He was a bit silly climbing trees the day before a big competition, wasn't he? He should've known something like that might happen.'

'Maybe, dear. But I wouldn't be surprised if it was all that Lawless lad's idea in the first place. Poor David is at his beck and call. Morning, noon and night.' I wasn't as sure about that as Bridie seemed to be, but I didn't say anything. David could do no wrong as far as she was concerned. My opinion wasn't going to change her mind. She sipped her tea. 'Of course, what can you expect when she's off out gallivanting with that new fancy man of hers? Not a care in the world and no idea where that lad is from one end of the day to the next.'

The 'new fancy man' had been on the scene for a few months. 'Uncle Vic', Shayne called him. He drove a maroon Mercedes with a sunroof and tinted windows and had gold-rimmed glasses like the ones Kojak wore. I'd spotted him in Mealy's one evening buying a box of Milk Tray and forty Silk Cut. He smelled of leather and spicy aftershave.

'And I suppose you've heard the latest from that quarter?' Bridie continued, carefully placing her cup back on its saucer. 'About the holiday?' She knew from my face that I hadn't. 'Herself's heading off to Spain on Friday, if you don't mind. With the fancy man. And leaving that child all alone in the house for the week.'

'Shayne?'

She nodded. 'On his own. No adult supervision.' She pushed the biscuit tin closer to me. 'Where would you hear the like?'

I took another coconut macaroon. I thought about Shayne being able to do what he liked for a whole week. But I didn't feel jealous. Not at all. I just felt sorry for him.

We were all out on the green that Friday afternoon when Liz left. She stood up in Vic's car as they drove alongside us and stuck her head out through the sunroof, waving a white straw sun hat and shouting something none of us could make out. Valerie said it sounded like 'Adios' but I doubted it. I couldn't believe Liz knew even a single word in another language.

Shayne had been out for the past half hour, circling around us on his bike. He didn't even look up when Liz and Vic drove by and I wondered if any form of goodbye had taken place between them. Had Liz given him a great big bear hug and left a list of do's and don'ts sellotaped to the fridge? Had her eyes glittered as she showed him the week's worth of frozen meals in the freezer and pushed a wad of notes into his hand? And when she'd lovingly placed a pile of freshly washed and ironed clothes in his wardrobe and put clean sheets on his bed, had she looked around his tiny attic room, then rushed downstairs and flung her arms around him, telling him she'd phone every day without fail? I almost laughed out loud at the scenario I'd imagined. She'd probably left barely enough food in the cupboards, the place in a mess, and a parting instruction that the house be clean and tidy on her return.

David was holding court under a cherry tree, his broken wrist lying heavy in his lap. The cast was still blindingly white; he'd refused to allow any of us to autograph it. A circle of girls – Valerie, Tracey and Sandra included – sat around him as he read aloud the words to 'Hotel California'. He often did that: copied out the words to songs and 'explained' their meaning to anyone who cared to listen. He broke off when Shayne came within earshot. His words showed that things were a bit strained between them.

'I see the Wicked Witch of the West has left us,' he said, using his preferred name for Liz. 'How I'll miss her sweet visage. Would that Mother and Father O'Dea might fly off to some far and distant land. 'What a tempting prospect.'

Shayne showed no reaction, save for a toss of his head. I doubt he even understood what David was saying. For him, his mam being away made little difference, seeing as she pretty much left him to his own devices most of the time anyway. For someone like David, it would've been an altogether different story.

'Now,' David said, turning once again to his audience. 'When the words of the song refer to checking out but not being able to leave, what do you suppose that means?'

Aidan Farrell had been watching the group and he began to run around the circle of girls, pointing to his bum and roaring with laughter.

'It's when . . . It's when you can't do a shite even though . . . even though . . . you're dyin' for it!' he shouted. 'And you're fartin' like mad! Great big stinkers, like!'

Tracey leapt up, eyes blazing, her face red with rage. 'Come on!' she announced to everyone. 'We're going down to the graveyard. At least we'll have some peace and quiet there.' She yelled at her brother, 'Go on home! And you can take them with you!' She pointed at the collection of Farrells playing in among the bushes. 'And if you don't do what you're told, I'll tell Mam what you said.' Aidan stuck his tongue out but then he slunk off, rounding up his siblings with a branch he'd broken off a tree.

We all obeyed Tracey and soon we were heading up the lane towards Churchview Park, where a narrow pathway would lead us to the graveyard. Mel ran into Mealy's for a bag of gobstoppers and Shayne cycled on ahead, disappearing from view while David led our small group, chattering away like some annoying tour guide. The way he walked annoyed me – each step measured and deliberate. As if he was on a stage, aware of an audience. Sandra decided to imitate him behind his back, careful not to let the twins see. Tracey's giggles encouraged her but Valerie didn't find it as funny. 'Be careful he doesn't catch you,' she whispered. 'I don't think he'd be amused.'

'I'm only messing,' Sandra said.

'David's not someone I'd mess with,' Valerie said. 'He can be quite . . .' She trailed off.

'Quite what?' I asked, curious.

'Well, he's . . . he's . . .' She slowed down, allowing the twins to walk ahead. Then she took a deep breath and looked at the three of us. 'Promise you won't say this back to him?'

'What?' Tracey asked in a high whisper. 'Say what back to him?'

Valerie leaned in close to us. 'He . . . well . . . he didn't fall out of the tree. He threw himself from it deliberately. To get out of that piano competition.'

'You mean . . . on purpose?' Sandra asked, her eyes wide. 'He did it *on purpose*?'

'Ladies, ladies!' It was David. He'd stopped and turned around to face us. 'No dilly-dallying now. Keep up with the group.'

'Sshhh!' Valerie hissed at us. 'Don't let on. He made me swear I'd keep my mouth shut.'

David gave us a big smile when we caught up. Then Mel arrived back, gobstopper in cheek. 'Wonderful!' David said. 'We're all together again.'

Soon we were walking alongside the churchyard. The branches of the copper beech towered up and out over the high stone wall, making the pathway dark and damp. As we passed under the canopy of purple-brown leaves, David held his cast out from his body and gave an exaggerated shudder.

'Pity about that piano competition,' I said, unable to resist. 'I mean, after you'd been practising so hard and all.'

Sandra gave me a dig and Valerie glared.

'It is indeed,' he replied. 'Especially as I was so looking forward to it.'

Just then, through the black railed gate that opened into the churchyard, I spied Father Feely. He walked slowly past the Virgin Mary in her concrete grotto, muttering to himself. He carried a big red book in one hand, and a huge bunch of keys jingled in the other. He looked up as we passed and we all stopped dead; his gaze had the power to root our feet to the ground. He made a beeline for us, crunching across the fine gravel, his face getting redder and redder with every step until, when he reached us, I half expected steam to start whooshing out of his ears. 'Well, well, well, and who have we here? Hmm?' he puffed. He looked around. 'Let me see.' He named us all, one by one, and stood beaming, his yellow eyes all googly and glassy and the long hairs that grew out of his nose quivering as he breathed. 'And how is young Master O'Dea?' he asked, eyeing the cast on David's wrist. 'That was an unfortunate mishap, was it not?'

'It was indeed, Father,' David said, plain-faced, meeting Father Feely's gaze straight on.

'And did I hear 'twas from our copper beech that you fell? What the divil had you up there in the first place, lad?'

David paused for only a split second. 'I was praying, Father,' he said. 'Praying to the good Lord to grant me the strength to do my very best in the piano competition the next day.' He ran his fingers over his cast as he spoke. Father Feely dipped his head to one side, his features softening while he listened. 'And . . . well . . . you see, Father, I . . . perhaps stupidly . . . I imagined my prayers might have more success if I was . . . closer to God, as it were.'

Father Feely reached out a hand and laid it on David's head. He closed his eyes and said something in Latin, then blessed himself. 'I knew. I knew as soon as I heard that there'd be a plausible explanation. I said to myself, there'll be a reason that lad was up that tree. Perhaps he was rescuing a little kitten, or returning a tiny fledgling to its nest . . .' He smoothed his plump hands over the fattest part of his belly. 'God bless you, my son. And know that this is merely the Lord's way of testing the strength of your faith.' He took David's wrist in one hand and made the sign of the cross over it with the other. 'In the name of the Father, the Son and the Holy Ghost.'

Valerie pinched my arm. Though she knew she could trust Sandra and Tracey not to blab about the truth of David's accident, she wasn't as sure about me. But she needn't have worried; I wasn't about to say anything at all. My feelings were confused. Witnessing the skill of his little act with Father Feely, I couldn't decide if what I felt for David O'Dea was admiration or disgust.

'Thank you, Father,' he was saying now, blessing himself and genuflecting.

'Ah, now, that's enough, that's enough.' Father Feely laughed, tousling David's hair. 'And next time you want to be closer to the Lord, come to me and I'll make sure to let you up into the gallery to say your prayers. No more climbing trees, do you hear me?'

'Yes, Father.'

'And don't forget. The Lord hears our prayers no matter where we are. He listens to us wherever we happen—'

'Yes, Father. Thank you, Father,' David said, backing away, anxious now to escape. He blessed himself again and turned solemnly on his heels, leaving the priest muttering under his breath.

We followed David until we were out of Father Feely's sight. Then everyone sort of exploded and collapsed in on top of one another with laughter. Tears welled in Tracey's eyes. Valerie made a sound like a donkey. Sandra squealed. Mel was clearly in awe of David's ability to keep a straight face; his way of showing it was to wallop David on the back and offer him a gobstopper.

'Jesus! What's keepin' ye?' Shayne called as he cycled towards us. He skidded to a stop and looked at the girls. 'What's so funny? What're ye all laughin' at?'

'Ah, nothing,' Mel said, spitting his gobstopper into his hand so he could speak. 'We were just talking to Feely, that's all.'

I stepped forward. 'David was explaining how he came to break his wrist, weren't you, David?' I said. 'About how you climbed the tree so you could be . . . closer to God . . . while you prayed for success in the piano competition.'

'And Feely was very impressed, wasn't he?' David said. 'Why, I'd even go so far as to say I made his day.' He laughed, picking a small stone from the path and firing it at Shayne's bike where it clanged off the mudguard and shot off into the air. 'What do you think?' he asked Shayne. 'Would you say he believed me?'

Shayne frowned. He rode up close to him, jamming on the brakes just short of David's legs. 'What do I care?' he said. 'Come on, will yez. Don't be takin' hours. There's a new grave and all.' He sped off, elbowing David as he cycled past. I watched David now as he walked through the graveyard gates, his steps so sure and precise and his voice so annoyingly loud.

And I found myself wishing he hadn't come away so lightly from the fall.

Once inside, Shayne zipped down the winding paths, past the old granite gravestones and crosses covered in ivy and moss. He stopped beside the new grave, waiting to show it off like it was some art project he'd spent ages working on. A freshly filled grave always attracted our attention. It was kind of thrilling to imagine that beneath the mound of newly turned earth lay a human body in only the very early stages of decay. A person that probably looked like they were asleep, even though they were just as dead as the piles of bones and teeth and hair in all the other graves. We gathered around it, our noses filled with the scent from the wreaths and bouquets that were piled on top. Mel's eyes watered and he sneezed, the sound of it almost deafening in the silence. There wasn't a headstone yet so Shayne leaned down to read some of the cards stuck in among the flowers.

'It's someone called Teresa,' he announced quietly. 'There's one from her kids.'

'Someone's *mam* is lying under all that muck?' Linda shrieked, horrified at the thought.

'We all have to face it,' David said to his sister, making no attempt to lower his voice. 'Don't expect Mother O'Dea to be around forever.'

'Shut up, David,' Valerie said, throwing him a sharp glance. 'Your mam'll be around a long time. She's not that old or anything. This Teresa woman was probably ancient.'

'Perhaps. Perhaps not. The grim reaper can pay us a visit at any time, I'm afraid.' He looked at Shayne. 'Isn't that so? Why, even the Wicked Witch of the West will leave us one day. Who knows, it may be sooner than we think . . .' He twirled around, the toe of one shoe grinding deep into the loose, dusty gravel. He placed the tip of a finger to his bottom lip. 'Let me see. Could it be the bite of a mosquito that does it? Or too much . . . what is it they drink over there? Sangria, isn't it? Yes, that's it, sangria . . . Too much of that and a badly timed lunge from Uncle Vic while they're watching the sunset from their balcony. Or, worst-case scenario, complete engine failure at thirty-five thousand feet.' He turned his eyes upwards, where, as if he'd planned it, a noiseless jet snaked across the sky, leaving a long white plume in its wake.

No one said a word. We watched the jet, almost waiting for it to burst into flames or take a sudden nosedive towards the earth. Shayne gripped his fingers tight around the handles of his bike, twisting hard. It was obvious he was ready to pounce.

David looked him in the eye. 'It wouldn't make any difference if she never came home, anyway,' he sneered. 'She's hardly ever around. She might as well be dead.'

Shayne crashed his bike to the ground. With the back of his hand he pushed the hair out of his eyes before curling his fingers into a tight, hard fist and landing a punch of some force on David's right cheek.

'Fuck off, O'Dea! OK? Just FUCK OFF!' His words ricocheted around the graveyard like bullets.

We stood, hypnotized.

None of us ever used the F word.

Not even on the green where we were completely out of our parents' earshot. And here was Shayne, shouting it out loud. Twice. And in the graveyard!

As we watched the colour drain from David's mole-dotted face, it wasn't clear what stunned him more: the stinging crack to his cheek or the shocking cut of the curse that had sliced right through the holy air. His eyes were round and wide and his mouth hung open in a big, trembling 'O'.

The twins started to cry. Much as they didn't get along with their brother, blood is thicker than water, as Bridie was fond of telling me, and so they rushed to David's side. But their sympathy changed to puzzlement when his lips began to curve into a slight but definite smile. Then we heard a familiar voice from behind.

'*What* in the name of the Lord God Almighty is going on here?'

It was Father Feely walking towards us, his face on fire. David couldn't hide his delight at the perfect timing.

'This is a *holy* place. A holy, *sacred* place,' Father Feely spat at us. 'And you –' he turned to Shayne – 'you dare to behave like a . . . a . . . *heathen*. Like a *hun*. Like a . . . a . . . bar*barian*.' He shook his head at each description, his cheeks flaming with scribbles of spidery, purple veins. 'And you needn't be looking at me like that, Lawless. I saw what you did. You *dare* to use violence and profanity in a blessed place? In *any* place? Shame on you! And this young boy here already injured.' He put his hand on David's shoulder and lowered his voice. 'Are you all right, lad? 'Tis the mercy of God there's no damage to your eye.'

David nodded, cradling his cast to his chest and managing

to keep his quivering lips from smiling. Father Feely waved his hands at Shayne. *'Off with you!'* he commanded. 'Go on! And take your filthy mouth with you!' He began examining David's swelling cheek, making him turn his head so he could see the bruise that had started to appear. David was loving it. I couldn't stand it.

'It's . . . it's not fair, Father,' I blurted. 'David's as much to blame. He was slagging Shayne about his mam, and—'

'And *nothing*,' Father Feely cut in. 'That's no reason to resort to violence and vulgar language, is it?' His boiled-egg eyes bulged. 'Well? Is it?'

It was no use. I might as well have been trying to defend the devil. Shayne had no chance against the holiness of Saint David. 'No, Father,' I sighed.

'Now,' Father Feely said to Shayne, sticking his stomach out like a penguin. 'I won't say it again. Off you go. And you can walk. Vehicles of any kind are prohibited in graveyards. *Prohibited*. Do you hear me?'

He turned his attention once more to David. As everyone crowded around for a closer look at his injury, Shayne lifted his bike and slowly wheeled it away. I stood watching him for a moment, listening to the babble of the group as they jostled for space. He shuffled along the path, his shoulders slumped and his head bowed.

It sickened me. David was getting all the sympathy even though he'd been the one who'd started it. It wasn't Shayne's fault that Liz didn't look after him properly. David had said those things to deliberately hurt Shayne. He'd deserved the punch. I left the group to themselves.

'Hang on,' I called after Shayne.

He glanced back but kept walking. 'What do ye want?'

'I . . . I . . . David O'Dea's a pig.' It was all I could think of to say.

I followed him through the gates. Under the shade of the copper beech, he stopped. 'Ye want a crossbar home?'

I nodded and climbed up. It was wobbly at first as he got used to my weight. Then he began to cycle faster. He leaned hard on the handlebars, his chest pressed into my back and his breath coming in hot blasts against my head. Apart from that time he'd squeezed my wrist, I'd never been so close to him before. I'd never been so close to any boy before. I hadn't expected him to offer me a crossbar home but I supposed it was his way of thanking me for sticking up for him. His left thigh thumped against the side of my leg as he pedalled. I'd left my hair loose that morning and I could feel it lifting into the air, sure it must be whipping across his face, finding its way into his mouth. But I didn't want to turn my head back to look.

We were almost into the cul-de-sac when Dad drove past, heading home. His eyes were fixed straight ahead and he didn't notice us. I felt Shayne's muscles tense when he saw the car. He leaned his face close to my head and whispered warm words in my ear.

'Would ye forgive yer da anythin'?'

I thought I'd heard him wrong and for a few seconds tried to convince myself he'd said something else like: Would you give your doll a ring? Would you live with the king? But nothing I thought of made any sense.

His mouth was at my ear again. 'Well, would ye?'

I twisted my head around a bit. 'What do you mean?'

'Ye know, if he did somethin' bad?'

'Like what?'

He pulled softly on the brakes and stopped at Bridie's gate. 'I dunno. Anythin' bad.'

'Don't be stupid,' I said. 'I know my dad. He wouldn't do anything bad.'

'Ye sure?'

I slid down off the bike. ''Course I am.'

'So . . . what would ye say if I told ye I knew he'd done somethin' bad?'

My heart bounced in my chest, slipping and sliding about like the ones in the silver trays in Boylan's window. 'I . . . I don't believe you.'

'All right, Ruth?' It was Dad. At our gate with Kev in his arms. He looked over and smiled. 'Dinner's nearly ready.'

Shayne leaned in to me and laughed. 'I was only messin'!' he whispered. 'Ye should see the look on yer face!'

'I knew you were only joking,' I said as I walked towards the house.

He followed me up the drive, still wheeling his bike. 'Really? Ye didn't look that sure to me.'

He was right. Much as I didn't want to believe him, there was something behind what he'd said. I could sense it.

Mam came flip-flopping out to the door in Dad's slippers, a tea towel in her hand. 'Where are the others?' she wanted to know. 'I'm after doing a huge pot of mash. There's enough to feed an army!'

Shayne's face lit up. 'Mash!' he said. 'Me favourite.'

They exchanged a glance and I knew what was coming next. Only someone completely heartless could've ignored him.

'Your . . . your mammy's away, isn't she?' Mam asked, smoothing down the front of her apron. 'Come on in, then. You can have a bit of decent food for a change.'

None of us said anything about what had happened in the graveyard. But we knew it was more than a little funny that only an hour since Shayne had shouted the F word in front of Father Feely, he was sitting at our table asking Mel to pass the tomato sauce. Dad was far less chatty than usual. I got the feeling he wasn't happy that Shayne was there. He only opened his mouth to fork food into it or to tell us off over things he normally ignored. He asked Mel three times to stop talking with his mouth full, told Sandra to stop daydreaming and eat up, and even asked me to take my elbows off the table and said my hair was in my food even though it clearly wasn't. Mam said nothing but I could tell she thought Dad was going over the top. He was definitely a bit edgy, and kept glancing at Shayne as if he was afraid of him. *Would you forgive yer da anythin'?* I couldn't get the words out of my head.

There was silence for a while, and I picked through the bones in my piece of fish, hoping for a distraction of some sort so that Mam wouldn't realize I wasn't actually eating it. Kev was almost a year old now and full of mischief, especially at mealtimes. He banged his spoon on the tray of his highchair and sent a lump of mash flying through the air. We all laughed, except Dad who wagged his finger and told him he was a bold boy. Kev just smiled and did it again. This time, a dollop of tomato sauce hit the wall with a splat, leaving behind a dripping splodge of red. I imagined the man in the tree had been shot and that blood was oozing out of the wallpaper. Dad was about to give out but Mam got in first. 'It'll wipe off,' she said. 'No damage done.'

A few more minutes of silence followed. Then, the doorbell rang. Dad jumped in his seat, slamming his knife and fork down on the table, in anger as much as in fright. Mam said it must be Mrs Shine, collecting the church money, and asked me to run out with the envelope. I was more than happy to leave the table, knowing my fish would be cold by the time I came back, giving me an excellent excuse not to eat it. Mrs Shine always kept me at the door for ages. Apparently I was the same age as her beloved niece, Nuala – a fact, it appeared, she found fascinating and she was forever asking me questions so she could compare the two of us. I opened the door, ready to be bombarded. But instead of Mrs Shine's anxious eyes, I saw the pale, rigid lips of Mr O'Dea and, beside him, the flushed and flabby face of Father Feely.

'We see young Lawless's bike in the driveway,' Father Feely said, all breathless, like he'd just climbed a mountain. 'We take it he's here?'

ELEVEN

We'd no choice then but to tell Mam and Dad what had happened. According to the others, Father Feely had insisted on bringing David home after Shayne and I left the graveyard. They said he'd run off – Father Feely could run? – to get his Morris Minor, so that the 'injured child' wouldn't have to walk 'all the way' to Hillcourt Rise. David had been allowed to sit in the front and had given them his queen's wave as the car choked and spluttered down the road. (Father Feely's driving was well known around Kilgessin – Bridie said he'd destroyed the engines of three cars in the last ten years.) Passing the O'Deas' house on their way home, the others had seen the Morris Minor parked in the drive and Father Feely looking out the front room window, wiping his blotchy face with a handkerchief.

Dad said there was no point in all of us traipsing over to the O'Deas'. 'If Eamon O'Dea wants Shayne to apologize, then I suppose I'll have to go over with him,' he said, with more than a trace of annoyance in his voice. 'But there's no point in everyone's evening being ruined. You lot stay here and finish your tea.'

'But Dad,' I said, 'we're all witnesses.'

'She's right, Mick,' Mam said. 'At least let's give the lad a fair chance. From what they've told us, it wasn't exactly black and white.'

Dad grumbled. 'I suppose so.'

Father Feely and Mr O'Dea hadn't got into any discussions at our door. They'd simply told Dad what had happened to David and said they wanted 'young Lawless' to go over and explain himself. Then they left, saying, 'We'll be waiting for you', not 'We'll be waiting for him', which made Dad feel like he'd no choice but to go as well. Shayne said he didn't mind going on his own, but Mam insisted he should have an adult with him. 'Sure wouldn't your mammy go with you if she was here?' she said, but I knew full well she didn't believe that for a second.

Dad, Shayne and Mel led the way across the green. Sandra and I walked behind. The grass on the green had been mown earlier and our toes kicked up sprays of cuttings as we walked. Geraldine came to her door with Fiona in her arms as we passed. She stood there, her face scrubbed as pink as the shirt she was wearing, not even trying to pretend she was being anything other than nosy. She said something over her shoulder, then Tracey came running out and sat on the wall to watch.

News of our convoy spread rapidly, and within seconds Nora Vaughan had joined Geraldine on the doorstep. Tracey was summoned to take Fiona and she slid off the wall reluctantly, a look of defeat in her eyes. Sandra nudged me as she walked up her drive – Tracey's skirt was caught in her pants, exposing her upper thigh. It was nearly as thin as my arm and the flesh – what there was of it – had a sort of blue tinge. I watched her take Fiona and noticed how Geraldine's shirt wasn't quite as baggy as it should have been.

'I bet Tracey's mam's having another baby,' I said to Sandra.

'I doubt it,' she said. 'Tracey said that after Fiona was born, her mam swore she wasn't ever having another one.'

It was Tina who answered the door. She didn't say a word, just stared at us with her big grey eyes, then went into the front room to get her father. He kept us waiting for ages as if we were kids selling raffle tickets and we'd disturbed him in the middle of watching the news. When he finally came out, he was clearly surprised to see all five of us. 'In you come,' he said, after taking his pipe out of his mouth. His cheeks were sunken – from all the pipe-sucking, I imagined – and he had deep lines at the sides of his seawater eyes. He didn't appear to have any eyelashes, and his crinkly ginger hair looked like lengths of unravelled washing line plastered flat across his head. He wore a shirt with little beige and blue squares, a yellow tweed tie, and an army-green cardigan with leather buttons and elbow patches.

We followed him into their front room, where David sat in a chestnut-brown leather armchair beside the fireplace, holding a strip of bacon against his cheek. Father Feely stood with his back to the window, his hands flat against the swelling mound of his stomach. He was leaning towards David, speaking in his droning, Sunday mass voice, but as soon as we walked in to the room he stopped short, straightened himself up and cleared his throat.

'Children, children,' he said, smiling and walking towards us with his arms outstretched. He touched Sandra's shoulder, ruffled Mel's hair and gave me a wink. He patted Dad's arm. 'Michael. Mick,' he said, as if he wasn't sure what to call him. 'Good of you to bring the lad over.' He went in close and whispered, 'I know the mammy's gone away. Somewhere foreign, I believe. Glad to know yourself and Rose are there for the lad.' Dad opened his mouth to say something but Father Feely turned away, beaming at Shayne and almost shouting. 'And Shayne! Good lad. How are we now? Anxious to get this over and done with, eh?' He winked again and his smile grew even larger, making his cheeks bunch up under his eyes like juicy plums.

Mr O'Dea stood beside David, one hand resting along the back of the armchair and the other holding his pipe, which he puffed on every now and then, filling the room with a sweet smell like the vanilla essence Bridie spooned into her cake mixtures.

Father Feely clapped his hands, making me jump. 'Now! Where will we start, Eamon?' David made a moaning sound and rubbed the rasher over the side of his face.

'With an apology,' Mr O'Dea said, his teeth clenched down on his pipe. 'An unreserved apology.'

'Shouldn't we get both sides of the story first?' Dad asked, his eyes flitting from Father Feely to Mr O'Dea. 'That's why I brought them all over. They did witness what took place, after all.'

'Children, I think it's safe to say,' said Mr O'Dea, 'make the most unreliable witnesses. David has told me what happened.'

'But is David not a child himself?' asked Dad.

Mr O'Dea scowled. 'Violence speaks for itself, Mr Lamb. Take a look at my son's face.'

'And don't forget, I was a witness to the incident too, Michael. Mick,' Father Feely said. 'I saw what I saw. Young Lawless landing a punch to David's cheek and using profanities I never thought I'd hear in a sacred burial ground.'

'But do you not think we should hear what went on before that?' Dad said. 'Wouldn't that be the Christian thing to do? Hear all sides?'

Father Feely scratched his nose. He walked over to the fireplace and took a silver-framed photograph from the mantelpiece. It was a picture of David, aged about three, dressed in a sailor suit and sitting stiffly on a big wooden chest. 'You're correct, of course,' he said, looking at the photograph. 'We should always endeavour to get to the . . . truth of things.'

Sandra said that, really, Valerie, Tracey and the twins should tell their sides of the story too, but Mr O'Dea said we'd had quite enough witnesses to contend with already and, besides, he didn't want the twins involved any more than was necessary in the 'whole affair', as he called it. Tina had disappeared after she'd opened the door and Linda was nowhere to be seen.

While the others recounted what had happened, I looked around the room. It had a sort of dull, museum feel, as if nothing had been shifted in years, and the air was fuzzy with dust. Most of the contents were made out of things that had once been alive: two leather armchairs and a matching couch with buttons pressed deep into its back; a zebra-skin pouffe with star patterns made from what looked like tiny white bones stitched into its sides; and in the middle of the dark, wooden floor – so shiny it was like you were walking on glass – was a long-haired sheepskin rug.

David's piano stood near the window. I walked across the room and stood beside it. Its lid was closed and the wood was polished to a high gleam, like the floor. On the top, faded dried flowers were arranged in a fan shape in a big pink seashell. And beside it, under a round-topped glass case, was a stuffed, open-beaked, yellow-eyed blackbird.

'And would that be how you remember things happening?' Father Feely was droning. 'Hmm?'

'Ruth,' Dad said. 'Father Feely's talking to you. Is there anything you want to add? Or have the others covered everything?'

The others had covered everything all right, but they might as well have been talking to the sheepskin rug. Eamon and Father Feely said nothing when Mel and Sandra explained what David had said about Liz. They simply chose to ignore it. It wasn't fair. David couldn't be allowed to get away with *everything*. I ran my palm along the smooth coldness of the piano and lifted the lid.

'Well . . . there is one thing,' I said, fingering the ivory keys. 'David didn't break his wrist by accident. He flung himself from the tree on purpose. To get out of taking part in the piano competition.'

David jumped up out of the armchair and flung the rasher to the floor, where it landed with a splat. 'I did not!' he said. 'Don't listen to her! She's lying! Why would I do that?' He stood before his father, his face as clear and angelic as it was in the sailor suit picture, except for the purple bruise on his right cheek. 'You know I wouldn't do something like that! I'd been looking forward to that competition for so long. I'd practised for months! I was expecting to do really well. I was sure of a placing. I—'

'What in the name of *God* is going on?' It was Mrs O'Dea. She breezed in from the hall, her heels clicking across the wooden floor. She bent down to pick up the piece of bacon and Father Feely told her what I'd said. 'And you expect me to believe that piece of utter *non*sense?' she said, laying the rasher carefully on the desk beside the door. She went over to the window and, although it was still bright outside, she drew the gold velvet curtains, fussing with the ends of them, pulling them in and out until she was satisfied with the way they sat on the floor. 'Well?' she said, widening her small, dark eyes and breathing loudly through her long, thin nose.

Her black backcombed hair sat stiffly around her head like the brim of a witch's hat and when she leaned down to turn on a lamp, the bulb, through its green satin shade, gave her skin a scary, emerald hue. She looked a lot more like the Wicked Witch of the West than Liz Lawless did.

'How can you say such a thing?' Father Feely asked me. 'David had a terrible fall. A truly terrible fall. He could've been killed! Why would anyone in their right mind do something like that on purpose, child? Hmm?'

'This is ridiculous,' Mr O'Dea said. 'Absolutely ridiculous.' He turned to me. 'And would you mind not touching the piano keys, please? We've only just had it tuned.'

Dad looked tired and angry. 'What's all this about, Ruth?'

'Father Feely said we should always try and get to the truth of things,' I said.

Mrs O'Dea folded her arms. 'Well, young lady, from where I'm standing it looks like you came up with a very successful way of diverting attention from the real culprit. I've never heard such rubbish in all my life.'

'Well, I don't see why Shayne should get all the blame!' I said.

Dad turned to Sandra and Mel. 'Is Ruth telling the truth here?' he asked. Mel had taken a sudden interest in a glass paperweight with a butterfly inside it and pretended not to hear Dad's question. When Dad asked again, he gave him a wide-eyed look and shrugged like he'd no idea what he was talking about. Sandra fiddled with the buttons on her blouse. 'I don't know, Dad,' she said. 'I'm not sure. I . . . I did hear something about David doing it on purpose but I . . . I don't know . . .'

'This is unbe*lievable*,' Mr O'Dea said. 'You people. You're hardly living in Hillcourt Rise a wet weekend and you're causing all this trouble. There was never anything like this before you arrived.'

'Now, hang on a minute,' Dad said. 'That's a bit unfair.'

'It certainly is!' said Mrs O'Dea. 'It's *very* unfair. Our child has been accused of being a liar. Look at his face! Destroyed! We were expecting an apology and all we've got is . . . is . . . abuse!'

'Look, let's all calm down,' Father Feely said with a false smile. 'We haven't heard a word from young Lawless here, have we?' He slapped a fat hand on Shayne's shoulder. 'What have you got to say about all this, lad?' Shayne stood very still. His face had turned pale. The skin under his eyes was white, almost glowing, and his lips were a dark purplish-blue. His forehead looked clammy and he swayed a little on his feet. 'Lad? Are you all right?' Father Feely gripped his shoulder tighter.

'I . . . I . . . don't feel well,' Shayne mumbled.

'Sit down, lad, sit down.'

Shayne took a few careful steps forward and lowered himself down onto the zebra-skin pouffe.

'Well, that's very convenient, isn't it?' Mrs O'Dea said. 'Feeling ill all of a sudden.'

'Now, now, Mona,' said Father Feely. 'It's hardly the lad's fault.'

Mrs O'Dea raised her eyes. 'This is a complete waste of time. I don't know why we bothered getting him over here in the first place. And surely you're not taken in with this . . . this . . . act?'

Father Feely shuffled his feet and cleared his throat. 'Well I . . . surely you can . . . can we not . . . Hmm?' He fixed his eyes on David. 'You fell out of the tree, is that right, lad? That was the truth you told me, wasn't it? About trying to be closer to the Lord so he might hear your prayers?'

David blinked then gave Father Feely a hard, unflinching stare. 'The truth is . . .' He glanced at Shayne, who was bent over, clutching his stomach. 'The truth is . . . that I fell, Father, like I said.'

The words were barely out of his mouth when Shayne gave a low moan, lurched forward and vomited all over the sheepskin rug. A bitter smell immediately rose up in the air and we all stood staring at what he'd produced. Dad went over and crouched down beside him.

'Oh, that's right,' Mrs O'Dea said through her tears, her voice thin and high. 'That says it all.' She put her hand down the front of her dress and pulled out a handkerchief, dabbing at her eyes then holding it under her nose. 'Easily known whose side you're on,' she whined.

'Shush now, Mona. You're upset,' Father Feely said.

'Upset? Of course I'm upset! My son has been accused of deliberately throwing himself out of a tree, his face is disfigured and we've received no apology, and now his . . . his . . . attacker appears to be getting all the sympathy. It beggars belief!'

Shayne moaned again.

'Look,' Dad said. 'I should take the lad home. He's not in any fit state for this.'

'Oh yes, off you go,' said Mrs O'Dea. 'Avoid responsibility at all costs.'

'Responsibility? He's not my responsibility. I've nothing to do with all this.'

'But he was in your house all evening, wasn't he? Eating at your table, I believe? In your care?'

'Rose asked him to stay for his dinner. It's hardly a crime.'

'Oh, did she now? It's all getting very cosy between the Lambs and the Lawlesses, isn't it?'

'Come on,' Dad said, looking at me. 'We're going home.'

Mr O'Dea came up behind me, waiting for me to move away from his precious piano. I touched one of the keys, smiling inside as a clear, high note sounded out in the room. Dad pulled me by the arm, gesturing at Sandra and Mel to follow. Father Feely ushered Shayne towards the door and David sank back into his armchair, closing his eyes.

When we got out into the hall, we heard the rumble of conversation starting up and Mrs O'Dea's high-pitched voice crying, 'And look at my sheepskin! It's absolutely ruined!'

'You should've kept your mouth shut,' Mel whispered in my ear. 'You're in for it when we get home.'

'It's not my fault,' I said. 'You can't blame me when I was only telling the truth.'

'But how do you know what the real truth is? You weren't there.'

'David didn't fall by accident. I just know it.'

Father Feely saw us out. He stood at the door making little grunting sounds as we squeezed past his stomach.

'I'm sorry we didn't have a better outcome to all of this,' he said, joining his hands together. 'But with the help of God, we'll find a resolution.'

It looked like the whole of Hillcourt Rise was waiting for us to appear: Tracey was wheeling Fiona along in her pram, with Valerie by her side; Geraldine and Nora had taken their conversation out to the Farrell's gate; Paddy was in his drive, looking under the bonnet of his van, scratching his beard; and Clem was on his hunkers in the Farrell's front garden, pulling weeds up from the lawn. Sandra and Mel ran up to Tracey and Valerie. Shayne followed but leaned on the pillar when he reached the gate, looking like he was going to puke again.

I hung back with Dad and tucked myself in behind him, tracing my fingers over the red bricks around the O'Deas' front door while I listened to Father Feely's mumbling. I could tell Dad was eager to get away from what was turning into a sermon but Father Feely kept going on and on about 'forgiveness' and 'God's love' and the 'power of prayer', barely taking a breath between sentences.

Then he started talking about David, saying stuff I was sure he wouldn't have if he'd remembered I was still there, hiding in behind Dad. He spoke about how Eamon and Mona were such loving parents and about all the sacrifices they'd made for David over the years and how things had been so difficult for them before it was arranged and how their lives had been transformed after it came about. *It?*

'You know, it can't have been easy for them,' he said. 'Ten years is a long time to wait. Thought they'd never have a family. Never. And then it was touch and go at the start, with him being nearly a year old when they got him. And they've always had high hopes for him, you know. Very high hopes. Poor David has a lot to live up to.' He lowered his voice. 'And, of course, with the girls being Mona and Eamon's own, well, you know, he's bound to feel a bit . . . put out. What I'm trying to say is, we should perhaps make allowances for him. At least sometimes.'

So that was what 'it' was. David was *adopted*.

Mr and Mrs O'Dea weren't David's real parents at all! But they were Tina and Linda's. How strange was that? Back in our old school, there'd been a brother and sister who were adopted. Despite trying not to, I thought of them as different. Sometimes when I looked into their eyes, I could tell there was an uncertainty there, like they weren't really sure who they were.

'. . . heartbroken about his wrist,' Father Feely was saying to Dad. 'Heartbroken. Months of practice down the drain and him so eager to do well. That boy has been nothing but a pleasure to his parents from the moment they took him home, let me tell you. I didn't know them at the time, of course. They weren't living in Kilgessin back then. But I know the lovely convent sisters and they assured me Mona and Eamon were the most deserving and appreciative of adoptive parents. Most deserving. That the Lord blessed them with the twins not long afterwards is surely evidence of his faith in their abilities.'

He went on and on. Dad kept saying 'Hmm' and 'Is that so?' I wondered if David knew. Or if Mr and Mrs O'Dea had managed to keep it a secret from him all these years. But I could hardly step out from behind Dad and ask. Surely it was something he'd have mentioned if he knew about it? Boasted about it, even? He was forever complaining about 'Mother O'Dea', so if he knew she wasn't his real mother, wouldn't he have been keen to let us all know? And even if he didn't, he must've questioned it sometimes. With his bleach-blond hair and skin that easily tanned, he looked nothing like either of his parents.

Father Feely was rambling on about 'making allowances' again and about how Shayne should've apologized for punching David and that it was impossible to believe that David had thrown himself out of the tree. Then he finally took a breath and Dad interrupted. 'To be honest with you, Father,' he said, 'I know what you mean but . . . well, I'm not responsible for the boy. Shouldn't you be saying all this to his mother?'

'Yes, yes, I will, of course,' he said. 'Indeed and I will, to be sure. As soon as she gets back. Young Lawless has always been trouble and the mammy . . . well, she's—'

'Look, I'll let you go, Father,' Dad said, irritated. 'I'm sure you're needed inside.'

With another grunt and a shuffling of his feet, Father Feely reluctantly closed the O'Deas' front door. I could tell Dad was really annoyed as I followed him up the drive. He took big, hard steps and held his arms rigidly down by his sides, his hands formed into tight fists. Shayne fell in behind us, still clutching his stomach as we walked onto the green, where the others were chatting to Tracey. I could hear Sandra giving her a detailed account of what had happened. Tracey was all ears but she kept glancing back at Geraldine and Nora, who were waiting, arms crossed, for the full story. As were Clem and Paddy, who were only half-heartedly going about their jobs. They didn't really need to be fixing engines and weeding gardens on a Friday evening; it was just an excuse to be close to the heart of the action.

Dad pounded his feet over the grass, sending clumps of green cuttings into the air. He had lots to be angry about. I was listing off all the reasons in my head and wondering what we were going to say to Mam, when suddenly he stopped, turned and let out a roar at the group of neighbours who'd gathered outside their houses for a gawk. 'Go on back inside, the lot of you! Show's over!' he yelled, flapping his arms.

I stopped dead, hardly believing my ears. That couldn't be my dad, could it? I'd never heard him shout like that before. Well, except maybe once, back in the South Circular, when Mel snuck a tin of blue paint in from the car to decorate the go-cart he'd made from bits of an old chair, and he'd spilled a small lake of it all over the sitting room carpet. But that had been inside and was just between ourselves. This was outside. In front of everyone. Dad looked so mad. His eyes were blazing slits under his black eyebrows and his whole face looked like it was on fire.

He stormed on over the green with his head down and we didn't need to be told to hurry up and follow him home. But I couldn't resist having a look over my shoulder. I saw Tracey bumping the pram over the grass towards her house, with Fiona screaming her head off inside. Clem and Paddy had joined their wives at the gate, along with the other neighbours who'd obviously heard Dad's outburst, and they stood huddled together with their arms folded, rolling their eyes and nodding their heads in our direction.

I glanced over at the O'Deas' and spied Father Feely's fat head poking through the gold velvet curtains then disappearing back into the sitting room. And then I saw a movement at an upstairs window. It was David. Up close against the glass, silent and stiff like the blackbird on top of his piano. His eyes found mine and held them for a moment. Even from that distance, I could see the flowering bruise on his cheek.

'You were long enough,' Mam said when we got home. 'Little man's just gone up. Dead tired, he was.' She began cutting slices from a block of banana ice cream and sliding them into the bowls of raspberry jelly she'd set out on the kitchen table.

'How did it go?' She looked up and saw Dad's face. 'I see. Not great, then.'

Sandra got in first, 'Ruth said that David—'

'That's enough,' Dad said. 'I'll tell your mother all about it later. Just have your dessert and get yourselves ready for bed.'

There'd be no arguing with him tonight. We sat down and started to eat. Mam scraped the last of the ice cream into my bowl. 'Anyone for more jelly? There's plenty. Shayne?'

Shayne shook his head and pushed his bowl away, untouched, rubbing his hand over his stomach.

'Shayne got sick,' Sandra said. 'All over the O'Deas' rug.'

Mam put her hands on her hips and looked at him with a frown. 'You did, did you? And what was all that about?'

'Dunno. I just don't feel well.'

'Have you a sore stomach?'

'Yeah.'

'Hmm.'

She picked up the laundry basket from behind the back door and went out to the garden. Dad followed. After a few minutes, they came back inside. Mam started folding the clothes she'd taken in off the line and sorting them into piles. Dad snatched the newspaper from the table and disappeared into the sitting room. Mel scraped Shayne's dessert into his own bowl and noisily slurped the jelly off his spoon. I noticed Mam had forgotten to wipe the smear of tomato sauce from the wall and it had started to harden into a dark red lump.

'I think I'll go home now,' Shayne said, squeaking his chair over the lino as he stood up.

'Mick and I were talking,' Mam said, folding a pair of Dad's underpants. 'And if you want to stay here for tonight, that'd be all right.'

If she'd said the world was ending we'd hardly have been more shocked.

'Here?' Mel asked. 'Why? Where'll he sleep?'

'I just don't think we could let you go home to that empty house and you after getting sick and all,' Mam continued. 'You can sleep in Mel's room. Mick'll bring in the fold-out bed for you.'

Sandra's mouth fell open and her ice cream dripped off her spoon. None of us had ever had a friend to sleep the night. And the fact that Shayne Lawless was the first was almost too much for her to take in. Mel squelched his jelly through his teeth and let it dribble out the sides of his mouth. Shayne turned away. If anything was going make him vomit again, it was that.

'Is that all right, Shayne?' Mam asked. He nodded. 'Now, finish up and go get yourselves ready. You heard what your father said.' She handed Shayne a pair of Mel's pyjamas from the pile. 'Take these. They're not ironed but they'll do you for tonight.'

It was far too early to be going to bed on a Friday night and really embarrassing in front of Shayne. But he was too ill to complain and even seemed relieved to be heading upstairs. Dad came up and pulled the fold-out bed from the hot press, dragging it across the landing into Mel's room with a lot of huffing and puffing.

Sandra and I sat on her bed. She'd spread two nightdresses out on the eiderdown. 'Which one do you think I should wear?' she asked me.

'Oh, definitely the lilac one,' I said, not caring in the slightest.

'Why?'

'It's Shayne's favourite colour.'

'Really?' she asked, her face all serious. 'How do you know?'

'He told me. "Ruth," he said, "I do so love a girl in lilac. Nothing gladdens my heart more than to see a young maiden in—"'

I was stopped short by a pillow in the face.

'Shut up!' she said. 'I hate you. And you know what? You sound just like David O'Dea.'

'I do not!' I said, even though I'd actually felt like him when I was saying it.

'And it's all your fault we have to go to bed this early. You had to blab, didn't you?'

'I was only telling the truth. Someone had to. And thanks for pretending you knew nothing about it, by the way.'

'Yeah, well, I don't know if he fell on purpose, do I? None of us do. We weren't there, were we?'

'Come on, you know right well what David's like. And I had to do something to make his mam and dad see. They think he's some kind of saint. You know they do! And anyway—'

'Shut up, Ruth. I'm sick of hearing about it. Just leave it.' She sat down at the dressing table then turned sharply, her hair swishing round and whipping her face. 'And get off my bed.'

She started to brush her hair with long, forceful strokes, something she never usually did before going to bed. Then she sprayed a cloud of 4711 all over her neck. It was obvious she was hoping to go in and talk to Shayne. But Mam came in to say goodnight and told us she'd left a basin in Mel's room in case Shayne got sick again and under no circumstances were either of us to go near him. And Dad peeped his head round the door to say more or less the same thing. Mam asked him did he think Shayne had thrown up because he was more used to the muck Liz Lawless dished up than the proper meal he'd had with us. She said you'd only have to look at Liz Lawless to know she used Smash instead of real mashed potato, and frozen peas and fish fingers instead of fresh veg from Pav the vegetable man and nice fillets of plaice from Boylan's. Dad said not to be ridiculous, that she'd no way of knowing what Shayne ate at home and he was sure he'd seen Liz making mash when he was round painting her kitchen. They started to go downstairs and I heard Mam saying that if he did, it must've been all for show because you couldn't be peeling potatoes every day and have nails like hers. Sandra hopped into bed and flicked through her latest copy of *Jackie* for a few minutes before sighing deeply and flinging it onto the floor. She was asleep in minutes.

I'd decided I wouldn't say anything about David being adopted. At least not yet. It was something I wasn't supposed to know and I felt I'd said too much that evening already. But as my mind wandered through all sorts of thoughts – what we were missing on telly, or the way I couldn't get the taste of banana ice cream out of my mouth even though I'd brushed my teeth – the word 'Adopted!' kept appearing in my head in a starburst shape, like 'Pow!' or 'Bam!' or 'Ka-Boom!' in a comic.

Adopted. The word kind of changed the way I thought about David. He might've been someone completely different if he hadn't been given to Mona and Eamon. Or maybe he'd have been exactly the same. Who knew how things would turn out if even the tiniest thing about our lives was changed? If I'd been given away when I was born, would I be me, I wondered? The me I knew. Or would I be another person altogether?

I tried to think about David as a tiny boy like Kev, asleep in a strange cot in a strange room, the very first night the O'Deas brought him home. Where was his real mam? And his real dad? Did he have real brothers and sisters who would've taken care of him if he hadn't been given away, the way we took care of Kev? And how did he feel when Tina and Linda came along? Caught forever between the solid pairings of his parents on one side, and his twin sisters on the other. A sort of stranger in his own family. A bit like me.

TWELVE

Shayne appeared to have made a complete recovery the next morning and was well able for the toast and boiled egg Mam made him for his breakfast. He sat at the table, stuffing his mouth and wiping his fingers on the front of his T-shirt. While he'd been asleep, Mam had taken his jeans from Mel's room and sewed patches over the rips and holes, and although he'd have to have been blind not to notice, he didn't say thanks or mention anything about them at all. Mam wouldn't come right out and ask him to stay longer, but she said a few things like: 'I hope you'll be all right on your own' and 'You know where we are if you need us'. And when she announced we were having sausages and mash for dinner and apple crumble for dessert, she searched his face for a reaction but there was none.

We didn't see much of him the rest of the week. Dad said he saw him in Mealy's later that day, buying a packet of Tuc crackers and a Choc Ice, and that Shayne ignored him when he asked how he was. He did much the same to me one evening when I saw him cycling back from the village with a bag of chips and a bottle of Cidona under one arm. It was hard to tell if he was avoiding us, embarrassed by the whole vomiting thing and wearing Mel's pyjamas, or if he was, as I suspected, simply making the most of having the whole house all to himself. I pictured him stretched out on the brown couch in their sitting room, eating Rice Krispies straight from the box and guzzling Liz's whiskey, watching horror films late into the night when we were all fast asleep. Mel asked to go down to his house a couple of times but Mam said 'under no circumstances' and if she caught any of us sneaking down while Liz was away, we wouldn't be let out for the rest of the summer holidays.

It didn't take long before the whole estate knew what had happened in the O'Deas'. Once Geraldine and Nora found out, it may as well have been on the *Nine O'Clock News*. Mam gave out to Sandra for relaying everything to Tracey but Dad said not to be too hard on her, that Mona O'Dea would've made sure she let everyone know anyway. He had to tell Mam how he'd let a roar at the neighbours. She was definitely not pleased but said she understood – to a certain degree – even though the whole thing had nothing to do with us. It was all Liz Lawless's fault, she said. If she hadn't gone and left Shayne on his own, Dad wouldn't have been the one bringing him over to the O'Deas' in the first place.

Despite David's predictions, Liz's plane made it back safely and when I saw Shayne cycling around the green clicking a pair of castanets and wearing a huge orange sombrero on his head, I knew she was home.

It must've been about two days later when I stopped him at the edge of the green on my way back from Mealy's and asked him if she'd had a good time. He said he didn't know; she'd gone to bed as soon as she came back and hadn't been up since. Uncle Vic had only dropped her off, he said, then had to go away 'on business'.

'Have you seen much of David?' I asked him.

'O'Dea? Nah. Not much. Keepin' clear of his ma now, amn't I?'

'I wonder did she get her rug cleaned?' I said and he sort of smiled.

I realized I must've grown a lot over the summer – my eyes were almost level with his. I was able to look straight into them now, and as I did, it was like they gave something to me. It seeped down into my body, deep and dark and endless, mixing with my insides, with my heart and blood and bones.

There was something about Shayne that would stay with me always. I could tell.

'I . . . I have to go and check on me ma,' he said, and in one swift move he was up on the saddle, pedalling fast towards his house. I followed after him, my legs not feeling like my own as I ran. My head tingled with sparks and flashes, with waves of hot and cold. He looked back when he reached his gate and I pictured myself as he did, racing down the road, my cheeks pink and my hair all over my face. The evening sun flashed between my eyelashes, golden and grainy. It was late August now; summer was nearly over. Soon we'd be back into the ordered, daily routine of school and homework and early bedtime. I still had a year to go in Kilgessin National, but Sandra, Mel and Shayne were heading off to Grangemount. Everything was changing. I was being left behind.

I got to his gate, breathless, and leaned my back against the pillar. He stood in front of me, blocking out the sun, took a length of Wrigley's from his pocket and bent it into his mouth. My heart still raced and my legs shook. Then he reached into his pocket again and handed me a piece. I unwrapped it slowly and folded it into my mouth. It zinged against my tongue as my teeth worked it into a soft ball.

'Ye can come in if ye want,' he said, shouldering open the side passage door. I pushed myself away from the pillar.

'Is she OK? Your mam, I mean. She's not sick or anything, is she?'

He reached the kitchen door and stepped into the house. 'Nah. Think she just got sunburned and stuff.' He took a glass from the sink and held it up to the light. I could see it was filthy. He rubbed it against his T-shirt and poured the last of a bottle of red lemonade into it, taking a gulp of it himself before heading out to the hall and up the stairs.

The kitchen was just as untidy as the last time I'd been there: the sink filled with dirty plates and glasses, the countertops littered with crumbs. I peered out to the hall. Liz's suitcase stood at the end of the stairs, half unzipped, some of its contents spilling out onto the carpet: a lime green swimsuit, a red, plastic, high-heeled sandal with a huge yellow daisy on the toe, and a multi-coloured towel.

'Yeah, OK!' I heard Shayne say, his voice raised. 'Fuck's sake. I'm gettin' them!' He thundered back down, sighing loudly, plunging his hand into the suitcase and rummaging around. He pulled out two packs of cigarettes and a bottle of red wine. Stuffing one pack in his pocket, he raced back up. There was some mumbling and heavy footsteps and the slamming of a door. Then silence.

I sucked on my chewing gum, pushing it from side to side with my tongue, and I waited. I watched how the dust floated in the shafts of sunlight that poured in through the crinkly glass panels beside the front door. I wandered back along the hall and peeped into the front room. It smelled like The Ramblers. The couch cushions were strewn about the floor, covered in cigarette ash and crumbs. A tower of LPs, stacked beside what looked like a brand-new record player, had collapsed and slid across the carpet in a line all the way to the window. Cliff Richard's dark eyes peeped out at me from under the hem of the curtain.

On the coffee table, a box of Sugar Puffs lay on its side, along with a half-empty bottle of Martini and a mound of greasy chip bags. It was more or less exactly as I'd imagined, but I felt none of the satisfaction I usually did when I got things right. It'd seemed funny when I'd thought about how Shayne spent his evenings when Liz was away, but standing in the stuffy room with the pathetic still life of his week laid out before me, I felt flattened, sort of squeezed and tired.

Shayne was taking his time. Maybe he'd forgotten about me. Or maybe . . . he expected me to follow him. I left behind the sour, vinegary smell and made my way up to the landing, where soft radio sounds seeped out from Liz's bedroom and eye-wateringly bitter smoke clouded the air. The smell of it followed me as I walked up the narrow attic stairs. At the top it was even stronger. I chewed harder on my gum and knocked gently on the door. I let about a minute pass before I quietly pushed down the handle and looked inside.

He was standing on the tea-chest, puffing on a cigarette and blowing clouds of the horrible, stinking smoke out the window. I coughed loudly and he turned around.

'Needed a fag,' he said when he saw me. 'Want a pull?'

'No thanks, I'm OK,' I said, walking into the room. 'You didn't answer when I knocked.'

'Didn't hear ye, did I? Me head was stuck out the fuckin' window.' He frowned but then gave me a false grin, showing his neat white teeth. 'Watchin' Goggin, I was.'

'Bridie, you mean? What's she doing?'

'Jump up and have a look.'

I put a foot on the chest and held onto the window frame

to haul myself up. I stood beside him, trying not to touch him. It was difficult.

'She's having a chat, that's all,' I said when I looked out. I could see Bridie at the Farrell's gate talking to Geraldine.

'With Ma Walton, though. Gettin' all the scandal.'

'I think she got most of it already. She wasn't too pleased when she heard what I said about David.'

'Thinks the sun shines outta his arse, so she does.'

'It's not her fault, really. David has most people fooled. Everyone thinks he's a saint. She was disgusted when David's mam told her I said he'd done it on purpose. She's not half as friendly with me as she was before.'

'Tut tut. Poor Goggin.' He blew a long plume of smoke in the air. 'Oh, oh, Ruth dear! How could you!' he mimicked her.

We watched her, so far away she was like a doll version of herself, patting her hair and glancing over at our house, her head leaned in close to Geraldine's. Shayne sucked the end of his cigarette and stubbed it out on a roof tile. He flicked the butt with his finger and it bounced down along the slope, disappearing over the edge.

Far below I saw Tracey, lying flat on her back with Fiona sitting on her chest, slapping her big sister's face. Things had been frosty between herself and Sandra since that night in O'Deas'. She'd lapped up the cream of the gossip then turned her back on her like a cat because of what I'd said about David. In the last few days, she'd made a display of the friendship she shared with Valerie, laughing and joking loudly with her when she knew Sandra was watching. I'd seen them both, linking arms and throwing nasty looks over their shoulders in an attempt to highlight the bond they'd formed long before Sandra had arrived on the scene. And whenever the twins were allowed out, Tracey marched over, grabbing their hands and making sure they stuck to her until they were called back in. During the past week, their mother had taken to rationing their time out on the green, watching them from her front door until she was sure Tracey had gathered them close, as if she was afraid Sandra or I might contaminate them.

The sun beat down on the roof and I could almost smell the heat that rose up from it. I noticed how a thin layer of vivid green moss covered the slates, except for a long strip that ran from the window down to the edge of the roof.

'Isn't that weird?' I said. 'The way there's moss everywhere but there?'

Shayne grinned and scratched his head. 'That's where I piss out me window in the night. Too lazy to go down to the jacks. Piss must be fuckin' poison, so it must.'

He didn't seem embarrassed telling me. It was almost a boast. I pictured him in my head, standing at the open window in the moonlight, his piss spurting out and dribbling down into the gutter.

We watched Bridie tottering home and Geraldine gathering a few Farrells in for their tea. Then David appeared. He stood at the edge of the green, looking like Action Man from so far away, and gave a signal to the twins, who immediately ran over to his side. Then I saw Sandra coming back from the village with Kev, the pram handle hung with bags of shopping. I had to squint, but I could tell David didn't take his eyes off them till they turned into the cul-de-sac.

'Look at O'Dea down there,' Shayne said. 'Thinks he's fuckin' great, so he does, with his stupid ma and da and his poxy piano.'

He swung to the floor in one swift jump, his feet landing steady and sure. I took my time climbing down and stood awkwardly beside him in the cramped space. He kicked at a worn patch in the carpet and I could feel the walls of the room sort of closing in around us. It seemed smaller than the last time I'd been there. Then I realized why.

'You got a new record player,' I said, looking over at the huge wooden cabinet that was taking up most of the space along the wall opposite the bed.

'A radiogram,' he corrected me. 'Me ma let me have it after me uncle Vic brought her over a new one.' He lifted the lid on one side. 'Took hours to get it up here. Fuckin' weight of it.'

'Must be good to have it, though,' I said, sitting down on his bed.

'Fuckin' magic.'

He selected an LP and slipped it out of its sleeve. Lifting the lid, he raised the arm and placed the record onto the turntable. 'Wait til ye hear this. It's me favourite.' He carefully dropped the needle then sat down beside me. The words burst into the room. 'Bohemian Rhapsody'. It was one of my favourites too. It'd been number one for weeks. I'd watched Queen loads of times on *Top of the Pops*. Dad said they all looked like girls with their long hair and sparkly outfits and it was the biggest load of wailing he'd ever heard in his life. But I thought it was the best song ever. Shane had a poster of Freddie Mercury on the wall beside his bed. There was no sign of the photo of his uncle Joe though; it wasn't stuck to his headboard any more. And he seemed to have forgotten all about the snake tongue. At least, he never mentioned it.

He closed his eyes and tilted his head back, mouthing the words. His chest rose as he breathed in before each line and I looked along the length of his body. He wore a washed-out, red T-shirt with yellow stripes on the sleeves, and a pair of faded jeans, the same ones he'd had on the night he stayed in our house. But the patches Mam had sewn were gone. He'd unpicked every single thread. I was wearing my brand-new Wranglers, my very first pair of real jeans. They'd cost four pounds, something Mam kept reminding me of every time I wore them, which was practically every day now. But they were too clean and new and although I felt bad for Mam that Shayne had unpicked all her work, I sort of understood why he'd done it.

The scar under his chin shone in the sunlight that flooded the room. I leaned in closer to get a better look. 'How . . . how did you get that scar?'

'Dunno,' he said, his eyes still closed. 'Me ma says the devil gave me a kick when I was born.'

It sounded like something Liz would say all right.

'So you've had it a long time?'

'Long as I can remember, anyways.'

'Did she . . . did she ever say anything else? About the day you were born, I mean?'

'Like what?'

'I don't know . . . anything.'

'She says I nearly killed her, I was such a fuckin' lump. And I came out legs first. Says I couldn't even get that right.'

'But, you know, does she ever say anything about . . . well, your dad or anything?'

He opened his eyes and reached his arms behind his head 'Nah. Nothin'.'

'Didn't you ever ask?'

'Nah. Never.'

'Never ever?'

'I said no, didn't I?' he snapped.

'So . . . you don't know who your dad is?'

'Nope. Don't care either.'

'What about your uncle Joe? Did you ever . . . think it could be him?'

'Look, I don't care who me fuckin' da is, OK? Maybe it's him, maybe it isn't. Whoever it is, he doesn't care about me so why should I care about him?'

I sucked the last bit of flavour from my gum. I was aching to tell him what I knew about David. I hadn't breathed a word. Even when Sandra and I had been talking in bed about some girl from the village who was only seventeen and who everyone knew had got herself into trouble, and who tried to hide it by wearing a huge woolly poncho all the time. 'She'll have to give it up for adoption,' Sandra had whispered. 'That's what Tracey says.' She'd also reluctantly told me I'd been right – Geraldine was indeed expecting Farrell number eight.

I took a deep breath. 'David doesn't know who his dad is either.'

He squinted at me. 'Huh?'

'He's . . . well . . . he's adopted. His mam and dad, they're not his real parents.'

He sat up slowly, pushing the hair out of his eyes. 'Who told ye that?'

I told him how I knew. He sank back down on the bed, stretching his arms above his head. 'Yeah, well, I knew that anyways.'

'You did?'

'Yeah. It's no big deal.'

'Oh. I wasn't sure if he knew.'

'O'Dea? Ah yeah, sure you'd have to know somethin' like that, wouldn't ye?'

'It's just he never said, that's all.'

'Yeah, well, he doesn't like talkin' about it.'

'I thought, you know, the way he's always going on about his mam and dad, giving out about them. If he knew they weren't his real parents, surely he'd have said?'

'Nah.' He picked at one of the holes in his jeans.

If David knew he'd spent the first year of his life in an orphanage, he must've wondered about it. What it'd been like. He had no one to ask. No one who could tell him when he'd first smiled. When he'd crawled. And all the funny little things babies do. He had to be curious. Maybe that explained why he'd taken Kev from outside Mealy's. And the more I thought about it, the more it made sense that it was David who'd got into our house to watch him asleep in his cot, But whether he was curious or not, it was still all very creepy.

I faced Shayne. 'What . . . what really happened that day? He did throw himself out of the tree deliberately, didn't he? I mean, I was right about it, wasn't I?'

He sighed and then he nodded, his face grim and pale.

'Why didn't you tell?' I asked him. 'And why do you even hang around with him?'

He chewed at his thumbnail, ripping off a length and biting it with his front teeth as we listened to the song filling the room.

'He made me swear. Said he'd fuckin' kill me if I told. That's what he's like. And I have to hang around with him. He makes me. I'm too scared not to. He's mental, so he is. But no one round here'd believe it.'

'I do. I mean, I can see what he's like. The very first day I saw him, I knew he was weird. I can sense stuff like that.'

'He's always been crazy.'

'Like how?'

He thought for a second or two, looking up at the sky through the open window. 'Well, one time, before youse came, we found a nest full of eggs in the bushes up near the church. I tried to stop him but he . . . he tipped the eggs out. Stood on them all, so he did. There was . . . there was bird guts and stuff everywhere.'

I swallowed, trying not to feel sick. 'That's disgusting. How could someone *do* that?' I imagined the mother returning to the empty nest, her babies stamped into the ground, bits of broken shell all over the place. 'I think . . . I think he got into our house on Christmas Eve. Someone got up our uncle Frank's ladder and was in watching Kev. My dad said it was you but . . .'

'Me? *Me*?' His face was scary. 'What do ye think I am? Who does yer da think I am?'

'I . . . I . . . Look, it wasn't me who said it.'

He relaxed a bit. 'Yeah, well, sounds like something O'Dea would do. He's crazy enough.'

'Do you think it's something to do with, you know, being adopted and all?'

'Dunno, do I? Don't think he cares much.'

'You mean he's OK with it?'

'Think so. I dunno who me da is and I'm not crazy, am I? And anyways, da's aren't all they're made out to be, half the time.'

'What do you mean?'

'Well, ye know, look at yers.'

I shifted myself around to look him in the eye. 'Mine? My dad?'

'Yeah. Yer da.'

'What about him?'

He managed to push his finger through the hole he'd been picking at in his jeans and he scratched at the skin on his thigh.

'Ye think he's the best, don't ye? Better than anyone else's?'

'He's . . . he's my dad.'

He looked at me, his eyes dancing all over my face. 'So, I asked ye before . . . Would ye forgive yer da anythin'?'

Slow but sharp, like stars pushing through the black of the sky, a million fiery needles prickled deep down in my flesh.

'You said you were only messing when you asked me that before,' I said.

'Well, I wasn't.'

The song filtered from the radiogram, each word clear and perfect and familiar. His face seemed to soak up all the light in the room. All around him was dark and distant and not part of now. He stared at me, hard and close and I knew he was going to tell me something bad. Tears rose in my eyes. I didn't try and blink them away.

'*What*?' I whispered. 'What is it that I need to forgive?'

'He tried to kiss me ma.'

I shook my head and felt a tear spill down my cheek. My body was like a sponge in water: heavy and soaking and ready to sink. But I wasn't shocked. How could that be? Was it that I knew from the very first day Liz Lawless knocked on our door something like this was going to happen? Had I pushed it to the furthest part of my brain, hoping that if I didn't think about it, it wouldn't really come about?

And was it that, in some terrible, roundabout way, I felt like I was partly to blame?

'You're lying,' I said.

'Swear to God. I wouldn't make somethin' like that up.'

'When?'

'Ages ago. When he was here paintin'.'

'How do you know?'

'I saw! That's how.'

'But maybe you're making a mistake! Maybe it's just what you think you saw?'

'Look, don't believe me if ye don't want to. I don't care.'

'You said . . . you said he tried to kiss her. But did he actually . . . you know . . . do it?'

'Just for a second. But only 'cos me ma said I was in the house. He must've been afraid I might see. He didn't know I was on the stairs, watchin' them.'

'But how do you know it wasn't all your mam's idea? Maybe it was her who kissed him?'

'It wasn't. I saw what happened. Swear! Look, don't be cryin' over it. It's OK.'

'*It's not* OK! How would you know? And why did you have to tell me anyway?'

'Dunno. Just thought ye should know. Ye'd want to hear the truth, wouldn't ye? Like ye wanted the truth about O'Dea. I was going to tell ye before, but . . .'

'Does your mam know you saw? I mean, did you say anything to her about it?'

'Nah. Sure, why would I do that?'

I felt heavy and sick. I thought about Mam in her Home Sweet Home apron, her hair in those silver clips and Dad's slippers on her feet. What would she do if she knew? Her whole world would fall apart. And how many times had it happened? She couldn't ever find out. I'd have to swallow it whole and keep it inside me for ever. If I let it out it would never go away. It would destroy everything we thought we were certain of. When things change, you can't ever change them back. You have to live with them, no matter how good or how bad they are.

Right at that moment, I would've gladly stayed in Shayne's room for ever. I knew that nothing would be the same for me once I climbed down the stairs. In a few short moments I felt like I'd grown older. Everything looked different. Even Shayne. There was a sharpness to the outline of his body, and every part of him – his hands, his mouth, his face – seemed crisp and super-real. And when I looked into his eyes, the whites of them almost dazzled me.

'How far did he get?' I wanted to know.

'What?'

'My dad. With the kiss.'

'Ah, it was nothin'. I told ye.'

'So they didn't actually . . . you know . . . touch?'

'Not really. Well, maybe kinda. Just a bit. I'll show ye.'

He shifted closer to me, turned his face, and pressed his lips on mine, flicking his tongue against the front of my teeth. I breathed in hard, gulping down my tasteless lump of Wrigley's in surprise. His hair brushed against my cheek, tangled and thick with the smell of tobacco, and his smoky, warm breath entered my mouth, following the gum straight down the back of my throat. He was swift, like he was scared of me. When he sat back he focused on the radiogram as it played the last few seconds of his favourite song.

Neither of us moved. I wanted to look at him but I kept my eyes on the turntable. Then, from behind the music came the faint but instantly recognizable screech of Liz's voice calling out his name. We both knew we'd wait until the song was over; it wouldn't have been right to stop it before the end. I wiped a tear from my cheek and felt his face against the side of my own.

'So, would ye forgive yer da that?' he whispered into my ear.

My hand touched his arm as I stood up to go. My head throbbed and I swayed a bit on my feet. I knew then and there that Hillcourt Rise wouldn't be our home for ever. We were only passing through. Everything was different now.

THIRTEEN

I tried to tell myself that everything would calm down and get back to normal when school started again. That we'd all figure out we'd made far too big a deal of things over the summer simply because we'd had nothing better to do. But I soon realized that whatever had happened couldn't be deadheaded like Bridie's roses: chopped, discarded and left to rot into nothing.

Going back to school was hard. Not just because the others were starting in Grangemount and I had a whole year of the awful Mrs Lally as teacher to look forward to, but because everything had become far too real. I'd lain in bed for nights and nights, playing a game of 'so what', trying to convince myself that nothing really mattered.

I'd told David's parents he'd thrown himself out of a tree on purpose. So what? It was the truth as far as I knew. I'd found out David was adopted. So what? Loads of kids are. Tracey had turned all the girls against Sandra and me. So what? Who'd want to be friends with them anyway? Dad had tried to kiss Liz Lawless. So what? Hundreds of men had probably done the same.

But it was no good; everything mattered.

Things got worse. Bridie began hiding her tin of coconut macaroons. Whenever I'd gone round before, she'd open the lid as soon as I let myself in, almost forcing me to help myself. Now, when she heard me calling at the back door, she'd tell me to 'wait a moment' and I'd hear her scuffling about while I stood with my hand on the door handle. And when finally she'd say I could come in, she'd be standing, all red-faced and breathless at the kitchen table, the biscuit tin suspiciously absent. And she rarely called me 'dear' any more. Whatever about the coconut macaroons, that was the thing I found hardest to accept. She didn't stop me from calling in to her and we continued to have our chats about this and that, but it wasn't the same. Sometimes I'd catch her staring at me when I was rearranging her knick-knacks along the mantelpiece or searching through some box of junk she'd allowed me to sort out. Her small eyes, ringed with short, powdery lashes, bore into me like pointed screws. It made me feel uncomfortable. Like she didn't trust me any more.

Every day, as I walked to school on my own, Dad would drive past me on his way to his latest job. He'd wave or give a little toot on the horn and I'd give him a sort of smile but I couldn't look at him without thinking about The Kiss. The idea of it was as heavy in my stomach as my schoolbag was on my back. And what made it worse was that I couldn't think about it without remembering Shayne's demonstration. While the picture of Dad's attempt with Liz weighed me down, the memory of Shayne's lips against my own seemed to lighten the load, but I wasn't sure if I should be grateful for that or not.

I suspected Aidan Farrell and the twins had started to wait until I passed their houses before they left for school themselves. It was far too much of a coincidence that every day they happened to come out as soon as I got to the top of the hill. I'd hear Aidan slamming his front door, and if I looked back, I'd see him belting down to the O'Deas' to call for Tina and Linda. Then I'd spy the twins, waving their mittoned hands at their mother as she stood at the door, pulling her quilted dressing gown tight around her chest.

For a while, with all the distractions of school, Sandra wasn't too fussed about Tracey and Valerie deliberately avoiding her. But when Tracey started trying to turn even Sandra's new friends against her, it was me who got the blame.

'I hate you, Ruth, you know that?' she said one evening while we were doing the washing up.

'Why's that?' I asked, squirting a long stream of Quix into the sink, not caring in the slightest what her excuse was this time.

'Everything was fine here till you opened your big mouth about David. Tracey and Valerie are being so mean.'

I sighed. 'They'll get over it. And anyway, I thought you said you'd absolutely loads of new friends at Grangemount?'

'I do. But Tracey keeps whispering to them when she knows I'm looking. I know she's trying to turn them against me.'

'Why do you care?'

''Cos she's my friend! And so are they!'

'How the hell could someone who does that be your friend? Grow up, Sandra.'

'Me grow up? At least I have friends my own age. The only one you have is Bridie.'

I was going to say that at least she was a real friend but I thought better of it when I remembered the coconut macaroons. I could've told her that I kind of regarded Shayne as a friend, but did I really? I wasn't sure. I'd never told her I'd been in his room – twice – and although I'd thought about it many times, especially when she was being mean to me, I was afraid The Kiss thing might slip out and that'd be disastrous. Whatever hope I had of keeping it from Mam and trying to act as if nothing was wrong every time I looked at Dad, Sandra would never be able to hold it in. She'd go absolutely mental if she heard I'd been up in Shayne's room. And if she found out that he'd shown me what The Kiss had been like, well, I dreaded to think how she'd react.

Since we'd moved in, Mam had been so busy with Kev and getting the house the way she wanted it, she'd barely had time to take a breath, never mind truly get to know all our neighbours. Although she'd been the one most keen to move to Hillcourt Rise, it was as much about wanting a better life for us as it was about having a modern house. She'd hoped we'd make good friends and knit ourselves into a safe and trusting community. *They need somewhere safe to play, Mick,* she'd said. *And some kids to play with . . .*

But it wasn't quite working out like she'd planned.

We didn't get to celebrate Hallowe'en that year. It wasn't our choosing; it turned out to be the day of Uncle Frank's funeral. He'd fallen from the roof of a bungalow on the Howth Road one morning and lay in the back garden for ages until the owner came home from work and found him. He'd survived a similar fall before and escaped with only a couple of broken bones so everyone was hopeful at the start. But then the doctors said to prepare for the worst.

Dad went to the hospital every day around lunchtime to sit at his bedside with Cissy, and Mam usually followed later on. We liked being on our own at first, but then Kev got chicken pox. Mam said it never rains but it pours and there was nothing we could do but let it run its course. We dreaded being left to look after him. He moaned and whinged and wouldn't sleep, even though he'd been awake all day. I think Mam was almost relieved when she handed him over and headed off to the hospital each afternoon.

Uncle Frank lasted a week. Cissy was on her own with him when he died and Dad said later that she made him feel really guilty because he hadn't been there with her at the end. Mam told him not to worry about it, that Cissy didn't know what she was saying.

We weren't allowed go to the funeral. Mam said we'd have to stay and look after Kev. I didn't mind. I didn't want to go anyway. I was afraid the coffin might be open and we'd have to sit looking at a dead Uncle Frank. Bridie called in to 'pay her respects' when she heard, breezing past me when I opened the door like I was invisible. Mam asked if she'd mind keeping an eye on us when they went to the funeral, but when she saw Kev covered in calamine lotion she threw her hands in the air and started bustling out to the front door. 'Oh God, no. Chicken pox! I'm sorry, Rose, I couldn't. Sure I've never had them and I don't want to be putting myself at any risk at my age. Hits adults far harder than children, you know.' I wasn't sure, but it seemed to me she was almost happy to have found an excuse not to mind us.

Because of Uncle Frank's accident, we hadn't been that excited about Hallowe'en. And since the others were now in secondary school, they weren't going to be dressing up anyway. It was an unwritten rule that once you finished primary, you didn't bother with that sort of thing. So as Mam and Dad were leaving to go to the funeral, we didn't mind too much that they told us to stay inside for the night. It was too dangerous to go out on our own, they said, what with the bonfire and all.

'We'll be going back to Cissy's afterwards but we should be home by half-seven,' Mam said at the door. 'Say a prayer for your uncle Frank.' She had tears in her eyes. 'And remember, no going outside.'

It was only once it started to get dark that we realized we hadn't asked if we were allowed to answer the door to callers. I said we shouldn't, that we weren't ever supposed to open the door to anyone when Mam and Dad went out at night. But the others felt the usual rules didn't apply because it was Hallowe'en. Sandra said it would look a bit strange if we didn't and Mel agreed, saying only complete weirdoes kept to themselves on Hallowe'en night. I said that since Mam had been preoccupied during the week and hadn't gone shopping, there was hardly anything in the house to give out to callers anyway, so it might be better if we pretended we weren't in. But I was overruled. Sandra said it was bad enough that Tracey and Valerie hardly talked to her now without giving them even more of an excuse to hate her. In the end it didn't matter; we only had about four callers. And they were all kids we didn't know, probably from Cherrywood and Churchview Park. Not one neighbour rang our bell.

At first, Mel and Sandra insisted that everyone must've been waiting until after the bonfire, even though the year before most of us had collected our goodies way before it had been lit. Then they suggested that maybe word had gone round Hillcourt Rise about Uncle Frank, and no one had called out of respect for the dead. I realized how stupid that sounded later on in the night.

We watched out the window for a while and saw the first sparks coming from the bonfire, then we pulled the curtains and flumped down to watch telly. It was the usual boring stuff: fiddle players in Aran jumpers in front of a fire on one channel, and a group of politicians in dark suits arguing about the state of the country on the other. Kev refused to settle in his cot but finally dozed off, stretched across Mel and Sandra's laps. They entertained themselves by counting his spots, afraid to even flinch in case they woke him up. Then a quiz came on the telly and they sat glued, trying to outdo each other answering the questions.

After a while I got up to get a drink. Before I got to the kitchen, I heard a sort of whooshing noise and then a hard, flat thump against the front door. Dead silence followed. Then the faint sound of footsteps echoing away up the road. Opening the door carefully, I peeped out, then stepped onto the drive and, even in the darkness, I was certain it was Tracey I saw running swiftly up the cul-de-sac on her skinny legs. And from the green, loud laughter rose high in the chilly air.

Then I noticed the lumpy parcel sitting on the doorstep, loosely wrapped in newspaper and stained a dark, brownish red. I cautiously nudged the bulky shape with my toe, feeling a solid but sort of spongy mass inside. I leaned down for a closer look and as I peeled back a corner of the paper, what I saw was a dark, dead eye staring into nowhere from a pulpy, bloody mess of skin and hair.

It was a sheep's head.

I staggered backwards in fright, the sickening, rotten smell flooding my nostrils and making me retch. My heart drummed hard and I covered my mouth with my hand as I half looked away and tried to toe the paper back around the 'gift' we'd been given. Then I ran inside and grabbed a plastic bag from a drawer in the kitchen.

'I'm . . . I'm just going into Bridie's,' I called out to the others, hoping I wouldn't be questioned on my sudden need to go next door. 'Back in a few minutes.' But all I got by way of response was a grunt from Mel and a loudly whispered 'Shut up, you'll wake Kev!' from Sandra.

Back on the doorstep, I used one of the empty milk bottles left out for the milkman to try and push the sheep's head into the bag. It wasn't easy. The damp newspaper tore into useless shreds and without it, the head slid across the step, leaving a rusty trail in its wake. I held the bag open by the handles and tried to scoop it under the head, like filling a bucket full of water at the seaside. After several attempts, I finally managed to hook it under the sheep's chin and pulled it up over the whole head. When I lifted it up, it slipped heavily down into the bag, its greasy weight straining against the thin film of plastic. I held it away from my body as I ran along the path up towards the green.

Paddy and Clem were walking round the bonfire with their hands in their pockets, kicking any stray bits of timber into the flames. Geraldine and Nora stood over by the trees in their woolly bobble-hats and quilted anoraks. Other parents huddled in small groups, chatting and laughing while their children chased each other around the green, their bags of goodies rustling in the wind as they ran.

'Well, well, and what do we have here?' David announced when he saw me approaching. He stood straight and tall in well-pressed jeans and a navy corduroy jacket, with a red polo neck jumper underneath. He'd had the cast off a good few weeks, but still held his left wrist in his right hand, massaging it slowly as he spoke. 'Here to help the Hallowe'en party?' he asked, nodding in the direction of the plastic bag swinging from my hand. Tracey, Valerie and the twins made their way over.

'You're a bit late, aren't you?' Valerie said with a snigger. 'Why didn't you come out earlier like the rest of us?'

'Maybe Mother and Father Lamb wouldn't allow their babies out, for fear of the big bad wolf?' David said.

'For your information, my uncle died,' I said.

Tracey looked at the others, unsure of what to say.

'Yeah . . . well,' Valerie said, fingering the necklace that spelled out her name. 'That's probably a lie. You're good at those, aren't you?' She looked at David.

'Me?' I said. 'You know right well you were the one who said David broke his wrist deliberately in the first place, so don't try and pretend it was something I made up.'

'Huh? Cheek of you, Ruth Lamb. Think you're so special, don't you? Well, guess what? No one round here likes you. Everyone wishes you never moved to Hillcourt Rise.'

'Yeah,' Tracey agreed. 'We all got along fine before you Lambs came. You're nothing but trouble. Even my mam says so. Why don't you all just go back to wherever you came from?'

I could feel my face beginning to burn. And my throat stung, like it always did when I was about to cry.

'And where's your daddy tonight then?' Valerie continued. 'Not showing off this year with his stupid fireworks?'

'I told you,' I said, trying to steady my voice. 'My uncle died. He's at the funeral if you must know. Not that it's any of your business.'

'So what're you doing out here now? It's nearly all over, or hadn't you noticed?'

'Well, I thought I'd give you this back,' I said, tipping the sheep's head out of the bag. It landed on the grass with a thud, glancing off Valerie's shoe. She screamed, grabbing David's arm and dragging him with her as she jumped back in horror.

'Jesus Christ! Get that away! Mammy! Mammy!' she yelled over to Nora.

'What do you think you're doing?' David said. 'Are you mentally deranged? You're sick, you know that?'

'I'm only giving it back!' I said, blinking away my tears. 'Tracey dumped it on our doorstep! If anyone's sick, it's her. And I bet you all knew about it too.'

'I did not!' Tracey insisted. 'You liar! Why would I do something like that? It's disgusting. And where would I get a . . . a . . . sheep's head, for God's sake?'

'You can easily get them in Boylan's. I know it was you, Tracey Farrell. I saw you!'

Nora and Geraldine came running over, elbowing their way through the small crowd that had gathered to see what was going on. Paddy and Clem followed and soon I was surrounded on all sides. Geraldine pointed to the ground. 'What in the name of God is that?' she demanded. 'Is it what I think it is?' She screwed her face up in disgust.

'Yes,' David answered. 'It is what you think it is. It's a sheep's head.'

Nora tutted and muttered 'disgrace' under her breath. 'Deposited here by Miss Lamb,' David continued, glancing at me. 'Ironic, wouldn't you all agree? I wonder what Mother Lamb will say when she finds out?' He touched the head with his foot, turning it over and kicking it across the grass towards me. He thought he was so smart, making fun of my name and my mam. But I could play that game too. I swallowed hard.

'At least I know who my mother is.' I stared into his face. 'My *real* mother, I mean.'

As soon as the words were out of my mouth, I knew Shayne had been lying. The effect was instant. Even in the twilight I could see David's face drain of its yellowish colour.

He hadn't known.

But I could tell from his eyes it was something he'd lain in bed at night wondering about.

'Wh . . . what do you mean . . . *real* mother?' he stammered.

Geraldine instantly turned and took off like a bullet across the green in the direction of the O'Deas', determined to be the first to deliver the news to Mona and Eamon. I wanted to run too, but I was surrounded. I hadn't a hope of escaping.

'Well?' David asked. His voice quivered as he tried desperately to keep his face from crumbling. 'What do you mean . . . real mother?' he pleaded to everyone gathered. 'What's going on? Paddy? Anyone? Tell me what she's on about.'

'Ah now, son,' Paddy said, putting his arm around David's shoulder. 'Sure, don't mind anything that's said in the heat of the moment. Words, that's all it is.'

Tracey and Valerie nudged each other and stared at me with their mouths open. The twins looked like china dolls, their huge eyes frozen and unblinking, and their perfect hair waving gently around their pink cheeks. David fiddled with the stud of his wristband, clicking it again and again as the small crowd began to mumble among themselves. Geraldine arrived back, out of breath, with Mona and Eamon behind her. She planted her hands on her hips and nodded at me. Her nostrils glistened and she sniffed loudly before she spoke.

'There she is,' she said, as if to show Mona and Eamon she hadn't been making it up. 'Happy with yourself?' she asked me.

'Mother?' David asked Mona. Her worried face said it all. She went to put her arms around him but he pulled away. He scanned the faces of the various adults around him; it was clear that they'd all known. Through their years of living in Hillcourt Rise, Mona and Eamon had confided in their neighbours. At coffee mornings, after mass chats and garden gate gossips, they'd each learned the secret about David O'Dea. A secret they'd all kept safe from their children. And safe from David himself. 'But I *asked* you about it,' David said, his voice thin and high. 'Remember? When I pointed out I looked nothing like you or Dad.' He zipped his jacket right up to his trembling chin. 'You told me not to be so . . . so ridiculous.'

'David. Dear. Come back inside. We'll talk about this at home.' Mona tried again to touch him.

'*Get away from me!*' he growled. He faced up to Eamon. 'And you. You make me sick. I don't want anything to do with either of you. You've lied to me my whole life.' He waved his arms around and shouted, 'And everyone knew about it except me!' It sounded as if he was choking, unable to catch his breath, and he pounded on his chest with his fists before dissolving into a fit of coughing. He fell to his knees and Paddy ran over, but David got to his feet and pushed him away. 'Fuck off,' he spat, between coughs. 'Fuck the hell off! All of you! You hear me?' He began to run, his legs like a newborn foal's to begin with – all gangly and wobbly under the weight of his body – then, as if mastering the trick of balance for the very first time, he took off like a bird released. We all watched him in silence. Then, slowly, the crowd began to thin. One by one, out of shame and embarrassment and fear, everyone made their way home. Some of them looked at me as they passed but no one said a word. In minutes, I stood alone on the green.

I shivered. I'd run out without my coat. Crossing my arms over my chest, I pushed my hands up into the sleeves of my cardigan to keep my fingers warm and started walking. I wanted to go home. But not home to forty-two Hillcourt

Rise. Home to the moon. Or the stars. Or the bottom of the sea. Anywhere.

Anywhere but here.

Suddenly, I felt my body lift off the ground and sail through the air. Stars flashed all around, burning and fading through the blackness. Bangers exploded. *Pop! Pop! Pop!* And from over the rooftops came the faint but certain sound of excited screams. Some other strange noise whistled about my head and it wasn't until I landed on the grass with a thump that I realized it was air squeezing out of my lungs. I slid along the damp grass for a few inches, stopping short of the sheep's head, it's slimy, bloody face only inches from my own.

David had slammed into me from behind. He'd launched the full weight of his body against mine, and had landed on all fours to my right without so much as a wobble. His eyes were fixed on me – steady and sharp and fearless, like an animal. His breath rasped in and out of his throat.

At that moment, David O'Dea hated me. More than he hated anyone. Even those who'd kept the secret from him for so long. As he stared at me, his lips twitched with the trace of a smile. I'd have felt less frightened if he'd roared at me like a tiger and sank his teeth into my flesh.

Slowly, he got to his knees, grinning. Then he began to laugh. It came from the back of his throat, softly at first, like an engine spluttering to life. Then it travelled down into his belly and came up again, bursting from his mouth, snorting out of his nose. He stood up, towering over me like a crazy giant. The moles on his face stood out against the paling of his skin and his hair hung down in sweaty spikes. He stepped closer. I pulled my knees up to my chest. He drew his foot back and I squeezed my eyes shut, readying myself for a kick, trying to tense my trembling limbs. I held my breath.

'David! *David*! Come on home now, lad! Let's have a little chat.'

I opened my eyes. It was Father Feely. Summoned by the O'Deas, no doubt, and waddling towards us, flapping his arms. David dropped his foot. I took a gulp of air and felt my body sink into the cold ground. 'Come on now, lad. Let's get you home.' Father Feely put his arm around David's shoulders, barely even glancing at me as he steered him away.

I lay there, watching the two of them heading across the green. And beyond them, Eamon and Mona stood at their front door waiting, their shapes black against the bright white light coming from their hall. I scrambled to my feet. My body felt as though it had been beaten. Pain shot up and down my legs. I was dizzy. The world around me whirled. Spun. Like water down a plughole. I was being sucked down with it. I could feel it. If Father Feely hadn't arrived, David would've kicked me.

And I was certain that it wouldn't have been just the once.

A few feet away from me was the sheep's head. Grotesque and all as it was, I didn't want to leave it there. I picked up the plastic bag and managed to push it inside with my foot. It bumped against my leg as I made my way home. Just before I rounded the corner to the cul-de-sac, I saw Shayne approaching from the left, hands in pockets, hair flapping up and down. When he saw me, he quickened his steps, running the final few yards until he caught up.

'Ye goin' home already?' he asked, his teeth chewing on something hard and sticky. I kept walking and he danced sideways alongside me, 'Ye got loads of stuff,' he said, nodding at the bag. 'Give us a look.'

I stopped dead on the path. 'Here,' I snapped. 'You can have it.' I slapped the bag into his chest. He pulled his hands out of his pockets to catch it.

He looked inside. 'Jesus *Christ!*' His face wrinkled up and he dropped the bag to the ground. 'That's disgustin'. *Stink* off of it. What're ye doin' with that?' I picked up the bag and started walking again, faster this time. He followed beside, his warm, strawberry breath finding its way up my nose. 'What's wrong with ye?'

'What's wrong with *me*? What's wrong with you that you can't tell the truth? I should've known not to believe you. You told me David knew he was adopted.'

'So?'

'*So*? Turns out he didn't. And you didn't either, did you? You just pretended you already knew. You couldn't stand that I found out something like that before you did.'

I told him what had happened.

'Yeah, well . . . d'ye not think it's better that he knows?'

'You're glad he found out, aren't you? Now he knows how you feel, isn't that it?'

His face turned sour. 'Yeah, well, he's always slaggin' me 'cos I don't know who me da is. Taste of his own medicine now. I told ye. Ye don't know what he's like. Thinks he's better than everyone else.'

'But I'm the one who's going to get in trouble for telling him, not you.'

'Nobody made ye go and blab, did they?'

'No, but . . . you shouldn't have pretended he already knew.'

He hung his head. 'I didn't mean for ye to get in trouble over it. I was goin' to tell him meself. Swear I was.' He looked up, still chewing on his sweets. I thought about his lips on mine.

'It's OK,' I said. 'I mean . . . it's not your fault. If that's what he's like then . . . then I'm glad he knows now. It's weird the way the truth can get you in as much trouble as telling lies.'

He half grinned. 'Yeah. Weird all right.' He held out a handful of red jelly hearts and I slipped one into my mouth. We were almost at our house.

'Why weren't you out with the rest of them on the green?' I asked.

'Dunno. I was just . . . keepin' an eye on me ma.'

'She's not in bed again, is she?'

'Nah. I had to wait till me . . . till me uncle Vic went out.'

'Why?'

'Dunno. She's . . . sort of . . . you know . . . scared of him, that's all.'

'Why would she be scared of him?' I couldn't imagine Liz being afraid of anyone.

'Ah, ye know. Goes a bit mental when he's had a drink and he was knockin' back the whiskey billy-o earlier on, so I thought I better hang around.'

'Oh. What do you mean, *mental*?'

'Ye know. Beltin' her round the place and stuff.'

'Vic? Your uncle Vic?' I tried to picture a scene in my head. 'But why . . . why does she stay with him then?'

'Got no one else, has she?' He swallowed his mouthful of sweets. 'If he does it again, I'll fuckin' kill him.'

My teeth began to chatter from the cold. He offered me another jelly heart. It was warm and soft from the heat of his hand.

'My uncle Frank died a few days ago,' I said as I chewed. 'It was his funeral today.'

'I wish me uncle Vic was dead.'

He walked off then without a word and as I looked back at him shuffling along, he seemed smaller and thinner than he had before, like he'd shrunk even in the time I'd been talking to him.

I breathed out a long sigh that hung like a cloud in the cold air. I didn't want to go back inside. It didn't feel like our house. It was simply a place where we happened to live: a collection of walls and floors and furniture. It didn't matter how many cushion covers Mam made or how much Dad prettied up the garden; something was keeping me from calling Hillcourt Rise my home.

I stopped outside Bridie's and very quietly opened her gate. I tip-toed up her drive and crept in behind her hydrangeas where she kept her dustbin. Lifting the lid, I emptied my plastic bag. *That'll teach her to hide her coconut macaroons,* I said to myself, as the sheep's head plopped heavily down into her bin.

When I let myself back inside, Mel and Sandra were arguing over their quiz scores and, surprisingly, Kev was still fast asleep. Mam and Dad came in at nine o'clock, apologizing for being late but Cissy, they said, had insisted on everyone staying for tea and ham sandwiches. Poor Cissy. Mam said that during the funeral, she'd whispered, 'I can't think where Frank's got to, Rose. He's not usually late for mass.'

I didn't tell them about the sheep's head or what had happened with David. They'd had enough upset for one day.

FOURTEEN

But it wasn't long before everyone heard about the Hallowe'en drama on the green. One evening the next week, I was lying on my bed, reading, when I heard Father Feely's voice vibrating up through the house like a swarm of bees.

'You're wanted,' Sandra said, poking her head round the door. 'Now.'

I groaned and slammed my book shut. I knew what his visit had to be about.

Mam ushered me into the sitting room. Dad closed the door.

'There you are, Ruth,' Father Feely said. 'I thought I'd call in for a little chat. You know why I'm here, I'm sure?' He stood with his back to the fireplace, air rushing out of his nose like a hurricane. 'I believe you had words with young David? You let him in on a little secret, hmm?'

'It was hardly a secret,' I said. 'Most of the grown-ups already knew.'

'Yes, well, his parents are most upset at the way he found out. Most upset. They'd planned to tell him soon themselves, you see. And now . . . well . . .'

'I didn't plan on telling him. It just sort of slipped out.'

'I see. You seem to have a history of allowing things to slip out,' he said. 'Isn't that so? All that upset over how he broke his wrist, hmm?'

'But—'

'Now, now, young lady,' he interrupted, wagging his finger. 'That tongue of yours has caused enough trouble already. I don't have time for any buts.'

'But I—'

'Ruth!' Mam said, raising her eyebrows. 'Do as you're told.'

'David is going away,' Father Feely announced. 'To the boarding school in Clonrath. I've just confirmed it with the brothers down there.' He brought the tips of his fingers together in a pyramid shape. 'Now, it's not been an easy decision, let me tell you. Not at all. Sending a young lad away from home. But Mona and Eamon, they, well, we . . .' He stared at me with his swivelly eyes. 'It's for the best. He needs a change of scene, poor lad.' Dad coughed and Mam fiddled with the buttons on her cardigan. 'It won't be until the new year,' he continued. 'But I wanted to let you know. I thought it might be better coming from myself.'

'Well, thank you, Father,' Mam said, as if we should somehow be grateful. 'It was good of you to call.'

I wanted to say something about the sheep's head and how everyone had been so mean to me, but I knew it wouldn't make the slightest difference. Up against His Holiness, Saint David, I didn't stand a chance.

Father Feely took a watch on a chain from his pocket and examined it closely. 'Yes, well, I'll be off now, if you don't mind.' He patted my head. 'I take it I'll see you in confession soon, Ruth. Hmm?'

Mam saw him out. Dad scratched his moustache and looked at the floor. 'I don't understand why you had to go and say that to David,' he said.

'I thought he already knew! Shayne said—'

'Lawless! I knew he'd have to be behind it! I don't want you listening to a word he says, you hear me? He's trouble.'

I bit down on my lip. *Why don't you want me to listen to anything Shayne says, Dad?* I wanted to ask him. *Because you're afraid he'll say something you don't want me to hear? About you and his mam?*

'It's not Shayne's fault he's the way he is,' I said.

'Yeah, well, you're better off away from him. And stop meddling in other people's affairs.'

'And you'd know all about them, wouldn't you?' I mumbled under my breath.

'What was that?'

I didn't think he'd heard, but I couldn't be certain.

Mam came back into the room. 'What's going on?'

'Nothing,' I said.

Dad gathered his eyebrows into a thick black line. 'I don't know what's got into you, Ruth. I really don't.' His face was close to mine now. 'Ever since we moved in here, you . . . you . . . I don't know!' He threw his arms in the air. 'If you've any sense, you'll keep your mouth zipped in future. Some things are none of your business.' He brushed past Mam on his way out to the hall. 'I'm going for a drink,' he said. 'I rue the day we ever came to this shaggin' place.' He slammed the door on his way out.

Mam wouldn't look at me. 'You can go back upstairs,' she said flatly, folding her arms. 'For the night.'

There was no use in me trying to go back to my book. I couldn't concentrate. I lay on my bed and looked at the ceiling, hot tears dripping into my ears. But I was glad Dad had said he was sorry we'd moved to Hillcourt Rise. It made me feel better about The Kiss. He regretted it, I could tell. We'd both done things we shouldn't have. But if I wanted him to forgive my mistakes, I had to forgive his too. I wished he hadn't stormed out. Even though I didn't feel everything was entirely my fault, I did have to take some of the blame. I wanted to tell him I was sorry. I wouldn't even have to say the word; Dad would know by looking at my face. He'd put his arms around me and hug me tightly and everything would be forgotten. I couldn't wait for him to come home. I wanted to do it now.

After I heard Mam putting Kev to bed, I waited a while before creeping downstairs. The sitting room door was open a crack and I peeped inside. Mel was in a kind of trance looking at the telly. *Charlie's Angels* was just starting. Sandra was staring, studying The Angels, every toss of their heads and spin of their heels. Mam had a paper pattern laid out on the floor and cut-outs of material spread across her lap. She was in the middle of making a pair of dungarees for Kev. I took my coat from the hall cupboard and a key from the table. None of them would be budging for at least an hour.

Once I was down the hill, it took five minutes to reach The Ramblers. Its mirrored glass windows glowed golden through the darkness and a smoky, sour stench wafted through its half-open door, along with a slurred chorus of 'The Wild Rover'. *No nay never no more* . . . I gulped as much fresh air as I could before poking my head through the door of the pub.

It was packed inside. I could barely see from the amount of smoke. Practically every person in the place was puffing on a cigarette. And the noise was deafening. Shouting and singing and laughing and 'Jaysus' this and 'bloody' that. I shoved my way through the dark crowd of bodies, hiding behind a bulky man in a musty brown overcoat. I scanned the murky room. It didn't take me long to find Dad. But he wouldn't have seen me even if I'd stood right in front of him. His gaze was drawn to the large expanse of flesh on show between the open buttons of Liz Lawless's black satin blouse.

They were sitting together on a bench. Dad said something and she shook her head, then something else and she nodded. She stared into her glass, as if she found the piece of lemon floating in the dregs the most fascinating thing in the world.

Dad offered her a cigarette and she took one, leaning in to the match he held out then throwing back her head and blowing a long, straight plume of smoke towards the yellowed ceiling. My stomach felt queasy. And it wasn't because of the smell of the place. I pushed my way to the door, stomachs, backs and bums squeezing up against me. When I got outside, I was gasping. I ran most of the way home, up the hill and across the green, only slowing down when I reached the cul-de-sac. When I let myself in, I tip-toed back upstairs, fell onto my bed and cried myself to sleep.

I didn't feel the way I usually did coming up to Christmas. I wasn't excited at all. I felt more alone than I ever had. Mam was running around after Kev all the time, often falling asleep soon after she put him to bed. And since they'd started in Grangemount, the others barely noticed my existence. Mel had joined the football team and succeeded in attracting the attention of some girl he'd fancied for ages. Sandra had made loads of new friends and she stayed back after school most days to play basketball. Dad was working around the clock to keep up with the usual demand for house decoration in the run-up to Christmas, even working weekends. That was one thing I was glad about. The less I saw of him, the better. I could hardly even bear to look at his face.

Auntie Cissy came to stay the day before Christmas Eve, along with Bertie the budgie in his battered old cage. We weren't too pleased to hear about the sleeping arrangements.

I was to have the pull-out bed in Mel's room, and Cissy would sleep in with Sandra. But we put up with it for Cissy's sake; we knew she would've been far too lonely at home without Uncle Frank. She tried to make herself useful when she arrived, helping to ice the cake and singing 'Pat-a-Cake' and 'Incy Wincy Spider' with Kev while Mam went about her work. But after that, she sat in front of the telly looking lonely and sad. Mel grumbled because she didn't bring any presents for us and Mam gave him a clip around the ear, telling him to keep his voice down and not to be so selfish. Whether Cissy heard or not I don't know, but on Christmas Eve morning, she handed each of us a five-pound note and told us to go to the shops and buy ourselves something nice.

We took Kev with us in his pushchair, wrapped up tightly against the cold in a stiff, quilted all-in-one suit that made him look like some sort of blow-up toy you could burst with the prick of a pin. The skin on his cheeks was cracked and red and his eyes watered as soon as we brought him outside. There was no one else about as we made our way along the path. Everything about the estate seemed different: sharper, clearer, fresher. A kind of electric silence buzzed in our ears and gulps of tingling air whooshed into our lungs, waking up our insides. There was no day in the whole year like Christmas Eve. It held the weight of so much expectation. And even though we didn't believe in Santa any more, it was still as magical as it'd ever been. The sun hung low in the sky. Its light was almost blinding. But it wasn't warm enough to melt the cover of crisp frost that had settled on the green in the night. We each took a turn to run across it, crunching over the hardened blades of grass and leaving behind a curving line of footprints.

When we came close to the lane that led to the shops, I noticed tracks criss-crossing the area in front of the trees. Whoever had left them had come from the far side of the green, walking over and back in a looping figure of eight. As we got nearer, I saw a small, dark shape against the white ground, lying not far from the base of a tree. I left the others and ran over, curious to find out what it was.

Long before I reached it, I noticed the blood. The footprints that came towards it were clean, but the ones that led away were coloured with smudgy splats of red. I slowed down, shielding my eyes from the flashing rays of yellow-white sunlight that sliced through the leafless trees. My steps joined the upper arc of the eight, following the tracks until they arrived at the shape.

As far as I could make out, it was a blackbird. Its coal-black wing feathers splayed out like a fan, twisted and broken by a deliberate, forceful stamp. Its once plump stomach had been crushed flat, sending its guts bursting out over the frosted earth in an oozing, mangled mess. Keeping my eyes down, I followed the bloody track lines that led away from the scene of death. The red staining faded slightly with each step until, as the footprints reached the edge of the green, it disappeared completely. Right opposite the O'Deas'.

I crossed the road to the path and heard the soft, sweet tinkle of David's piano drifting out over the silent estate. Through the window I saw him, bent over, his head swaying from side to side and his hands rising up and down in slow, graceful waves like a pair of swans diving underwater. I stared hard, wishing my gaze was a red hot beam that could pierce the glass and bore a hole right into his brain. But he kept on playing his airy tune, deep in concentration. Then he suddenly stopped and swivelled around on his stool. I could tell from his face that he knew what I'd seen. He gave me a weak sort of smile before turning back to play.

I walked slowly back to the others. Mel couldn't understand why I was making such a fuss. 'Won't you be eating dead bird for dinner tomorrow?' he asked. 'With roasters and bread sauce and everything?'

'But that's . . . that's not the point,' I said. 'At least there's a purpose to killing a turkey, isn't there?'

'I'd say that blackbird was already dead before someone stamped on it,' Sandra said. 'Birds always die when the ground is hard, don't they?'

'But who'd do something sick like that, anyway?' Mel asked.

'There's only one person round here sick enough,' I said. 'You can hear him now if you strain your ears.'

Sandra swerved the pushchair into the lane. 'David? David O'Dea? You think so?'

'Can't think of anyone else.'

'Sure it could've been anyone,' Mel said. 'Forget about it.' He ran ahead of us. 'Come on! We've money to spend!'

What had David been thinking about when his foot came down on the bird's body? And how could he just smile and wave at me knowing what he'd done? David O'Dea wasn't just strange; David O'Dea was sick.

Sandra and I agreed we should buy Auntie Cissy a present in Sheila's Fashions. Mel said he'd contribute but wasn't going into a ladies shop so he'd wait outside and mind Kev. But he warned us not to be more than five minutes or he'd pull out of the deal.

Because it was Christmas Eve, Sheila actually had a few customers in the shop when we went in. Dolly Flynn, who ran the bingo in the parish hall every Thursday night, was there, trying to decide between two equally awful outfits. Sheila was trying to convince her to buy both.

After a scan of the display cases, we spotted a small gold brooch in the shape of a cat. I was sure Auntie Cissy would love it but Sandra wasn't convinced. She argued for a few minutes but then we saw Mel making signals through the window and she gave in. We quickly paid for the brooch and almost knocked each other over running for the door. I got there first and pulled it open, throwing myself through.

Straight into Bridie's batch-loaf bosoms.

She scowled down at me, her nose glowing red from the cold. 'Well! Of all the . . .' She turned to her companion. It was Mona O'Dea. 'I don't know, Mona. Manners don't cost anything, do they?'

Mona clasped her handbag to her chest. 'They were free the last time I checked, Bridie,' she sniffed.

I was about to open my mouth to apologize when the two of them elbowed Sandra and me out of the way and barged into Sheila's, muttering under their breath. Sandra's face was pink from embarrassment. I could feel my own cheeks heating up too, but not from shame – from anger. I might as well have been some stranger, some brat Bridie had never seen before in her life. She knew perfectly well it was an accident. If it'd happened a few months ago, *she'd* have been apologizing to *me*.

I let the others go into Mealy's while I waited outside with Kev. I'd lost any desire for sweets. Bridie may as well have punched me in the stomach. And Mona O'Dea – I was sure the tin of coconut macaroons was left open on the counter whenever *she* called round. They were welcome to each other. They were blind to almost everything going on around them. They only saw what they wanted to see. The truth about David was plain and simple but they chose to pretend he could do no wrong. I knew what he was really like. My mind was in tune with these things. I took my time and looked for clues to the truth. They stumbled about, missing out on the most obvious hints.

Walking home, I told the others we should bury the blackbird, but they didn't agree. Sandra said wild creatures die all the time and no one goes around burying them. Mel shook a box of wine gums under my nose and said he'd better things to be doing than kicking bird guts into a hole. And then Kev started to moan because he wanted more chocolate than we were prepared to put in his mouth and that made them walk even faster towards home. But it didn't seem right to leave the poor thing lying in the open with its insides squirting out all over the place, so I told the others to go on without me and, ignoring their mocking, ran back across the crunchy grass to the scene of death.

When I got there, I began searching around for something I could dig a hole with. It had to be sharp, able to cut through the hardened ground. I bent down and lifted the bottom branches of a bush. Scrabbling around among the crisp packets and sweet wrappers, I found an empty Coke bottle. I struck it against a rock but it just bounced off, sending a tremor up my arm. I gripped it tighter and tried again. This time, the base of it broke away, leaving me holding a sort of glass scoop with a nicely jagged edge.

I pictured Bridie's face in my head as I stabbed at the earth and gouged out lumps of frozen dirt. Puffy white clouds of my breath rose up in the air as I worked and though I knew I must've looked strange, I carried on. It wasn't long before I attracted attention.

'Yuck.' It was Valerie, with Tracey in tow. 'What did you do to that poor bird?'

I breathed out a long sigh. 'Nothing. I'm just burying it.'

'Looks like you slashed it open with that bottle,' Tracey said. 'Its guts are all over the place.'

I looked up at them. 'I found it like this, OK? Someone stamped on it. Can you not see their footprints all across the grass?'

'Sure that could've been you,' Valerie said.

'And why would I do that?'

''Cos you're weird, that's why.'

'No weirder than you.'

'Ha! That's funny.' She put her hands on her hips. 'That's really funny. I'm not the one down on my knees in the freezing cold burying a dead crow on Christmas Eve.'

'It's a blackbird, if you must know.'

'Whatever it is, it's weird,' Tracey said. 'Everything you do is weird. You're a weirdo, Ruth Lamb. A weirdo.'

'Me a weirdo?' I said. 'I wasn't the one leaving sheep's heads on people's doorsteps at Hallowe'en, was I?'

'Can't take a joke, can you? It was hardly the end of the world.'

'I always knew it was you,' I said. 'Even though you swore it wasn't.'

Tracey sniffed and looked away.

'You think you know everything, don't you?' Valerie said. 'Always poking your nose into other people's business. And because of you David's going away now.'

'Don't be so stupid. That's nothing to do with me,' I said. 'I only told him the truth. And what do you care, anyway?' I stood up, as much to stretch out my legs as to look them both square in the eye. 'You should be pleased. You're always saying how much you can't stand him. You only pretend you don't like him when really you fancy him like mad.'

'I do not!'

'You do too, Valerie Vaughan! And so do you, Tracey!'

Tracey took a few steps closer. 'Well, if you can say we both fancy David O'Dea, then we can say you fancy someone like

–' she rolled her eyes in her head as she searched for a name – 'like . . . Shayne Lawless!'

I didn't think about what I did next. I just saw her horrible, pathetic face and her dirty little mouth with its curling lips. And although her flesh was covered, I pictured it under her clothes: chalky and bruised and brushing against me, goosebumped and cold, like the scrawny dead turkeys hanging in Boylan's window. As her face leaned into mine and she opened her eyes wide in defiance, I raised myself up on my toes and held the broken bottle to her cheek. 'Shut up,' I said, through gritted teeth. 'Shut up, Tracey Farrell, or I'll burst your fuckin' face.' She was stunned, I could tell. She tried to cover up with a nervous laugh.

'I'm straight telling on you,' Valerie said. 'You're in deep trouble.'

'Tell whoever you like,' I said, lowering the bottle. 'I don't care. Go away and leave me alone. In fact, leave all of us alone. None of us can stand you!'

'Yeah, well, we hate all of you too,' Tracey said. 'My mam says you're nothing but trouble and everything was fine till you came along.'

'Well, maybe we'll just leave. And you can find someone else to blame for everything.'

'That's exactly what we're wishing for,' Valerie said. 'In fact, that'd be the best Christmas present ever.'

Tracey was about to add another comment when across the green came the distinctive call of her mother. Clem had reversed the car out of their driveway and Geraldine stood at the gate in her anorak and woolly hat, ready to climb in. Over the last few weeks, her stomach had grown huge. Farrell number eight would be arriving soon and for Tracey, the prospect of even more responsibility. She closed her eyes and sighed. I got the feeling that, given the choice, she'd prefer having a broken bottle held up to her face than yet another few hours looking after a houseful of snotty Farrells.

'Come on,' she said to Valerie, linking her arm. 'Let's go. There's a horrible smell around here, anyway.' She glanced back as they walked off, thinking I wouldn't be able to resist throwing another remark their way. But I didn't give her the satisfaction. Geraldine and Clem drove away when they saw her coming across the green, so if she was thinking of telling on me, it would have to wait till later on.

I got back to my digging and when the hole was big enough, I used the bottle to push the blackbird's body into its grave. I covered it with earth and when I stood up, I levelled it softly with the sole of my shoe. A small, fluffy feather lay on top of the trail of guts left behind on the frosty grass. I stuck it into the grave and it shivered, though there was hardly a breeze.

As I walked home over the whitened green, I found myself wondering if the person who'd held the bottle to Tracey's cheek and said the F-word could really have been me. It was like it was someone else; someone I didn't know at all.

FIFTEEN

On Christmas morning, Auntie Cissy came down to breakfast
fully dressed in her drab 'Christmas rig-out' while we were
all still in our dressing gowns. She gave Bertie a handful of
seed, then sat at the table fiddling with the neck of her blouse.
Dad whistled as he fried rashers and sausages, looking over
his shoulder every now and then to ask, 'Are you all right
there, Cis?' I felt sad for her. It was the first Christmas in
years and years that she wasn't with Uncle Frank in their own
home. Mam had told us the evening before that no presents
would be opened till we came home from mass. That was
what Cissy would expect, she said, and we should do our
best to make her happy. So we were ready for the earliest
mass at nine o'clock; the sooner we could get it over with,
the sooner the ripping of the wrapping paper could begin.

All the way through mass, I kind of knew something was going to be wrong when we got back to the house. I hadn't a clue what it might be but I definitely felt it wasn't going to be an ordinary Christmas Day. I was sorry I hadn't said as much to anyone on the way home because when we walked into the kitchen and saw Bertie lying lifeless at the bottom of his cage, I couldn't very well turn around and say, 'I told you so'. I knew it wasn't right that I was more disappointed at my failure to warn everyone than I was at the budgie's death but even so, when Mel asked when we were going to open our presents, I told him not to be so selfish.

Auntie Cissy sat crying and wringing her hands, asking, 'Who's next? Who's next?' Because deaths, she told us, always happen in threes. 'First Frank, then Bertie,' she said, wiping her eyes. Dad said a budgie hardly counted as Number Two, even if you did believe in all that sort of superstitious stuff, and that made her cry even more. He tried to say he was sorry and it wasn't that he thought Bertie meant nothing to her, but the damage had been done. She waved him away whimpering, 'You were always the same, Mick. Insensitive to the last.' Mam rowed in then, attempting to make Cissy feel better by siding with her.

'Don't mind him, Cis,' she said. 'Heart like a brick, he has.' And then to Dad she whispered, 'Have you no sense? Don't you know that bird was like a child to her?'

Dad puffed up his cheeks and blew out a sigh. 'And a merry shaggin' Christmas to you, too,' he mumbled, taking a bottle of beer from the fridge and disappearing into the sitting room.

'Don't be too upset,' Mam said, stroking Cissy's hand. 'Sure you have had that bird for . . . what? It must be ten years, isn't it? They don't last forever, Cis. It was his time to go.'

'Twelve years, Rose. I have had him nearly twelve years. Don't you remember you were there the day Frank brought him home? Ruth was only a baby.' She looked at me and smiled through her tears.

'I remember it,' I said. 'Uncle Frank lifted me up to see Bertie in his cage.'

'Don't be silly, Ruth,' Mam said. 'You can't have been more than a few months old.'

But I could see the image clearly. And I could 'feel' Uncle Frank's hands around my middle, the grip of someone unsure of how to hold a baby.

'Vivid imagination, she has,' Mam said, tousling my hair as if I was about three. 'Always has to know more than she possibly can.'

I gave her a bit of a scowl. 'No I don't. I can't help if I know things. And I do remember it!'

'Yeah, yeah, OK. We believe you,' Mel said, clearly desperate to get the present opening started.

'I even remember what Uncle Frank was wearing, so there,' I said.

Cissy took hold of my hand and squeezed it. 'Tell me then, dear. Because I remember too.'

'A red jumper. A really bright red. A Christmas kind of red.'

'That can't possibly be right,' Mam said. 'Sure Frank never wore anything but brown.'

'She's right, you know,' Cissy said. 'I bought it for him the week before. It was the only day he ever wore it. Hated it, he did. Said it was bright enough to stop traffic.'

'Told you,' I said to the others. 'Now do you believe me?'

'Who cares anyway?' Sandra said. 'It was years ago.'

'You're just jealous because I was right.'

'I am not. Why would I be concerned about what you can remember? You think you're so special with your psychic powers or whatever it is you think you have.'

'I never said I was psychic. You and Mel did. Just because I pay attention to what's going on around me and spend time thinking about things.'

'Waste time, you mean. No one cares what you think, anyway. We're all too busy living our own lives to be worrying about everyone else's.'

'Shut up, you.'

'No, you shut up. If you're that smart, why didn't you know Bertie was going to die? Or Uncle Frank? Maybe we could've saved them and poor Auntie Cissy wouldn't be sitting here in tears, would she?'

'Stop it now, the pair of you!' Mam said. 'For God's sake, it's Christmas Day.' She handed Kev to Sandra. 'Take him into the sitting room. And tell your father I want him. Sorry, Cis, but we'll have to, you know, get rid of . . . I mean, we'll have to do something with Bertie.'

'Bury him, you mean,' Cissy said, dabbing at her eyes with her handkerchief.

Sandra shouted in from the hall, 'Ruth'll do that for you. It's her favourite job.'

Dad came into the kitchen, not looking very pleased. Mam handed him an empty tea-bag box and nodded her head in the direction of the cage.

'Come on in to the sitting room, Cis,' she said quietly, taking Auntie Cissy's arm. 'Mick'll take care of everything.'

If it had been any other day, we might've had a bit of a ceremony. Like the one we'd had for our goldfish back in the South Circular. We'd wrapped it in toilet paper and placed it in an empty Bisto box. Then we'd carried the 'coffin' out on a cushion and buried it in the corner of the front garden, scattering the grave with rose petals. But as it was Christmas Day, Bertie was given a simple send off. While Mam poured Auntie Cissy a Babycham and kept her chatting about this and that, I followed Dad out to the back garden and, in not much more than a minute, Bertie was laid to rest.

Dad brought his bottle of beer out with him, and when the deed was done, he stood looking up at the house and took a long slug. 'Burying a bird on Christmas morning,' he said, wiping his moustache with the back of his hand. 'Eating one, yes. But digging a hole in the back garden for one?' He shook his head. 'Sure you'd have to laugh.'

'It's not really funny though, is it?' I said. 'Auntie Cissy's upset.'

'Ah, she'll get over it.'

'Do you think death really comes in threes? Like she said?'

'Sure that's all rubbish.' He dribbled the last of his beer into his mouth. 'I didn't think nonsense like that'd scare you.'

Lots of things scare me, Dad, I wanted to say. *Like seeing you down in The Ramblers with Liz Lawless.*

'But what if she's right?'

'She's not, do you hear me? She's superstitious. Always has been.'

'I suppose we'll soon find out.'

'Find out what?'

'If she's right. If someone dies, I mean. Then we'll know this was a sign.'

'Look,' he said, not even trying to hide his annoyance, 'no one is going to die. That –' he said, pointing the beer bottle at Bertie's grave – 'is a budgie. A shaggin' budgie! It's not a sign for anything. It was old. Probably diseased! It was always going to die.' He started walking back up to the house, turning to face me when he reached the back door. 'You need to grow up a bit, Ruth. Stop all your airy-fairy notions.'

I stared at him. In the past few weeks, he'd allowed his hair to grow out of its usual neat cut, and it rippled out from his skull in little kinks, making his head seem bigger. His moustache was thicker too, more bushy, and I wondered was it because he couldn't be bothered trimming it any more or because he actually liked it that way. He had a strange expression on his face, like he was looking at someone he thought he knew but couldn't quite place. We stood there for what seemed like ages and I could've used a million words and still not have been able to explain what passed between us.

After that, the day got worse and worse. No matter what we did, none of us could cheer up Auntie Cissy. She sat staring at the fire, tears welling in her eyes. She opened our present and said, 'Thank you, my dears,' but instead of pinning the brooch to her jacket, she put it back in its box and slipped it into her handbag. Mam and Dad gave her a clock made out of a china plate and when she took it out of its box, she said, 'Lovely, Rose. Don't know if I've a whole lot of time left to be counting, but thank you all the same.'

I tried my best to act over-the-moon with the presents I got, and although there were quite a few books I knew I'd enjoy and a crystal-making set, nothing was really going to cheer me up.

Dinner wasn't much of an improvement. The turkey was left in too long and got dried out; Kev flung a Brussels sprout and hit Cissy on the nose; and Dad kept avoiding me, even asking Sandra to pass the bread sauce when it was clearly far closer to me. Then we discovered that not only did the crackers not bang when we pulled them, there were no jokes inside them either, and the paper hats barely fitted our heads. Mam said sure, what could you expect when we'd got them in Mealy's, and Dad sat there stony-faced, because it was him who'd bought them. I didn't think things could get any worse.

But then, to top it all, as Mam got up to get the pudding, the doorbell rang.

'Ah now here,' Dad said, slapping his hands on the table. 'It's Christmas feckin Day! Who in the name of God?'

Mel answered the door. I'm not sure if he asked our callers into the house or whether they barged in uninvited, but either way, in the space of ten seconds, Mam was offering Geraldine Farrell and Nora Vaughan a seat at our Christmas dinner table.

'No, we won't, if you don't mind,' Geraldine said, speaking for both of them. 'And we're sorry to be arriving in the middle of your dinner, but, well, this can't wait, can it, Nora?' She stood with her feet spaced apart and her arms crossed over her huge belly. I knew it wasn't easy to find nice things to wear when you were having a baby, but surely, I thought, she could've made some sort of an effort on Christmas Day. She was dressed exactly the way she always was, whether pregnant or not, and wore one of Clem's floppy jumpers and a pair of stretchy slacks. Nora, by contrast, looked as though she might be a good example of what Bridie would term a 'dog's dinner' – all frilly and flowery in a dress I was certain I'd seen in Sheila's Fashions, with a string of large purple beads around her neck and her hair newly dyed a sort of squirrely-red.

'This girl put a broken bottle up to my Tracey's face yesterday,' Geraldine announced, looking directly at me. 'Now before you say a word, I want to let you know that Valerie was witness to the event, wasn't she, Nora?'

'She was. She saw the whole thing,' Nora agreed.

Dad glanced at Mam, then turned to me. 'Is this true?'

I knew it could go either way. There was just as much chance of me saying 'yes' as saying 'no'. It was like tossing a coin. Mam stood at the table holding the pudding on a plate, watching my face for clues to the truth. I juggled the possible answers in my head. Whatever I was going to say, it'd cause trouble. There was no easy way out.

'Well?' Dad said, realizing his paper hat was still perched on top of his head. He pulled it off, screwing it into a ball and stuffing it in his pocket. I could feel the man in the tree looking at me from behind his cover of pots and onions. Watching, watching, waiting . . .

'We're not here for the good of our health,' Nora said, wagging her finger at me. 'And we have our own Christmas Day to be getting along with, don't we, Geraldine?'

'We do, Nora. But we had to come over and get this sorted. Now, if you'll admit the truth and apologize, we can all get back to enjoying our day. It's been spoiled enough already with this. Tracey's very upset.'

'Well, I'm sorry . . .' I began, watching the look of satisfaction that spread over Geraldine's face as she thought she was getting her apology. 'But I've no idea what you're talking about.'

Her wishy-washy eyes bored into me. 'You're quite sure about that, are you?'

I nodded.

'So our girls are lying, then?'

I shrugged.

'And why would they make up something like that?' Nora wanted to know.

'Look,' Dad said, 'she says she didn't do it. What more do you want?'

'Just the truth,' Geraldine said. 'That's all.'

'Well, you've got it. Now, if you don't mind, can we finish our dinner in peace?' He took the pudding from Mam and put it in the middle of the table. 'Get the bowls,' he said to Mel. 'Ruth, bring over the brandy sauce. Sandra, see our visitors out, like a good girl.'

Nora looked at Geraldine. 'Well! Of all the—'

'Happy Christmas,' Dad said, giving them a false smile. 'Enjoy the rest of your day now.'

'There was no need to be flippant,' Mam said, as soon as our 'visitors' had left the room.

'Ah, come on, woman. Don't give me that. Marching over in the middle of our Christmas dinner! Did you ever hear the like?'

The pudding was served in silence. Auntie Cissy picked the cherries out of hers and pushed them into a little pile, which she spooned onto her placemat. Dad wolfed down his then helped himself to some more. Kev spat out the bit Mam allowed him to taste, rubbed it into a streaky brown mess on his tray, then wiped it into his hair.

Sandra smirked at me from across the table. 'Why do you think Tracey would've made up something like that?'

'I don't know. Why don't you ask her?'

Before she could reply, Mam butted in. 'I don't want to hear any more about it, do you hear me, both of you? We'll get to the bottom of it another day. Let's forget about it for the moment. Isn't that right, Cis?'

Auntie Cissy's face was blank. 'Cis? Isn't that right?' Mam said again. 'We'll just forget about it.'

'What? Oh . . . yes . . . yes, Rose . . . We'll do that.'

By the looks of things, Cissy had forgotten about it already. Mam and Dad didn't believe I'd done it. I could tell. It wasn't only because it was Christmas Day that Dad had rushed Geraldine and Nora out; it was because he thought Tracey had made the whole thing up. He wouldn't be able to believe I'd done something like that, as much as he'd said I'd changed. Did that mean he trusted me? Or did it mean he didn't know me at all? I wasn't sure. There was a lot I wasn't sure of any more.

I pictured Tracey's face, how close it'd been to mine. I remembered how angry I'd been. Burning angry at the way her mouth had curled around the words 'Shayne Lawless'. Like she knew them better than anyone else. Like she'd more of a right to use them. Like she owned them. I saw her cold, see-through skin, her icy veins like frozen rivers underneath. I watched myself press the jagged glass to her cheek, and felt a rush of relief inside when I imagined I'd drawn blood. I pictured it oozing thick and black, flowing freely to the ground in a steady drip-drip that settled in a circular pool on the frosty grass. I watched the whole thing like it was a film.

But I told myself it wasn't really me that I saw. Not the proper me. Not the me who'd moved into Hillcourt Rise a year and a half before. But the me I thought this place had turned me into.

As usual, *The Wizard of Oz* was on in the afternoon. While everyone else settled down to watch it, I lay out on the rug to look at my books and eat some chocolate from my selection box. Auntie Cissy soon fell asleep, the only indication being that her eyes closed. Her body remained as stiff and upright as ever, her hands in her lap, and her head not even slightly bent to one side. Kev sat on Mam's knee and on more than one occasion, she had to pull him back as he leaned over and tried to prise open Cissy's eyelids.

By half past four it was dark outside, and the heat from the fire and the glow of the fairy lights made me drowsy. With the sounds of Dorothy's silly little-girl voice telling us there's no place like home, I laid my head on a cushion and closed my eyes.

I'm not sure how long I was asleep, probably no more than half an hour, but when I woke up, Dad's chair was empty. 'Gone out for a breath of fresh air,' Mam whispered when I asked where he was. Cissy was still dead to the world and Kev had joined her. He lay curled in a ball on the couch beside her with his bum in the air and his hair still sticky with bits of Christmas pudding. 'He said he wouldn't be long.'

The others were playing with the present Uncle Con had given us – some board game with question cards and counters and very complicated-looking rules. When he saw me awake, Mel asked really nicely if I'd like to play, but I wasn't fooled by his burst of Christmas goodwill. It was just a trick to try and lure me in. It'd make him feel so much better if he could cheat his way to beating both his sisters.

I couldn't remember Dad ever going out on Christmas Day before. Once he sat down in his chair after dinner, he usually only got up to get another bottle of beer or to go to the bathroom.

'Did Dad say where exactly he was going?' I asked Mam.

'I told you. He's gone out for a bit of air. He'll only go around the green, or to the bottom of the hill and back.'

I felt like asking her if she was sure, and how did she know he wasn't going around the green and down to the bottom of the hill by way of the Lawlesses' house? If Bridie hadn't decided at the last minute to visit Dick's brother and his family on their farm somewhere in County Meath for a few days, I could've told Mam I was slipping out to wish her a happy Christmas and then had a good look around for Dad. Mam didn't know how far downhill my friendship with Bridie had fallen. If I'd told her, she'd only have brushed me off in a 'don't mind her, she doesn't mean anything by it' kind of way.

'My head's a bit stuffy,' I said. 'Can I go round the cul-de-sac for a few minutes?' It was better than nothing.

'Well . . . all right then. But ten minutes at the most. It's freezing out there and we don't want you coming down with a bad cold if we can help it.' She stroked Kev's back and he threw his arm out to the side, whacking Auntie Cissy's knee. She half opened her eyes and swivelled them from side to side, then closed them again, mouthing what looked like 'Bertie, Bertie' with her thin lips. 'And we'll have tea and cake when you both get back,' Mam said, smiling.

Once outside, I scanned the whole of the estate, along the path past Bridie's, down one side of the green and across to the other. There wasn't a soul around. The cold stung my eyes and made them water. It dried my lips and hurt my ears and crept into every part of my body. I shoved my hands right down in my pockets as I walked. The sky was alive with stars. I couldn't make sense of the amount of them. I stood for a moment and threw my head back to get a better look, nearly toppling backwards I got so dizzy. I was about to cross the road and go around the corner when I saw a movement in the distance up ahead.

It was Dad.

Running up the path from the direction of Shayne's house.

I quickly slunk into a gap between a lamppost and a wall, breathing in to make myself as thin as possible, and hid there while he passed. I watched him slow his pace as he neared our house, then stop to catch his breath, leaning forward and putting his hands on his knees. I slipped out from my hiding place and, as he began to walk, followed behind him all the way to our front door.

'Where were you?' I asked. He spun around, nearly dropping his keys.

'For fu— Jesus, Ruth! You put the heart shaggin' crossways in me! What are you doing out here?'

'Getting a breath of air. Like you.'

His eyes were jumpy and his face was all red.

'Were you running or something?'

He poked around at the lock, his hands kind of shaky, finally getting the key in and opening the door.

'Well?' I asked.

'Well, what? What is it you want now?' He raised his voice. 'Just this once, could you cut the questions and let a man go about his own business on Christmas Day? I don't have to answer to you or anyone else.' He flung his coat over the banisters and went into the kitchen, slamming the door behind him. Mam came out of the sitting room, patting her hair back into place and having a good yawn. 'What's going on?' she asked.

I had hundreds of things in my head, but I couldn't say them. It was like trying to eat toffee without making noise – just sucking on it and waiting for it to dissolve, when all you really wanted to do was get your teeth into it and chew and chew and taste the flavour in every part of your mouth.

'I don't know, Mam,' I said. 'I just don't know.'

The days that followed grew even colder. The temperature fell further each night and Mam said she'd heard we might be in for a bit of snow. Auntie Cissy agreed and said she wouldn't be surprised if we were in for more than a bit, she could feel it in her bones. She started to fret over Thomas, her cat, concerned that the neighbour who'd promised to feed him wouldn't bother to bring him in at night and he'd freeze to death.

'He's all I have left now,' she said, as if we didn't rank at all.

Mam said whoever heard of a cat freezing to death? Didn't they always find themselves somewhere warm to sleep? But Cissy couldn't be convinced and said she kept having visions of him frozen solid on her windowsill, his fur all stiff with ice. So she packed her case and Dad drove her home. She wanted to leave Bertie's cage with us but Mam said we'd no use for it and sure she might want to get another budgie at some point in the future, so she may as well take it home. 'That bird could never be replaced,' Cissy said, horrified. 'I don't know how you could even think it, Rose.' As she bent to kiss each of us goodbye, we noticed she'd pinned the cat brooch to her blouse.

The next night was New Year's Eve. That was when the Big Freeze started. Auntie Cissy had been right; it was more than just a bit of snow.

I had no real reason to explain the way I felt when we looked out at the blizzard from Mam and Dad's room. My mind was a jumble of suspicions I'd no way of knowing how to prove. I'd no idea if they even made sense. But it was as if the snow was trying to silence me, to lull me into believing that everything in Hillcourt Rise was pure and perfect and trouble-free. I thought I'd suffocate under its thick, heavy layers if I didn't tell them then.

'Something bad's going to happen this year.'

That was what I said.

Not that I thought warning them would change anything; I just felt I needed to let them know. And if they'd pushed me on it, what would I have said? What clues could I have given them to try and make them understand? There was nothing concrete, no one thing I could put my finger on. But that night, the last night of the year, I sensed it was more than the snow that was freezing us out. We were never really meant to live there in the first place. The only reason we came at all was because of Kev. If it wasn't for him, we'd never have moved. We'd still be living on the South Circular in the house where Dad had been born. And if Kev was the reason we came to Hillcourt Rise, what would be the reason we'd leave?

SIXTEEN

Because of the snow, David's departure for Clonrath was delayed. Every school in the country had extended their holidays. While the rest of us were delighted and wanted the Big Freeze to stay forever, he went around wishing the snow would hurry up and melt. Boarding school, he claimed, was something he was actually looking forward to. Despite Tracey and Valerie blaming me for David being sent away, he himself seemed weirdly relieved to be going, as if some sort of weight had been lifted from him. He became less serious, more relaxed. I saw him at mass the Sunday he finally left and noticed he'd left his coat unzipped and the top button of his shirt undone.

On my way back from Mealy's one evening with Kev, I met Shayne. Though Mam had told me dinner was almost ready, and not to be long, I stopped to talk to him. There was something I had to ask. I needed to start clearing things up if I was to make any sense of the bad feeling I'd been having. I hadn't mentioned anything about seeing his mam with Dad in The Ramblers. It felt safer to keep it secret. But I had to find out if Dad had been telling the truth about his 'breath of air'.

We stood at the top of the lane. He had that faraway look in his eyes, only this time it seemed he was more unconnected to his thoughts than usual.

'Did anyone call to your house on Christmas night?' I asked, watching his face closely.

He took a while to answer. 'Christmas night? Um . . . I dunno. Can't remember. Why?'

'It's just that . . . well, my dad went out for a walk and I saw him running back from the direction of your house and I thought maybe . . . well . . .'

His gaze became more steady. 'Oh, yeah . . . Christmas night. Yeah . . . I remember now.' I saw his pupils shrink. 'Me ma went to the door. Yeah . . . she thought it might've been me uncle Vic.'

'But it was my dad?'

'Yeah . . . yeah . . . yer da . . .'

'What did he want? Did you hear what he was saying or anything?'

'Nah. Had me music on, didn't I? Me ma let me use her record player, ye know, 'cos it was Christmas and all.'

'Oh. So you don't know what he wanted?'

'Me? Nah.' He bit his thumbnail. 'I could . . . ask me ma if ye like?'

'No! No. It's OK. It . . . it doesn't matter,' I said as I wheeled Kev on towards home.

So. My suspicions had been right. Dad had called to Liz on Christmas night. Who did he think he was fooling? *'I needed a breath of fresh air . . .'*

I knew it. I just knew it.

And the more I thought about it, the more I became convinced that this was part of the something bad I'd told the others about. Whenever I thought of Dad and Liz, I got that awful stinging-nettle feeling that crept through me like a rash. I knew I'd have to tell someone soon – Mam, the others, Father Feely, even. I wouldn't be able to stop the bad thing happening if I didn't.

School was as boring as ever when it started up again. The only good thing was Aidan Farrell was out for a few days. Geraldine had squeezed Farrell number eight out into the world the night before we went back (a boy – Brian) and Tracey and Aidan were left in charge while their mother was in hospital. I saw them at the door one morning, while Clem cycled off to work – Tracey with Fiona on her hip and another Farrell hanging off her leg, and Aidan with a potty in one hand and a wooden spoon in the other. When he saw me looking, he stuck his tongue out and gave me the two fingers.

It was easier to pass the O'Deas' house now that David was gone. It didn't feel half as creepy as it had before. But in some ways, it was as if his absence was more noticeable than his presence had been – the way you notice the hole a missing tooth leaves far more than you ever noticed the actual tooth. His piano tunes had been part of the air around Hillcourt Rise, and not hearing them was kind of strange.

In early February, Dad announced that he'd got some big contract to paint an estate of new houses, miles away in County Kildare. It meant he had to leave really early, and every morning I woke to the sound of his whistling ringing through the house. He rarely got home before eight. Mam always looked weary when we came down for breakfast. Kev had become a bit of a handful, whinging and moaning if he didn't get his own way. He'd started to say a few words, his favourite being 'no', and Mam was worn out trying to get him to do what he was told. I knew she hated the way Dad had to leave so early and wasn't home till late, and while she did say she was happy he'd got the work, she said she wished it wasn't so far away. But I was glad he had to spend so much time away from Hillcourt Rise. It meant there was less chance of him having any contact with Liz. I didn't care how far the houses were from anything. The longer it took Dad to paint them, the better.

Bridie stopped me at the gate one afternoon on my way home from school, all fidgety and breathless, to tell me that her daughter, Majella, had got engaged to her garda boyfriend on Valentine's Day and the wedding was planned for 'June twelve months'. If she thought she could pretend that everything between us was all right, she was mistaken. I just said, 'That's nice' and walked off, leaving her muttering something about her crocuses being very late for the time of year.

Shayne didn't seem to be around as much now that David was gone. Whenever I did happen to see him, he was always in a world of his own, like he didn't quite know what to do with himself. I think he felt a bit lost. Despite everything that had happened between them, I suppose he felt that David was better than no friend at all. Some evenings, he cycled round and round the green with his head lowered and the neck of his T-shirt pulled up over his chin, not seeming to care that he couldn't possibly see where he was going.

I was heading home from school one afternoon when I saw him cycling towards me on the path. He'd obviously skipped off class early again. Mel said he was doing it a lot lately. Sandra told me Liz had been called up to the school the first time it'd happened and she'd arrived wearing her knee-high boots, a very short skirt and loads of make-up. She'd spent ages in the headmaster's office and after that, Shayne never got in trouble for anything.

He whizzed past me, banging his elbow off my schoolbag and knocking me off balance. I toppled against the wall, scraping my hand, and yelled after him, 'Watch where you're going, will you! You don't own the bloody path!'

That evening, I took Kev for a walk down to the bottom of the hill to wait for Dad. It was a Friday and he'd told Mam he was finishing up early and would be home in time for dinner. When he saw the car, Kev got all excited. I got in the back and Dad sat Kev on his knee so he could 'drive' us home. As we turned slowly into the estate, I saw Shayne sitting lengthways on the O'Deas' wall with his back pressed up against the gate pillar. He was munching a packet of crisps and held a can of Fanta between his knees. He barely raised his head but I could tell he was watching us.

We crawled along, Kev all delighted he was holding the steering wheel and Dad going *vroom vroom* into his ear. Shayne lifted his eyes as we approached, but I don't think he even saw me sitting in the back of the car. His gaze was fixed on Kev – a cold, blank, scary stare.

Dad was about to say something when Shayne grabbed the can from between his knees, took aim and fired it at the windscreen of our car. It clattered against the glass, sending bubbly orange splashes all over the bonnet. Dad got such a fright that he pushed his foot down hard on the brake and Kev bumped his forehead on the rim of the steering wheel.

'What the . . . ? Christ alshagginmighty!' Dad shouted.

Kev screamed, instant tears flooding down his face. Dad gave him to me and I tried to comfort him, stroking his cheek and cuddling him tight. I expected Shayne would hop on his bike and disappear. But when I looked, he was still there, eating his crisps and staring at Kev as he snuggled into my chest.

'I'll wring his bloody neck,' Dad said. He waved his fist at Shayne. 'I'll wring your shaggin' neck, you gurrier! Do you hear me?'

I couldn't believe Dad was still sitting in the car. 'Are you not going to get out?' I asked.

He shook his head and drove off, breathing heavily down his nose. It was only when we got to our house that he spoke. 'I don't want to see you hanging around with him any more.' His voice was low and even. 'It's gone far enough. Stay away from him. That's an order.'

That Monday, I got the letter.

Mam handed me the light blue envelope when I came in from school. I think she was as curious as I was to see who it could be from. My name and address had been written with a fountain pen in what Mrs Lally would've described as 'beautiful copperplate script'. I rarely got letters. In my whole life, I'd probably only got a handful.

'I'll open it in my room,' I told Mam.

She was hovering over my shoulder like a fly. 'Ah, sure open it here. I'll make us a nice cup of tea while you read it.'

I didn't wait around to argue. I took the stairs two at a time, my schoolbag still on my back.

The letter was from David.

Written in the 'beautiful script' on five lined pages the same colour as the envelope.

Dear Ruth,

I've been meaning to write for ages but there's so much to do every day here it's hard to find the time. I'm writing this during study. Hope I don't get caught (!) Brother Cornelius is looking down and I'm supposed to be learning my Latin verbs. We have ANOTHER test tomorrow (aaagh). It's not so bad here though. In fact, I actually like it a lot more than Grangemount. I've made real friends too. I share my dorm with two boys from Cork and one from Tipperary and we all get along very well.

I've been thinking a lot about everyone and I have a few things I want to say. Things I probably should have said before but it's easier to put them in a letter. I know you were blamed because I was sent down here but it wasn't really your fault. They should have told me before. My parents, I mean. About being adopted. I know how you found out and I know Shayne pretended I already knew (he told me) but I would've been sent down here anyway. My parents had been thinking about it for ages. They don't like Shayne. They were never that happy about us being friends. They were always saying he was bad news and I used to tell them they were wrong. Shayne's been my friend for all the time I've lived in Hillcourt Rise. When we were small we used to pretend we were brothers. He shouldn't have said he already knew about me being adopted but I think he was upset that you found out about it before he did. I used to always feel bad for him because he didn't know who his dad was and when he found out that I didn't know who my real dad was either, he thought that maybe I'd been keeping it a secret from him. I was mad at first when

I found out from you about being adopted but it's OK now. In fact, I'm glad because it made my parents make up their minds to send me down here. And I don't have to worry about covering for anyone when I'm here. Because that's what I had to do all the time for Shayne. Remember all the stuff about when I broke my wrist? Well, to tell the truth here and now, you were right. It wasn't an accident. But you were wrong when you told my parents that I did it deliberately. That wasn't what happened.

What happened was that Shayne pushed me.

I was climbing the tree quicker than he was and I called him a fairy or something and he got mad and he pushed me.

I pretended to my mother and father that I fell. And then when Valerie asked me if I'd done it deliberately, I never denied it and that was how that spread all around the place and I suppose I liked the way that all of you thought I'd done it myself. I know it was stupid to cover for him but he made me do it and I was afraid if I told the truth he'd get into serious trouble and be sent away. And most of all, I didn't ever want my parents to be able to say they were right about him.

Mam poked her head round my door. 'You all right?' she asked.

'Yeah. I'm fine.'

'So? Are you not going to tell me who it's from?' She was putting on a real cheerful voice like she wasn't that interested when really she was dying to know.

'David.'

'Oh. I see. That's nice . . .' She was waiting for more.

'Just telling me about his new school and stuff.'

'Well? Does he like it?'

'Maybe when I get to read it all I can tell you,' I said, frowning. Her head disappeared and she went back downstairs.

It's only because I'm away from Hillcourt Rise that I can see how stupid I was. And I know you think I'm weird and I'm sorry I scared you that day I took the pram from outside the shops, but I only did it because he made me. He said if I didn't maybe one of the twins might fall into the bonfire or something and I was scared. I just did everything he said. And I always thought that if I told on him, it would just make everything worse.

I'm only telling you now because I think you should know. Just be careful because he might start trying to do the same thing with you. AND DON'T TELL HIM I TOLD YOU ANY OF THIS. I KNOW I CAN TRUST YOU.

You can write back to me if you want but it's all right if you don't want to, I won't mind.

Vale (= goodbye in Latin) for now.

David (O'Dea)

P.S. I wrote out the lyrics to 'Bohemian Rhapsody' (Queen) for you. Shayne told me you liked it. They're the actual correct words. One of the fifth years got them from a song words magazine. It's good to see the actual correct words because where they say 'Bismillah' I always thought they were saying 'Wish me luck' (!)

I opened out the separate sheet – the double centre pages of a copybook – where he'd written the song words. I read them through then put them back in the envelope. My chest was sizzling inside, the heat rising up through my neck and all the way to my face. I looked at myself in the dressing table mirror and saw my cheeks were flaming red. The silence in the room was suffocating. I felt like I was caught in the middle of a bunch of balloons.

I didn't believe him. It was all lies.

There was no way Shayne would've pushed him. He wasn't that bad. And David was hardly that desperate that he'd have covered for him. No one would be so stupid.

It was all a big joke. I could picture him, grinning all the while he was writing, with Brother whoever-it-was sitting at the top of the hall smiling down at him, thinking he was writing out his Latin verbs. David would've enjoyed that, fooling a teacher into believing he was such a goody-goody when really he was a sly and spiteful liar.

And the way he started off the letter all happy-go-lucky like I'd be interested in how many friends he had and all that stuff. Real friends, he said. I couldn't care less. And why would I want the words to the song anyway? I could've written them out myself if I did. I knew them off by heart. I didn't need him to be doing it for me.

And then trying to convince me it was Shayne who was being mean to him when it was really the other way around. And what made him think I'd believe that Shayne had forced him to take Kev from outside Mealy's? I'd seen his face that day. I knew what he was like. He thought he knew everything, but I didn't believe a word he'd said. The way the letter was written didn't even sound like him. It was far too . . . normal. I tore it into pieces, shoved it back in the envelope along with the song words and hid them at the back of my underwear drawer.

At dinner that evening, Sandra was killed quizzing me about the letter. 'Mam says you got a letter from David O'Dea. Why would he be writing to you? What did he say? Does he hate Clonrath? Is he—'

'Stop,' I said. 'It was just a letter. He probably only wrote it because he's so bored he didn't know what else to do.'

'Bored? I thought he'd be doing loads of stuff!'

'Well, it is called boarding school, don't forget,' Mel said, laughing at his own joke.

'But why did he write to *you*?' Sandra asked me.

'How should I know?'

'Unless . . . unless you wrote to him first? In secret . . .'

'Why would I do that?'

She shrugged. 'Only you'd know that.'

'Well, for your information, I didn't. OK? And you're just jealous you didn't get a letter.'

'Yeah, I'm really jealous weirdo O'Dea wrote to you. I've far more exciting things to be concerned about.'

'If you're that uninterested why were you asking me all the questions?'

She sniffed, tucked her hair behind her ears and stuffed her mouth with a large forkful of macaroni cheese. We had Dad to thank for such a tasty dinner. Since he'd started the job in Kildare, Mam had begun making us things he would've turned his nose up at. She cooked a dinner especially for him when he came home later – usually pork chops or a mixed grill, which he ate on his own with a pot of tea and a tower of bread and butter.

'If Ruth doesn't want to tell us what was in the letter, that's her own business,' Mam said. That was a laugh, seeing as she'd been trying to find out herself earlier on.

'Yeah,' said Mel, sniggering. 'It's your own private business, isn't it? Just between you and O'Dea. Maybe it was a love letter. Wooooh.'

'You could be right there,' Sandra agreed. 'Why else would she be keeping it all to herself?'

'Now stop that, the two of you,' Mam said, clearly annoyed. 'Leave your sister alone. None of that nonsense.'

'I just thought it'd be nice to know how he was getting on,' Sandra sulked. 'I've always wanted to know what boarding school is like.'

'Well, keep up your teasing and you might find out sooner than you think,' Mam told her, getting up from the table. 'Now, you're on the washing up if I'm not mistaken, miss, so make sure you do a good job, all right? And no messing.' She lifted Kev from the highchair and brought him upstairs for his bath.

As soon as Mam was out of the kitchen, the others started again. Sandra kept wondering out loud about what had been 'going on' between David and me, and how had she not spotted it? Mel went through every possible reason he could think of for David writing, watching my face for some sort of reaction to each thing he suggested. I ignored them both and got on with the drying up.

Later, I went up to my room and addressed an envelope to David. I took out my ladybird-patterned notepaper and thought about what to say to him. But every time I had an idea that sounded right, a second later it sounded stupid. In the end, I decided not to reply at all. The last thing I wanted was David under his blankets at night, re-reading my letter by torchlight, sniggering at how he'd managed to stir up trouble even when he wasn't anywhere near Hillcourt Rise. I had a better idea.

I had to talk to Shayne.

SEVENTEEN

I found him outside Mealy's the following afternoon. He'd propped his bike against the wall and was standing beside it, one foot resting on a pedal while he messily licked his way through an Iceberger. He wiped the back of his hand over his mouth when he saw me.

'I want to talk to you,' I said.

His tongue skimmed his lips for smears of ice-cream. He stuffed the last of the Iceberger into his mouth and began wheeling his bike away. I walked beside him, noticing he was almost a head taller than me now. We passed Boylan's and rounded the corner into the lane. When we were halfway up he stopped.

'So?' he asked.

I breathed in hard, giving myself a few more seconds to figure out if I was doing the right thing. What good would telling him about the letter actually do? Maybe it'd be better to leave it and not say anything at all. He leaned his head to one side and started chewing on a yellow jelly he'd pulled from his pocket. I let the bag of groceries I'd bought for Mam slip to the ground.

'I got a letter from David,' I blurted, the words tumbling out before they'd even formed in my head.

He chewed for a while before he spoke. 'Oh yeah? Nice of him. Never bothered writin' to me, the spa.'

'I didn't ask him to. I mean, I wasn't expecting him to write.'

'All excited, were ye?'

'No. I'm just saying I was . . . you know . . . surprised.'

Aidan Farrell came belting into the lane from Hillcourt Rise, slapping his thigh and yelling, 'Giddy up! Giddy up!' He shut up when he saw us, walking past with his head down, embarrassed that we'd seen his little display.

'So. What was O'Dea sayin'?' Shayne asked when he'd gone. 'Bet he hates the place.'

'No, he likes it. Made loads of friends and all, he said.'

'Ha ha, sure. Ye wouldn't want to believe anythin' he says. Probably shittin' himself every night, bawlin' his eyes out for his mammy.'

'Maybe. I don't know. But . . . well . . . he did tell me something that I don't believe . . .'

'Yeah? What was that?'

'That you pushed him out of the tree.'

He turned his head and spat, leaving a line of yellow-tinged phlegm on the ground. 'Fuck's sake! Ye know why he's doin' this, don't ye? Just loves stirrin' shit.'

'He said you got mad because he climbed the tree quicker than you, and you pushed him.'

'Fuckin' O'Dea. I'll bleedin' burst him when I see him, I will.'

'Please don't say anything. Just leave it. I wasn't supposed to tell you.'

'Bet he knew right fuckin' well ye'd go and tell me. Loves pissin' me off, so he does.'

'What really happened that day?'

'I dunno, do I? I wasn't as high up as him. Maybe he fell, maybe he threw himself, I dunno! I don't fuckin' care, OK!'

He kicked at the wheels of his bike then bent to pick a few pebbles from the ground, twisting his face up and firing them over the wall.

'I better go,' I said. 'I'm not even meant to be talking to you.'

'Who said?'

'My dad. After you threw the can at our car. He said I wasn't to be hanging around with you.'

'That's the reason he gave ye, is it?'

'What do you mean?'

He flung more pebbles into the air, trying to clear the telephone wires that criss-crossed over the lane above our heads.

'Ye know why he told ye to stay away from me, don't ye?'

I shook my head.

'He's mad 'cos he knows I seen him and me ma again and

he's afraid I'll be rattin' on him. They're at it, ye know, the two of them.'

The ground felt hard and cold under my feet. 'At it?'

'Yeah. At it. Ye know . . . I seen them.'

I put my hands on my hips, trying hard to ignore how I felt inside. 'What exactly did you see?'

'What do ye think?'

'I don't believe you. My dad's not even around here much now, anyway, so he wouldn't have the time. He's working way down the country. He's gone before we get up and it takes him ages to get home. He doesn't even have dinner with us any more he gets home so late. You're making it all up.'

He laughed out loud and pushed his face close to mine. 'Keep tellin' yerself that, why don't ye? Takes him ages to get home, does it? Takes his time down the woods around Westgorman, ye mean. Yeah. That's where they go. I seen them. I seen them all the time. Where do ye think I go on me bike when I'm mitchin' from school? He'd be home for his din dins a lot earlier if me ma wasn't waitin' for him up the back roads every evenin'.'

For a second, I thought he'd punched me in the chest. I could hardly breathe and I felt all woozy, the way I did when I went too high on a swing, or slid head first down the stairs so fast I got carpet burn on my stomach.

It couldn't be true. It just couldn't.

While we were eating our macaroni cheese or our beans

on toast, was Dad really 'at it' with Liz Lawless in the woods in Westgorman?

This was the something bad. I knew it.

It was like a wave. I could see it. Rolling towards us in the distance, gathering speed and strength as it approached. Coming closer and closer. Very soon it would rise up over us and come crashing down, washing everything away for good.

Everything we owned. Everything we loved. Everything we were.

I started walking fast down the lane. Shayne followed and caught up, pedalling slowly beside me until we reached the estate. I kept my head down and didn't say a word.

'Ye needn't be blamin' me,' he said.

'Just shut up and leave me alone.' I started running across the green.

'I was only tellin' ye!' he shouted after me. 'I thought ye should know. Isn't it better ye know the truth? Isn't that why ye told me what O'Dea said in the letter?'

I stopped dead, almost toppling over myself. I swung around.

'Is it?' I yelled, not caring if anyone else could hear. 'Is it really?'

He was cycling on the road now, sailing along with his hands swinging down by his sides and his hair waving out from his head. He grinned over at me and I ran towards him, standing on the edge of the green as he swerved over and pulled the brakes. 'Well, that's what everyone says, isn't it?' he snarled, showing his teeth. He reached over and grabbed my arm, pressing his fingers into my flesh. 'Ye know I'm tellin' the truth. And ye know I was right to tell ye, don't ye?'

'Let go of me!'

He gripped even tighter and laughed as I tried to free myself. It was only when I stopped resisting that his fingers relaxed their hold and I broke away. I rubbed at my arm as I galloped across the green, feeling the row of half-moon-shaped marks his nails had left in my skin.

When I got home, Dad was out in the back garden with Kev, clipping dead bits from the creeper that grew up one side of the tree. Kev stood close beside him, trying to imitate every move Dad made. I watched them through the kitchen window while Mam rummaged in cupboards and clattered around in the cutlery drawer. Dad lifted Kev up and sat him on a branch of the tree, holding his body tight in his big hands to make sure he wouldn't fall. Kev kicked his legs and his wellies fell off and he laughed like it was the funniest thing in the world. Dad turned around and saw me looking, and he pointed at Kev and grinned, as if to show me what a great time they were having and what a truly wonderful dad he was. When he took Kev in his arms and began swinging him up in the air, I had to turn away. A horrible taste came into my mouth and I thought I was going to get sick.

'Have you got those eggs, Ruth?' Mam asked me as she poured a mound of sugar into a glass bowl of melted margarine.

'Eggs?'

'Yes. Eggs. They did have some in Mealy's?'

Only then I remembered I'd left the bag of groceries in the lane.

'I . . . um . . . I don't know what I did with them.'

'You what? What are you talking about? Where did you put them?'

'I . . . I must've lost them.'

'Lost them? Sure how could you lose half a dozen eggs?'

The back door opened. Kev pushed his way in through Dad's legs.

'I . . . I don't feel well, Mam,' I said, watching Dad wipe his feet. 'I think I'll have to go up to bed.'

'But what about this cake? I can't make it without eggs.'

'Ask . . . ask Bridie for some. She always has loads.' I made my way out to the hall.

'What's up with her at all, at all?' I heard Mam say to Dad.

'Ah, just let her lie down,' he said, wiping his feet. 'She doesn't look the best. Like a ghost, she was, looking out the window. Fierce pale altogether. Fierce pale.'

When I heard Dad leaving the house the next morning, I lay in bed and prayed that he'd surprise us all and be home in time for dinner. I imagined him coming in the door and Mam being all delighted he was home so early, and fussing about when she realized she'd have to hurry up and get his chops under the grill. But that evening his chair sat empty at the top of the table and I watched the others stuffing their food in their mouths while I picked at mine and tried to force it down. I didn't care how delicious macaroni cheese was; if Dad could only be home to eat dinner with us, I'd gladly have put up with liver.

I started watching out the sitting room window in the afternoons, to see if I could spot Liz making her way out of the estate and down the hill to wait for the bus to Westgorman. I saw her once, belted into a shiny black 'wet-look' mac that made her look like one of the sea lions in the zoo. She wore her knee-high boots and wiggled her bum as she trotted alongside the green, but she was too far away for me to see if her face was dolled up like she was going on a date.

I knew deep down I wouldn't be able to keep the stuff about Dad and Liz inside for ever, no matter how hard I tried. It was bad enough hearing about The Kiss and seeing them in The Ramblers together and knowing the real reason behind Dad's 'breath of air' on Christmas night and all. But this news about them being 'at it' in the woods was another thing entirely. The something bad was coming closer, and even though I couldn't stop it crashing down, I felt I should at least send some sort of signal that it was on its way.

The Friday we got our Easter holidays, I expected Dad might try and be home early and that I'd bring Kev down to meet him at the bottom of the hill and I could at least pretend everything was normal. But when Mam told me there was no need to lay a place for him at the table, a wave of dread rose up from my stomach and down again, and I had to hold on to the back of a chair. 'Is Dad not coming home early? It's Friday,' I said, trying to keep my voice as steady as I could.

'I know, but he's not able to manage it this evening,' Mam said. 'He has another job to look at when he finishes up today. Strange on a Friday evening. But sure if someone wants a price for a job they need doing, you don't tell them you have to be home for your dinner, do you?'

'So what time will he be home at then?'

'God knows. It's some place even further out he has to go to, he said. So it could be all hours by the time he gets back.' She saw the look on my face. 'I know you miss Dad. I do too, love. But he has to take the work where he can get it. This job he's pricing, he said it's a big one. He said he might even have to take someone on if he gets it.' She wiped her hands down her apron. 'But I have a little treat for you all.' She smiled. 'Fish fingers. And chips. And Angel Delight for after.'

I was puzzled. 'I thought you said fish fingers were muck?'

'Did I? Sure what harm can they do once in a blue moon?'

'You did. You said they were the sort of thing Liz Lawless would have.'

'Well . . . maybe I did. But there's a difference in having them the odd time and having them every day of the week.'

'But how do you know how often she makes them? How do you know anything about her?'

'Well . . . I know what I see. I have eyes. That woman spends more time on her face than she does standing at a stove, that's for certain. And sure you'd only have to look at young Shayne to know he's not fed properly. All pasty and hollow-eyed, he is. I'm surprised he even has the strength to be riding that bike around the place day in and day out. Chips for breakfast, dinner and tea, no doubt. And as for school, sure Mel says he's forever skipping off after lunch and going off on his bike. God knows what he gets up to. But sure it's not as if she cares. I mean . . .'

She babbled on and on while she took the fish fingers out from under the grill and turned them over. I laid out the knives and forks, but my mind sort of switched off and I didn't even check if I'd put them down the right way. I couldn't think straight. He was watching me. The man in the tree. I knew it. Waiting to see how far I'd go, if I'd say the words that were in my head. He could tell exactly what I was thinking.

He knew all about the something bad.

I watched Mam arrange the fish fingers on the plates. She gave us three each and spread them out in a fan shape, tipping a mound of crispy chips beside them. She told me to call the others and they came running, Sandra with Kev in her arms and Mel with a moan on his face because Mam hadn't timed the dinner in line with the programme he was in the middle of watching. He attacked his food, cramming a whole fish finger in his mouth in one go. Mam had to tell him to slow down, that it didn't matter how quickly he ate his dinner, she wasn't going to allow him back in to watch telly until everyone else was finished too. He groaned, looking at my plate and wailing that if he had to wait for me, he wouldn't get to watch anything all evening.

I'd hardly touched my food. It wasn't that I didn't like what Mam had made, it was just that I kept thinking about the reason we were having fish fingers and chips in the first place. It was because Dad wasn't here. And Dad wasn't here because he was, at that very moment, probably 'at it' with Liz Lawless. How could I sit here munching and crunching when all that was going on up in the dark woods?

While Mam was busy making sure Kev got his chips into his mouth instead of on the floor, I signalled to Mel that he could help himself to my dinner if he wanted. His eyes lit up and he slid my food onto his plate, demolishing it in seconds, delighted that he'd managed to get two dinners *and* speed up his return to the telly. He begged to be allowed to bring his dessert in with him and when Mam said, 'All right then, go on', he ran off, with Sandra close behind him carrying their bowls of Angel Delight.

'The Lord save us!' Mam said with a jump when we heard the sitting room door slam. 'Could they be any louder? Thank God your father isn't here. They'd know all about it then.'

I swallowed hard. 'Mam,' I said, feeling the man's eyes on my back. 'I . . . I don't think Dad's off pricing a job.'

'No?' She laughed. 'And where else would he be?'

'I mean . . . not now. Maybe he was earlier on but . . . well . . . I don't think that's where he is now.'

She frowned at me and shook her head. Then Kev spat out a piece of fish finger and mashed his last chip flat on his tray. 'Ah, now, don't be making a mess, you little rascal,' she said.

He smacked his bowl down, then lifted it above his head and flung it on the floor. Mam let out a heavy sigh and leaned down to get it. Her face was all red when she sat back up. 'Now, what were you saying?'

And then it all spilled out.

Everything. The Kiss. The Ramblers. The breath of air. And being 'at it' in the woods in Westgorman.

It didn't take half as long as I'd imagined it would. I'd thought about it so often that it was almost like a poem or a part in a play that I'd rehearsed and knew off by heart. When I finished, Mam's face was even redder, and she kept looking at me in a really weird way, her eyes kind of bouncing in her head, as if someone had turned her upside down and shaken her.

My cheeks burned and I bit the inside of my mouth while I waited for her to speak. I could hear the others laughing and then the telly being turned up really loud. Kev started whinging to get out of his highchair and Mam got up from the table like a robot and plonked a bowl of Angel Delight on his tray. He stuck both his hands in it and splodged a big, pink mess all over his face. She sat back down and stared at him, but didn't tell him off or wipe his face or take the bowl away.

Her eyes wandered all over the room. Up to the ceiling and down to the floor. Over the cupboards and the counters and the table and the wall. Ages went by and I started wondering if I'd actually said anything at all or if I'd only imagined that I'd told her. I was about to smile, almost relieved, when finally she spoke. She sounded so strange; all quiet and far away and dreamy. 'You know,' she said, still looking at the wall like she was in a kind of trance, 'I never really liked that wallpaper. Not really.'

'But . . . you said . . . you loved it,' I said, puzzled, wondering why she was talking about the wallpaper. 'So . . . you were only . . . pretending?'

She started gathering the placemats up. 'Your father picked it out when I was in the hospital. I didn't want to hurt his feelings.'

'Oh.'

A long, loud moan came from the sitting room, followed by a series of screams. Then Sandra came running in, clutching the top of her arm. Mel had punched her several times, she said, because she'd changed the channel. He ran in after her, protesting his innocence, saying she'd started it. Mam got up from the table and took Kev from his highchair. 'Upstairs. All of you,' she said.

'But —' Sandra began.

'Just go.' She handed Kev to me. 'Give him his bath. Then into bed with the lot of you.'

'But Dad's not even home yet! And it's Friday!' Mel whined. 'We always stay up later on Fridays!'

'Regardless of your behaviour?' Mam asked, her voice getting louder and much more cross.

Mel knew not to argue. He gave a big sigh and deliberately shouldered Sandra on his way out the door. 'Now look what you caused,' he said. They were still belting each other as they stomped upstairs.

I hung back, waiting for Mam to say something. Anything. But she just continued clearing the table, then began filling the sink with hot water. Kev laughed in my face and rubbed his sticky fingers in my hair.

'Mam, I—'

'Up you go. Now.' It was her 'no arguments' voice.

I shuffled out of the kitchen and was about to climb the stairs when she came out to the hall. She had her rubber gloves on and a blob of suds wobbled on her cheek. She reached out her arms and I thought she was going to give me a hug, but it was Kev she wanted. She took him from me and squeezed him tight. He clung to her and whimpered, and she rocked him gently, making a kind of muffled, humming sound when she pushed her face in against his neck. Then she kissed him loads of times and stroked his head, sniffing all the time because her nose was runny.

'You're the only one,' she said as she kissed him one more time, her voice all squeaky and cracked. 'The only one.'

I lay awake for ages after I got into bed. Kev had gone down easy; the bath had tired him out and he'd only cried for a couple of minutes before he fell fast asleep. Sandra had hopped into bed with a bag of cotton balls and a bottle of Anne French and had spent about twenty minutes 'cleansing' her face. She kept calling me to show me how much dirt she'd taken off, holding up a cotton ball and saying 'yuck,' every single time. I finally told her I didn't find the subject of her face filth even mildly interesting and when she leaned over and threw one of the used balls at me, the open bottle of lotion slid off her eiderdown and spilled all over the carpet. She blamed me but I got her back by saying it was her and Mel's fault that we'd been sent up to bed in the first place. She said it had to be more than that, that Mam must've been in a bad mood or something to have sent us all up after only a couple of punches.

I suppose I could've told her the reason Mam was in a bad mood, and I did think about it. But I wanted to see what was going to happen once Dad got home. For all I knew, Mam mightn't even say anything to him, at least not straightaway. And there'd be no point going to all the trouble of explaining everything to Sandra unless I really had to. She fell asleep not long after she turned her light out and I lay there with the sound of her breathing filling the room while I strained to hear Dad's key in the front door. I willed myself to stay awake for what seemed like hours, but I fell asleep without hearing him return.

The next morning, Mam was gone. Dad was in the kitchen when I came downstairs. He was 'shaggin'' this and 'bloody' that while he stirred a pot, the smell of burning rising up through the house. Kev sat in his highchair, playing with his plastic cup and spoon.

'Your mother said to give him scrambled eggs,' Dad said when he saw me. 'Shaggin' scrambled! Do you suppose fried would be out of the question?'

'Where is she?' I asked.

'What? Who?'

'Mam! Who else? Where is she?'

'Hmm? Oh, she's . . . she's gone to your Auntie Cissy's for a night or two.' He cracked an egg on the side of the frying pan and cursed when half of it dripped down onto the top of the oven.

'Auntie Cissy's? Why?' They must've had a fight. She must've told him everything I'd said and she'd stormed off. 'She never said anything about going.'

'I know, I know. She just decided on a whim. Said she needed a bit of a break.'

'From . . . what?'

'From you lot! What happened last night, anyway?'

'Um . . . only some punching. The usual stuff. Did she not say?'

'Ah, she didn't go into the ins and outs of it. Just said there'd been trouble. They'll have to be taught a lesson, those two.'

She hadn't told him at all. She'd let on it was the others fighting that had her in bad form.

'So . . . that's why she's gone to Auntie Cissy's?'

'Yep.' He flipped the egg over and put a slice of bread in the toaster.

'Without saying goodbye?'

'She wanted to get the first bus. No point in waking the house, was there?'

'And she left Kev?'

'Looks like it!' he said with a forced sort of laugh, pointing the egg slice at Kev. 'Stuck with you while your mammy's away, aren't we, mister?'

'But what about Easter and all? And who'll mind him if she's not back for Monday?'

'Easter's not till next weekend. She'll be back before then. And if she's not home before I go to work on Monday, well, then you'll just have to look after him yourselves, won't you?'

'Why didn't she take him with her? Will she not miss him?'

'Stop your moaning, Ruth. The one time you're asked to mind your brother and you're complaining.'

'I was only wondering.'

'That's what you call it? Sounds a lot like complaining to me.'

'So . . . if she's not home by Monday, when do you think she'll be back?'

'I don't know! Give the woman some time! It's this sort of thing has her head frazzled. Questions, questions! Just accept it. A bit of responsibility won't do you any harm.'

He whistled about the kitchen, buttering toast, throwing sausages onto the pan, and making tea. He filled the burned pot with hot water and a long squirt of Quix, then slung a tea towel over his shoulder and did a silly dance for Kev. He thought he was being funny but he just looked a bit stupid. He put a sausage and a slice of toast on the table and told me to sit down and eat. I stabbed the sausage with my fork and nibbled at it while I watched Kev trying to stuff his crusts into the pocket of his pyjamas. Dad sat across from me and bit into his toast.

'You must've been home very late last night,' I said.

'I was.'

'Mam said you were pricing a job somewhere.'

'That's right.' He cut his sausages into little pieces.

'So . . . how come it took that long?'

He coughed and took a gulp of tea. 'These things always take time. You can't rush. If you make a mistake, there's no going back on your word. People always hold you to your price.'

'But that long? I mean . . . it must've been way after ten before you got in.'

'Eleven, if you must know.'

'Was Mam really upset about the fighting? What . . . what did she say?'

'Not much. Just that she'd done her best to make you all a nice dinner and that was how you repaid her. By belting the livin' daylights out of each other.'

'It wasn't me, though. I didn't do anything.'

He stopped chewing and pushed his food into his cheek. 'No, you never do, do you? Good as gold. Our little angel.'

I didn't like the way he looked at me. Like he didn't really mean what he'd said.

Mel came into the kitchen in his bare feet and poured himself a bowl of cornflakes. He asked where Mam was and made a face when Dad told him. Sandra arrived down fully dressed and announced she was going into town with Diane

Grogan, her new best friend from the basketball team. Dad took one look at the thick black lines she'd pencilled around her eyes and the scruffy denim jacket she'd borrowed from Diane and said, 'Not looking like that, you're not.'

I managed to slip upstairs during the argument that followed and flopped down on my bed. Why hadn't Mam said anything to Dad about what I'd told her? Maybe she just needed time to think about it all, and what she was going to do. But I felt bad that what I'd said had sent her to Auntie Cissy's. Her house was dark and gloomy and always freezing, even in summer. And Thomas the cat's eye-watering stink was all over the place. He was always miaowing to be let out, clicking over the slippery, cold lino with his tail in the air, showing off his wrinkly bum-hole. If anyone deserved to be staying in that smelly, icy, cave of a house, it was Dad.

And what if Mam decided to stay there for ages? What if she never wanted to see Dad again? What would happen to us?

I lay there wondering if perhaps I shouldn't have said anything at all.

EIGHTEEN

David was back.

I saw him on the green the next day after dinner. I'd taken Kev out for a run while the others did the washing up. With Mam away, Dad had had to do the cooking and had flopped down in his armchair to read the Sunday paper when we were finished eating. Kev was happy I was bringing him outside and he held my hand without moaning. Sunday afternoons in Hillcourt Rise were always quiet; dead, even. I wasn't expecting we'd see anyone. But as we got nearer to the green, I saw a lone figure standing beside a cherry tree. Even though I knew he'd be home from Clonrath for Easter, it was still a bit of a shock to see him after all the weeks he'd been away. He waved when he noticed me but I didn't wave back. Kev pulled free from my grip and raced across the grass, flinging himself at David's long legs and hugging his knees. David held his arms out and took a step backwards, clearly surprised.

'At least someone's pleased to see me,' he said, lifting Kev up and tossing him in the air.

'What did you expect?' I asked. 'Yellow ribbons round the cherry trees?'

'Well, nothing quite that elaborate. But perhaps a smile might've been nice.' Kev clung to his neck and David laughed. 'Unhand me, you fiend! He's a clingy beggar, isn't he?'

I took Kev from him, relieved to have him back in my arms. I didn't like David touching him.

'No more than any little boy,' I said. 'You were probably exactly like him once upon a time. I'm sure your mother would tell you if you asked her.'

'I suppose you think you're being smart,' he said.

'Well, I do think of myself as intelligent, yes.'

'Smart as in sarcastic, I meant. Not smart as in brainy.'

'You can think whatever you like. I was only making a comment,' I said.

'And which mother do you suppose I ask?'

'Whichever one will tell you the truth, I suppose.'

'Unfortunately there's only one that I actually know, so I'll just have to trust her, won't I?'

'Well, you can hardly expect other people to be truthful if you're telling lies yourself,' I said, putting Kev back down on the grass.

'Lies?'

'Yes, lies. Your letter.'

He laid his hand on his chest. 'I didn't lie in my letter. It's the honest to God truth. I swear.'

'I don't believe you. You threw yourself from that tree. I know you were lying when you said you fell. And Shayne's not exactly pleased about what you said.'

'I did ask you not to tell him I wrote.'

'You knew right well I'd tell him. That's what you wanted, wasn't it? Stirring up trouble even from so far away.'

'I thought I could trust you not to say anything. I thought you'd understand.'

Kev was running around me, slapping my legs and pulling at my jeans. I shook him off and he waddled away.

'Understand what?' I asked.

'Not to take everything Shayne says as gospel.'

I watched Kev tottering towards the edge of the green. He flapped his arms and nodded his head, happy in his own little world.

'And what about everything *you* say?' I said. 'How am I supposed to take that?'

'Look, I don't really care, OK? I'm only trying to let you know. I've lived here a lot longer than you and I know what he's like.'

'So, you're looking out for me, is that it? Is that what you're trying to say?'

'Sort of, I suppose. I know you like him. I wouldn't want you to get hurt in any way.'

'I don't know what you mean.'

'Look, I know you fancy him and I—'

'No I don't!' Heat rushed to my cheeks. 'Shayne Lawless?''

'Oh, come on, Ruth. It's obvious!'

I wanted to punch him. He didn't know what he was talking about. Why did everyone think I fancied Shayne? I mean, I didn't hate him or anything, not like I did when we first moved in. I knew he was good-looking and I did feel sort of hot inside whenever I looked at his face, but that didn't mean I fancied him, did it? *Did it?*

It made me mad the way people thought they knew things when they clearly didn't know anything at all.

'Shut up! You don't know what you're talking about. He's a friend, that's all. And you're pissed off because you're not around any more. Well, we're all getting along fine without you, David O'Dea. And if you're trying to warn me off hanging around with Shayne, it's not going to work!'

I shoved my hands in my pockets and stormed over to Kev. David followed after me, his long legs easily keeping up with my strides.

'Everything I wrote in that letter is true,' he said. 'You have to believe me. He's not what you think he is. I thought you of all people would figure that out.'

I looked into his face. 'What do you mean, me "of all people"?'

'You're different to the others around here. I know you are. The very reason you think I'm lying shows that. You don't accept everything you're told. You're always looking for the truth that lies underneath.'

Was he being serious or was he mocking me? I wasn't sure. But it shocked me that he knew me so well.

He touched my arm. 'But this time, Ruth, you've got it wrong.'

The way he looked at me made me feel hollow. Like I had no brain to think with, no heart to feel with. Could he really be telling the truth?

And if he was, did that mean everything Shayne had told me was a lie?

I had a million questions. I opened my mouth, not knowing which one I was going to ask. But another voice spoke before mine.

'Yer back.'

David let his hand fall from my arm. Shayne bumped his bike over the kerb then threw it down on the grass.

'I . . . yes . . . looks like it,' David said, his eyes moving between my face and Shayne's. His voice had changed. 'Glad to see me, I presume?'

'Glad to see ye? Can't wait to see the back of ye. And ye needn't be writin' to anyone else about me, ye hear? If ye want to say stuff, say it to me fuckin' face, right?'

'I can write to whom so ever I choose, I'll have you know.'

Shayne screwed his face up. 'Whom so ever? *Whom so ever*? What the fuckin' hell does that mean?'

'*Who*ever then. I can write to *who*ever I choose. Perhaps that offends you less?'

'Why can't ye just talk English?'

Kev came over and whined at me. I picked him up. His

trousers were damp from the wet grass.

'You understand me, don't you, Ruth?' David asked.

'I . . . I . . . sometimes,' I stammered.

Shayne grinned and jabbed a finger into David's chest. 'See! I'm not the only one. Even she hasn't a fuckin' clue what you're on about half the time.'

'I'll thank you not to lay a hand on me again,' David said, his voice shaky now.

'Thank me, would ye? Ye can thank me all ye like but ye won't stop me punchin' yer fuckin' face in if I want to.'

David clenched his fists but kept them down by his sides. Shayne spat on the ground and puffed out his chest. He pushed his shoulders back and stepped forward, narrowing his eyes and tossing his hair away from his face.

'Go on, then, hit me if it'll make you happy,' David said. He tensed his jaw and a bulgy vein at the side of his right eye throbbed.

Shayne tilted his head to one side as if he was thinking about his next move. Then his fist shot straight out and he landed a loud smack on David's open mouth. David barely flinched. Then he lashed back, punching Shayne's forehead with his right hand and throwing a dig to his stomach with his left. Shayne staggered back a few steps, clearly surprised at the speed and sharpness of David's reaction.

Then they came at each other, arms swinging and legs kicking, loud grunts escaping from their mouths as they rained punches down on one another's bodies. Shayne managed to get David in a headlock, pushing his arm hard against his neck. But David jabbed him fiercely in the ribs with his elbow and hooked his foot around Shayne's leg. Shayne released his grip and David lurched forward then swung around, launching the full weight of his body against Shayne's side, toppling him to the ground. He lay like a beetle on his back, arms and legs grappling in the air. David paused for a split second and Shayne rolled over and tried to get up. He wasn't quick enough. David pointed his toe and, with all the force he could gather, drove his foot into Shayne's back. Then he did it again. And again.

Shayne writhed and squealed, 'Fuck off, ye filthy lookin' bastard ye! Get off me. Get off ye fuckin' bollocks!'

All this time, Kev was in my arms, watching the scene unfold with curiosity. At first he pointed and laughed, and although I knew I shouldn't have let him see, I was as fascinated as he was and couldn't bring myself to walk away. But his wonder turned to fear when Shayne started to yell and his little body stiffened in my arms. Despite being less than two years old, he knew that what was happening wasn't right.

The fight continued. They rolled about on top of one another, thumping and kicking and belting. I called out for them to stop, my voice sounding weak and useless against the scuffle. Shayne had David pinned to the ground, straining to get at his neck. David struggled to keep his hands away, at one point catching the flesh of Shayne's arm in his teeth. I started to run, holding Kev's head close to my neck. If I couldn't get them to stop, I'd have to get Dad to help. But I'd only got to the edge of the green when I saw him, running towards me, his eyes all dark and fierce.

'Christalshagginmighty! Is it the bloody *zoo* we're living in or what? Didn't I *tell* you to keep away from that . . . that . . .' He sped past, yelling over his shoulder at me to take Kev home. But I stood rooted, scared at how angry he was, how he ranted and raved. 'Animals!' he shouted when he reached the fight. 'Bloody *animals*! That's enough, you hear me!' He kicked out at David and Shayne. 'You're like a pair of dogs! Have you no shame?'

'Fuck off!' Shayne shouted. 'It's none of yer business!'

Dad was furious. 'You think you can speak to me like that, you little pup?'

'I'll say what I like. Ye can't stop me.'

David saw an opening and punched Shayne on the chin. Dad tried to muscle his way between them to break them apart, but got elbowed in the ribs. He slipped on the damp grass and toppled onto the two of them, his shoulder slamming into David's face as he fell. David hit out, trying to push him away, and Shayne began kicking at Dad's legs. Dad grabbed Shayne's T-shirt and twisted the neck of it till his fist was shoved right up under his chin. Then David dived on Shayne, grabbing his hair and slamming his head onto the ground.

'For the love of *Jaysus*!' Dad cried out, trying again to push his body in between them. He managed to shoulder David away and ended up sort of straddling Shayne on all fours.

Shayne looked up at him with disgust, set his mouth into a snarl and headbutted Dad right across the eyes. Dad reeled, moaned and fell back to the ground, lying flat on his back with his hands on his face.

Shayne scrambled to his feet, his hair wild and flapping all about his head. He smoothed his T-shirt and shook his jeans back down to his ankles, a sideways grin on his lips. David sat up with his legs bent, resting his arms on his knees, breathing heavily. His right eye was puffy and the cheek underneath was swollen and pink. For a few moments, nobody spoke. Then Kev took his finger out of his mouth and pointed.

'Daddy down,' he said.

'Did I not tell you to take him home?' Dad said, screwing his face up in pain and easing himself into a sitting position.

'I . . . Are . . . are you all right?' I asked.

'Of course I am!' he said, frowning up at me. 'Of course I'm all right! You hardly think this pair of . . . of . . . bowsies could get the better of me?'

Shayne laughed. 'Bowsies? Yer some old man, you know that?'

Dad leapt to his feet and leaned into Shayne's face. 'Old man? Old man, is it? I'll . . . I'll . . .' He held his fist an inch from Shayne's chin, leaving it hovering for a second before taking it down and slapping it against his own thigh. 'Waste of time trying to get through to the likes of you.' He turned to David. 'And I'd have thought better of you. What'll your friend Father Feely say when he hears about this? He won't be too pleased, will he? After all his efforts getting you into that fancy school.'

He came over and took Kev from me and I noticed his nose had begun to swell. 'Now do you see why I told you to stay away from him?' he said. 'This is the real Shayne Lawless you're seeing here. Vicious thug.' He started walking. 'Come on. We're going home.'

'Yeah, go on. Ye big coward, ye,' Shayne called after us. 'Don't know what me ma sees in ye.'

Dad stopped dead. Then he turned and made a run at him. Kev was scared as he bobbed up and down in Dad's arms. 'You see him?' Dad growled to Shayne when he reached him. 'This little boy? Look at his face. *Look at it!*' He shook his head and sneered. 'This was you once upon a time, you know. Now look at you. What the shaggin' hell went wrong?'

'What the fuck are ye talkin' about?' Shayne roared. 'Think yer such a great da, don't ye? Think the sun shines out of yer precious baby's arse. I don't give a shit what ye think. What any of youse think! I FUCKIN' HATE THE WHOLE LOT OF YOUSE!'

He picked up his bike and got ready to swing his leg over but David got to his feet and held onto the handlebars. 'Wait. Don't go yet. Hang on. Look, I . . . I'm sorry for, you know, the letter and stuff. I didn't mean anything by it. I was only trying to . . .' He looked at Dad. 'We're sorry, Mr Lamb. Everything got out of hand.'

'We're *sorry*?' Dad said. 'You needn't be apologizing for him, do you hear? He can speak for himself.'

Shayne shrugged and spat but said nothing.

'Well, you know what?' Dad said. 'I don't want your shaggin' apology anyway. You can stuff it up—'

'Shayne and I would've sorted it out, Mr Lamb,' David cut in. 'We've always sorted things out by ourselves before.'

'Oh, really? I can see how you'd have sorted it out all right,' Dad yelled. 'You wouldn't have been happy till one of you was half shaggin' *dead*! You're a disgrace, you know that? An absolute disgrace!' He stroked Kev's head as he spoke. 'I'd be ashamed of my life if any son of mine ever behaved like that. It's your fathers I feel sorry for. God help them. What did they ever do to deserve the likes of you? I've a good mind to . . . to . . .' He trailed off, shaking his head and gulping, knowing straightaway he'd put his foot in it.

'To what, Mr Lamb?' David said, his face drained of colour, his voice flat and grave. 'You've a good mind to what? Have a word with them? Have a word with our fathers?' He nodded at Kev. 'Your dear little angel might not grow up like me and Shayne, if you're lucky. But he's had a bit of an advantage right from the start, hasn't he? At least he knows who his father is.'

Shayne stayed silent. His mouth hung open as if he wasn't sure what had just happened, but his gaze grew tight and steely and he stared over at Dad. David caught my eye and my breath quickened, wheezing in and out of my chest so fast I could hardly catch it. His jaw clenched as he bit down hard, and behind the mask of his face, I could tell his whole insides were on fire.

Dad didn't reply to David's words. There was no way back from what he'd said. And I knew there wasn't a hope in hell he'd say sorry. He wasn't going to let them think they'd won. He reached up and touched his swollen nose, then turned and walked away. I followed after him, watching Kev's head resting on his shoulder. Before we got to the house, I looked back and saw the two boys still standing on the green where we'd left them, their bodies dark, rigid shapes against the bright green growth of new grass.

Bridie came out her front door as I passed. 'Just waiting for Majella,' she said, fussing at the lacy scarf around her neck and trying to sound all important. 'We're off to the Westgorman Park Hotel for afternoon tea.' She obviously hadn't seen the fight. 'Kevin's getting as big as a house. Saw your daddy bringing him in there. Mammy away again, is she?' I gave her a thin smile; I wasn't going to give anything away. She frowned but then Majella's car appeared in the cul-de-sac and she gave a little yelp, teetering down the drive in her too-tight shoes.

Dad handed Kev to me as soon as I stepped into the hall. 'Your mother phoned earlier on,' he said, his voice all flat and grim. 'I'm going to collect her now. Can I trust you to look after your brother for an hour or so?'

I nodded.

'And I want to talk to you when we get back.'

I didn't need to be told what it'd be about.

Kev bawled when Dad left. I could tell it was because of the fight. It wasn't his usual cry – the screechy, whiny one that made me want to plug my ears and dive into the hall cupboard. It was more like what you'd call sobbing or weeping, and his eyes were filled with a sadness I'd never seen in him before. It was like he'd just figured out there were other people in the world besides himself, and he wasn't the only one who could feel pain. He looked more like Dad than ever, and as the tears streaked down his cheeks, it was almost like watching Dad cry.

The others had been told to hoover the sitting room and give the place a general tidy up before Mam came back, and they knew from the tone of Dad's voice not to argue. They didn't know about the fight but Sandra said Dad's nose looked funny and she asked what had happened. I wasn't in the mood for explaining so I said I'd tell her about it later.

I had a feeling that a lot of things would be out in the open once Mam and Dad came back from Auntie Cissy's.

I couldn't calm Kev. No matter how many faces I pulled or toys I showed him or funny noises I made, he continued to cry. After a while, his sobs turned shivery, rippling through his body and causing loud, shuddery sounds to escape from his throat. I knew the only thing that might make him stop would be to put him in his pushchair and take him for a walk. The appearance of a dog or a flock of birds was usually enough to have him smiling again. I told the others I was going and they looked relieved; even the hoover didn't mask the sound of Kev's crying.

It was beginning to get a bit chilly, but by the time I realized it, I'd reached the top of the lane and I figured it was too late to go back to get Kev's coat. I knew it'd be dark soon anyway so we wouldn't be out for long. As the pushchair rattled down the lane, the sight of a scrawny black cat put a smile on Kev's face and he finally began to quieten down.

All sorts of thoughts ran through my mind. I wondered what Mam and Dad would talk about on the car journey home. Would Mam sit there in silence, holding all the things I'd said about Dad and Liz inside, making Dad ask her what the shaggin' hell was wrong? Would Dad tell her about the fight on the green, leaving out the bit where Shayne said he didn't know what his ma saw in him? Or maybe he'd say nothing and just pretend he'd been horsing around with Kev and that's how he'd got the bump on his nose. And I thought about how it'd all be different once they came home. Dad had said he wanted to have a talk.

The truth – whatever it was – was going to come out. I knew it.

Things had gone too far to be kept secret now.

I walked through Churchview Park then out onto the path that ran around the church grounds and, before I realized it, I was heading through the gates of the graveyard. Kev was asleep now, his head lolling to one side and his arms and legs dangling out of the pushchair like a rag doll. I knew Mam would probably go mad because I'd allowed him to fall asleep so late in the day, but the poor thing was exhausted from all the crying and he needed a bit of a rest.

The graveyard was deserted. All the Sunday visitors had long gone. Fresh flowers had been left at the graves: cellophaned bouquets of pink roses; bunches of bluebells and buttercups stuffed into jam jars; wreaths of red and white carnations. The air was soaked with the scent of them all and as I pushed Kev past the rows of grey headstones, it was as if we were cutting through a thick mist of expensive perfume. I breathed it in deeply, its sweetness rushing up my nostrils, filling my lungs and filtering up to my brain. It made me kind of light-headed and woozy, and my legs wobbled slightly as I walked deeper into the middle of the graveyard. I turned a corner and stopped beside a tree, its branches like an umbrella over my head. Closing my eyes, I leaned against the thick trunk, feeling the hard, knobbled bark pressing into my back.

Everything was going to change once I got back home. There'd be no pretending any more. The wave of something bad was almost on the shore now. I could feel it. I could hear it. I could sense it in the air. It was going to crash down once Mam and Dad came in the door and our lives would never be the same again. Even if Mam hadn't told Dad what I'd said, she wouldn't be able to keep it inside for ever. It would all have to come out.

Kev shifted and gave a little moan. I opened my eyes. It was beginning to get dark and the air was getting colder so I slipped off my cardigan and draped it over his legs. He smiled in his sleep and I touched his cheek and, at that moment, I pictured Mam's face the last time she'd held him, after I'd told her about Dad and Liz. She'd said he was 'the only one' and I wondered what she'd meant. Maybe that he was the only one of us who didn't give her any trouble, the only one she could depend on not to cause her any grief. The only one she could count on not to make her sad.

I passed by Dick Goggin's 'final resting place', as Bridie called it, with its newly laid layer of fine blue-grey stones and cement vase of red plastic roses at the base of its headstone. 'Because they don't wither, dear,' Bridie had told me when I'd asked her why she kept fake roses on Dick's grave even in summer, when she could've picked bunches of real ones from her own garden. They were better than nothing though. Lots of graves had been forgotten about, their headstones casting black shadows across their flowerless stone beds.

Only minutes had passed since I entered the graveyard, but already a murky dusk was filtering down from the sky, turning the air grainy and making it hard to see. It was time to head for home. A clammy dampness descended all around as I made my way towards the gates. I shivered. I looked down at Kev. He was still fast asleep, slumped down with his head on his chest. But his legs were bare. My cardigan had slipped off and was nowhere to be seen. Though I thought about leaving it and going back to find it the next day, I didn't want Kev to be cold. And it was my fault he didn't have his coat in the first place. So I left him at the side of the path and started walking back.

For the first time ever, I was scared in the graveyard. Maybe because it was getting dark or maybe because of what I knew was going to happen once I got home. There was a heaviness in the air, a dull kind of pressure that made things less clear. My eyes were cloudy and my ears were muffled and the path felt sort of spongy beneath my feet. The light had almost gone and colours were fading. I thought I could see my cardigan lying at the edge of the path ahead, but when I ran up, it was only a clump of weeds.

Things began to swirl. Shapes swam together in twisting, blurry spirals. And then I could see shadows: waving through the trees, sliding across the ground, slipping in between the headstones. Kev would have to put up with the cold; I was going home. But as I turned, I saw something.

A movement. A slight shuffle. A figure.

Someone was standing beside a cross.

A man. Rigid and frozen like a statue, his face turned up to the sky.

I slunk down behind a headstone for a closer look.

The shape of him was dark and bulky against the white of the cross. As I watched him, I felt myself drain. After all that had happened, I was tired. I pressed my cheek against the smooth, cold headstone and knew that he wanted me there. That his presence meant something. Then he snapped his head around and stared at me, the black holes of his eyes holding my gaze. Like he'd known all along I was there.

He was bleeding me. Of all my thoughts and memories and pictures.

All the laughter. All the colour. All the life.

Then slowly he turned and spread his arms wide. His big black coat opened up and I gasped out loud at what I saw: a dark red shirt; mucky brown trousers; big black boots with straps and silver buckles.

It was him.

The man in the tree. The one I'd drawn on the kitchen wall. The one I'd seen the day Kev had been born.

Kev . . .

I felt my insides burning, freezing, burning, my bones scorching raw under my flesh. In a blind dread, I clambered back between headstones and crosses, tripping over a grave edge, falling hard, scraping my hands and knees. As I crawled back down to the path, the sound of birdsong echoed all around. Sharp and stinging, like poison in my ears.

I tried to convince myself as I ran that the falling darkness was playing tricks with my eyes. That the pushchair really was still there. That I could see it. And Kev too. His little legs twitching . . . his eyelids flickering as he dreamt . . .

Please.

Please, please, please.

Seconds passed like hours . . . Days . . . For ever.

But I knew.

Kev was gone.

I ran up and down, spinning around, stupidly hoping I'd made a mistake about where I'd left him.

But there was no mistake.

He'd been wheeled away.

Trembling, I tried to find tracks in the dusty grit of the path. But the light had faded . . . Tears swam in my eyes . . . I could barely see.

I didn't know what to do. The world I knew was whirling round my head like a tornado.

Where was I going? Why couldn't I do more than run?

I should've been screaming. Kicking, yelling, punching. Tearing down the walls. Toppling the headstones and crosses. Unearthing everything in my way.

And then I was outside the graveyard, running past the high stone wall. The dark branches of the copper beech towered above my head, scribbling and scratching against the blue-drained sky.

I reached the churchyard gates and heaved my weight against them.

They wouldn't budge. The latch was locked on the inside.

I pushed my hand through the bars and tried to flick it open.

It was no use. My fingers could barely stretch to touch it. But the gates had been open when I'd passed them earlier. They were always open. Why were they closed now?

I couldn't see anything through them but dark shadows.

No life. No movement. No Kev.

I tried to climb over them but they were far too high. And even if I could, what if I didn't find anything on the other side?

I might be wasting precious time. Whoever had Kev could be halfway to Westgorman by now. Or on a bus into town. Or in a car headed to . . . anywhere.

'Kev! Kev!' I yelled, rattling and kicking at the gates.

I kept calling and calling but there was nothing. Not a sound. Just a deep, black, empty silence.

I strained my ears for something . . . anything . . . and then I heard the weak sound of crying coming from . . . from where, I wasn't sure.

It grew louder and stronger and more familiar, and I almost laughed as I yelled Kev's name and waited for him to come running out from the shadows of the copper beech to find me.

But my voice, when I heard it, was quivery and strange and I struck my head against the cold bars of the gate when I realized the crying I'd heard was my own.

Help. I needed help. 'Help!' I screamed as I ran. 'Help!'

Someone else could do this. I didn't want to. All I wanted was to sink down into my bed, soft and warm and sleepy, and then to wake up and find it was all a dream. A stupid dream.

What are you talking about? Mam would say. *Kev's here. Kept me up half the night, didn't you, you little monkey?* And he'd snuggle his face into her neck and she'd squeeze him tight and smile.

I was in the lane now and still I hadn't seen a soul. I burst out into Hillcourt Rise, my footsteps loud and hard, echoing out over the rooftops. Then the noise of them stopped as I belted across the green, the grass soft and squishy under my feet.

How could the houses look the same as they always did? With lamplight filtering through curtain cracks, and chimneys puffing smoke into the night sky? I wanted to bang down the doors. Roar in everyone's face. Drag them from their armchairs and punch them out into my world.

Didn't they know? Didn't they know Kev was gone?

I ran into the cul-de-sac. I slammed into our front door and held my finger on the bell. My eyes were on fire, my mouth was dry. I was sure I was going to throw up.

I fell into the hall when Mel answered, unable to speak. I wasn't even sure I remembered how to. 'What's wrong?' he asked. 'What happened?' He grabbed my arm and shook me. 'What is it? Tell me, Ruth! *What*?'

I lay on the floor, hugging my knees to my chest. How was I going to say it? How long ago was it? I didn't know how many minutes had passed. Five? Ten? I'd no idea.

It seemed like I'd known a whole lifetime.

'What is it? God, Ruth! What happened? Are you OK? Where's Kev?' It was Sandra, her hand reaching down to take mine. Her grip was strong and safe. The touch of living flesh against my own was like a slap that brought me round. She helped me to my feet and I stood facing the two of them, my stomach rolling, my legs shaking, my body not my own any more.

I opened my mouth . . . and Mam came through the door.

'There you are!' she smiled, all bright and cheerful. She rustled a plastic bag in front of our faces. 'Cissy sent over your

Easter eggs. Big ones they are, too. They're all different but she told me whose was whose, so there'll be no arguments over them, all right?' She studied our faces. 'All right?'

Then Dad came whistling in, swinging his keys around his finger.

'Something's wrong,' Sandra said. 'Something's wrong with Ruth.'

Mam looked at me. 'Right,' she said, her voice more matter-of-fact. She handed the bag to Sandra. 'You and Mel go into the sitting room. And no trying to get at the eggs. They're not to be opened till Easter Sunday.'

'But—' Sandra began, her voice desperate.

'But nothing! Just put them on the sideboard and sit down quietly. I hardly have to order you to watch television, do I?'

They did as she said and I was left standing there. Time was ticking. And still I was the only one who knew Kev was gone.

'Look, Ruth,' Mam said, her voice all soft and kind. 'All this stuff about your father and Liz Lawless. It's . . . it's, well, it's all rubbish, love. None of it's true.'

Dad's face was stern, but not cross, and he sort of half-smiled as he nodded. 'I'm sorry, love, but your mother's right. It's my fault in a way. I should've told you ages ago. You got the wrong end of the stick. I—'

'Stop, Dad,' I managed to whisper, tears running down my face. I didn't care what he was saying. Not now. I wasn't even sure I understood what he was talking about.

He put his arm around my shoulder. 'It's all right. No crying, you hear? Everything's going to be OK. Don't be feeling bad. You weren't to know.'

'We had a good talk on the way home,' Mam said. 'We know you thought you were doing the right thing telling me. And I should've said last night I knew it wasn't true. But . . . I don't know . . . just hearing that thing about the woods, it put doubt in my mind.' She looked at Dad. 'It shouldn't have, but when your daughter comes out with something like that, it . . . well . . . it knocks you for six. And I don't know why, but I felt I had to get away for a night. I'm sorry, love. Me going off like that probably made it all a whole lot worse. I'm sure you thought it was the end of the world.'

'I told your mother about the fight on the green earlier too,' Dad said. 'You see now why I wanted you to stay away from that gurrier? God only knows what he's capable of. I can only—'

'Kev's gone.'

Mam's chin went back and she looked at me all confused. Then her eyebrows shot up. 'Now, see here, if this is another one of your . . . your—'

'We were in the graveyard. I only left him for a minute!' My head was pounding. I thought I was going to faint.

'The graveyard? What were you doing there?' she asked. 'And what do you mean he's gone? Gone where? He's all right, isn't he?'

'I . . . I don't know! I don't know where he is. I ran home all the way! I tried to get into the churchyard to see if they took him there but the gate was locked and it was too high to climb over and it was all dark and I—'

'Hold on. Slow down.' Dad let his arm fall from my shoulder. 'You mean . . . someone . . . took him? Someone took Kev? When? When, Ruth?' He grabbed my arms and shook me. 'How long ago?'

'I don't know! Just now. Fifteen minutes, maybe twenty. I'm not sure.'

'*Jesus Christ almighty*! Holy Mother of God!' Mam covered her mouth with her hand. 'Jesus, Mick! Call the guards! Jesus *Christ*! What are we going to do?'

Dad had already picked up the phone. 'Did you see anyone? Was there anyone around? Anyone in the graveyard?'

'No. No one,' I said. 'Just some old man, that's all.'

'What old man? What did he look like?'

'Like . . . like . . . I don't know! Like some old tramp.'

'Think, Ruth!' Mam said through her tears. 'You have to remember!' Dad was talking into the phone now. 'Tell them, Mick,' she cried. 'Tell them she saw someone there. Jesus, Ruth, what was he like? The guards will want to know.'

'It wasn't him! He didn't take him!'

'How do you know? If there was no one else around he—'

'No! Someone took Kev when I was watching the man!'

'*Watching* him? *Why*, for God's sake? It was more important to spy on some old tramp than keep an eye on your baby brother?' She collapsed onto the stairs in a heap, her head in her hands. 'We have to go and look for him. Mick?

Mick? Are the guards coming? Are they on their way?'

'A couple of minutes. Said they'll be here as fast as they can.'

'What's going on? What's wrong?' Mel appeared, with Sandra right behind him.

Dad told them. Mel went white and Sandra burst into tears.

'This man, start writing down what he looked like,' Dad said, scrabbling for a pen in the hall table drawer.

'I don't need to! I know what he was like. But it wasn't him!'

'*Do it!*' he shouted. 'Just do what you're told! Don't cause any more trouble than you already have!'

I grabbed the pen from his fingers and flung it on the floor. 'I don't need to write it down, OK?' I screamed. 'If you really want to know, I'll show you!'

I ran into the kitchen and shoved the table away from the wall. They all followed me in and watched as I reached down and found the edge of the wallpaper, scraping at it with my nails till I had a grip on one corner. Then I pulled it up and away from the wall in one long, narrow strip. Then another. And another. Each one revealing a part of the man. His boots, his legs, his body.

No one said a word.

I found the blackbird with his yellow eye and the notes coming out of his beak. Then the tree trunk, the leaves, the branches.

Then I finally found the man's face, and even though I hadn't looked at it that day in the park, it was exactly the face of the man in the graveyard.

'There,' I said, crying. 'That's him.'

'That's *crazy*,' Mel said. '*How*? You did that when Mam was in the hospital! That was ages ago! How could it be him? You mean you've seen him before?'

'I . . . I think so. But . . . maybe I imagined him. I don't know! But I know he didn't do it. Maybe it was some sort of warning or something. Maybe he—'

'Shut up, Ruth!' Mam roared at me. '*Shut up, shut up, shut up!*' She slapped me across the face, then started thumping me with her fists, screaming and wailing. 'Warning you? *About what, for God's sake? About what?*'

Then Dad ran to answer the door. The guards had arrived.

NINETEEN

They took one look at Mam and told Dad to phone for Dr
Crawley. He didn't want to but they insisted. They said it
was for the best. The situation 'called for calm', and the most
important thing was getting all the facts together. It couldn't
be done properly with Mam 'in that state'. Dr Crawley came
in minutes and gave her something that made her all drowsy
and quiet and Dad helped her upstairs to bed.

There were two guards – big, tall men with country
accents and unhurried movements – and they tried to make
us feel that we weren't really in the middle of a disaster, that
everything was going to be all right if we simply let them do
their job. It kind of worked in a way. While they were speaking
to me, asking me the same questions over and over, Dad lit
a cigarette, Sandra put the kettle on and made sandwiches

without being asked, and Mel even went back to watching telly. I suppose it helped to do normal things; it wouldn't have done any good if we'd all been tearing around screaming our heads off like Mam. I couldn't get the image of her mad face out of my mind. I'd managed to avoid most of her thumps by holding my arms over my head, but my cheek was stinging from where she'd slapped me.

One of the guards asked Dad about the bruise on his nose and Dad said it was nothing, just the result of some 'horseplay'. They both nodded silently and there was an awkward kind of pause, then one of them wrote something down in his notebook. Dad puffed nervously on his cigarette and asked if he shouldn't be out searching for Kev, but the guards said they already had that under control and it was more important for him to stay with his family.

It wasn't long before Bridie came to the door. The guards wouldn't let her in but she managed to extract enough information to understand roughly what had happened. Then Mel came into the kitchen to tell us a large crowd had gathered on the green.

When I showed the guards the man on the wall, they rubbed their chins and nodded again, asking if I was positive this was an 'accurate representation', but making no remark about the fact that his picture was on our wall or about all the bits of stripped wallpaper on the floor. No matter how many times I told them I was sure he wasn't the one who took Kev, they just ignored me. They quizzed me again and again about the 'suspicious individual', making me repeat everything I'd already told them. They spoke to me as if I was a little kid, and far too young to understand the way they had it all figured out.

When they said they were finished with me for the time being, they spoke quietly to Dad while I sat at the table, biting the inside of my cheek and shaking my head at the ham sandwich Sandra was pushing towards me.

Dad tried to light another cigarette, striking match after match that fizzled out or snapped in half. He growled in the back of his throat, crushing the cigarette in his fingers and flinging the matchbox across the room. The guards made him sit down, telling Sandra and me to go and watch telly with Mel. I was about to protest but Dad gave me such a look I knew it wouldn't be a good idea, so I kept my mouth shut and slid down off my chair.

Mel was slumped on the couch, staring at *Little House on the Prairie*. I felt like kicking the screen in when I saw Pa and Laura trekking off in the wagon with stupid smiles all over their faces. Sandra went to the window and looked out through the dark at the crowd on the green.

'Everyone's out there,' she said, beginning to cry again. 'Why aren't we? We should be looking for Kev.'

'The guards said they're already out looking for him,' I said.

'But we should be with them! He's going to be so scared when they find him. He'll need someone he knows to calm him down.'

'How do you know they're even going to find him?' Mel asked, looking at me. 'He shouldn't have gone missing in the first place.'

'Of course they'll find him!' Sandra said, coming away from the window. 'A little boy can't just disappear!'

The door opened and one of the guards called me out. Dad was standing at the front door. 'Get your coat on,' he said, his voice low and grave. 'Sergeant Pearce is coming to take us to the churchyard.'

Mel and Sandra poked their heads round the sitting room door.

'It's all right,' Dad told them. 'You two stay here with the guards. We have to go down to the . . . the graveyard for a little while, so Ruth can show us where Kev was when he . . . We'll be back shortly.'

A car pulled up, driven by a young guard, with the sergeant in the passenger seat. Dad looked straight ahead and swallowed hard before telling me the station had radioed in to say a pushchair had been found in the churchyard, at the base of the copper beech.

It started to drizzle as we drove alongside the green, and the throng that had gathered huddled together in small groups. Geraldine stared at us as she pulled the hood of her anorak up. Paddy half raised his arm in a sort of wave. Mona turned away, as if she was afraid we might catch her eye. I glanced over towards her house and saw that the curtains had been opened. Through the window, I saw David at his piano, practising away in a pool of yellow lamplight, his head bent in concentration. Dad saw him too and we exchanged a look in the back of the car. I knew from his face that I wasn't the only one who thought it was strange. A lump rose at the back of my throat and I swallowed it down, remembering the day he'd taken Kev from outside the shops . . .

To get to the churchyard by car, we had to go down the hill towards the village and take the road that went up behind Churchview Park. As we slowed down to turn the corner, we spotted Liz coming out of The Ramblers with Vic. The path was sort of greasy from the rain and one of her heels skidded on the slippery concrete. She let out a yelp and grabbed onto Vic, yanking him halfway to the ground. They steadied themselves then started to laugh and plonked down on one of the low windowsills, where Vic kissed her on the cheek and she gave him a playful slap on the arm. I wondered how she could seem to be so happy with a man who was beating her up. She caught sight of me in the back of the police car and her slitty eyes followed us as we drove on up the road. Dad opened his mouth to say something but closed it again when Sergeant Pearce turned around and smiled at me, saying, 'This won't take long. We'll have you back home in no time.'

Could I really believe what Mam and Dad had said when they came in from Aunty Cissy's? That there was nothing going on between Dad and Liz? That I'd 'got the wrong end of the stick'? Mam said she knew what I'd said about Dad and

Liz wasn't true, but hearing the stuff about the woods had put doubt in her mind. That was why she'd wanted to get away for the night, she said. Maybe to put a bit of fear into Dad and let him sweat while she decided whether she believed it or not. So that meant that if I'd said nothing about The Kiss, or the woods, or anything, just kept my mouth shut, she wouldn't have gone to Auntie Cissy's at all.

She'd have been home with us.

We might even have gone out for the day somewhere, for a drive up the mountains maybe. But she'd gone, and Dad had to make the dinner and he'd been exhausted afterwards and had made me take Kev out on the green and then he'd got into that fight. And Kev was so upset and I couldn't calm him so I'd taken him out for the walk . . .

If Mam had been there . . . If she'd only been there . . .

She'd have been able to comfort Kev. She wouldn't have let me take him out so late in the day when it was getting cold and nearly dark . . .

It was all very well saying to myself that I'd kind of known all along about the something bad, but now it was starting to dawn on me that I might've actively played a part in making it happen.

When we got to the churchyard, the drizzle had turned into proper rain and we got soaked as we walked from the car, through the gates and across the grass towards the copper beech. It was completely dark now; I could hardly see a thing. I wished Dad would reach out and take hold of my hand. He sniffed and cleared his throat, then asked the sergeant if no one had thought to bring a torch.

The sergeant called up ahead to the guards who'd made the find, 'Give us some light there, lads', and a white shaft cut through the blackness, the spitting raindrops in its beam glowing like a million bits of splintered glass. Under the spreading branches of the copper beech, two guards stood beside a pushchair and I knew from yards away that it was definitely Kev's. I nodded when the sergeant asked if I was sure, the tears starting again.

'Don't touch it!' he said when I tried to grip the handle. Then he smiled at me and softened his face. 'Not for the moment, anyway. We'll get it back to you as soon as we can.'

The copper beech gave us some shelter, but the rain gathered on up the leaves and, every few seconds, big blobs of water splashed down to the ground. The torchlight filtered part of the way up, lighting the undersides of the twisted branches, making them show silvery grey against the tarry-black layer of the sky beyond.

Had Shayne really pushed David? Was he capable of something as bad as that? Who was telling the truth? And in the middle of all that was happening, did I even care?

The sergeant seemed to think it was a good sign that Kev's pushchair had been found. I heard him saying to Dad that it showed whoever had taken him couldn't have gone too far, because it'd be difficult to carry him a long distance. I didn't agree. It didn't really prove anything. And just because Kev might've been close by, it didn't mean he was going to be OK. I knew the sergeant was only saying it to make Dad feel better.

The guard with the torch came with us back to the car. The beam jigged about as he walked, lighting up the gates, bouncing off the stone wall, and showing up flashes of glistening wet grass under our feet. And when it zig-zagged over the soft ground in front of the Virgin Mary in her grotto, I noticed, criss-crossing the earth, the twisty, twirly pattern of bicycle tracks.

David was still at his piano when we drove back into Hillcourt Rise, his head and shoulders jerking as he played, and his hands moving fast up and down the keys. It was creepy the way he was practising when everyone else was out on the green. It didn't seem right. Like he was trying too hard to be normal. Dad didn't notice him this time; he was staring out at the growing crowd on the green. Liz and Vic had joined it, along with people I recognized from Churchview Park and Cherrywood, as well as a few guards who stood with their arms crossed, slightly apart from the rest of the gathering. Everyone turned their heads as we passed.

'What are they shaggin' well looking at?' Dad asked. 'And what are they all doing out there anyway? They're no use to anyone hanging around in the rain.'

'Human nature,' Sergeant Pearce said. 'Just showing their concern.'

'*Concern*? Wouldn't it be more in their line to be out searching? Trying to find him? What good is it standing there?'

'Our men are out in force already, Mick.' He turned around to face us. 'Garda units from all over the city, checkpoints, tracker dogs, the lot. Descriptions of the suspicious individual have been circulated. House searches will start shortly. We'll call in the assistance of a volunteer team as soon as we feel it's warranted.'

'It's warranted *now*, surely? It's been over two hours! He's not even two years old, for God's sake!' Dad rattled at the car door in a panic. 'I have to get out! What am I doing just sitting here? This is bloody crazy!'

'Take it easy, Mick. We're doing all we can. We have to . . . go at this the right way. You understand that, don't you?'

Dad thumped the sergeant's seat. '*He's only a little boy*! Do you understand? It's dark and cold and raining, and he's only a little boy!'

'I know, I know. Just . . . take it easy, all right? Keep it together for the sake of . . .' He glanced in my direction.

Dad's breath shuddered in his chest and I knew he understood what the sergeant meant. I laid my hand on the seat, expecting him to reach across and take it, but he turned away and stared out the window.

'You two go on inside now,' the sergeant said when the car pulled up at our house. 'I'll follow you in. I'm going to radio in and get the latest.' He caught my hand as I was getting out. 'Good girl,' he said, trying to smile. 'I'm sure we'll have him back to you in no time.'

Dad smoothed his hair down then wiped his hands over his face when we walked in the door. Mel and Sandra came rushing out, asking if there was any news. 'Not yet, not yet,' he said. He ruffled both their heads then put his arms around them. 'Everything'll be OK. Don't be worrying, you hear me?' They nodded and he ushered them back into the sitting room.

I hated the way he was soft and caring with the others, while he'd been all hard and cold towards me. Tears stung my eyes as I watched them. I blinked them away, wondering where Shayne was and picturing the whirly lines of the bicycle tracks I'd seen in front of the grotto.

Dad went up to check on Mam. When he came back down, I heard him saying in a low voice to the guards that she was out for the count and it was just as well they'd insisted on calling Dr Crawley. 'She wouldn't have been able for all this,' he said as the sergeant came in the door. 'I hope to God it's over soon.'

We went into the kitchen. The floor was clean. Sandra had swept up all the bits of wallpaper while we were gone.

'No news yet, I'm afraid,' the sergeant said. He pulled out a chair and sat down, facing the man in the tree, studying him closely and drumming his fingers on the table. 'So, tell me, Ruth,' he said. 'How do you like living in Hillcourt Rise?'

'I . . . it's . . . we . . . Fine. It's fine. We haven't been here that long, really.'

'But long enough to know if you like it? And long enough to make friends, hmm?'

He was a grey man. Everything about him was grey: his skin, his eyes, his hair. Even his teeth. Nothing about him stood out. Nothing about him was distracting, and there was no one thing on his face to focus on. His nose wasn't big, his eyes were neither dull nor twinkly, his mouth was . . . just a mouth.

'I suppose. A few.'

'And who would those few be, eh?'

Dad stood over by the sink, lighting a cigarette with a match from the box he'd flung on the floor earlier. Sandra had tidied them up too. And she'd washed all the cups and put them away and wiped down all the worktops.

'I don't know . . . everyone,' I said with a shrug.

The sergeant smiled. 'Everyone! Well, aren't you the popular girl?'

'What's all this got to do with anything? What does it matter who she's friends with?' Dad said, angrily flicking ash into the sink. When he turned back around, his face scared me. His skin was ghostly and his eyes were sunken into his skull. His hair was flecked with white and, for a moment, I puzzled about how that could be when it was Sunday and he hadn't been out at work. Then I realized it wasn't paint, but lots of little white hairs showing up under the fluorescent tube. Dad looked old.

'Just exploring all the avenues,' the sergeant said. 'She was the last one to see the little lad.'

'She told you who was there when he disappeared, didn't

she? It's him you should be quizzing. Assuming you shaggin'
well find him.'

'I'm aware of what she told us.' He waved his hand at the
wall. 'That this . . . I don't know, tramp, down-and-out, wino,
whatever you want to call him, was hanging around. But just
because she says she saw him, it doesn't mean we have to . . .
well, that we have to . . . What I mean is, we have to keep all
our lines of inquiry open.'

'So what you're saying is you don't necessarily think he's
your man?'

'I . . . suppose you could say that, yes.'

I nearly smiled. Finally, they were coming round to
believing me. I felt sort of free, and light as air. But then I
remembered why the guards were there in the first place
and the feeling began to fade. When the sergeant spoke
again, it disappeared completely. Everything went black.
I was thrown into a deep and silent lake, weighted down
with a hundred bricks.

'There wasn't anyone else in the graveyard, was there, Ruth?'
the sergeant said. 'It was only you and your brother, wasn't it?'
He leaned closer to me. 'Now . . . is there anything you'd like
to tell us?' I was sinking now. Melting blobs of faces floated in
the air, voices were muffled and faint. I felt the heat of more
tears in my eyes, the weight of a hand on my shoulder. 'Now,
now. It's all right. Don't be upsetting yourself. Whatever it is,
we're here to help. Isn't that right, Mick?' The sergeant patted
my arm. When his face came into focus, I could see he was

smiling; the kind of smile people use when they're pretending they care how you feel.

'What? What do you mean?' Dad asked him, blowing smoke out of his nose.

'I'm not sure we're getting the real truth here.' The sergeant stood up and walked over to Kev's highchair. He picked up his blue bowl and looked at it as he spoke. 'What were you doing in the graveyard in the first place, Ruth?'

'I . . . I was taking Kev for a walk. I already told you.'

'To the graveyard? On a chilly evening? And it nearly dark?'

'I didn't *plan* to go there. I just kept walking and that was where I ended up. I like going to the graveyard.'

'You like going to the graveyard? What little girl likes going to the graveyard? And by herself?'

'What are you trying to say?' Dad asked him. 'Why all these questions? What does it matter anyway, for God's sake?'

'Just doing my job, Mick. Just doing my job. Hers is the only story we have.' He placed Kev's bowl carefully back on the tray of the highchair. 'We have to be sure it's the right one.'

'The right one?' Dad asked.

'She could've been anywhere . . .' The sergeant's voice started to rise. 'With anyone! And the only person she says she saw is some . . . some *cartoon* man she conjured up nearly two years ago!'

Dad's face turned grim and hard. He spoke through his teeth. 'Just because you lot haven't been able to find him, you think he doesn't exist! Is that it?'

'Look. Let's be realistic here. Little girls don't go off to the graveyard of a cold and dark Sunday evening on their own. There must be something else to this. She must be leaving something out. You said yourself she was great at spinning yarns.'

I glared at Dad. *Spinning yarns?*

He put his head in his hands and spoke into his palms. 'That's not what I said and you know it. I said she had a great imagination.'

'Same thing, isn't it? Didn't you say she thought you were carrying on with the Lawless woman? Wasn't she trying to convince her mother you were having it off with her up in the woods after work every evening? Well? That's what you told me, isn't it? Or maybe you're the one spinning the yarns, Mick? Maybe you really *are* playing away? No smoke without fire, eh?'

Dad picked up Kev's bowl and fired it onto the floor. 'For *Christ's* sake! What are you trying to do? You're supposed to be helping us here! My son is out there somewhere! Do you not understand? I want him back here when his mother wakes up, do you hear me? Do you fuckin' well hear me?'

Sergeant Pearce stood looking at Dad, his eyes not blinking and his mouth set into a straight, hard line. 'Put the kettle on there, lads,' he said. The two guards who'd been standing by the back door nodded and followed their orders.

'Put the *kettle* on? *Put the shaggin' kettle on*! Is that all you can do?' Dad roared.

'Take it easy now, Mick. You're not doing yourself any favours here, you know.'

'I'm not shaggin' well interested in doing favours! Not for you or me or anyone. I just want you to do your job and get my boy back!'

The sergeant sighed. 'That's exactly what I'm trying to do, and I'd appreciate a bit of co-operation, if you don't mind.' He sat down again. 'Now. Let's go over everything that happened today, Ruth.'

'I've told you everything already,' I said, wiping my nose with my sleeve. 'And what's the point in going over it again when you don't think I'm telling the truth?'

'Look. We'll go back a bit further this time. Give me an outline of the day since you got up this morning.'

Dad paced up and down the kitchen as I spoke. The guards put the teapot on the table and the sergeant listened and nodded while he poured. I stopped a couple of times, trying to figure out whether or not he believed me, but his face gave nothing away. He sipped quietly at his tea, saying, 'Go on' or 'Continue' or 'Keep going'. It was only when I got to the part about the fight on the green that he finally asked me a question.

'So your dad got involved in this fight, did he? This is the . . . eh . . . horseplay he mentioned?'

'Well, he . . . I mean, he . . . It wasn't his fault, he—'

'What was I supposed to do?' Dad interrupted. 'Stand by and let them kill each other? I had to try and stop them.'

The sergeant scratched his ear. 'So you think it was a good idea to roll around on the ground with two lads less than half your age?'

'For God's sake, it wasn't what I wanted! I didn't come out intending to get my head bashed in, did I? It was the natural thing to do, to try and break it up.'

'And tell me, what was this fight all about anyway? Any idea?'

My head started to spin. I couldn't get my brain to concentrate on one thing. Millions of 'whys' and 'because ofs' and 'if onlys' swam around my head. What had it been about? I couldn't remember. I knew it'd been clear earlier on but now, after all that had happened, it was fuzzy and coming through only in bursts.

Lies . . . It was something to do with lies. Someone was telling lies. That was it, wasn't it? Or someone wasn't telling the truth.

Was that the same thing? I wasn't sure.

'No . . . I . . . no . . . I don't know.'

'Wouldn't have had something to do with your dad and the Lawless lad's mother, would it?'

I looked at Dad. 'I . . . don't think so.'

'You don't *think* so?' Dad said. 'There's NOTHING GOING ON! It's all in his twisted little head!'

'But what about all the things he saw?' I yelled. 'And the things *I* saw!'

'What things? *What things, for God's sake*?'

'The things I told Mam. Like kissing Liz.'

'That's absolute rubbish!'

'But why would he lie?'

'He's winding you up! I thought you were more intelligent than to be taken in by something like that!'

The sergeant sipped his tea, his ordinary eyes watching us over the top of his mug.

'Even if that isn't true,' I said, 'you were with her down in The Ramblers.'

'I was sitting beside her. That's all.'

'I know what I saw!'

He came over and leaned in to me, gripping the edge of the table. 'I'll tell you what you saw, shall I? Then maybe you'll shut up and we can get on with finding your brother. What you saw was that woman in bits, after being beaten about by her own son. Terrified of him, she was! What was I supposed to do? I only went down for a quiet drink. I didn't arrange to meet up with her!'

I searched his face for something that would show me he was lying. But I couldn't find it.

'Shayne?' I said. 'You mean . . . Shayne?'

'Yes! Shayne! Precious Shayne! Why do you think I warned you to stay away from him?'

'But . . . what about . . . his uncle Vic? Shayne said he was beating his Mam. That's what Shayne said. He said—'

'He said! He said! *Forget about what he said!* Just discount whatever he told you, all right? You can't believe a single word out of his mouth!'

'And . . . and Christmas night?' I asked him. 'When you went for a walk?'

'What about it?'

'He said . . . I mean . . . You did call to their house, didn't you?'

'I went out for a breath of air! If he told you anything else, he's shaggin' well lying! And all that stuff you told your mother about the woods? A load of shit! A complete heap of crap! What do you take me for, Ruth? What sort of man do you think I am?'

'But if it's all lies – if Shayne's been telling lies and hitting his mam and everything – why did you never tell me?'

Dad thumped his fists on the table. The sergeant's mug tipped over, the tea splashing out in a pool that spilled over the edge and dripped down to the floor. 'BECAUSE I'M YOUR FATHER!' he screamed into my face. He slumped down in a chair and put his head in his hands. 'And I brought you to this place! This godforsaken . . . *Jesus Christ.* I don't know! I don't know.'

Sergeant Pearce stood up and carefully lifted his chair back in under the table. 'So. You've been angry with your father for quite a while, Ruth. Is that right? He was doing something he shouldn't have been, that's what you thought, and you . . . maybe you wanted to . . . hurt him in some way for that? When he asked you to look after your brother, perhaps you weren't as . . . as careful as you should have been. Hmm?'

Dad raised his head. 'Tell me that's not true, Ruth,' he said, looking into my eyes.

'It's not! It's not true! *I swear!* I'd never do anything to hurt Kev! I was looking after him. *I was!*'

The sergeant took a dishcloth from the sink and threw it over the pool of tea on the table. 'We have to look at the whole picture here. And we won't know how deep the water is until we dive in, isn't that right?' He walked around the room, then stood behind me. 'What you're saying, Mick, is that the Lawless lad is violent towards his mother. Am I right in thinking that?'

'What? He . . . Yes, yes, I suppose that is what I'm saying. I—'

'You're quite sure about that?'

'Yes! I . . . Look, that's not what's important! Find out what's happening to my little boy!' Then Dad reached out his hand for mine. 'Look, Ruth. I know I should've told you about all this before. But I thought things would settle down. And maybe I thought you were too young to deal with it all, I don't know. I just wanted it to go away. I wanted you to have friends, to be happy here. That's all I wanted. For you to be happy here.'

I gripped his fingers tight in my own. I could see it in the way he looked at me, the way his eyes were sort of pleading and sad and . . . helpless.

It was the truth.

He wouldn't lie to me now. Not today. Not when Kev was missing and the guards were here and Mam was . . .

Oh God. What was happening? Where was everything that I thought was true? I knew things, didn't I? I was the one who understood. I sensed stuff. I noticed everything. I watched more closely than anyone else. I . . .

Shayne. I had to find him.

Mel appeared, fidgeting with the buttons on his shirt and looking anxious. 'There's someone at the door.'

The sergeant nodded at the guards and one of them went out into the hall. A soft hum came filtering down to the kitchen. It was Father Feely. He bustled in, bringing with him the smell of cabbage and candles. And slipping in silently behind him was a pale and frightened-looking David O'Dea.

'Good of you to come, Father,' the sergeant said. He looked at David. 'Young O'Dea, isn't it?'

'It is,' Father Feely answered. 'It is indeed.' He ushered David into the middle of the room. 'This is a terrible business. A terrible business altogether. I was just out there having a word with all the neighbours and this young man came out to me. He has something he'd like to tell.'

Dad fired the questions at David. 'What? What is it? Do you know something? Did you see someone? Do you know where Kevin is?'

'Hold on, Mick,' the sergeant said. 'Let the lad talk.'

David clicked the stud on his wristband and kept his head down as we waited for him to speak. Father Feely coughed. The sergeant sniffed. Then we strained to hear as David lifted his face to Dad's.

'You should've just left it,' he said in a cracked whisper. 'Why didn't you? Why didn't you just . . . leave it?'

'Leave what? What are you on about?' Dad asked, clearly puzzled.

I knew. I didn't need David to say it. It was written all over his face.

'What you said after the fight. To me and Shayne.'

'You're over here complaining about that when . . . when all this is going on? I don't believe it!' Dad was raising his voice. *'I don't bloody well —'*

'Now, now, Mick. The lad is only trying to help,' Father Feely said.

'Trying to *help*? Over here with his tittle tattle, you mean!' He prodded David's shoulder. 'I don't have time for a troublemaker like you. You get me? I stand by everything I said. You're nothing but a little . . . a little . . . You and Lawless! Gurriers, both of you. One's as bad as the other. Now, if you don't mind, we're in the middle of a crisis here, in case you hadn't shaggin' well noticed.'

David looked at the floor and cleared his throat. 'Shayne followed Ruth into the graveyard.'

Dad's eyes went flat and still. He held onto the back of Kev's highchair.

'We . . . we went into the churchyard after the fight,' David continued. 'Shayne wasn't saying anything. He was really quiet. But I knew he was mad. It was like he went into a kind of . . . trance or something. He even let me cycle around on his bike and he never does that. Then he climbed up into the tree and just sat there, looking out over the wall.'

'Go on,' the sergeant said when David paused. 'Tell us what happened next.'

'Well, he was just . . . sitting there, not moving and then . . . he jumped down out of the tree like he was in a real hurry and he started running to the gate. I cycled over and asked him where he was going and he said . . . he said . . . Ruth had gone into the graveyard with that little . . .' He stopped and swallowed hard.

'That little what?' Dad asked. 'That little what? If you've something to say, just shaggin' well say it!'

'Now, Mick, give the lad some time,' Father Feely said. 'He's doing his best.'

'Time? He's had a couple of hours and he's only telling us this now? How much more bloody time does he need?'

The sergeant touched Dad's arm. 'Take it easy, Mick. Now, David, what was it Shayne said?'

'He said . . . Ruth had gone into the graveyard with that little . . . that little . . . *bastard*. And then . . . and then . . . he got down from the tree and ran in after her.'

Father Feely blessed himself and muttered under his breath. The sergeant nodded his head slowly. Dad slapped his hands against his sides and whimpered. *Jesus Christ, Jesus Christ, Jesus Christ.*

'And you didn't see him, Ruth?' Sergeant Pearce asked me. 'You definitely didn't see anyone except this . . . this . . . man?'

I shook my head. 'No.'

'You're quite sure about that? There's nothing you want to . . . get off your chest, is there? There was no arrangement to meet up with young Lawless? No agreement that you'd see each other there?'

'NO! I already told you!'

'Well, I suppose we'll have to look into it, have a word with him. You haven't seen him since, I take it?' he asked David.

'I waited a few minutes,' David said. 'Then I just went home. I . . . I don't know where he is.'

'If he thinks he's being smart,' Dad said, 'I'll . . . I'll . . . I mean it, if he thinks this is funny . . .'

'Don't be jumping the gun, now, Mick,' the sergeant said. 'Shouldn't you go up and check on Rose?'

'I'll come with you,' Father Feely said. 'I believe Dr Crawley came earlier? Best thing, Mick. Best thing for her. The poor . . .'

His voice faded as he followed Dad upstairs. The sergeant spoke quietly to the two guards. I strained to listen but all I could make out was 'careful' and 'time' and 'search'. David kept his eyes to the floor. I could tell he felt awkward. 'I think I should go home,' he announced after a minute. 'I mean . . . if that's all right . . .'

'You go on, lad,' the sergeant told him. 'Garda Murphy will escort you. We might be needing to talk to you again. In the meantime, if you think of anything else, you will let us know?'

David nodded and shuffled out into the hall with his head down. I followed after him and saw he was holding his wrist, the one he'd broken, his fingers pressing hard into the flesh like they were trying to find their way through to the bone. The sergeant was still talking to Garda Murphy in the kitchen, and while we waited for him at the door, David gave me the same kind of look that had been in Dad's eyes: pleading, sad and helpless.

'I'm sorry,' he said. 'I tried to tell you. I—'

I caught his arm. 'What you said in the letter – it's all true, isn't it?'

He looked at where my fingers gripped him. He nodded.
I let his arm drop. It was like my skin had been scalded. I
slumped against the wall.

Shayne had pushed him out of the tree. He'd made him
take Kev's pram.

What else had I got wrong?

'Did you ever climb up on our roof? And hide in the corner
of Kev's room?'

David frowned and shook his head. He didn't know what
I was talking about.

'And the blackbird,' I said. 'On the green. Did you . . . kill it?'

'Yes.'

'You did? But why? *Why*?'

His voice was thin and high. 'I didn't want to! I hated doing
it but I . . . I had to. I saw Shayne from my window. The bird
was all weak from the cold and he kicked it around like a
football. He laughed at it struggling on the ground. Then he
just . . . he just went off and left it. It was cruel to leave it in
pain. I had to put it out of its misery.'

Something burst inside me. It was like I'd woken up from
a deep and crazy dream. I searched his face.

'You know, don't you?' I said.

And he nodded, before walking out the door.

They didn't notice I was gone for a while. It gave me just
enough time.

I imagine Dad sat with Mam for a few minutes, glad she

was in some other world, and hoping that when she woke up he could look into her eyes and smile and tell her everything was all right. Father Feely probably stood at the end of the bed, whispering prayers under his breath for Kev's safe return and reassuring Dad that Sergeant Pearce was doing his very best. I imagine Mel and Sandra, for once sitting quietly together on the couch, afraid to speak, barely breathing, aware that the life we knew was in the balance and that one tiny movement could tip us over the edge.

I wondered what was going through David's mind as I saw him walking across the green with Garda Murphy. He was smart enough to know it was over. That this was the end of Hillcourt Rise as he'd known it all his life. But he'd already made his bid for freedom, made the leap to a wider, open world. Things had changed for him when he'd left for Clonrath.

Only then could he stop acting. Only then did he feel safe to tell the truth.

And what about all those who had gathered on the green? I glanced over at them as I came up out of the cul-de-sac and ran tight in along the shadow of the wall. None of them saw me, so close was their grouping under their hoods and their umbrellas, and so great was their interest in what David had to say. But he ignored their call for detail and continued walking over to his house with his head bowed and his steps unsure and faltering. The way they were supposed to be.

I was somehow aware of the depth of the ground under my feet as I ran – of the layers of concrete and rubble and sand. Of clay and rock and boiling liquid reaching down for miles and miles to a solid mass of something hard and dense and black. I wanted to understand it, to feel the weight of my bones and my flesh against it. To remember what the world I'd known had felt like. Very soon, I knew I'd take off. I'd lift up into the air and float for . . . who knew how long? I might never touch earth again.

His bike lay on the driveway, mud packed into the ridges of its tyres. I looked up at the front of the house, at the gaping black squares of the windows, the peeling paintwork, and the cold, damp emptiness that seemed to ooze from every brick. The side-passage door had swollen in the rain and it shuddered out of its wooden frame when I shouldered it, slapping back against the wall when it gave way. Fingering the knobbled surface of the pebbledash, I remembered the way I'd felt when he told me about The Kiss. The way it had seemed so . . . so right and so . . . real. So true. How could that have been? What had made me so sure? It was like I'd closed my eyes and just accepted I was blind.

The tap in the kitchen was flowing, rushing onto the pile of dirty dishes and splashing over the worktop in a fan of sprinkled drops. I reached in and turned it off, seeing sodden butts floating in an overflowing bowl. I watched them for a moment, the way they whirled around in circles, bobbing about like tiny swollen bodies in a flood. My world was getting smaller now, shrinking down. Shrivelling. Soon it would disappear. There'd be nothing of it left. I'd have to make a new one, build it up, grab at things that had no meaning, things I wouldn't recognize from any place or time. Everything made sense to me, and nothing did. I walked out of the room, across the carpet of roses, and began to climb the stairs. *One, two, three . . .*

I reached the landing and looked up at the steps that led to his room. Only then did I get scared. I knew they'd all be close behind me, but I couldn't let them be the ones. This was my task. No one else could do it. Not Mam. Or Dad. Or the others. Not David or the sergeant or Father Feely. It wasn't their job. I had to be the first.

That was how it was meant to be.

It seeped out from the room, through the gap under the door and down to reach me as I climbed. Silence. Thick and cloudy and dead. Far too much of it. It settled around me like a cloak and, for the last few steps, I almost allowed it to weigh me down. It would've been so easy to just lie there and wait for them to find me. But I dragged myself on and stood outside his room, pressing my face to his door.

When I pushed down on the handle and slipped inside, I entered the place of endings. This room at the top of his house, looking out over the green and beyond to the mountains, was as far as I could go.

I'd never escape.

This was where I'd be stuck for the rest of my life. No place on earth would hold me as close, however far I travelled. I'd always be there. Always. Nothing would ever change that.

I wanted to know so many things. A hundred whats. A thousand whys. But I didn't know what to believe any more. Had I made my own path, or had I followed one laid out for me? Was every twist and fork already on the map? Every bump and bend?

Or did the corners only exist because I turned them?

The stench of secrets. The hidden smell of happenings. I walked across the floor and stood under the window, looking up to the sky. Whatever was written in the stars had been read. The words were a story. My story.

The only one I would ever tell.

TWENTY

I'm not sure why I lifted the lid. I suppose it just seemed logical at the time. I remember sitting down on his bed for a moment and trying to figure out what I would've done if I were him. Because I know the truth now, I'm not sure if I recall exactly what went through my head. The real gets mixed up with the imagined. I think I realized that there wasn't anywhere else, no other place he would've used. And I know I was certain that the answer was there, in his room. I was sure of it.

I tried to be him. I conjured myself into his clothes, under his skin, replaced my bones with his. I lay down on the bed, the smell of him sneaking into me, the shape of his body accepting the sinking weight of my own. This was what it was like. This was the place.

This was the only place.

I got up and flicked the switch by the door. The weak yellow bulb in the ceiling smeared the whole place with a misty, dreamy glow. It showed up cloudy, softened versions of what I knew to be there. The grubby bedclothes, the threadbare rug, the chipped and hacked-at headboard. And the huge monstrosity of his radiogram, the bulk of it dwarfing everything else in the room. On top of the side that held the turntable was the small, square photograph of him with his uncle Joe. Only now, uncle Joe's face had been scribbled over in careful, detailed whirls, the lines so many and so close that his features could barely be seen.

I thought about the way he'd shown me how Dad and Liz had 'kissed'. Were his lies only lies because I believed them? And would I have been standing in his room now if I hadn't?

The rain drummed louder against the roof, the noise of it making me almost thankful I was there. Sheltered, safe, unseen. Some days now I want to remember it all; other days I want to forever forget. But it seems cold and hard to deny the memory, to want to hide the truth of what I found.

How could I not want to remember Kev? Every minute of him.

In life. And in death.

He was so perfect, curled up as though asleep. Stored away, soft and silent under the lid of that great, wooden beast. I've lifted it a thousand times in my mind since, over and over, hoping I'll find nothing more than a stack of favourite records, a prized collection of familiar songs. Sweet tunes to sing along to, with words I think I know the meaning of. But once the lines have been written, they can't ever change. You know them by heart and think you understand them, until one day you find out they're not what you thought they were at all.

I don't think I screamed, or cried, or made any sound. For one beautiful second, the relief at having found him was stronger than the realization he was dead.

I knew he was.

But it couldn't be the sort of dead I'd come to know, could it? Not the for ever and ever Uncle Frank sort of dead? This was Kev, not even two years old. His was surely a different kind of dead. This was a line that could be re-written, couldn't it? It had to have another meaning. It couldn't be the end. Not really, truly, absolutely . . . The End.

I reached down and scooped him up in my arms. His clothes were damp. He was cold. Cold, cold, cold. And he was heavy; heavier than before.

Before.

Before was over.

I held him the way Dad had sometimes held me: laid across my outstretched arms, his head to my left, his feet to my right. I pulled him close to my chest and kissed his pale forehead. His flesh was like stone. I swayed a little, back and forth, rocking him gently in my arms.

*

It wasn't long before they came. Minutes, seconds maybe. A blur of sounds and motion. Of strokes and rushing air. Of arms and prayers and whispers. The smell of wet hair and damp skin; the touch of soft palms and warm blankets. The silence. Then the screams.

Before they led me away, I saw Shayne.

His face like the moon at the window, hollow-eyed and silvery. His gaze unconnected to the world, as always. He stared at me from behind the glass – unblinking, blank, empty.

That's how I remember him. That's how I'll always remember him.

He was sitting in the shadow of the chimney. Sergeant Pearce said he'd never seen anyone so at ease at such a height. Like a bird, he said. Like it was his home. He was taken to the garda station straightaway. Dad tried to keep it all from us and, for a while, he succeeded. But we learned the truth in dribs and drabs, from half-heard conversations and snatched sentences.

He'd wheeled Kev to the churchyard, taking care to lock the gate. Then he'd lifted him, still sleeping soundly, from his pushchair. He'd held him with one arm, his little head slumped over his shoulder, and stepped up easily onto the strong, low branches of the copper beech.

And when he'd climbed as high as he could go, far up inside the dark web of leaves and branches where he felt safe and sure . . . he let him fall.

That's what he said.

It wasn't an accident. He didn't slip. There was no sudden stumble. He just . . . let him fall.

And when he picked him up from the ground, he heard me rattling at the gates, calling out Kev's name. It had been that quick.

When I was gone, he took off home on his bike in the dark, carrying Kev's lifeless body bundled up inside his jacket. He'd waited in the lane, watching me run across the green, only speeding off when he was sure I'd reached our door. Mam and Dad, coming up the hill in the car with the bag of Easter eggs from Auntie Cissy, must've only missed him by seconds.

The doctor's examination showed there were no broken bones in Kev's body. Not one. Because he was asleep – a deep, deep sleep after all the crying that he'd done – he'd been completely relaxed. But he'd fallen on his head and his brain had died and his insides had all been shaken up.

The one thing Dad did tell us was that his death had been instant and there was never any chance he could've been saved. I suppose he thought that might've made us feel better. But it didn't. Not at all.

Father Feely stayed with us into the early hours of Monday morning and convinced Mam and Dad to have the funeral as soon as possible. He said it was better for everyone concerned if the matter was dealt with quickly. If these things drag on, he said, it only prolongs the tragedy.

I doubt if Mam even heard what he was saying. Dad had woken her up when Kev had been found – against Sergeant Pearce's advice – and although she seemed sort of aware of what had happened, she was muzzy and confused and she didn't really understand.

Dad went along with Father Feely and a Mass of the Holy Angels was arranged for the Tuesday morning. Before he left, Father Feely gathered us around in the sitting room to say some prayers for Kev. Mam sat on the couch and stared into the deadened fireplace, her hands like withered lilies in her lap. Mel, Sandra and I knelt on the carpet and cried silently as we listened. At one point, Dad looked over at us with a sort of panic in his eyes like he'd no idea where he was or who any of us were. Then he bowed his head and started to shiver so bad we could hear his teeth chatter.

Kev was taken straight from the doctor's to the funeral home. We never saw him again. We didn't get time to accept he was dead. We should've had time to hold him, to stroke his cheeks and tell him how much we loved him and maybe save a lock of his jet-black hair.

Father Feely was wrong; it wasn't better that way.

The church was packed for the funeral. Liz stayed away. I suppose it wouldn't have been right for her to go. Almost everyone else from Hillcourt Rise was there. It was clear they were all upset, but they mostly kept their distance from us after it was over. None of them really knew what to say. Bridie stood beside me for a moment on the steps of the church, dabbing her eyes with a lacy handkerchief, and I got the feeling she hoped I might collapse into her arms. But I turned my face away. I was glad we'd become distant.

Paddy and Clem shook Dad's hand. Nora and Geraldine made sympathetic faces. They meant well, I suppose, but none of it seemed real to me. I think they all knew we'd be gone soon enough and there was no point in wasting too much energy trying to be supportive. Our arrival had upset the way things had been run in Hillcourt Rise, and the sooner we were gone, the sooner everything could get back to normal. We should never have expected we were going to slot ourselves into the tightly knit grouping that had existed for years before we came. Eamon and Mona hovered at the edge of the crowd with David and the twins. They looked over but came no closer, and were gone before we drove away.

Mam didn't want Kev buried in Kilgessin graveyard. Apart from it being the place where he disappeared, there was nobody there, she said, to look after him. She wanted him in Wicklow, where her own mother and father were buried, so, after the funeral, we made our way there. Once through the city, we drove past Bray and Greystones and on down twisty, green tunnels of winding country roads, where the spring sun flashed through the trees and the hedgerows were splashed with clumps of yellow primroses.

I went in Uncle Con's car, with Trevor and Auntie Cissy. Trevor sat beside me in the back and had a pocketful of cough drops he kept insisting on offering me. I said 'no thanks' every time but it didn't stop him asking.

Mam clung to Dad in the graveyard. She could barely stand up. Sandra and I held hands and Uncle Con kept his arm around Mel. Auntie Cissy walked on her own, ahead of everyone else, like she was showing us what to do. I suppose because it was only six months since she'd buried her husband, she felt she knew more about grief than the rest of us. We had to wait a while for Father Feely. He apologized for being late, saying his car wasn't up to the 'narrow boreens'.

None of the neighbours made it down for the burial. I thought maybe Bridie might've asked Father Feely for a lift, but he arrived alone. Not that I really cared if she was there, but it would've been nice if she'd made the effort. I heard Father Feely telling Dad later on that nobody from the estate came because they assumed we only wanted family and they didn't want to intrude. Dad said that was just an excuse and if they'd really wanted to make it down, they would have, and it wasn't as if Wicklow was the other side of the world.

Mam managed to keep upright until Kev's coffin was lowered into the ground. Then her knees kind of gave way and Dad had to grab her and stop her from falling into the grave. I think if he hadn't, she wouldn't have cared. She'd have let herself be buried alive. I won't ever forget the sound she made. Not ever.

The days that followed were the worst. Everything was turned upside down. Auntie Cissy offered to have the three of us and Dad wanted us to go. But Mam said she wouldn't be able to bear the house without us. Even though she said that, she acted as if we weren't there. She lived in some sort of in-between world and took to staying up for most of the night and sleeping in snatches during the day. I'd come into the kitchen and find her slumped with her head on the tray of Kev's highchair and she'd spring up in fright when she heard me, her eyes wild with fear and her hair stuck to her head with sweat.

At night, the lights were left on and all the doors were kept open, and we'd hear strange sobs and all sorts of shuffling and moaning. We'd come down in the morning to find plates of cold scrambled eggs and hard toast on the table that she'd made hours before. And in the evenings, she filled the bath with warm water and bubbles and sat on the lid of the toilet for ages, with a towel in her hands, just staring into space.

On Easter Sunday, we broke our chocolate eggs into pieces and melted them in the fire. The thought of them made us feel sick. Even Sandra, who'd given up sweet things for Lent and had been looking forward to breaking her fast, wasn't tempted. Mel seemed to take the greatest pleasure in the task, smashing his eggs with his fists and stamping on the boxes till they were flat. When Dad came in and saw what we were doing, all he said was to make sure we didn't leave too much of a mess.

We discovered later on that Shayne had been charged with Kev's murder on the day of the funeral. Dad had cut the piece about it out of the *Evening Press* and kept it in his wallet. I found it when Mrs Shine called for the church dues the following Friday and he asked me to take the fifty pence myself because he was doing the washing up and his hands were wet. I didn't think Mrs Shine should be calling at all. It didn't feel right, and I said as much to Dad. But he said something about life going on and her only doing her job. She didn't mention Kev; she probably hoped the pained expression on her face was enough. But seeing as it wasn't any different to the one she usually wore, I couldn't tell. She did ask how Mam was and went off on a ramble about some cousin of hers who'd lost a son in a farming accident, but I wasn't in any mood for her and closed the door before she'd finished.

I sat on the stairs after she'd gone and read the words on the small rectangle of newspaper. 'Youth on Murder Charge', it said. It didn't give Shayne's name, just called him 'a fourteen-year-old youth' and said he'd been 'charged at a special sitting of Kilgessin court with the murder of twenty-one-month-old Kevin Lamb of forty-two Hillcourt Rise, Kilgessin, on Sunday last'. It said he was to be 'remanded in custody to St Patrick's Institution to appear before the District Court again on Thursday'. That was over a week before. I wondered what had happened. I folded the piece of paper up and put it back in Dad's wallet. There was no use in asking him; I knew he wouldn't tell.

Father Feely called round the next evening and said we should try to get back to normal, that we'd feel a lot better if we followed our old routine of school and work and going to mass on Sunday. Dad told him it was good of him to call but, if he didn't mind, we had our own way of doing things, thank you very much, and there wasn't much point in us going to all the trouble of settling into our old routine when we weren't going to be around very much longer anyway. That was the first time Dad had said anything about moving. Since I'd always had a feeling it was going to happen, it didn't surprise me, but the others were shocked and Sandra started to cry. Father Feely got all red-faced and asked Dad if he was sure he was doing the right thing, would he not think about it for a while longer, and what about all the good friends and neighbours we'd be leaving behind? Dad got mad then and said not one person had asked how we were since we'd buried Kev. And none of these so-called 'friends' had come round to ask any of us out to play. Father Feely said not to be so hard on people, that it was a difficult time for everyone and no one really knew what to say, and maybe people thought we'd prefer to be left to grieve and didn't want to intrude. But how could we stay after all that had happened, Dad wanted to know. It was because of Kev that we'd come here in the first place, he said. He'd been born the day we moved in, for God's sake. We'd never even begin to get over it if we stayed. Father Feely said people were very sorry for what had happened, but no one could've foreseen such a terrible event, and if any of us had known things like the fact that the Lawless lad had been violent to his mother, then maybe some sort of action could've been taken sooner.

'And what about David?' Dad said, boiling up because he thought Father Feely was trying to make out he was in some way responsible. 'Covering up the fact he was pushed out of that tree? Maybe if he'd said something back then, Lawless would've been locked up long ago.'

Father Feely said we had to make exceptions for children; they couldn't be expected to have the same sense as adults when it came to doing the right thing. 'Shayne is a most unfortunate child,' he said. 'A most unfortunate child.'

'What about my unfortunate child?' Dad said. 'That . . . monster might be getting locked up but my child is gone for ever.'

'Maybe we're all guilty in one way or another for not saying things we should have,' Father Feely said, looking at me. 'But life is a test and none of us know what the good Lord has in store for us. Isn't that so? Hmm?'

I think Dad might've taken a swipe at Father Feely if Mam hadn't appeared. She sort of floated into the room in her nightdress, carrying the box of photographs from under her bed. She'd been crying again and she asked Dad why there didn't seem to be any pictures of Kev. Dad put his arm around her and tried to explain that they wouldn't be in the box, that any we had of Kev would be in the sideboard. But it was like she didn't hear him and she put the box on the table and began pulling out handfuls of pictures, studying each one and tossing them to the floor. Father Feely coughed and shuffled around a bit before manoeuvring his stomach out the door and into the hall, saying it was time he left us in peace and maybe he'd see us at mass in the morning. We heard him droning at the front door with Dad for a few minutes while Mam continued flinging photos all over the place. Then she closed her eyes and seemed to fall asleep. Sandra and I gathered them up and put them back, not pausing to look at any of them, not even for a second. It was as if they were pictures of some other family, with no relation to us at all.

Dad came back in and Sandra asked him if was true that we were really moving house. He stood looking at her for a moment, like he was trying to figure out exactly how he should answer. Then Mam woke up with a jolt and opened her eyes wide. She saw the box of photos on the table and took it onto her lap, saying she must have a good look through and see if she could find any of Kev.

'Yes, it's true,' Dad said. 'I think it's for the best.'

That night, Sandra and I pushed our beds together but neither of us could get to sleep. We lay on our backs and held hands under the covers and, after a while, we both began to cry. Mel must've heard us as he crept into our room, asking if we were all right. He sat on the edge of my bed in the dark while we listened to Mam moving around downstairs in the kitchen.

'Do you think Mam's gone a bit . . . crazy?' he asked.

'Don't say that,' Sandra whispered. 'She's not crazy. She's just . . . I don't know . . . not herself, that's all.'

'Do you think she'll get better?'

'Of course she will. She still has us, hasn't she?'

Mel laid a hand on my foot. 'What do you think, Ruth?'

'I don't know,' I said, wiping my tears with the sheet. 'I think maybe she'll get better. But she'll never be the same as she was before.'

'I suppose none of us will,' Sandra said. 'I mean . . . not really.'

'I hate Shayne Lawless,' Mel said. 'He's a fuckin' bastard.'

I could almost taste his words in the silence that followed.

'What's going to happen to him?' Sandra eventually asked.

I answered. 'Locked up. That's what Dad said to Father Feely.'

'I hope that's true,' Mel said. 'I hope we never have to look at his stinking face. Ever again.'

He lay down across our beds, curling the end of the eiderdown around his body. Sandra and I moved our legs up to give him some room. The smell of burned toast found its way up from the kitchen and, after a few minutes, we heard Dad walking heavily down the stairs.

'You were right, Ruth,' Mel said, slipping in under the covers. 'When you said something bad was going to happen. Remember? On New Year's Eve, when we were looking out at the snow?'

'Did you know it'd be this bad?' Sandra asked. 'Did you know it'd be . . . you know . . . about Kev?'

'No! Of course I didn't!' I sat up. 'It was just a feeling. Just some kind of . . . feeling. It wasn't . . . I mean . . . I didn't . . . I thought all kinds of things were happening. All sorts of bad things. But I was wrong about them. I was wrong.'

'But you weren't wrong! You said something bad was going to happen and it did.'

'Yeah,' Mel agreed. 'You really must be, you know . . . psychic.'

'No, I'm not. I'm not. It's not like that.'

'You saw that man before, didn't you? The one in the graveyard. You drew him on the wall the day after we moved in. Where did you see him? Who do you think he is?'

'I don't know. I saw him in the park when Mam was having Kev. Remember I went off on my own? He was there . . . watching me. And then when I drew him on the wall, it was like he was still watching me, even when he was covered up with the wallpaper.'

'Maybe he was some kind of . . . spirit or something,' Sandra said, sitting up and cuddling into me.

'It's weird you saw him the day Kev was born,' Mel said. 'And then the day he . . .'

'He might've been warning you about Kev. About . . . you know . . .' Sandra said.

'Maybe. Do you think Kev . . . If we hadn't moved here, if we'd stayed in the old house, would he . . . ?'

'But we only moved here because of Kev,' Mel said. 'If we didn't move here, it'd mean he wouldn't have been born.'

'So do you think it was all planned out or something?' Sandra said. 'That he was always going to . . . ?'

'I don't know,' I said, sliding back down into the bed. 'And I don't ever want to find out.'

Next morning, Dad announced we were all going to Auntie Cissy's to stay. Just till we'd sold the house and found ourselves a new one. I was sure I saw some sort of relief in Mam's face. She hadn't wanted the three of us to go, but she seemed happy that we were all going now, together. Dad said he'd thought long and hard about it and he felt it was for the best. The house could take months to sell and we weren't hanging around in Hillcourt Rise all that time. He told us we could start packing as soon as we were finished breakfast. We were going to leave that day. None of us complained. As much as we hated Auntie Cissy's house, we didn't mind the thought of going to live there now, and we were used to the idea after only a few minutes. Dad said to pack everything into boxes, but only to take essential stuff for the time being. Anything else could be kept in the house until we found a new place of our own.

Mam walked around in her dressing gown, opening drawers and cupboards. She selected the rolling pin, the sugar bowl and a stainless steel teapot that she never used, and asked Dad to find her something to pack them into. He told her he'd look after it and sent her into the sitting room for a rest on the couch, putting each item back in its place after she'd gone. When he was sure she was asleep, he asked Mel to help him carry Kev's cot downstairs and they lifted it into the garage, along with his highchair and his playpen full of toys.

It didn't take long for Sandra to pack. I think she surprised herself at how little she felt she needed to bring. Nothing seemed to be that important any more. When she was finished, she left me to it, managing a smile on her way out, saying she didn't know how on earth I was going to sort through all of my rubbish. Mel poked his head round the door minutes later, saying it hadn't been hard. He'd thrown everything he owned into a large box, and chosen to bring with him only a few comics and his collection of Dinky cars.

I decided to bring some books, some markers and a drawing pad. The rest of my stuff I dumped into a tea-chest Dad had given me from the garage, left over from when we'd moved in. I cleared my side of the wardrobe, my shelves and finally my drawers. The last one was my underwear drawer. After I'd taken everything out, I found the two things I'd hidden there: the tongue from Shayne's snake on its bed of cotton wool, and David's letter torn into pieces. I twirled the red, forked tongue around in my fingers, watching the way the 'V' of it wobbled about. I wondered if I'd never taken the snake or held onto the tongue, would things have turned out different to the way they did? I knew I had no way of knowing, but I couldn't help thinking that they might have.

I took out the letter, pieced it together like a jigsaw, and read it again. I'd been so sure it was full of lies, that it was some sort of joke, a twisted tale of David's that he was trying to lure me into.

How could I have been so wrong? How could I not have known?

I took out the song words and read them through again. It was true: there was no escape from reality. Then I put them back in the envelope, along with the tongue and the pieces of the letter, and went downstairs. Sandra and Mel were in the sitting room with Mam. She was awake now, and Dad had told them to stay and keep an eye on her. They sat holding her hands and talking gently about going to Cissy's, while she stared into the fire, her eyes all glassy and still.

I walked in and bent down in front of the hearth, shovelling a piece of coal from the bucket into the grate and tossing the envelope in with it. None of them saw what I did and the paper had almost disappeared by the time I stood up. A thin, bluish flame whizzed into life and sped up the chimney as I left the room and I guessed that was the tongue, finally disappearing into nothing.

I went into the kitchen and found Dad standing in the middle of the room with a brush in his hand, like he was waiting for me. Sitting on the table in front of him was a tin of white paint. He nodded at the wall. 'We can't leave it like that,' he said. 'Not with the estate agents coming round to have a look at the place. It won't be perfect but I'm not about to start papering the whole room again. I thought you could have a go at it.'

I rolled up my sleeves and dipped the brush in the paint. 'Mam never liked this wallpaper,' I said as I wiped a broad stroke over the man's boots. 'Did you know that?'

'Is that so?' Dad said, sitting down at the table.

'She just pretended she did because she didn't want to hurt your feelings.'

'How did you figure that one out?' he said, lighting up a cigarette.

'She said so. The night I told her about . . . the night before she went off to Auntie Cissy's.'

'I see. Well, no harm in that, I suppose.'

I swept the brush up over the man's legs and body. 'Do you not mind, then?'

'It hardly matters now, does it?'

'I suppose not.' I painted over the blackbird, whitewashing his yellow eye and the notes coming out of his beak. My throat burned and I knew I was going to cry. 'Dad,' I whispered. 'Do you wish we'd never come here?'

I heard him sucking deeply then blowing out a long, slow puff. 'Do you?'

I looked at the man's face on the wall, the brush hovering over it before I brought it down over his eyes, blinding him for ever. There'd be no more watching me now. 'There's no point in thinking about that, really, is there?' I said.

'No,' he said. 'No point at all.'

When we drove away from Hillcourt Rise that Sunday evening, we may as well have been going off for a spin up the mountains or to the park. It was hard to believe we weren't ever going back. The cherry blossoms were in full bloom on the green, their clusters of pink petals waving against the clear blue sky. We saw no one except Tracey, standing at her front door, balancing baby Brian on her hip, but it was like she didn't know who we were. Mam looked away as we passed; something she would do for months – years – afterwards whenever she saw a little boy.

TWENTY-ONE

Living with Auntie Cissy wasn't that bad. I suppose we didn't really care where we were as long as we were together. Her old, draughty house was in Phibsborough, a mile or so north of the city centre, on a busy street with a shop on the corner and lots of noisy traffic. It was like being back in the South Circular again and I think, in some ways, that helped. None of us went to school while we were there. It wasn't long till the summer holidays and Dad said there was no point starting somewhere new just for a few weeks when we'd be moving again very soon. Auntie Cissy did her best to keep us occupied. Sandra and I got up early in the mornings and did whatever jobs she had for us, like cleaning out her old range, polishing all her brass or going to the shops. Mel had to look after Thomas, letting him in and out and giving him his favourite food at various times of the day. He was also in charge of the fire. Because the house was so cold, it was lit every day, regardless of the weather. He had to take out the ashes, fill the coal scuttle, and set everything in the grate. All of which he did without the slightest complaint.

Most days, Mam didn't get up until the fire was blazing. She'd sit staring at the flames with a blanket wrapped around her shoulders and Kev's favourite teddy in her lap. We'd snuggle ourselves in beside her and one or all of us would eventually end up crying. Mostly, our tears fell silently, the tracks on our cheeks glittering in the firelight. But sometimes Mam would start sobbing: deep, wracking wails that lurched up from her chest and made it sound like she was choking.

Dad went back to work after a few weeks. Apart from the fact that we needed the money, I think he preferred to be kept busy. He took things easy, though, often coming home long before dinnertime, but even then he always found some job to do around the house. He grew quiet and began to smoke more, and did everything much slower than before. His hair turned completely white and he got very thin. Cissy said he'd turned to skin and bone.

It didn't take long to sell number forty-two. Majella and her garda fiancé made an offer on it not long after the sign went up. Well, Bridie made an offer on their behalf, the estate agent told Dad. But they were obviously in agreement and happy to live next door as they followed it through and the deal was done. It seemed right to me that it was someone like Majella that was moving in. I didn't like to think of another family of strangers trying to settle into Hillcourt Rise.

At first, Mam had no interest in looking for a new house. Dad would mark rings around property ads in the papers and make calls to estate agents and auctioneers. Lists and brochures arrived in the post and he'd pore over them at Cissy's big kitchen table, scribbling numbers and calculations on the backs of the envelopes. When he showed Mam places he liked, she'd listen in silence as he spoke and just mumble, 'Whatever you think, love' when he was finished.

But one morning, that changed. Dad had decided to widen his search. Instead of looking close to the city, he began considering places further out. Houses in the country. With land around them. And views of mountains and fields. I heard him talking to Cissy, telling her how much more you could get for your money if you were prepared to live 'out in the sticks', as he called it. Cissy looked doubtful. She reminded Dad he was born and bred in the city and she didn't think he'd be able to cope with country smells and having to drive miles for a pint of milk.

I went upstairs and told Mam. She was propped up against the pillows, her eyes fixed on a holy picture hanging on the wall, and her untouched breakfast tray sitting beside her. She turned to look at me and took my hand in hers.

'We could find somewhere in Wicklow,' she said. 'Somewhere close to Kevin.'

It didn't take long. Dad narrowed it down to three potential houses and viewed them all one day the following week, reporting to Mam on his return. He had hoped she might go with him but she couldn't be persuaded.

In the end, there was only one contender: a stone-built lodge on the outskirts of the village of Glengolden. Sitting on half an acre, and bounded by thick woodland on one side and open fields on the other, it was definitely the prettiest of the houses Dad had viewed. But there was only one reason Mam decided it should be our new home – it was just a little under a mile to the graveyard.

We all cried when we left. Even Dad. Cissy stood on her doorstep with Thomas circling her bony ankles and hugged Mam for the longest time. 'I'll be out in a few weeks for a visit,' she said, rubbing Mam's back. 'If you want me sooner, just let me know.' Mam nodded and pulled away, and Dad had to help her get into the car.

The journey took around an hour. I don't think there was one word spoken for the length of it. I was scared. I knew the others were frightened too. I could see it in their faces; sense it in their silence. I caught Dad's eyes in the mirror when we'd almost left the city behind and I could tell he was afraid. We'd been cocooned in Auntie Cissy's since leaving Hillcourt Rise and she'd looked after us well, better than I'd ever have imagined. We'd felt safe there. As safe as we could have in the circumstances. There were things Mam didn't have to think about while we were there, like making dinners and washing clothes and changing sheets. I worried that she might not be able to do those kinds of things any more. That she'd forget the way we used to live. The way we used to live before.

Dad had arranged for the removal men to collect all our stuff from Hillcourt Rise and bring it straight to the lodge, and as soon as we arrived that afternoon, he told Sandra and me to take Mam for a wander around the garden. I discovered later that he and Mel spent those twenty minutes taking Kev's things apart – his cot, his playpen, his highchair – and hiding them away in the attic. I'm not sure if Mam ever knew they were there.

Though the lodge was old and needed work, none of us cared, least of all Mam. Dad said it had 'character' and it'd be a shame to start 'tarting it up'. He was right, in a way. It wasn't tatty or scruffy; everything was just nicely worn or faded, and no surface had a hard edge. And the bubbled glass in the arched windows let in only a gentle, grainy sort of light that made the rooms all soft and dim.

I can't talk about how much we missed Kev in those early days in our new home. I don't have the words to describe it. Sometimes I try to figure out how we coped, how we got through things, and I can't for the life of me understand. But I know it helped that we were near to him. And that he was in such a beautiful place. All that summer, Mam liked to go and visit him in the evenings with Dad. They'd head off down the road after dinner, Mam picking cornflowers and poppies from the hedgerows to leave on the grave. And though the three of us might be doing our own separate things, after a while we'd all wander out to the garden gate and wait for them to return.

Sandra and Mel usually went together in the morning-time. They'd always ask if I wanted to go with them, but I preferred to go alone. In the late afternoon, when the air was heavy and warm, I'd take a shortcut across the fields and sit on the crumbling stone wall for a while, listening to the buzzing of bees and the faraway sound of cattle being led in for milking. And I'd think of all the things I wanted to tell Kev: how we were, what we were all doing, how much we loved him. But when I'd get to the grave, I could never remember a single one. The words wouldn't form in my head. All I could do was cry.

The weeks passed. We started in another new school but it was hard to make friends. People knew what had happened to us. And though it was hardly mentioned, it was always there, hovering in the air, separating us from them. Perhaps it might've been different if they'd known us a long time, if we'd been living in the area for years. The school wasn't bad, and we had some really nice teachers, but for those first few months we looked forward to coming home before we even got to the bus stop in the mornings.

Mam tried. Really hard. She got back into the ordinary things: cooking dinners, ironing clothes, hoovering. I used to think about her when I was at school, in the house on her own, with all those hours to pass until we got back. If Dad was working not too far away, he'd go home for his lunch. And a nice woman who lived in the farmhouse down the road called in every week or so with a bowl of eggs or a box of potatoes. And Cissy came to stay often too. Mam cried less at home as time went on. At least, she seemed more able to control it there. But outside it was different. It was always when she was in a crowd, as if being surrounded by people she didn't know made her realize who she was, and she'd break down sobbing, taking ages to stop. It happened in town one day when we were queuing to get new schoolbooks and Sandra got mad because people were staring. And one Saturday we went to see Mel's football match and missed his goal because we had to help Mam back to the car.

Dad spent all his spare time in the garden. He planted trees and shrubs and flowers, made a rockery, and laid a crazy-paving patio, like Mam had always wanted. In later years, he made a special place in a corner down the end, where a rose-covered arch led to a wooden bench set in a gravelled square. He'd sit there reading the paper, hidden from view except for the telltale wisps of cigarette smoke rising up in the air.

We each had our own bedroom in the lodge. Mine was the smallest, with a tiny metal fireplace and a window with a deep, stone ledge where I'd sit and look out over the fields and mountains. For months after we moved in, my stuff remained in boxes. Though my room had shelved alcoves and a tall wooden cupboard left by the previous owners, I wasn't in any hurry to fill them. I unpacked in dribs and drabs. It wasn't something I could do in one go. Everything I owned belonged to before.

By early spring, I had just one box left to empty. I tackled it on a crisp, cold Sunday afternoon when Dad had gone for a walk with the others and Mam was snoozing by the fire. After I'd shoved it across the floor, I sat down on the edge of my bed and started taking things out one-by-one. The envelope fell from the pages of a book. I watched it flutter slowly to the floor. I let it lie there on the wooden boards and stared at it for ages.

It was the one I'd addressed to David in Clonrath after he'd written to tell me the truth.

David O'Dea. I read it like it was another language. The words sounded bizarre in my head. Even the way I'd printed them was strange. I didn't write like that any more.

I picked it up. Inside I found two blank sheets of notepaper: the letter I'd never written. I laid them out flat on the book, found a pen and went over to the window. Looking out, I could see for miles. The whole countryside was quiet and still. The sky was pale blue, fading to white over the horizon, and above the frosted rooftops of Glengolden hung the silvery ball of the moon. Trees were still bare and the peaks of the mountains were lacy with snow. I settled myself sideways onto the ledge and began to write.

When I started the letter, it wasn't with any intention of sending it. I'd barely thought of David, or anyone from before, since we'd left Hillcourt Rise. I think my mind had shut that part of my memory down, blocked it out, so I wouldn't have to keep re-living what I might've done wrong. What I could've done differently.

What I wished I hadn't done at all.

I asked him how he was, if he still liked Clonrath, whether he'd made any more friends. I wondered if he did much study after school, what his favourite subjects were, if he still played the piano. I told him our new address, described our new house, said it was near the graveyard. I didn't mention Kev's name. Or what had happened. I didn't mention any of that at all. But at the very end, before I signed my name, I wrote: *I'm sorry I didn't believe you.* I folded the pages and slipped them in the envelope. Then I went downstairs and took a stamp from the tin Mam kept on the kitchen windowsill. I ran all the way to the postbox at the crossroads and didn't think about sending the letter until it was out of my hands.

After three weeks, I gave up waiting for a reply. Not that I'd really expected he'd write back. And in a way, I was glad. I'd said what I'd wanted to say, that I was sorry I hadn't believed him. There wasn't any need for him to respond. But I felt better knowing that I'd told him.

Mam and Dad planned to have a headstone on Kev's grave in time for his first anniversary. It wasn't something they'd been able to think about before then. They talked about it in the evenings, and I saw Dad scribbling designs on a folded-out cigarette box. They didn't include us in their discussions and though I felt I should be annoyed about that, I wasn't. I preferred the grave as it was. I liked the way only we knew who lay there. Kev's name carved in stone – I wasn't sure any of us were ready to see that.

On a sunny April Saturday, I set off across the fields for a visit. I'd spent the morning helping Dad in the garden and had only just managed to convince the others it was time they did their share. Auntie Cissy had come to stay, and she and Mam were sitting at the kitchen table having a cup of tea when I left.

When I got to the graveyard wall I sat down. I picked at the powdery stone, grinding chips of loose slate into dust and brushing it to the ground. I wondered how long the wall would survive, if it'd still be there years into the future, when there was nobody left who remembered us. It scared me there was so much I didn't know. So much I would never find out. I looked up to the sky – to the vast, pale blue blanket that covered the place where my baby brother lay. This was his home now. Close by him were my grandparents, Mam's mam and dad, and it comforted me to know they were there. Though they'd never met each other, they were family. They belonged together.

I dropped down from the wall and made my way into the graveyard, turning the corner after the big yew tree. When I got to Kev's grave, I gasped.

I saw his name.

The letters straight and hard and exact. Lines cut into a heart of smooth white marble. Deep and lasting. Like scars that would never heal.

Kevin Lamb
Beloved Youngest Son of Michael and Rose
Safe in the Arms of Jesus

I read the words over and over. I didn't want them to make sense. I didn't want to understand them. But there was no way around the truth that they told. Through my tears I whispered a prayer. And for the first time as I stood at his grave, I was able to tell Kev that I loved him.

That we all did. And that we would never stop.

I bowed my head. An airy silence rang in my ears, taut and fragile, waiting to be broken.

And then it snapped.

'Hello, Ruth.'

I knew without turning around. And for a moment, I didn't want to. But he came closer and touched my arm and I had to.

'I got your letter,' he said. 'I . . . I didn't know if I should reply.'

He'd changed. Grown so much taller. His hair was longer, parted in the middle now, unbrushed and curling down around his neck. Golden brown hairs that caught the sunlight grew above his lips and all around his chin. He wore a striped shirt with no collar, the tail of it hanging out over frayed and faded jeans.

'It's OK,' I said. 'I didn't expect you to.'

'I hadn't planned on coming. Just decided this morning.' He still wore his leather wristband, clicking it open and shut as he spoke. His voice trembled slightly. 'A lad at school, his parents took him out for the day. To Bray. For his sister's communion. I asked for a lift.'

'But it's a long way,' was all I could think of to say. 'How will you get back?'

'It's grand. They'll collect me from the village later.'

I bit my lip as I looked at him. 'Why did you come?'

He glanced towards Kev's grave. He swallowed. 'I wanted . . . I just thought . . . It's nearly a year now, isn't it?'

I nodded.

'Doesn't seem like it,' he said.

I couldn't tell. Time had lost the meaning it once had. In some ways, it seemed like yesterday, and in others, it could've been a hundred years.

'When did you get here?' I asked him.

'Couple of hours ago.'

'And you've been here all that time?'

He nodded. 'I . . . I was going to call to the house. But I wasn't sure if . . .' He took a deep breath. 'Then I saw his name and I . . . I don't know . . . I just stood looking at it. For ages.'

'It's new,' I said. 'The headstone. It's the first time I've seen it. It feels . . . different now.'

'Does it make it worse?' he asked. 'Seeing his name, I mean.'

'I'm not sure. All I know is it's not the same.'

I moved back towards the wall and he followed. We sat down together, our feet kicking against the flaking stone. We were silent for a few moments, neither of us knowing what to say. Then he began to speak, answering the questions I'd asked in my letter. He was happy in Clonrath, he said. He'd made a few more good friends. He still played the piano, but had given up entering competitions. Some lads from school had formed a band and he'd joined – he played keyboards and wrote all their songs.

'We're going to be huge,' he said, grinning. 'You'll be seeing us on *Top of the Pops.*'

I gave him a smile. 'I'll watch out for you.'

He cleared his throat. 'That day,' he said. 'The fight. On the green. I—'

'It's OK,' I said, shaking my head. 'It—'

'It's not OK! I shouldn't have dared him to hit me. And I shouldn't have hit him back. If we hadn't had that fight . . . If—'

I slid from the wall and faced him. 'Stop! There's no point. It won't do any good.' I looked away, tears burning my eyes. 'I should've believed what you told me. I should've guessed he was making all that stuff up. But there's no point in wondering about the ifs and buts. None of it matters. Not now.'

'But I do wonder,' he said. 'All the time. I think about how things could've been so different.' He turned his head to look out over the fields. 'If only . . . Sometimes I hate him, you know. Then other times . . . I kind of think I understand. Not what he . . . what he did, but . . . I could've been him.'

'What do you mean?'

'My mother. My real mother, I mean. She could've kept me. She could've tried. And Liz, she could've given him away. To a family. Like mine.' He faced me. 'I'm not sorry I tried to be his friend, Ruth. I'm just sorry it worked out the way it did.'

'It's not your fault,' I said. 'It's not anyone's.'

He stood down from the wall. 'Sometimes I think it's all of our faults.'

We started walking, stepping on shadows the sun cast along the path. We were silent until we reached the gate.

'I just feel so bad for you,' he said as we left the graveyard. 'For all of you.'

'Don't,' I whispered, turning my face away. 'We'll be fine.'

He said I didn't need to go any further with him but I wanted to. He'd come all that way. It was only right that I should. When we got to the village, we sat on the shop windowsill, squinting against the sun.

I could have asked him lots of things. But I didn't want to know. I had all the story I needed. I thanked him for coming, and I hoped he knew I meant it. He promised he'd write but I didn't say I would. I wasn't sure.

I left him waiting outside the shop for his lift back to Clonrath. Before I turned the corner, I looked back and he waved.

I walked the long way home; I wanted to follow the road. Once out of the village, it was straight all the way. No twists and turns. As I came closer to the house, I could see Dad at the door, surveying the front garden with a mug of tea in his hand. He saluted when he saw me and came out to the gate.

'There you are,' he said with a smile. 'I was beginning to wonder where you'd got to. Dinner's ready.'

I went inside and sat down at the table with my family. Mam, Dad, Cissy, Mel and Sandra.

We'll be fine.

I wondered if I'd meant what I'd said to David. If I really thought we would. It wasn't something I could be sure of. It was something I'd just have to trust.

ACKNOWLEDGEMENTS

I began working on *The Story of Before* during my Masters in Creative Writing in University College Dublin, so thanks are due to those who inspired me during that year: Éilís Ní Dhuibhne who so generously pointed me in the right direction and gave such valuable instruction; James Ryan for his words of wisdom and kindness; and my fellow students, many of whom read and critiqued first drafts of early chapters, particularly Colin Barrett and Mariad Whisker, and most especially, the two who continue to be with me every step of the way – Jamie O'Connell and Claire Coughlan.

I am hugely grateful to my agent, Lucy Luck, and would like to thank her for her commitment, advice and enthusiasm. Likewise, my editor, Sara O'Keeffe – her suggestions and guidance have made this a better book. Thanks to the team at Corvus, and also to the Arts Council of Ireland for their assistance while I was writing *The Story of Before*. And to my family – my parents, my children and my husband, for their unfailing support, encouragement and belief – thank you.

Read on to discover more about

THE
STORY
OF
BEFORE

Q&A with Susan Stairs

1. What inspired you to start writing?

I can't remember a time when I wasn't creating in one form or
another. Words and pictures have always gone hand in hand
for me. As a child, I was constantly drawing or painting. When
I was read to, and when I began reading myself, I loved using
the words on the page to create pictures in my head – whole
worlds that only I could see. And once I was able to write, I
regularly made up stories and poems of my own. I went to art
college and later, when I worked in the art business, I wrote
several books about Irish artists. I also wrote some fiction at
this time – two (unfinished) novels and some short stories.
Then I did an MA in Creative Writing and the tuition and
advice I received there gave me the confidence I needed to
not only just start, but actually *finish* a novel. So I think the

inspiration to write, to create, to give life to the 'pictures in my head' was there from a very young age.

2. Who are the writers you most admire, and who are your biggest influences?

Transferring what's in one's head onto the page and persevering until it's a fully formed piece of work, independent from its creator, is a difficult and solitary process. So I have huge admiration for anyone who manages to produce a novel, or a collection of short stories or poetry, regardless of whether their work is to my taste or not. When choosing a book to read, the first page has to grab my attention, the voice has to 'speak' to me and lure me into another world. In the last number of years, while I've been writing fiction myself, some of the writers who have brought me into that other world and inspired me to keep writing myself include Donna Tartt, Sarah Waters, Sadie Jones, Alice Sebold, Jeffrey Eugenides and Maggie O'Farrell.

3. What compelled you to write *The Story of Before*?

When I was a child, a tragedy occurred not far from where I lived. Growing up, it was something I thought about often: how and why it happened; the people involved; how their lives were changed forever. It was too strong a memory to remain in my head, and when I was faced with the challenge of producing a novel plan while doing my MA, it was this memory that triggered the basis for *The Story of Before*. Whilst my novel is purely fiction, the real-life event was the catalyst that spurred me on and was never far from my thoughts while I was writing.

4. Did anything surprise you during the course of writing this book?

The most surprising thing for me was how difficult I found it to allow my characters to make bad choices. I felt very responsible for them all – I had created them and wanted the best for them – and it was very hard to see some of them choosing to do the wrong thing. I did feel in control of them, but only to a certain extent; there were many times when they steered the narrative in a particular direction and I was as surprised as I hope the reader will be. I had no idea what was going to happen from one chapter to the next, but to quote Robert Frost: 'No tears in the writer, no tears in the reader. No surprise for the writer, no surprise for the reader'.

5. What advice would you give to aspiring novelists?

Read, read, read and write, write, write. Write about the thing that interests you, that drives you, that you can't stop thinking of, and your passion will come through in your words. And never give up. It might be a cliché, but it really is the best advice I can give. While I was writing *The Story of Before*, not knowing if it would ever see the light of day, I'd often walk around a bookshop or look at my own bookshelves and tell myself that none of the books I saw there were written by writers who gave up. We only see the ones written by those who kept going. Persevere. It *is* possible.

6. Can you tell us a little bit about what you are working on next?

I'm working on another novel, also set in Ireland – in the early 1980s this time – and in a more rural location. As in *The Story of Before*, I'm exploring the differing ways adults and children see the world and how keeping secrets from each other can impact upon our lives. It's told through the eyes of a young boy who is sent by his parents from his home in England to spend the summer in Ireland with an aunt and uncle he has never met. What he discovers while he's there will rock his world and by the summer's end, his life is changed forever.

Reading Group Questions

1. The theme of family is central to *The Story of Before*. How does the author explore the relationship between Ruth and her parents?

2. The book presents an acutely observed and unsettling portrait of family secrets, lies and familiar childhood moments. How do you think this affected your response to the characters?

3. The setting of the novel is a very prominent theme. What impression are we given of the community in Hillcourt Rise? How does the author evoke a sense of place?

4. How does Ruth's psychic belief that there is a 'bad thing coming' alter your reading of the rest of the novel?

5. 'Where was everything that I thought was true?' As the story progresses, Ruth doubts everything she believes she has witnessed. How does the author explore Ruth's development as an individual?

6. What is it that draws Ruth to Shayne? In your opinion, what makes him such an intriguing character?

7. How did your response to David change as the book progressed? Were you convinced by his declaration of the truth to Ruth? Do you think he is presented sympathetically?

8. A recurring theme of the book is that of a mother and father's bond with their children. How were you affected by the author's depiction of these fundamental relationships?

9. Discuss the novelist's representation of grief.

10. What did you think of the novel's ending? Do you think the family will ever be able to recover from the events that have broken them in two?